Curse of the Bayou Beast

THE WATCHMAKER REVELATIONS BOOK 3

MICHAEL L. HAWLEY

HELLBENDER
BOOKS

an imprint of Sunbury Press, Inc.
Mechanicsburg, PA USA

HELLBENDER BOOKS

an imprint of Sunbury Press, Inc.
Mechanicsburg, PA USA

For information about special discounts for bulk purchases, please contact Sunbury Press Orders Dept. at (855) 338-8359 or orders@sunburypress.com.

To request one of our authors for speaking engagements or book signings, please contact Sunbury Press Publicity Dept. at publicity@sunburypress.com.

FIRST HELLBENDER BOOKS EDITION: October 2023

Set in Adobe Garamond | Interior design by Crystal Devine | Cover design by Amber Rendon | Edited by Jennifer Cappello.

Publisher's Cataloging-in-Publication Data
Names: Hawley, Michael L., author.
Title: Curse of the bayou beasst / Michael L. Hawley.
Description: First Trade paperback edition. | Mechanicsburg, PA : Hellbender Books, 2023.
Summary: A serial killer in New Orleans uses a monstrous beast to mutilate and collect victims systematically. Assisted by the Watchmaker, serial killer sleuth Edward Dunham, young Rob Faulks goes into action, but he quickly realizes the fiend's wrath is too much for the authorities, especially when he—or it—owns the night.
Identifiers: ISBN : 978-1-62006-839-7 (softcover) | ISBN : 979-8-88819-157-6 (ePub).
Subjects: FICTION / Mystery & Detective / Police Procedural | FICTION / Thrillers / Crime | FICTION / Thrillers / Supernatural.

Product of the United States of America
0 1 1 2 3 5 8 13 21 34 55

Continue the Enlightenment!

chapter 1

Suspect Number Twelve
Jackson, Mississippi

Chuck Engles glanced around the police station's waiting room at the others being reinterviewed. *So, all these idiots own white vans too?* he thought to himself. He shook his head and smirked. He knew these cops were no closer to finding the killer than they had been three months ago when they first questioned him. According to the detectives back then, someone saw a person in a light-colored Caravan throw a large, wrapped object off a bridge and into the Pearl River upstream from where they discovered the body of a woman.

A police officer walked by, escorting someone in handcuffs.

Engles scratched the exposed portion of his portly belly as he watched them, then stretched his T-shirt down in a futile attempt to cover his skin. He wiped sweat from his balding head and glanced up at the clock. "This van thing must be the only clue they have," he muttered.

The door of the interview room opened, and a relatively young police officer with short hair and an athletic build walked out with a man, closed the door behind them, then escorted him through the waiting room.

Before the door closed, Engles spotted the two detectives who'd questioned him months ago sitting in the interview room. He chuckled and shook his head. *Little do these boneheads realize, the killer they're so desperately searching for is sitting in this waiting room right in front of their very noses!* He knew he gave them a solid alibi, which was obviously the reason the cops hadn't bothered him until now.

The police officer walked back into the waiting room and approached Engles. "Mr. Engles, the detectives are ready for you now."

Engles eagerly got to his feet. *Now, let's see how much these guys really know,* he thought as he followed the cop into the room.

"Take a seat, Mr. Engles," a thin, elderly, gray-haired detective directed. "It's been a few months since we last met. Let me reintroduce myself. My name is Detective Hobbs." He turned toward the other detective in the room. "This, again, is Detective Nebelecky, also on the serial killer task force."

Engles nodded to both of them.

Hobbs glanced up at the police officer who'd brought Engles into the room. "Officer Mitchell, did you read Mr. Engles his Miranda Rights?"

Mitchell nodded as he positioned himself in the back corner, standing in professional cop-stance with his legs apart and his arms straight, hands clasped in front of him. "Yes, Detective, he received his rights when we arrived at the station thirty minutes ago." He glanced at Engles. "He then voluntarily waived his right to have an attorney present for this interview."

Engles nodded with a confident, almost cocky grin. "Nothin' to hide, Detective; just like before, I'm here to help y'all." He paused, then added, "Pity about those women being tortured and murdered." That was the first of his lies today, and he was enjoying every minute of their attention. When this Officer Mitchell escorted him to the station and told him a new serial killer task force member wanted to reinterview the entire list of white van owners, he thought it would be kind of fun to toy with the new kid on the block.

Hobbs studied his clipboard as he penned 'Engles' at the top of the page, then he raised his eyes toward the suspect. "As you can see by the crowd in the waiting room, we've brought back everyone even remotely connected to the case to be reinterviewed. You see," he paused, "we recruited an out-a-towner to help us in our investigation, and he's asked to retrace our steps from the beginning." Hobbs glanced at the other detective. "Before we begin the interview, Mr. Engles, I want to again offer you the opportunity to have a lawyer present."

Engles shook his head. "Thanks; I'm fine," he replied, reveling in outsmarting the police. It gave him almost as much pleasure as the torturing and mutilating of his lovelies. Well, that was an understatement, but the excitement of playing with these cops for a second time was incredible. Oh, the power he felt running through his veins! At that moment, a second door to the room, situated behind the detectives, opened up, and Engles eyed a thin, middle-aged man with steel-gray eyes wearing a gray tweed suit coat with elbow patches.

Detective Hobbs nodded to Engles. "OK, but if at any time you want to end the interview, we'll stop." He glanced up at the thin man who'd just entered the room. "Mr. Engles, allow me to introduce you to Dr. Edward Dunham, special agent and chief scientist for the FBI."

Dunham stared at Engles over his wire-rimmed glasses. "You're number twelve of thirty interviews planned for today."

Engles nodded confidently, then watched the detective give his seat up to this so-called expert—a Yankee, if he had to guess. Engles grinned and purposely stared into the eyes of the slender stranger. *Although FBI, he's clearly a weakling*—and Engles loved to bully weaklings.

Dunham nodded to Hobbs, then smiled at the suspect. "Good morning, Mr. Engles." He dropped the smile. "I want to be upfront with you." Dunham paused. "In a court of law, you are considered innocent until proven guilty," he shook his head, "but we are in no court, and I am no judge." He leaned forward. "I shall begin by assuming you're guilty, Mr. Engles, yet I'm giving you the opportunity to prove your innocence to me." He paused again and purposely stared into Engles's eyes. "Only then will I take you off the suspect list."

Engles jerked his head back, taken off guard by Dunham's abrupt, aggressive approach. On top of that, this guy's intense eyes seemed to penetrate his thoughts, as if he were unraveling his lies. Engles quickly dropped his gaze. He shook his head and regained his composure; he didn't want to give any of his guilty thoughts away to this outsider. "Hey, I didn't do anything wrong. I just own a white Caravan." He pointed to the officer. "I only agreed to come down here because I thought I could help."

Dunham nodded. "We appreciate that, Mr. Engles, but think back for a moment. I've read your statement from three months ago." He flipped through the pages in the file. "The victim's body was estimated to have been dumped at a bridge on a Friday evening—the time a witness saw a white Caravan identical to yours on that bridge—but she was kidnapped four days earlier, on a Tuesday." Dunham read further, then glanced up at Engles. "Why were you traveling north on Emerson Road around one in the morning on Tuesday night?"

Engles nodded, fully prepared for this question. "Coming back from a late night of fishin' at Briar Lake, like I do every Tuesday. It's my day off."

Dunham flipped to the first page of the file. "I see you work as a night watchman at a local business, is that correct?"

Engles nodded. "Yep; I'm one of two watchmen on duty at all times. My partner can vouch for me."

Dunham paged further into the file. "Mr. Engles, think back a few years. I notice you lived in Vicksburg, Mississippi, in the mid-1990s." He popped his head up and stared into Engles's eyes. "There was a series of unsolved murders near Vicksburg in the mid-nineties. These victims were mutilated, not unlike the victims recently found here in Jackson."

Hobbs and Nebelecky shot each other a glance, both realizing they'd never picked up on this coincidence.

Engles's eyes opened wider. "What're you trying to say?"

Dunham ignored the question. "You wouldn't mind giving our detectives an account of your whereabouts at the time of these Vicksburg murders, would you?"

Engles frowned. "Not at all." He then shot his hands up and waved in mock surrender. "Well, you'll find that I was real close to one of those murders one night, actually, and I think I even saw the killer. He was my neighbor; this guy who owned a scary-sounding dog that he kept cooped up all the time. It howled and bayed at night. Never did actually see it until that night."

"Oh?" Dunham asked.

Nebelecky rolled his eyes at Hobbs, who shrugged in response.

"I saw his dog on the loose around those woods where the woman was killed that night, so I figured he must have been in there. Later that evening, I saw him walking back to his apartment."

"Why didn't you inform the police?" Dunham asked.

Engles shrugged. "I dunno. No one asked me."

Hobbs chuckled quietly and shook his head.

Dunham nodded, still scanning the folder. "Are you familiar with an Annie Witherspoon?"

Engles sat up straight in his chair; anger filled his eyes. "Yeah, she was my neighbor, and that should not be in my record. I was proven innocent! Cleared of all charges!" He'd tortured and abused young Annie in the woods behind her house more than a decade ago, but besides her emotional testimony, there was no evidence connecting him to the attack, especially when he luckily drummed up a convincing alibi. It was the moment he realized the key to getting away with anything was a solid alibi. But that should've been expunged from his record since the cops hadn't been able to nail him for it.

Dunham shook his head. "Being proven innocent is impossible in the court of law, Mr. Engles, since you're presumed to be innocent at the onset. Proving something that's legally mandated to be presumed is, in a way, a violation of law." He sat back and shook his head. "No, the available evidence in this case merely precluded the jury to convict." He pointed to himself. "Now, from a presumption of guilt perspective for our suspect list, I read this same evidence as . . . not proving you innocent. Thus, in my eyes, you tortured and molested that twelve-year-old girl."

Engles tilted his head in confusion then grasped his hair and shook his head. "Wha . . . I was found not guilty! And, and I didn't kidnap this McKenzie lady two days ago!" He stared forward, puffing, his fists clenched.

Hobbs whacked Nebelecky's leg under the table, grinning.

Nebelecky nodded back to Hobbs, beaming, and quietly mouthed, "Nice."

"Well, before we get to the McKenzie kidnapping, Mr. Engles," Dunham read the file for a few moments, "I'd like to ask you about the Peeping Tom incident you were convicted of seven years ago."

Engles shook his head and continued to glare at the wall. Yes, he was convicted in the case, but little did they realize his true intentions were to assault and murder that woman in her own bedroom, but a nosy neighbor got in the way and called the cops. He replaced his frown with a grin. "Now, that did happen. So what if I like to stare at nude women? They like it anyway."

"And the duct tape and knife found on your person?" Dunham asked. "You weren't intending on entering that home, were you, Mr. Engles?" He shook his head. "You're not doing a very good job of convincing me to take you off the suspect list."

Anger filled Engles's eyes. "I always carry a knife, and, and I don't remember why I had the duct tape. That was years ago."

"So," Dunham said, interrupting purposely in an attempt to catch him off guard, "where were you two nights ago when Janice McKenzie was kidnapped?"

"Working; check my timecard." Engles stopped abruptly and shook his head. "Oh, I mean I was fishing at Briar Lake by myself."

Dunham glanced down at Engles's hand. "I see that you have a fresh cut on your left index finger. How'd you get that?"

Engles unconsciously closed his fingers into a fist and placed his other hand over it, hiding the cut from view. He recalled cutting himself while slicing off his lovely's bra before tying her up. He quickly opened his hand, exposing the cut, then noticed Dunham and the detectives exchanging a glance. "Oh, I cut myself filleting a bass." He felt sweat beading on his forehead again, so he wiped it off with his sleeve.

"May I see that knife?" Dunham asked.

"Sure," Engles replied, "but I cleaned it."

"That's OK. That won't affect the test for latent bloodstains. I'll have a deputy pick it up tomorrow."

Engles's jaw dropped slightly, and some of the color faded from his face.

Hobbs glanced over at Nebelecky and quietly snickered.

Nebelecky grinned and nodded in approval.

Engles shook his head. This interview was not as pleasurable as he thought it would be. He leaned forward. "You're a Yankee-bastard asshole, and this interview's done. I'd like to go home now."

Dunham paused. "OK, Mr. Engles. Thank you for being forthright with us." He glanced up at the police officer in the corner. "It's late, and we still have many more interviews, but before we have Officer Mitchell take you home, I have one final question."

Engles said nothing but glanced up at Dunham, waiting for the question.

"We happen to know that the six recent Jackson victims—all discovered in or near Pearl River—were tortured multiple times with a cattle prod prior to being murdered."

Engles tilted his head in surprise. Nowhere in the papers did it say the police knew he used a cattle prod. He was sure he left no burn marks on his lovelies.

"I'm not claiming that we confiscated the very same cattle prod during a raid yesterday on a . . . hideaway, but," Dunham paused, "do you mind if we take your fingerprints before you leave?"

There's no way they could have found *his* cattle prod! Although, he realized, it was hanging out in the open on the garage wall of his mountain getaway, a secluded place he'd inherited from his dead parents just last year. *Ah, so what!* If they did raid his getaway and confiscate his cattle prod, he knew there was no way his fingerprints were on it—he always wore gloves.

"I'd be glad to cooperate," Engles responded.

Dunham stood. "We've taken up enough of your time. Thank you, Mr. Engles."

"Follow me, Mr. Engles," Officer Mitchell said.

Hobbs watched Engles through the open door as the suspect walked into the hallway. "I thought we weren't going to reveal your discovery of the use of the cattle prod, Dr. Dunham?"

Dunham nodded, also staring out of the room at Engles. "He's our man, Detectives, and the priority is finding Janice McKenzie alive." He paused. "I believe he's going to check to see if we did indeed discover his cattle prod, and wherever that location is, Janice McKenzie is nearby."

Nebelecky glanced over at Hobbs and shook his head. "Dr. Dunham, we eliminated Mr. Engles from the suspect list three months ago because he had a solid alibi at the time the victim's body was dropped off that bridge at 11:06 p.m. on Friday. The eyewitness recalled checking his watch."

"He was working with his fellow night watchman," Hobbs interrupted. "His timecard showed he clocked in at around nine p.m., and he clocked out around six a.m. This other watchman confirmed he was at work."

"He did admit to leaving work to pick up food at McDonald's at eleven but immediately returned," Nebelecky continued, "and his credit card receipt stated 11:04 p.m. McDonald's is ten miles in the other direction from the bridge, a full twenty miles away, making it impossible for him to have been at the bridge at 11:06 p.m."

Dunham placed his index finger on his lips, contemplating. "I purposely put Engles in a state of agitation before asking him where he was two days ago, in hopes of detecting a rehearsed response. The glitch you saw in his reply was textbook deception, indicating he's using his alibi as his safety net."

"What are you getting at?" Nebelecky asked.

"Are you able to contact Engles's coworker?" Dunham asked. "I'd like to find out if Engles has ever given him his credit card, offering to pay for lunch if the coworker drives and picks it up."

Hobbs grinned. "I get it. Engles offers to buy, and the coworker flies!" He glanced over at Nebelecky. "And when the coworker left to pick up lunch, Engles sneaked out the other way and dumped the body into the river then returned to work before the coworker got back with lunch!" He nodded. "We certainly will contact the other night watchman."

Dunham pointed his finger in the air. "I don't believe McDonald's requires a signature on small credit card purchases anymore, but if they did in this case, we need to get it and compare signatures."

Hobbs glanced at Dunham. "That was brilliant questioning, by the way, Dr. Dunham. Working his emotions, then seeing him covering up that cut on his finger; another classic case of deceptive behavior." He paused and shifted his gaze at the folder on the table. "Guilty until proven innocent; I love it."

Dunham grinned. "You set him up perfectly for me, Detective Hobbs. He believed he had the advantage."

Nebelecky nodded and grinned. "Dr. Dunham, if you're convinced he's our man, so am I. Let's haunt him tonight. Apprehending the serial killer and simultaneously finding Janice McKenzie alive would be a satisfying night's work. Wouldn't you say?"

"Why did you say we found a cattle prod at a 'hideaway'?" Hobbs asked.

Dunham nodded. "The case files show that this offender takes great care in trying to reduce his DNA signature, and he's very effective at it. In other serial killer cases I've encountered with a similar MO, the offenders used a separate location other than their domicile to torture and murder their victims in order to reduce their DNA signatures. Chances are he has a hideaway, and if he does, he might think we've found it."

"Let's hope we don't lose him if he does sneak off to it," Hobbs replied.

Engles peeked at his watch; it read 11:05 p.m. He scanned the dark streets in his neighborhood from behind the overgrown cedar shrubbery in his front yard. He'd purposely unscrewed his driveway light earlier in the day, so the closest light source, a distant streetlight, created almost imperceptible, dim, long shadows. *Perfect for a quick getaway*, he thought. There were no strange vehicles and no unusual activity. The neighborhood was as boring as it always was, and this time, it gave him comfort. He hadn't planned on visiting his mountain getaway for another few days, when his lovely was even more exhausted, less obstinate, and closer to death . . . but he had to know. *Did the cops really stumble upon my hideout? It's too coincidental. How many people in this area own a cattle prod—and have it hanging at a hideaway?*

Satisfied he wasn't being watched by the police, he slipped next to his Caravan, which was parked in his darkened driveway. Opening the door, he jumped into the driver's seat. He sat motionless in the dark interior of the van for at least ten minutes, ensuring that no one was watching him. Again satisfied, he started the van, pulled onto the street, and drove off. After about a hundred feet, he turned his headlights on and turned out of the neighborhood. He drove around in a random pattern through the mountain roads until he was convinced he was not being followed, and once he felt safe, he headed straight to his mountain getaway.

Engles quickly got out of his van, entered the garage, and held his breath as he shined his flashlight onto the wall where he kept his torture toy. There it was, his special cattle prod. Relieved, he exhaled. *Those bastards are far from catching me.* They'd rummaged around in the wrong man's hideaway. His cocky grin returned, and he shifted his gaze to the trap door in the center of the garage.

I wonder how my lovely is, he thought. "Oh, Lovely," he called out. "I'm here! Did you miss me?"

He grabbed his cattle prod and approached the trap door. Opening it, he shined the flashlight around, spotting Janice McKenzie, tied up and gagged where he had left her. He could see that she was dazed but certainly alive.

"I'm back sooner than I said I would be, I know. But, since I'm here, Lovely, it's time to play." He climbed down the ladder. He watched his prisoner's eyes open and widen as she recognized him. The immediate fear in her face made him shudder with excitement. "Hello, my Lovely. I see you remember me. How sweet."

Janice shifted her body away from Engles as he approached.

"Oh, don't be shy," he teased. "It's—"

Crash! Engles heard window glass breaking from inside the garage, then the sound of it raining onto the concrete floor. In an instant, he saw four SWAT agents pointing their rifles directly at him.

"Get on the ground!" one of the SWAT team members screamed. "Face down! Now, now, now!"

Engles quickly dropped to the ground, and in seconds his hands and feet were bound.

Outside, Hobbs, standing next to Nebelecky, swept his eyes over the mountain getaway, which was teeming with law enforcement officers and medical personnel. "The press will be here soon."

Nebelecky turned and peered down the road. "I bet you're right."

A detective sergeant and two other officers approached them. "Well, Detectives, our perp has been carted off to the station, and Janice McKenzie is on her way to the hospital."

"Have our crime scene investigators started on the room under the garage yet?" Hobbs asked.

The detective sergeant nodded.

"Good," Hobbs replied. "I don't want anything missed. This asshole needs to stay off the streets."

One of the officers glanced over at a thin, middle-aged man speaking to the crime scene investigators. "Is that Dr. Dunham?"

Nebelecky nodded. "Yes, Officer Henderson, that's the Watchmaker himself. He's got a perfect record for catching serial killers, and he did it again today." He shook his head and smirked. "Took him only two days; amazing."

"So, that's him," the officer said again. "Some say he's got a supernatural gift."

"If you ask him, he'd say it's just a lucky streak mixed in with lots of training and experience, but mostly teamwork," Hobbs replied. "He's not too into that religious, hocus pocus stuff. He told me himself."

The detective sergeant turned and glared at him. "So, why the hell did he team up with a priest when he caught the October Serial Killer last year in Boston?"

Hobbs and Nebelecky turned and stared at the detective sergeant, both with perplexed looks.

The detective sergeant nodded. "That's right. My buddy saw the whole thing. He's a detective out of Boston. The Watchmaker found the killer, and then this priest did some kind of exorcism on him." He pointed to the officer. "Henderson here is right. That guy's got some kind of connection with the Almighty."

Hobbs glanced toward Dunham. "Who gives a shit how he solves these cases? It works."

Dunham turned and noticed the Channel 4 News van speeding up the road. He walked over to Detectives Hobbs and Nebelecky. "If you don't mind, gentlemen, my job here is done, so I'm going to sneak off. I'd like to avoid making the news. It makes my job difficult if I am recognized by everyone."

Hobbs nodded and shook his hand. "No problem, Dr. Dunham, and thank you for everything. I'll keep you updated."

Nebelecky shook his hand. "It was great working with you, Dr. Dunham."

chapter 2

**Off the Coast of the Philippines,
US Navy frigate, the USS *Ouellette*,
1989**

Two of the four naval aviators assigned to the USS *Ouellette*, Lieutenant John Hanes and Lieutenant Junior Grade Alan Walker, walked into the wardroom for an impromptu meeting and realized from the crowd that they were the last of the officers and critical personnel to arrive.

The commanding officer of the ship, Commander Nast, or 'Captain,' was standing in the front glaring at them.

"My apologies, sir," Hanes said. "We just finished preflight, and the helicopter is good to go; one hundred percent mission ready. Waiting for a green deck."

Realizing that the two Air-dales—a term used by surface warfare officers when referring to naval aviators—had a legitimate reason for being late, he lost his glare, then gave an approving nod. "Take a seat."

Hanes and Walker found seats next to the other two aviators, Officer in Charge of the aviation department Lieutenant Commander Hap Tanner and Aviation Operations Officer Lieutenant Fred Peeler. Hanes leaned close to Tanner. "The captain seems on edge," he whispered.

Tanner shook his head. "I dunno what's up, but he did rush off to CIC and speak with the admiral on the satellite phone," he whispered.

"Quiet. everyone!" the executive officer belted out, then he eyed Commander Nast once the room was silent. "All yours, Captain."

"Thank you, XO," the captain replied. "This meeting has been classified Secret, so if anyone does not have the appropriate clearance, you need to leave now." The captain paused, staring directly at the supply officers.

The two supply officers stood up, slightly taken aback by the captain's directness, then walked out of the wardroom. The ship's medical corpsman, Petty Officer First Class Jared LaRue, unofficially known by the entire ship's company as 'Doc,' stood to leave as well.

"Petty Officer LaRue, wait in the passageway until we're done, and I'll have someone retrieve you in a few minutes," Commander Nast ordered.

"Yes, sir," LaRue said before exiting.

Nast watched LaRue leave then returned his gaze to the officers. "Gentlemen, a US spy plane just crashed some forty miles away from us, just a mile off the Philippine coast, and we've been tasked to take control of the waters until the salvage ship arrives in four days. Unfriendlies would love to get their hands on the highly sensitive equipment on that plane. A Special Forces team recently arrived on the beach from Clark Air Base and has made contact with the local village chief." He paused for a moment, then continued. "Apparently, there are Communist factions in the area, but the chief assures us he is no friend of theirs."

The ship's operations officer raised his hand, and the captain acknowledged him. "Sir, do you know if the pilots in the spy plane survived and, if not, are we tasked to recover the remains?"

Commander Nast gave a slight nod. "They survived, and apparently they will be returning on scene to assist in salvage operations. Now, moving on from the classified op to the humanitarian part of the mission—" he glanced over at the XO, "bring in LaRue."

The XO quickly exited and immediately returned from the passageway with LaRue; the captain nodded to the doc as he entered, then eyed everyone. "Our mission for the next four days, other than to control these waters, is to win the hearts and minds of the local villagers by whatever means necessary. As we know from real-world experience, these operations go more smoothly when we interact positively with the locals." He turned back to LaRue. "Doc, you are to organize teams to go into the village and give medical assistance and any other kind of assistance you can think of." He paused. "Hell, if they want their buildings painted haze gray, then by all means, paint them to look like ships."

"Yes, sir," LaRue replied.

The captain paused for a moment then said, "I want Petty Officer Reynolds on the team for Tuesday morning."

LaRue raised his eyebrows. "I'm sorry, who is Petty Officer Reynolds, sir?"

"He just joined ship's company," the XO interrupted. "I'll send him to you, Doc."

Commander Nast glanced over at the XO, nodded, then addressed the aviators. "Commander Tanner, coordinate with LaRue and the XO and set up a flight schedule." He paused. "The village is situated in the middle of a jungle. Where will you drop them off?"

"Right on the beach, sir," Tanner replied. "It's the quickest and safest place."

The captain nodded. "Flight quarters in thirty minutes. That is all." He abruptly walked toward the exit.

"Attention on deck!" the XO bellowed, and everyone stood at attention as the Commander Nast left the wardroom. Once the door shut behind him, the XO said, "We have our orders, gentlemen. Flight quarters in thirty minutes. Doc, set up a meet and greet, and bring gifts and hugs."

As everyone queued to exit the room, Tanner glanced at the other three aviators. "Hanes, Walker, are you two all set? Do you even remember how to land on a beach?"

Hanes grinned. "Beach landings are my forte, as you well know, sir," he boasted. "Do a quick flyby to look for electric wires or other obstructions on the beach, keep the helo's nose into the wind, land softly to see if the wheels sink into the sand, and if not, drop the collective and settle in for a landing."

"And takeoff?" Tanner asked.

"A quick hover and takeoff away from the beach immediately. Don't sit there and let the sand blow up and block our vision. A whiteout is never a good thing," Hanes replied.

"Good recall. Remember, that's exactly what happened when President Carter ordered the rescue of the hostages in Iran with helicopters. The pilots hovered and crashed in whiteout."

Petty Officer LaRue approached the aviators. "Gentlemen, I guess you're my chauffeurs for the next few days."

"Walker and I are honored to take first shift, Doc," Hanes answered. "Maximum of four people per flight, so your meet and greet will be a small contingent."

"No problem," LaRue replied. "Later, we can take advantage of the utility boat and bring bigger numbers with supplies."

Peeler gave an inquisitive stare. "Interesting accent, Doc. Are you Cajun?"

LaRue grinned. "True dat, sir, through and through. I'm from the Bayou in southern Louisiana.

"Isn't there another Cajun onboard?" Peeler asked.

LaRue nodded. "Yes, sir, Petty Officer Joe Castle." He frowned. "He's a dick, so don't think all Cajuns are like him. I'm gonna bring him along with us tomorrow and the next day. Maybe he'll get lost in the jungle or somethin'." He glanced over at Hanes. "I'll get the first contingent ready in a jiffy and see you in the hangar, sir."

"See you there," Hanes agreed.

Thirty minutes later, Hanes and Walker were seated in the cockpit of the SH-2F Seasprite helicopter with the engines blasting and rotors turning. The helicopter was still secured to the ship's flight deck by chains, fastened from the helicopter landing gear to deck hooks in the helo pad, pitching and rolling with the aft end of the ship. Hanes saw Petty Officer LaRue and three other sailors twenty feet away exit from the hangar and stand next to the wall, decked out in helmets and safety gear and ready to board the helo. "Are you ready for our passengers, Petty Officer Sanchez?" Hanes spoke over the helo's intercom to his air crewman, who was standing just outside the fuselage door of the helo.

Sanchez pushed the intercom button on his helmet wire. "All set, sir; I have their seats and harnesses ready."

Hanes pointed to the contingency and gave the deck officer a thumbs up. The deck officer, standing in front of the helo on the flight deck just outside the circular path of the moving rotors, nodded then directed the four to embark. They nodded back, rushed under the massive main rotors, and slipped into the helo then secured themselves in their seats.

Sanchez pulled the landing gear safety pins then jumped in the helo after the passengers and took his seat at the radar screen. "Ready for flight, sir."

Hanes radioed the helicopter control officer in the tower, which was located on the port side of the helo pad twenty feet up the hangar wall. "Tower, Easyrider 53, ready for takeoff."

"Easyrider 53, wait one," the helicopter control officer replied, then contacted the captain on the intercom radio. "Captain, HCO here, we have a thumbs up; request takeoff."

Sitting in the captain's chair on the bridge, staring straight ahead, Commander Nash could make out the coastline of the Philippines. He quickly eyed some gauges then picked up the phone. "Good winds, pitch one, roll three, green deck."

"Green deck, aye," the helicopter control officer replied, then he flipped a switch and the flashing red light located at the top of the hangar changed to flashing green. "Easyrider 53, pitch one, roll three, you are cleared for takeoff."

"Fifty-three, Roger." Hanes gave the flight deck officer a thumbs up.

The flight deck officer glanced up, spotted the green light, then directed four flight deck personnel to rush under the helicopter to take the chains off the landing gear. Once they released the chains and were cleared away from the helicopter, the deck officer gave the signal for a takeoff.

"We're off," Hanes commented over the helo's intercom as he brought the aircraft up off the deck into a hover, shifted off to the starboard side of the ship, then, once clear of obstructions, flew toward the bow of the ship. After flying over the ship and setting an initial waypoint on the computer, Hanes flew straight for the beach at 160 knots, or 184 miles per hour.

"Sir, I've connected Doc to the intercom," Sanchez commented. "He can now hear you."

"Doc," Hanes yelled, "once we land on the beach, I'm going to give Sanchez the OK for you to exit the helo. Special Forces should be greeting you. I'll wait for a thumbs up from you, and then we're departing the beach."

"Sounds great, sir!" LaRue yelled.

"We'll be in the air for another three hours, so if you need us, call on your handheld radio," Hanes directed. "We'll hit the beach in minutes."

"Will do, sir," LaRue replied.

LaRue had a clear view of the ocean's surface rushing by just fifty feet below them; it was exhilarating since the helo's side door was off and he was open to the elements. He glanced over at Sanchez and pushed his intercom button. "How cool is this!"

Sanchez grinned. "Just wait for Lieutenant Hanes's beach landing."

LaRue gazed out the six-foot wide helo fuselage door at the Philippine coastline just a few miles ahead.

Walker pushed the intercom button. "Landing site's at your twelve-thirty" he reported to Hanes.

"Roger, I've got a visual," Hanes replied then pointed to his two o'clock position at some smoke emanating from a clearing in the jungle. "See the smoke billowing south? Looks like I'll keep the nose pointing north for landing." As they neared the beach, Hanes clicked the intercom button. "Eyes open for obstructions, everyone. I'm doing a flyby."

Walker turned toward the others in the back. "Watch for those huge fruit bats with the four-foot wingspans too."

Once they reached the shoreline, LaRue noticed the Special Forces team on the ground watching them. They seemed to have cleared a large area on the beach.

"Landing checklist," Hanes directed Walker.

"Wilco," Walker replied, read through the checklist, then lowered the landing gear. "Gear's down, brakes on, landing checklist complete."

Hanes jerked the controls left, causing the helo to make an abrupt left turn over the water. He kept the controls to the left and dropped the power, resulting in a decreasing-altitude spiral. Once the landing zone was back in front of the helo, Hanes further dropped the power and popped the nose up, and the aircraft responded with a quick but perfect descent over the landing area. After a quick hover, Hanes landed the helo on the beach.

"Clean landing. It's all yours, Sanchez," Hanes reported.

"Roger," Sanchez replied, then addressed the passengers. "You're cleared to disembark. Give us a call when you're ready to be picked up." He then helped them exit the helicopter.

LaRue and his team debarked and quickly joined the Special Forces team. He turned around and gave the pilots a thumbs up, then the helo rose and left the beach just as fast as it had arrived.

"That pilot's a nut," the Special Forces team leader commented to LaRue, grinning. "My kind of pilot." He slapped LaRue on the back. "Come, follow me, gentlemen. We'll introduce each other en route to the village. The chief's waiting."

* * *

Three days later, in the village . . .

Petty Officer Castle stopped painting the side of the shack for a moment, wiped the excessive sweat off his brow, then glanced around at a couple of monkeys screeching in the jungle canopy. He turned to the other sailor who'd teamed up with him on paint detail. "Where's that lowlife LaRue with our chow? I'm starving."

The other sailor, Petty Officer Lasher, pointed to an old Filipino lady roasting some eggs over a fire. "Why don't you partake in the local cuisine?" He grinned. "I hear the balut is delicious!"

Castle cringed. "No thanks. What the hell is balut, anyway?"

"A hardboiled egg with chick embryo in it," Lasher explained. "You crack open the egg and eat everything; bones, beak, skull, and all."

"Figures they'd eat somethin' like that in this godforsaken place," Castle complained then stared at two very young Filipino girls running by. "Now, there's a dish I'd like to try."

Lasher glanced over at the girls then shook his head. "You're a sick bastard, you know that, Castle."

"To each his own," Castle replied.

LaRue walked up to Castle and Lasher and handed them their boxed lunches and drinks.

Lasher raised his drink to LaRue. "Thanks, Doc."

"What took you so long, LaDick?" Castle blurted out in a nasty tone.

LaRue grinned calmly. "Four more long hours until the utility boat comes and picks you up." He pointed to two SEAL team members speaking with the new guy, Petty Officer Reynolds, and three rough-looking locals carrying machetes. "Why not pick a fight with them, Castle?" He yelled loud enough for them to hear. "No longer king of your castle, eh, Castle?" he added sarcastically. LaRue walked away, then stopped momentarily and pointed at the half-painted shack, grinning. "Hey, you missed a spot."

Castle glanced nervously at the SEALs and company as they walked toward a path; the two SEAL team members glared at him until they vanished into the jungle. He turned back to LaRue and gave him the finger, then he spit on the ground. "See? They ran away just like you, bitch!" He sat on a makeshift seat next to a patch of three-foot high weeds and began to eat his lunch.

"Be careful, Castle," Lasher warned, pointing to the weeds. "This place is filled with poisonous snakes and bugs."

Castle shook his head. "You forget; I'm from the Bayou. I sleep with gators and poisonous snakes." But his eyes followed the two young girls as they ran into a shack just thirty feet ahead; he grinned ominously. "Once I finish my lunch, maybe I'll have to take a short nap in that shack over there."

"We're supposed to steal the hearts and minds of these villagers," Lasher replied, "not their children. Don't you even care if you emotionally scar them?"

"Not my problem." Castle finished his sandwich and crumbled up his cardboard box. "Well, nothin' wrong with just takin' a peek at how the locals live." He glanced around for somewhere to throw out his box then opted to hide it in the weeds. When he shoved the box into the grasses, he felt a prick on his hand. "Ouch!" He jerked his hand back and rubbed it. "What the hell?" he snarled as his vision went blurry and his head whirled like a top.

"You OK, Castle?" Lasher asked, but instead of answering him, Castle spun on his heels and crashed to the ground onto his back. Lasher rushed to him and shook his shoulder. "Castle! Oh shit!" He turned and spotted LaRue speaking to two other sailors and an old Filipino man. "Doc! I think Castle's been bitten by a snake!"

LaRue and the others sprinted over. He glanced up at one of the sailors. "Call the helo in—we have a medical emergency!" As the sailor rushed away, he glanced over at Lasher. "Lasher, go in our tent and grab my medical bag! Now!"

The old Filipino man searched the bushes and killed the snake with a walking stick.

Lasher returned with LaRue's medical bag.

LaRue searched through the bag, grabbed a sealed package containing a needle, and gave Castle a shot. "I'm not sure if it's going to help in this case." He shook his head. "That helo has to come, and soon."

The old Filipino man touched LaRue's shoulder. "He needs Adelfa leaves and Kamatgui flowers, now, or he will die. We need to take him to our medicine woman immediately."

LaRue nodded, as he understood that the locals had been treating snake bites for generations. "OK." He glanced up at the old man. "Where do we go?"

Minutes later, Castle was lying on a table with the village medicine woman rubbing a pasty substance on the wound and inside his cheeks. No more than four feet tall and shabbily dressed, the old woman pulled out an egg and rolled it with her right hand along Castle's chest and neck, chanting in Tagalog. Her left hand was raised to her shoulder level, and she shook it while she chanted.

The old Filipino man touched LaRue's arm. "She must call in the spirits to help. It is very serious."

LaRue patted his hand, convinced that it was not these so-called spirits that would save Castle but the pasty substance she'd applied all over him—along with the generic anti-venom shot.

A sailor rushed up to LaRue. "ETA for the helo is thirty minutes, Doc. The plan is to land right here in the village and med-evac him straight to Clark Air Base."

LaRue nodded.

The medicine woman suddenly stopped chanting and grabbed the arm of the old Filipino man, fear in her eyes as she spoke to him in Tagalog.

The old man's eyes and mouth opened wide. He turned to LaRue. "In order to save him, our medicine woman had to remove a powerful blocking protection spell on this man—an old spell from before his time."

LaRue stared at the old man and woman. He did not share their concern since this spirit thing was way out there in left field, but he also remembered his orders to respect the local customs. He nodded. "OK, but does she think he'll live?"

The old man nodded. "Yes, but she says his soul is dark; Aswang no longer dormant."

LaRue had no idea what an 'Aswang' was, but he had always known Castle to be a loser. Out of courtesy, he nodded again.

"We need to prep him for flight, Doc. The helo will be here soon," the other sailor interrupted.

LaRue stared at the old man and the medicine woman. "Thank you so much. You've been so helpful, but I need to prepare him for his flight to the hospital."

The medicine woman frowned and moved away, making room for LaRue to prepare Castle for the flight to the base hospital. She then grasped LaRue's arm and spoke to him in broken English. "Believe and beware." After a few seconds, she released him and rushed out of the shack.

chapter 3

Home of Sarah's Aunt Fran and Uncle Gary,
New Orleans, Louisiana

Rob pulled his compact rental car into the large, U-shaped driveway, stopped, then stared out the window at a massive white two-story home with a dozen or so windows adorned with thin black shutters. In front was a small-roofed entrance with large, black-framed wall lanterns on both sides of the doorway. He turned to look at his girlfriend in the passenger seat. "Sarah, you didn't tell me your Aunt Fran was well off!"

Sarah grinned and swept back her straight blonde hair. "I told you she married the owner of the company she works for." She raised her hand. "Well, I take that back. Uncle Gary's a partner, but he holds major stock, therefore, he *runs* the company. His passion, though, is cooking, so I'll have to watch my diet this summer."

Rob grinned, shaking his head. "So, I have to stay on a college campus run by conservative Jesuit priests, most likely set up in austere living quarters, a room with a single bed and a sink, eating only bread and apples, while you lavish in the luxury of a mansion, filling your face with gourmet food. How unfair is that!"

"Ha!" Sarah blurted out then leaned over and kissed his cheek. "Someone has to rough it, sweetie, so be a good boyfriend and take the bullet."

At that moment, a middle-aged man and woman walked out of the front door. The woman was beaming, and she rushed to the passenger side door as the smiling man continued in the same direction but at a slower pace.

"I think they're excited to see you," Rob commented then opened his door.

Sarah glanced back at him as she opened her door, wearing a huge grin. "I'm her favorite, so you'd better be nice to me," she teased. As she got out of the car, she landed right in the arms of her aunt.

Aunt Fran gave Sarah a big embrace. "Sarah! Oh, it's so good to see you, and to have you for three full weeks!" She held onto her niece and kissed her cheeks multiple times. "I want to hear all about your first year at Boston University."

"I'm so glad to be here, Aunt Fran. I missed you," Sarah replied, returning the huge hug.

Uncle Gary put his hand on Aunt Fran's shoulder, who then let Sarah go. He gave Sarah a gentler hug. "Hi, Sarah. I'm so glad you came. This summer's going to be awesome with you here. I've got my chef partner back."

"Hi, Uncle Gary," Sarah replied. "I missed you guys, and I can't wait to cook with you."

Aunt Fran eyed Rob with a grin. She took in his short dark hair, medium height, and relatively thin but athletic body frame. He was standing a few feet away, still on the other side of the car. "So, Sarah," she said, then paused, winking at Rob, "this must be the good-looking young man I've been hearing so much about from your mother."

Rob dropped his chin and blushed, then he approached them.

Sarah and Rob walked toward one another, then Sarah turned toward Aunt Fran and Uncle Gary. "Guys, I'd like you to meet my boyfriend, Rob Faulks."

Rob nodded. "It's nice to meet you. Sarah's told me so much about you."

Aunt Fran reached out and pulled Rob into a hug. "We hug in this family, Rob, so get used to it. Nice to finally put a face to the name."

Uncle Gary stepped closer to the couple, placed his hands on his hips, and stared at Rob suspiciously. "Rob, do you like bacon?"

"Love it," Rob replied. "I put bacon bits in my eggs every morning."

Uncle Gary grinned and nodded approvingly then shook Rob's hand. "You're a winner in my book, young man; a fellow bacon lover."

Sarah chuckled at Rob. "I forgot to tell you. Uncle Gary's a fanatic about bacon."

"And there's something wrong with that?" Uncle Gary demanded jokingly.

Aunt Fran grabbed Sarah around the shoulders and led her into the house. "Come, dinner's ready. We'll eat first and grab your things later."

Rob followed Sarah and Aunt Fran, walking next to Uncle Gary. "Gorgeous home, Mr. Smith."

Uncle Gary glanced up at the house. "Thank you, Rob. We've put a lot of work into it."

They walked inside to the entryway and foyer. The entire floor was checkered with two-foot black-and-white tiles, and above them hung a huge crystal chandelier. In front of them was a large staircase hugging the wall and spiraling upward to a landing with a coffee table and two large sofas. Rob stopped and just stared, marveling at the interior. To the right was the entrance to the living room with a large, white-framed fireplace. Above the mantelpiece was a six-foot tall mirror in an oak frame.

Sarah turned around and giggled. "Catch up, Rob!"

Aunt Fran also turned and grinned. "The dining room's this way."

They walked into the dining room through an entrance with open oak doors. A large glass dining table was in the center of the room, surrounded by ten cushioned chairs. To the right, the dining room opened into a family room finely furnished around a gorgeous white rug, a bar dominating the space. Rob glanced back at the dining room table, which was filled with food.

"Whoa!" he blurted out.

Uncle Gary's lips curved as he said, "I hope you're hungry, Rob!"

"Gary and I went all out tonight," Aunt Fran commented. "Time to dig in!"

They all sat down and attacked the food. As time went by, the conversation was mixed with lots of laughter, and Aunt Fran and Uncle Gary's oft-used wine glasses ensured even more revelry. Rob could tell that family was important to them, and they loved Sarah.

Uncle Gary glanced over at Rob. "So, Rob, Fran gave me a 'Reader's Digest' version a while ago, but why are you and Sarah in this summer course?"

"Well," Rob began, "Sarah and I were approached by the forensic department chair at Boston University, and he told us we were handpicked to participate in a three-week pro bono forensics/law enforcement college-accredited course at Loyola University, run by the Vidocq Society. All expenses paid."

"Handpicked!" Sarah interrupted. "Only a handful of the top college professors and experts in forensic and law enforcement were asked to make recommendations."

"Wow!" Aunt Fran commented. "You two certainly must be doing well at college."

Sarah stared at Rob with a meaningful gaze. "It's because Rob helped solve two big serial killer cases—the Niagara Falls and October Serial Killer investigations."

Uncle Gary glanced back at Rob. "Very impressive."

"Dr. Dunham," Rob explained, "chief scientist at the FBI Lab, was asked to recommend just one person on a list, but he insisted upon two." He stared back at Sarah. "He also chose Sarah because of her help with the October Serial Killer investigation." He turned back to Uncle Gary and Aunt Fran. "And when the Watchmaker insists on something, he gets it."

Aunt Fran gave both Sarah and Rob an inquisitive look. "Watchmaker?"

"That's the nickname everyone calls Dr. Dunham," Sarah answered. "When a serial killer task force is stumped, they call on the Watchmaker. He's amazing, and he's such a humble man." She paused. "Just like Rob."

Rob blushed and shook his head, grinning slightly.

"Wasn't he involved in that famous Cincinnati serial killer case a few years back?" Uncle Gary asked. "The 'Watchmaker' name rings a bell."

Rob nodded, then glanced over at Aunt Fran. "He solved that case and many others, but I'm not surprised you've never heard of him. He tries to keep a low profile."

"Like I said," Sarah interjected, "he's humble."

"I can see him fitting in with the Vidocq Society then," Uncle Gary commented. "I came across them when I was researching the history of certain French cuisines. Apparently, Vidocq was a French criminal-turned-detective who started France's entire detective bureau a couple hundred years ago. Scotland Yard even modeled themselves on this guy's work. The Vidocq Society, if I recall, is based out of Philadelphia and is a group of detective and forensic experts who volunteer their expertise in solving crimes."

Rob nodded. "They have a big reputation."

"The forensic chairman at BU said, if all goes well, this kind of invite is a golden ticket for any future jobs in law enforcement and forensics," Sarah explained, "as long as we don't screw it up."

"I highly doubt you will," Aunt Fran assured then leaned toward her niece with a non sequitur: "After dinner, I have to show you my newest additions."

Uncle Gary raised his hands animatedly then pointed at Rob. "Pray Sarah doesn't catch the shoe-bug from her aunt! You know, we built an addition off of our bedroom just for her 'new additions'!" He pretended to be bowled over by her shoe collection, but his slight grin spoke volumes.

Aunt Fran brushed both hands forward. "Oh, you and your teasing!" she said to her husband. Then, to the young couple: "Just ignore the grumpy bear. Bacon's gone to his head." She stood. "OK, time for dessert."

chapter 4

Foliage Park, New Orleans

Frankie Hambone peeked from behind one of the many trees in the wooded park, spying on a very young girl swinging alone in her secluded backyard some twenty feet away. His clothing, an earth-colored shirt with tan cargo shorts and a soft-sided outback hat, blended nicely with the bushes and trees. He spotted the neighbor in the adjoining yard, grilling on his back porch. The neighbor was popping in and out from the living room, obviously keeping one eye on the cookout chow and one eye on the baseball game, as he'd called out to his loud friends inside about the game several times. When the neighbor finally went back inside and closed the sliding glass door behind him, Frankie grinned at the sight of the solitary swinging figure. *Perfect*, he thought to himself. For weeks, he had been sneaking through the woods after work, casing all of the backyards for just this kind of opportunity; a little girl ripe for the picking. He rubbed his groin in anticipation and glanced up at the setting sun. *Just a few more minutes*, he thought. At that moment, he spotted a woman opening the sliding glass door of the house. Anger flooded his senses at the possibility of his opportunity slipping away.

"Katie!" the woman yelled to the young girl,. "Ten more minutes, then you need to come in and get ready for bed." A large German shepherd was in the kitchen next to the lady, halfway out the door, whimpering to go to the little girl.

"OK, Mommy," the young girl replied, still swinging.

The mother pulled back on the collar of the shepherd. "Back up, Bronson." Then she closed the sliding glass door, leaving the dog to nose at the glass.

"Yes," the man in the woods whispered. He noticed the shepherd pacing back and forth, still watching the girl, but the mother was no longer in the kitchen. He moved out from behind the tree and into the darkened path but then stood still once he realized the ever-watchful shepherd had stopped pacing, as if it were staring right at him in the woods. "Shit." He waited for a moment. Although the dog still stared, it didn't bark. *It's now or never*, he thought to himself. Just as he was about to rush into the backyard and snatch the girl, he heard a branch break close behind him. He froze and listened. A low, deep growl caused the hair on the back of his neck to rise. He slowly reached into his pocket and grasped a knife with a four-inch blade. As he pulled the knife out, he spun to face whatever was behind him. Mere feet away, a massive wolflike creature glared at him. Frankie's jaw dropped in fear, and his knife slipped through his fingers and fell to the ground.

In an instant, the animal emitted a piercing screech and attacked the man, who stepped backward and fell. His scream was cut short by the animal's jaws tightening around his neck.

Little Katie heard the strange sounds and stopped swinging. She stared into the woods. Her dog was barking loudly in the kitchen. She could still hear some kind of noise going on in the woods. Wondering what it could be, the four-year-old left the swing and ran to the edge of her yard, to the tree line, stopped, and peeked into the darkness. She almost turned back to go and tell her mom, but Katie's curiosity got the better of her. She slowly walked into the woods onto the well-worn path, following the sound. After a few more steps, she stopped when she saw a large, dark, hairy animal just behind a tree, wiggling low to the ground like Bronson did when he was trying to teach a rope toy who was boss. Katie ran up to the tree and stared. She could see what the animal looked like and what it was doing; a huge dog, bigger than any dog she'd ever seen, was attacking a man. She flinched when blood spattered onto her face.

The animal stopped when it realized it was being watched, then it glared at the little girl. It raised its head and shifted all of its attention to her.

Little Katie froze in fear.

The creature gave a deep growl low in its throat and stalked toward the girl.

Katie screamed and ran back as fast as her short legs would carry her, but she tripped. She rolled to her back and saw the creature coming toward her quickly with its jaws wide open. Its oversized teeth glimmered in the faint light. She screamed, closed her eyes, and raised her arms just as it was about to bite.

Out of nowhere came the German shepherd, streaking past Katie, and he attacked the creature, biting into its massive neck. The momentum of the shepherd's body colliding with the other animal knocked the creature back, away from the girl. The massive animal, twice the size of the shepherd, regained its balance, stood up on two legs, and swiped the dog off to the side. The shepherd landed, turned back, and instantly challenged the creature again, barking ferociously, purposely keeping himself between his girl and the behemoth.

Katie jumped up and ran along the path back into her yard.

"Katie!" her mother shouted from beside the empty swing set. Her screaming daughter ran out of the woods, and in an instant, she met her and scooped her up. Blood was on Katie's face and shirt. "What's wrong, Katie? Are you all right?"

Katie just screamed.

The woman realized her shepherd was fighting something—or someone—in the woods.

"Bronson!" she yelled, but she only heard the continued sounds of fighting, the dog seemingly ignoring her. "Bronson! Come!"

The man next door walked out onto his back porch, opened his grill, and picked up a spatula. Then he noticed the commotion going on across the yard: little Katie screaming, their dog growling and barking out of sight in the woods, and his neighbor clearly upset. He turned to his noisy companions. "Bob, quiet! Quiet!" He raised his hand as they stopped talking. He dropped the spatula and sprinted off the deck. "Come on, guys!" he shouted over his shoulder. "Something's wrong!"

Two men rushed out of the house and followed their friend.

"Bronson!" Katie's mother screamed for a third time, but instead of her dog coming out of the woods, it was a man stumbling, his clothes ripped to shreds and bloody from head to toe. She screamed and backed toward her house. The man dropped, facedown and motionless, in front of the swings.

The neighbor and his two friends finally crossed into the yard. "Linda!" he yelled, positioning himself between Katie's mother and the bloodied man.

Seconds later, Bronson ran out of the woods but stopped at the tree line, turned around, and faced the path as if something were about to come out and attack. The dog was drenched in sweat mixed with blood. Bronson scurried from side to side, agitated and barking frantically.

A loud howl followed by a shriek emanated from just inside the woods, followed by a deep, guttural growl.

Something vicious was in those trees, and the neighbor didn't want to find out what. He turned toward Linda and bellowed, "Take Katie, get into the house, and call 9-1-1!"

Linda squeezed her daughter tightly, ran into the house, and locked the sliding glass door behind her. As she placed her weeping daughter onto the kitchen floor, Linda grabbed the phone, dialed, and put the receiver to her ear. She glanced out the glass door and watched the neighbor and his friends inspecting the bloodied man; her shepherd was still zig-zagging in front of the path like a sentinel on patrol duty. Luckily, nothing was coming out of the woods . . . yet.

Katie curled up in a ball and rocked.

Linda sat next to her and held her as she explained the emergency to the 9-1-1 dispatcher.

Detective John Bakula stood in the backyard, sipping a cup of coffee, looking over the body of the mutilated man. In his late thirties, relatively tall, and with an athletic build, Bakula's clean-shaven face and short, well-groomed, dark hair gave him a youthful look. He had been in the business long enough for everyone working crime scene to know he was extremely competent. Crime scene specialists hovered near the body, which was lit up by portable, high-luminosity lamps. Police officers swarmed the area, from inside Linda's house to the backyard, in and around the neighbor's house, and searching through the wooded park. Flashing police lights colored the nighttime sky. Bakula looked to his right and saw his senior partner, Detective Harold Oglesby, approaching from the direction of the house. Bakula glanced behind his partner to take stock of the homeowner. "How's Mrs. Afton? Still freaked out?"

Oglesby nodded. "A little bit, but better. The girl's still traumatized though. Won't say a thing, poor kid." He stared into the woods. "They find anything in the park yet?"

"No, nothing; just the attack site about fifteen feet past the tree line," Bakula replied. "The park forest is thin and long and butts up against a dozen backyards."

Oglesby peeked over at the body. "Wow, that is a nasty attack—entrails sticking out. It's a wonder he made it out of the woods." He bent and studied the mutilated man's face.

Bakula flagged down one of the crime scene specialists. "Initial assessment, Caz. Is this an animal attack, or do we have a homicide on our hands?"

The specialist pointed to one of the wounds on the body. "These wounds are consistent with bite marks from a large animal, Detective. To me, the tears indicate a relatively narrow muzzle." He looked up at Bakula. "Initially, I'd say this was a dog attack. As of yet, I can't discount more than one attacker, especially with the severity and sheer number of wounds."

"Like a pack of dogs," Bakula commented then paused. "How about a gator attack? The canal behind this park goes right into Lake Pontchartrain."

Caz shook his head. "I don't think so, but we'd better get an animal attack expert's opinion to be safe."

"I think I know this guy, John," Oglesby interrupted, wiped his balding head, and nodded. "Yep. Frankie Hambone. He's a convicted child sex offender. He's some kind of tour guide on a swamp boat. I pulled him in for questioning three weeks ago about the kidnapping and murder of a child."

Bakula thought he and Oglesby were an excellent fit. Generally, it was the older detective taking the younger detective under his wing, but in this case, he was purposely partnered with Oglesby to keep an eye on him until he retired. Bakula sipped his coffee and thought for a moment. Although the department may have lost their confidence in Oglesby, he hadn't. The old man had a knack for detective work, and he knew everyone—even this Frankie Hambone. Bakula glanced at the woods. "That explains why he was lurking around just behind this particular house, the bastard." He eyed his partner. "Oges, do you think Mrs. Afton's shepherd did this, maybe protecting the kid after Mr. Hambone pulled her out of the backyard? It's the most logical explanation so far."

Oglesby shook his head then gazed at the victim's face. "Not if we're going to believe her and the neighbor's testimony. They said her shepherd was still fighting something when Frankie ran out of the woods and fell dead at their feet." He pointed at the entrance to the path. "Then the dog came out of the woods and turned around, waiting for something to follow him."

Bakula nodded. "Right; with this kind of mutilation, the shepherd's muzzle would have been covered in blood . . . and we did see blood, but nothing that would indicate the canine was the primary attacker."

Oglesby shook his head again. "Here's the freaky thing. The neighbor and his two friends claim that when the dog left the woods, some kind of animal was screeching and howling just inside the pathway and kept it up for a few minutes."

"We should take a blood sample of the German shepherd," Caz recommended. "Also, I'm sure the victim's body is covered with the attacking animal's DNA-filled saliva."

Bakula nodded. "Let's make it happen. If it doesn't match the shepherd, it looks like we have a Cujo—or a killer pack—on our hands." He glanced over at Oglesby. "There've been some feral dog pack sightings and animal mutilations just west of here. Maybe there's a connection."

A group of police officers with a canine unit came out of the woods and approached the detectives.

"Find anything?" Bakula asked the lead police officer.

"The scent continued to the other side of the woods but then stopped abruptly as though the animal disappeared," the police officer explained. "We did find a few items—trash, really—and they could've been there before. There wasn't any sign of blood."

"Doesn't look like much but bag it anyway," Bakula replied.

As the canine unit left, Oglesby said, "I think you're onto something, and with the ferociousness of the attack, maybe we should contact the zoo to see if all their predators are accounted for."

Bakula nodded. "One thing's for sure, regardless of how Hambone died . . . that dog saved the little girl's life. He should get a medal."

chapter 5

FBI Lab, Quantico, Virginia

Dr. Dunham sat in the back of the conference room watching members of his team setting up a video call with two detectives from the Big Rapids Police Department. Lately, he tried not to get directly involved with each criminal case that came to Behavioral Analysis Unit 2 at the National Center for the Analysis of Violent Crimes, since he had a habit of taking over while his team merely watched. Everyone in his department was highly trained and well qualified to assist local law enforcement in their investigations. He believed backing off would allow space for his subordinates to build their confidence, especially Jack Stride, one of his special agent supervisors. Jack was a brilliant scientist, just a little insecure. Slightly bald, wearing wire-rimmed glasses and having a thin, medium-build body was quite a contrast to many of the physically powerful special agents, which didn't help his confidence. Lately, though, Dunham noticed Jack was coming into his own.

Jack was standing while the four other team members were seated. He glanced up at the video monitor. "Can you hear us, Detective?"

"Loud and clear, Special Agent Stride," the detective replied.

Heather Kennedy burst into the room as if she owned it, but everyone allowed her this latitude because of her amazing ability to keep everyone ahead of the ballgame. Heather was another one of Dunham's special agent supervisors. She was small in stature, though stocky, and her dark glasses matched her equally dark cropped hair. Even though she had a habit of telling everyone what to do, including her bosses, they all welcomed it. They knew her mantra, since she repeated it to everyone on a weekly basis: 'We need to be proactive, not reactive.'

"Jack, you'll need the results of the database search," Heather exclaimed as she gave each special agent a copy.

"Thank you, Heather. This is what we were looking for. You're the best," Jack replied.

She walked up to Dunham and handed him his iPhone. "Here's your phone, Dr. Dunham. You forgot to pick it up from the security guard at the front desk."

"Thank you, Heather, you're the best." Dunham complimented.

"Didn't Jack just say that?" Heather joked then walked to the door.

"Show me someone who doesn't believe it," Dunham returned, ensuring Heather heard him as she closed the door behind her.

"Do you mind if we begin outside the apartment, Detective?" Jack asked.

The detective nodded. "Sounds good."

Michael Peters, assistant commissioner for the FBI's Critical Incident Response Group—and Dunham's boss—opened the door, spotted Dunham, and quickly sat next to him. "I heard you were back in town," he whispered. "How was New Hampshire?"

Dunham gave a slight grin. "Great; very friendly people."

"I heard you solved the serial killer case for them," Peters commented.

Dunham nodded. "The offender was initially on their suspect list, but they excluded him early in the investigation because of a seemingly solid, but false, alibi." He glanced over at Peters. "I tripped him up when I interviewed him. He led us straight to the kidnapped female."

Peters turned and watched the video monitor and grinned. "The guy underestimated you, didn't he?"

Dunham shrugged. "His ego was his undoing."

"What's going on here?" Peters asked, nodding toward five members of Dunham's team video conferencing with two men in suits and ties walking around a residential area.

"The Big Rapids PD requested our assistance on a burglary/murder/sexual assault case," Dunham explained. "We're watching two of their detectives in the victim's apartment complex, where her body was discovered. She was an elderly woman, found facedown in her apartment hallway. There was facial battery and evidence of sexual assault. The apartment was torn apart and burglarized.

Jack Stride's running this. Our team just finished reviewing the case file, which prompted them to ask for a video conference with the local detectives at the crime scene."

"Why are you in the back of the room?" Peters asked.

"I'm trying to stay out of it. In fact, I haven't even spoken to them about the case yet." He thumped his copy of the case file with his thumb. "I began reviewing it only an hour ago."

"I see Jack has two criminal profilers with him," Peters commented.

Dunham nodded. "The local detectives believe the unemployed, middle-aged son murdered his mother, but they don't have enough evidence to convict. Neighbors saw him having a heated argument with his mother the night before about borrowing money, and when the police went to his apartment two blocks away, they found graphic satanic and sexual drawings all over the place. Besides acting strangely, he refused to cooperate with the detectives. Some bloodstains were found in his car, but the results aren't back from the lab yet."

Peters eyed the team. "Sounds plausible to me, so why the profilers? Wouldn't crime scene technicians be more appropriate?"

"Jack and his team are not convinced of the son's guilt—nor am I. They want the detectives to consider that the son really doesn't fit the profile. If they reallocate their limited resources and invest more time on other potential suspects, maybe they'll be able to break the case." He grinned. "And, as far as my hunch, remember the name Alvin Fresco."

"Would you walk out to the street in front of the apartment complex and direct the video camera toward the apartment, Detective?" Jack asked.

The detective did as instructed, and the cameraman scanned the apartment complex for all to see.

"Just as I thought," one of the criminal profilers said. "Detective, this is Special Agent Graham, criminal profiling specialist."

"What do you have, Special Agent?" the detective asked.

"The view of the victim's front door is blocked from the street," Graham explained; he glanced at his fellow criminal profiler, and they nodded to each other. "This suggests that your victim was targeted, meaning the offender was not an opportunistic stranger committing a crime right off the street. He entered and exited from the front door, which is situated inside the apartment complex facing not only the inner parking lot but also dozens of front doors and balconies. The offender felt some level of comfort with the inner parking lot environment and was not threatened by all those potential witnesses."

"Exactly," the detective interrupted, "and her son was very comfortable with this location."

Graham nodded. "Very true, and a family member as the prime suspect is warranted in a case of a victim being murdered in their own home, especially when there is no evidence of forced entry."

"He's clearly a sexual deviant," the detective interrupted, "and the victim was sexually assaulted."

"Yes, but this is actually why we believe the son is innocent," Graham interjected. "In case study after case study, when a son murders his own mother and is motivated by anger, rarely is there a sexual assault involved."

The detectives remained silent.

"Also," Graham continued, "more often than not, the son will cover the body of the deceased mother, seemingly out of respect, but the victim in your investigation was not covered."

"The bruises and wounds to the face are very telling," Jack added. "This is an angry crime and not just a burglary. The offender clearly has a violent streak. Yes, the son was apparently angry at the mother the day before, but your investigation of the son's background shows a generally caring son with no history of violent behavior toward her."

The detective shook his head, frustrated. "OK, if we eliminate our prime suspect, where does that leave us? Back to the drawing board?"

"We don't think so," Graham answered. "That level of comfortability points to a resident of the apartment complex knowing the habits of their neighbors." He glanced over toward a blonde-haired woman to his far right.

"Hello, Detective," the woman began, "Special Agent Judy Durnell here; I'm a document analyst and researcher, and I was given a list of those living in the apartment complex. I believe this list came from you. I ran the names through our databases, then through a behavioral analysis program, and one particular individual was red-flagged—an Alvin Fresco."

Dunham glanced over at Peters, grinning.

"Did they tell you the results of the database search?" Peters asked.

Dunham shook his head.

"Show off," Peters whispered.

"He has a history of violent behavior against males and females," Durnell added, "domestic abuse, and three years ago he was charged with sexual assault against an elderly woman in Pennsylvania, although she suspiciously dropped the charges."

"Yeah, we interviewed Fresco," the detective began, "but we put him on our B-list because his girlfriend gave a convincing alibi." He paused. "And to be honest, once we had the son in our sights, we focused our time there. But, in our defense, we didn't know about the out-of-state sexual assault charge."

Jack nodded. "Yes, we're adding to our national databases on a daily basis, so it's no surprise we had this information and you did not." He paused. "That's really all we have, other than recommending searching Fresco's vehicle and his girlfriend's home."

"Thank you, Special Agent Stride, and everyone," the detective said. "This clarifies our next step."

Peters's cell phone rang, and he pulled it out as he stood, opened the door, and leaned into the hallway. "Assistant Director Peters." He paused. "Oh, hello, sir."

"Yes, sir, right away." Peters hung up, turned, and approached Dunham. "Edward," he whispered, "that was Director Allen. He's tasked me to escort you to NCIS Headquarters immediately."

Dunham stood. "What does the Navy want with me?"

"I'm not sure, but we've got to meet with their director in a half hour. It must be important." He looked at his watch. "We can easily make the six-mile drive across base in fifteen or twenty minutes. Do you need to make a pit stop before we leave?"

Dunham shook his head. "I'm ready. Let's not keep him waiting." As Dunham followed Peters to the door, he glanced back, made eye contact with Jack, and gave him an enthusiastic thumbs-up.

Jack beamed and waved.

Thirty minutes later, Assistant Director Peters and Dr. Dunham were just outside of the director's office at NCIS Headquarters. Peters glanced over at Dunham. "Director Allen is very approachable, but from what I've seen, he's all business and prefers no small talk."

Dunham nodded. "No problem. I'm not a big talker anyway."

Peters snickered. "I know, but I am. Elbow me if I start to ramble." He knocked on the door then opened it at the command from the voice on the other side.

Director Allen was an older gentleman with a full head of well-groomed white hair. "Come in, gentlemen, come in," he said, standing to greet the newcomers and straightening his high-end gray suit.

Dunham noticed a second man seated in the director's office, who also stood as the pair walked into the room. The man appeared to be in his forties, very fit, with short hair, and wore a suit and tie—the classic look of a special agent.

Allen shook Peters's hand. "Nice to see you again, Michael, and thank you for coming on such short notice. You'll see why in a moment." Then he turned to Dunham.

"Director," Peters began, "this is Dr. Edward Dunham."

Allen shook Dunham's hand. "Introductions are unnecessary. Hello, Dr. Dunham, I am fully aware of your background. Excellent job on that October Serial Killer case last year."

"Thank you, sir," Dunham said as Allen abruptly turned away, clearly not interested in any details from him about the case and confirming Peters's assessment of him.

Director Allen indicated the other man in the room. "Dr. Dunham, this is NCIS Special Agent Dick Turner. He works out of the Cold Case Homicide Unit at NCIS."

Turner shook Dunham's hand. "It's great to finally meet you, Dr. Dunham."

"Thank you," Dunham replied. "Nice to meet you."

Allen went back to his desk. "Please, take a seat." Once everyone was settled, Allen leaned forward. "Let's get right to the point. The Navy needs you, Dr. Dunham. In a few months, a whistle-blower will be publishing a book on a massacre that occurred in the Philippines in the late 1980s, which includes the deaths of seven US sailors. They were found mutilated in a local jungle village." He glanced over at Special Agent Turner. "The subsequent investigation was extensive, but it came up with nothing, and to this day, it basically remains unsolved."

Dunham's spine stiffened. "I don't recall hearing about this case."

"For good reason," Allen replied. "Up until yesterday, the case was classified because the humanitarian mission that these sailors were on was part of a larger sensitive mission to recover a secret spy plane that had crashed a few hundred yards off the coast of the Philippines. Because of this, the family members of these fallen sailors were not given an explanation as to how their loved ones perished. They wanted answers then, and they still want them now. Some are convinced there's been a military cover-up."

"And it being classified fed into their belief in that," Peters interrupted.

Allen glanced over at Peters. "Exactly." He paused. "Although the president has an excellent grasp of sensitive information vital to our national security, he also believes transparency will improve the mistrust the press and many citizens have with the military." He paused again. "Instead of allowing the popularity of the book to further entrench this mistrust, the president has ordered the declassification of the entire mission, allowing the investigation to be publicly scrutinized."

Dunham nodded. "So, the public will see there was no military cover-up. But the fact that the case remains unsolved may suggest Navy ineptitude. Is this the concern?"

Allen nodded. "Yes, in part, but the bigger concern is what the author is claiming . . . negligence on the part of Navy leadership. Word has it that he believes the village was in a pro-Communist stronghold and the villagers were Communist sympathizers, and that the CO of the on-scene Navy warship, directed by his chain of command, ordered his sailors to go ashore and do a humanitarian mission in the village armed only with paint brushes and medical equipment. Once the sailors were there, angry villagers and their armed fighters attacked them and ruthlessly mutilated their bodies with machetes. The fighters then vanished into the jungle. Somehow, some photos of our dead sailors have surfaced, supporting his claim—and he's publishing them."

Dunham glanced over at Peters, then back at Allen. "*Was* the village a Communist stronghold?"

Allen shook his head. "Not at all, as confirmed by the Special Forc—" he stopped and coughed. "Excuse me, confirmed by the local intel who was sent there just after the plane crashed off the coast. The closest pro-Communist stronghold was hundreds of miles to the east. Once our US warship was on scene and positioned itself just off the coast, security was in place on land, and the ship's company was mingling with the villagers that very day. The sailors were working hand-in-hand with the villagers for three full days with absolutely no negative incidents. In fact, the villagers even put on a ceremony on behalf of the US sailors." He pointed at Dunham. "Thanks to an executive order, you have the authority to report this."

"Since Dr. Dunham will be the one to reveal this, and not the United States Navy, it'll demonstrate to the world that the US military not only properly secured the area but also doesn't cave to public pressure demanding answers," Peters surmised.

Allen nodded. "Hell, just the fact that villagers were also mutilated should show they weren't Communist sympathizers . . . but there's more. Our concern is to break the case and not just eliminate blame." He glanced over at Turner. "I tasked Special Agent Turner to assist you in the investigation in hopes of breaking this cold case before the book is released. That is, of course, if you take it."

Turner eyed Dunham. "To be honest, the CCHU is in over our heads." He raised his palm. "Not that we aren't up to the task, but a resolution in such a short time gives us an extremely low probability of success. For one thing, I personally reviewed the case over ten years ago, and I came up empty."

"Post 9/11 has changed NCIS priority to anti-terrorism, Dr. Dunham," Allen interrupted, "and low on the funding agenda are cold cases, so CCHU has only six full-time special agents, all working a constant full load. This cold case investigation has been given top priority at the highest levels of government, but realistically, we can't do it without your help."

"I agreed with the suggestion to have you investigate this, Dr. Dunham," Turner added.

"Thanks for the confidence." Dunham glanced over at Peters. "If it's OK with my boss, I would be honored to assist."

"Of course," Peters replied.

"Will you give me a brief overview of the case before I read the folder, Special Agent Turner?" Dunham asked.

"The USS *Ouellette*, a Navy frigate, was sent to the coast of the Philippines when a spy plane lost hydraulics in-flight and crashed a few hundred yards off the coast," Turner explained. "The frigate was the closest warship available. While the subsequent salvage operations were taking place, the commanding officer was directed to give humanitarian assistance to the local village. Three days into the operation, one of the sailors sent into the village, a Petty Officer Joseph Castle, was bitten by a venomous snake, which prompted a call on the radio for an emergency med-evac." He glanced over at Director Allen, then back to Dunham. "Here's where it gets real strange. When the Navy helicopter arrived on the scene, the air crew reported seeing what looked like a tribal warzone. The entire village of around thirty locals and seven of the eight sailors were found dead; their bodies were mutilated. The only person found alive was the unconscious sailor bitten by the snake, although his clothes were torn to shreds."

The phone rang, and Director Allen answered. "Excellent; everyone's here." He hung up.

"We quickly eliminated the surviving sailor as having any involvement in the killings," Turner continued, "because the extent of the total carnage—all occurring in just minutes, mind you—matched that of what a small army could do." He glanced over at Allen. "Besides, he was unconscious at the time of the radio call, then he was found weaponless in the jungle just outside the village, clothes nearly torn off, with a puncture or bullet wound in his side, consistent with running and hiding from the attackers."

Dunham nodded. "Did he recall anything?"

"Absolutely nothing," Turner answered. "As if the snake venom gave him insomnia."

"Did you consider a local Filipino gang or warring group, armed with machetes or other weapons, rushing into the village?" Dunham asked. "The Filipino people are well-known within the martial arts community as experts with cutting weapons."

"That's the first thing they investigated, but not all of the wounds were consistent with sharp instruments." Turner paused. "But before I go into the details of the crime scene, you'll probably want to review the entire case." He handed Dunham a large file.

Dunham took the file and nodded. "Indeed, I would. We think alike. I'd like to spend a few days looking it over."

Turned nodded. "That's just the official report. I'll have the boxes of additional material sent to you today through secured inter-department mail."

"Excellent. What happened to the aircrew of the spy plane?"

"They survived unharmed," Turner explained, "and were even sent to the *Ouellette* to help in the salvage operations."

Dunham nodded. "Who suggested I help?"

Director Allen stood, followed by Turner. "Coincidentally, I was about to tell you, Dr. Dunham," Allen replied, grinning. "The reason why this case has been given high priority is because the uncle of deceased Petty Officer LaRue is none other than the vice president of the United States, and if my timing is correct, he's now in the hallway."

Both Peters and Dunham leaped from their seats, taken completely by surprise.

There was a knock on the door, and a Secret Service agent entered. He quickly scanned the room and then nodded to the vice president, who rushed in straight to Director Allen.

"Hi, Jerry, it's great to see you again!" Vice President LaRue greeted.

"Hello, Mr. Vice President," Allen replied, then went on to introduce everyone. "You've met Special Agent Turner."

The VP shook Turner's hand. "Great to see you, Dick."

"Thank you, Mr. Vice President."

Allen gestured to Peters. "Assistant Director Michael Peters."

Vice President LaRue smiled and shook Peters's hand. "Pleasure to meet you, Michael. I hear good things about you."

"I appreciate that, Mr. Vice President," Peters replied.

At last, Allen turned toward Dunham. "And this is Dr. Edward Dunham."

The vice president grabbed Dunham's hand, pulled him closer, and placed his free hand on Dunham's shoulder. "Dr. Edward Dunham—the Watchmaker! It's great to finally meet the man ridding our country of serial killers."

"Thank you, Mr. Vice President," Dunham replied. "I'm doing my best." He was shocked that the vice president of the United States, himself, knew the nickname given to him by the law enforcement and forensic community. Although Dunham had never promoted the moniker, the fact that many used it as a kind of battle cry against violent serial crime and gave officers and agents a level of hope made him comfortable with it.

"I assume they've been debriefed?" LaRue asked Allen.

Director Allen nodded. "All set, sir."

"Excellent. Years ago, when I was a senator, I asked the Cold Case Homicide Unit at NCIS to reinvestigate the murder of our sailors, including my nephew, and they obliged, but nothing new came of it." He paused. "The president is concerned that my name will be brought into this mess with some people screaming abuse of power and the wasting of resources for a personal agenda." He shook his head. "He even reconsidered his decision to declassify the case to keep my name out of scandalous discussion, but I insisted he follow through with it."

"I'll do my best, Mr. Vice President," Dunham replied.

"If anyone can solve this, you can," the vice president stated confidently. "I must be off, but I wanted to personally thank you in advance for your efforts." He glanced over at Allen. "Will you keep me updated, Jerry?"

"I certainly will, Mr. Vice President," Allen replied.

"Mr. Vice President," Dunham began as the man turned to leave, "not that I presume my investigation will lead me this way, but," he paused, "will I be able to contact you directly?"

Vice President LaRue glanced over at one of his men. "Am I allowed to give him my private number?" he muttered quietly.

The man shook his head. "No, Mr. Vice President, but," he tilted his head at Assistant Director Peters, "he can be transferred to your direct line at the director level."

"Well, Michael, I'll put that in your hands," LaRue answered.

"I'll take care of it on behalf of Dr. Dunham, should the need arise, Mr. Vice President," Peters replied.

After farewell handshakes, the vice president said, "Take care, everyone," and he and his Secret Service entourage rushed out of the room as fast as they'd entered.

Peters and Dunham stared at each other, still stunned.

Allen grinned. "Well, I believe we'll end on that note. Turner, keep me in the loop."

After Peters and Dunham made their way back to the car and drove out of the parking lot, Peters glanced over at Dunham and said, "If you need anything, Edward, the funding and resources will be there."

Dunham stared out the passenger side window. "Thanks," he muttered.

Peters noticed Dunham was deep in thought. "What's up?"

"My 'Spidey senses' are telling me they're holding back. They're not telling me something."

"Any ideas?" Peters asked.

Dunham shook his head and stared at the file on his lap. "Not yet, but I'm going to review the material with a fine-toothed comb. I'll let you know what I find."

chapter 6

Vidocq Crime-Solving Course,
Loyola University, New Orleans, Louisiana

Rob studied his campus map then glanced up at the building before him. "Here it is, Sarah; Stallings Hall."

Sarah grabbed Rob's arm and gasped. "This is so exciting. Ready to start our first day of crime-solving with the best of the best?"

"Sure am." Rob replied. He squeezed her hand, and they walked together into the building. Rob spotted a cardboard sign with an arrow:

Best Practices in Forensics and Criminal Investigation

Vidocq Society, Room 122

They followed the arrow and found the room set up with five tables, each having three chairs. Most of the chairs were already filled with fellow students. Everyone was silent. The instructors were not yet in the room. "Here we are," Rob said as he and Sarah approached two empty seats with nametags in front of them.

As they sat, the student already seated at their table gave a smile and a nod. He was stocky, slightly overweight, and his dark hair was wavy and unkempt. Rob reached over and shook his hand. "Hi, my name is Rob Faulks, and this is Sarah Blaine."

"Pleasure; my name is Jared Dugas."

"Is that a Cajun accent?" Sarah asked.

"Indeed it is," Jared replied. "I live just east of town, but I'm a student here at Loyola."

"'Town,' meaning New Orleans?" Rob asked.

"Sorry, yes," Jared began. "Down here we affectionately call New Orleans 'Town,' 'the Big Easy,' or 'NOLA.' It makes us folks in the Bayou feel like we own the place."

Rob snickered. "As you can probably tell by our accents, we're not from here. Sarah and I go to Boston University."

"Yankees are welcome, my friend," Jared jested back in good fun.

Four more students entered the room, and Rob noticed that all of the seats were finally taken. Then he heard two men talking in the hallway, and their voices grew louder as they neared. They walked in, and one of the men approached the front podium.

The man glanced around the room. "Excellent; I see everyone has made it. Good morning. My name is Dr. Bill Perry, chair of the Criminal Justice Department here at Loyola University. A little bit about myself; I am a forensic criminologist and the director of the Master of Criminal Justice Program, and lately, I've had the opportunity to work with local task forces in a consulting capacity." He paused and grinned at the sea of eyes before him. "But enough about me. I take great joy in having been asked by the Vidocq Society to coordinate this important three-week seminar, which has been sponsored by them. The Vidocq Society is an esteemed group of investigators and forensic experts who offer pro bono advice to any law enforcement agency with especially difficult unsolved cases, including cold cases. Their successful record speaks for itself." He gestured toward the students. "Your mentors, the men and women who recommended you for this exclusive session, are today's forensic and law enforcement movers and shakers. They were approached by members of the Vidocq Society to select students they believe are the future leaders in crime-solving. Because of this, I'm confident tomorrow's super-sleuths are sitting right here in this room." He raised his index finger. "Oh, before I forget, if you have any administrative issues during your stay, please run them by my secretary, Dorothy Clay. She's a miracle worker. My office is just down the hall." Then he pointed to Jared. "Also, Jared Dugas is an undergrad here at Loyola." Dr. Perry paused and grinned. "He's an extreme extrovert," he added, then paused again at the students' laughter, "and has offered to be the class's social coordinator."

Jared waved, stood up, and faced the students. "Dr. Perry is not far from the truth. I tend to talk people's ears off. Lunch is provided for us today, so at that time, I can answer all your questions about New Orleans—where to eat, where to go, where not to go. Thursday night is our first dinner function, and I'll be giving you the lowdown on that." He shot a nod at Dr. Perry then dropped back into his seat.

Perry waved a hand, a serious gleam to his eyes. "Word of warning," he said, "do not get Jared going on his . . ." he raised his eyebrows, "jokes."

Jared stood again, beaming, and turned to the class. "So, there's this biker dude who came into town wearing a leather jacket with a broken zipper."

Perry dropped his head then shook it, grinning slightly, allowing Jared to continue with his joke.

"He finally stopped the bike and said, 'Man, I can't drive anymore with the cold air hitting me in my chest.' So, the biker dude put his coat on backward to block the wind. He continued driving, and when he went around the bend, he lost control and crashed, right in front of Hector Two-tones's house."

Sarah glanced over at Rob, grinning.

"Hector saw the accident, so he called the police and explained what happened. The policeman asked him, 'Mr. Two-tones, is the guy showing any signs of life?' Hector replied, 'Well, he was until I turned his head around the right way!'"

The class responded with laughter and groans, and Jared sat down.

"I warned you," Perry commented, throwing his hands up in mock surrender. He turned and pointed to the man standing behind him. "I am honored to introduce you to your instructor for this prestigious course. This is Dr. John Taylor, retired professor of psychology at Houston, a fourteen-year veteran of the Houston Police Force in psychological services, specifically dealing with violent crimes. He currently lectures here at Loyola in criminal psychology. Dr. Taylor is also a member of the Vidocq Society. Students, I give you Dr. Taylor."

The class politely applauded as Dr. Taylor walked up to the podium. "Thank you, Dr. Perry, and thank you for making this all-important class a reality."

Perry waved and started for the door. "Remember, if anyone needs anything, I'm down the hall," he said as he closed the door behind him.

Taylor faced the students. "Good morning." He shifted his eyes toward Jared and paused. "The very first time I gave a lecture here at Loyola, Jared was in the class, which, coincidentally, was my introduction to Hector Two-tones."

Jared chuckled.

Taylor shook his head, grinning. "Life has never been the same."

Laugher echoed from the students before him.

"So," Taylor began, "just as Dr. Perry said, this course is sponsored by the Vidocq Society, and its purpose is to groom the best and the brightest of you for excellence in the field. The very reason for the society's existence is justice and the discovery of truth. We wholeheartedly believe people are the solution rather than technology, no matter how far it advances. In view of this, we've decided to expand our role from just advising investigators and forensic specialists to also offering crime-solving training, although on a very limited basis." Taylor approached each table and handed out a course curriculum. "The society only deals with difficult active cases; thus, by extension, you will be investigating actual active cases," he grinned, "and possibly solving them."

Jared leaned over to Rob and Sarah and whispered, "How cool is this!"

"It's legit!" Rob whispered back.

Taylor raised his finger. "Now, because these are ongoing investigations, there is a legal confidentiality component, meaning you cannot discuss these cases with anyone outside the class. Hopefully, this'll promote constructive class discussions for everyone's benefit." He paused and tapped the table in front of him. "As you can see, the class has five large tables, with three of you at each table. The second half of the class, each table will be working on individual cases, and your partners will be your tablemates."

Rob, Sarah, and Jared glanced at each other, giving thumbs-ups and nodding.

"The large tables will allow you elbow room when reviewing case files with photos, maps, etcetera," Taylor explained. "The last couple of days will be each table presenting their results to the class."

Taylor acknowledged a student who had raised her hand. She was short, thin, and had dark, curly hair.

"Lacy Gonzalez, Dr. Taylor," she said confidently. "Where will these cases come from?"

Taylor nodded. "The New Orleans Police Department is allowing us to assist them. All of you will be allowed to select from a list of active cases and cold cases." He paused. "In the words of the popular TV game show, each of you are allowed to 'phone a friend,' so to speak."

The students glanced around at each other, totally confused.

Taylor grinned. "Each of your mentors has given permission for you to ask their assistance," he raised his finger, "but only once!" He walked over to Rob's table and tapped on it. "For example, one of the FBI's chief scientists, Dr. Edward Dunham, will be assisting this table."

Rob noticed every head in the room turn in his table's direction. He blushed, surprised that Dr. Taylor remembered Dunham had selected him and Sarah.

Jared leaned toward Rob and whispered, "You know the Watchmaker?"

"This is Rob Faulks," Taylor explained, "and if you've read the papers on both the Niagara Falls Serial Killer and the October Serial Killer investigations, you may recall his name. According to Dr. Dunham, neither case would have been solved without Rob's help." He turned away and headed for his desk. "Now, it's time for him to help you."

Sarah, grinning from ear to ear, elbowed Rob, whose face was now beet red. "You're almost as famous as Dr. Dunham," she whispered.

"Hey, you helped too," Rob reminded her.

Taylor returned and handed each table a copy of today's daily newspaper. "In a minute, I'm going to have everyone stand and introduce yourselves to each other, one on one, but I'd like to begin the course by discussing a case that's been all over the local news. You may want to take it on in our second session. Take out the local section of the paper and turn to page two." As the students opened their respective papers to page two, Taylor turned and faced a white screen in the front of the room and clicked a projector screen remote. A satellite image popped up on the screen. "The article I am referring to is the recent mutilation of a man in Foliage Park. As you can see on the map, Foliage Park is a small, tree-filled park in a residential area just north of here. It is surrounded by the backyards of a dozen or more homes. Although it may not have been a homicide, it's an excellent exercise for everyone to begin to think like investigators. Take a few moments to read the article."

Sarah held the paper so both Rob and Jared could read it as well. After a few moments, Sarah glanced up at them. "Wow, the family's German shepherd saved the little girl's life."

Jared stared at the adjoining photo showing the mother holding the daughter, then pointed at the screen. "I know this park. It's next to a canal that goes into Lake Pontchartrain. My girlfriend's parents live about a block away."

"Even though it may just have been a vicious animal attack," Taylor explained, "as onsite investigators, we must treat the death as a homicide and the location as a crime scene. If we find that it was a homicide, critical physical evidence will not have been compromised—ideally. Crime scene investigation theory states that physical evidence, especially trace evidence, is always left behind. Latent prints, hair and fibers, and DNA." He paused. "Now, we will assume that the New Orleans PD has followed proper crime scene protocol and has blocked off the location, searched the area around the crime scene, such as the park and neighbors' backyards, and has interviewed the locals for any possible eyewitnesses."

Another student raised his hand. Taylor eyed his name tag and acknowledged him. "Cedric Brown."

"Dr. Taylor," Cedric began, "do you think there was evidence collected that was not reported in this newspaper column?"

"Yes, but hold that thought for the time being." He faced the class. "The mutilated body of a convicted child molester was discovered in the wooded park just behind a child's backyard. Eyewitnesses swear they heard the sound of a large growling animal among the trees." He paused and placed his index finger on his lips, then he raised it. "Hypothetical situation: the detectives who are assigned to the case approach you and ask you for assistance. They have one question for you: 'Was this a homicide?' Discuss this with your partners for a few minutes, and then we'll have a class discussion."

Jared, Sarah, and Rob faced each other. "It's clearly an animal attack," Sarah answered, "so, not a homicide. I bet it was a large dog."

"Apparently, there were extensive wounds," Rob added, "so maybe there was more than one animal, like a pack of dogs?"

Jared nodded. "We just had a feral dog pack attack on some farm animals just outside of town, so it makes sense. But I have another thought. Maybe it was a gator," he suggested as he pointed to the image of Foliage Park on the screen. "The park is next to Lake Pontchartrain, and a twelve-year-old boy was attacked by a gator in the lake a few years ago."

"I like it," Sarah answered, "but it doesn't account for the eyewitnesses hearing the growling."

Jared shrugged.

"If we assume they heard correctly," Rob surmised, "then it seems we have a dog or dog pack attack, but the problem I have with this is that no one in the neighborhood had seen any animals roaming before or after."

"Maybe they did but it wasn't reported in the paper," Jared added.

"True," Rob replied. "Still, something doesn't make sense."

Sarah grinned. "Uh-oh, Rob's got that gut-feeling thing again."

Dr. Taylor waved his hands. "OK!" he said loudly to get the class's attention. "Let's bring it back."

The room went silent as everyone looked up at him. "So, with a show of hands, who has concluded that this is not a homicide and merely an animal attack?"

Everyone in the class but Rob raised their hands.

"I see the class consensus is an animal attack. As I walked around the room, I heard you speak of the possibility of a pack of dogs, a big cat, or even an alligator attack. Now, let me add some evidence none of you were privy to." Taylor paused. "I contacted Detective Bakula, lead investigator, and he informed me that the wounds were examined by an animal attack expert, a local biologist. Apparently, the bite patterns and marks exclude an alligator attack and instead resemble that of a large, narrow-muzzled canine jaw. A partial footprint was discovered that exhibited clear claw marks in front of the pads, which seems to exclude it being a large cat, since they have retractable claws. He also noted that the pattern of the bite marks came in one size, suggesting one attacker and not a pack." He took a breath. "Here's the problem. Even though the bite marks resembled a canine, the bite pattern does not."

Students glanced at each other, surprised.

"Let me explain," Taylor continued. "According to the animal attack expert, fatal domestic dog attacks and feral dog pack attacks on humans exhibit a concentration of wounds to the extremities and not to the internal organs. The same goes for wolf pack attacks on humans—albeit an extremely rare event, apparently. Besides defensive wounds to the victim's arms, the Foliage Park victim had just the opposite—a lack of wounds to the extremities, and a concentration of wounds to the internal organs."

Jared raised his hand and Taylor acknowledged him. "How about a black bear attack? There have been black bear sightings just across the Interstate 10 Bridge in the Honey Island swamps."

Taylor nodded. "The detectives discussed this as well. The biologist told Bakula that, consistent with ursid attacks, there were claw marks on the skin in addition to a bite pattern, but the bite marks appeared canine, although she couldn't be entirely sure."

Taylor acknowledged Cedric.

"Dr. Taylor, in the article, it stated the witnesses heard deep howls followed by a scream or screech. Wouldn't this suggest a wolf or wolf-dog hybrid?"

Taylor nodded. "It would, indeed. They did do DNA swabs on the fluids surrounding the wounds, and although the results aren't back yet, this should let us know with more certainty."

Taylor called on Rob.

"Dr. Taylor, I'd like to revisit the question of homicide."

Taylor grinned. "I was hoping someone would."

"Now, I'm not saying that a human bit the victim, but it doesn't make sense that an animal dangerous enough to rip apart a man leaves the crime scene in a populated residential area of a large city without someone seeing it." He raised his finger. "Did the detectives have anyone report seeing a large animal in the area?"

"I did ask," Taylor answered, "and no one has."

Rob nodded. "It's only a small patch of woods surrounded by concrete and houses. Where is it hiding? The article did say they searched the entire park and surrounding area." Rob paused. "To me, this kind of elusiveness suggests human intervention. Also, how coincidental that a child molester, the type of person hated even by ruthless inmates in a prison, was murdered before he could kidnap a young girl."

"So, what are you suggesting?" another student asked.

Rob shrugged. "What seems to best fit the evidence is a big dog or hybrid under the control of a human, someone who trained it to kill. He or she could have ordered the animal into a van, hidden from sight, and then fled the scene."

Taylor nodded. "Sounds plausible." He glanced up at the class. "Any thoughts?"

"I agree with Rob," Lacy replied, "but the only problem I have is that training a dog to kill on demand can't be an easy task. I have a Lab, and I have a hard enough time teaching him to stay off my furniture."

Taylor grinned as a number of students chuckled. "Fair enough. Since our job is to pass on advice to the investigators," he raised his hand, "how many consider Rob's idea plausible enough for me to suggest it to Detective Bakula?"

Everyone raised their hand.

"Consider it done," Taylor commented. "If the Foliage Park mutilation is a homicide, any other possibilities?"

"It was the Rougarou," Jared blurted out.

Everyone, including Dr. Taylor, glanced over at Jared, confusion marring their expressions.

"Rougarou?" Rob asked.

"Yeah, the Rougarou has been in Cajun folklore for years. It's a swamp monster/werewolf. My uncle swears he saw it in the swamps."

A thin-framed student with red hair raised his hand. "Hi, my name is Sebastian Rohrbach, self-proclaimed expert in cryptozoology and the paranormal. Just ask me," he joked, then he cleared his throat. "There are many versions of the French Cajun Rougarou story. Some are centered upon obedience; obedience to Lent, as in, 'Catholics! If you don't follow the rules of Lent, the Rougarou will hunt you down and kill you!' Even Cajun parents and elders have used the threat of the Rougarou to scare children into obedience. Some stories are of shape-shifting werewolves cursed until they bite another poor soul. It's probably not a coincidence that the term 'werewolf' in French is, '*loup-garou*.'"

"I guess you do know something about the Rougarou," Jared complimented.

Sebastian pointed his finger in the air. "There's more, but I'll keep it short. Interestingly, in the early 1960s, there was a hairy beast roaming the swamps of Honey Island just northeast of New Orleans. Some say it was the Rougarou."

Taylor smiled. "It may be true, but I'm not sure if I want to pass *that* theory onto the detectives."

"This is New Orleans, Dr. Taylor," Jared replied. "The Big Easy. Nothing's strange here, so I'm sure it's already crossed their minds!"

Taylor shrugged, and the class laughed. He walked around to his students and handed each table a case file. "Detective Bakula has promised to inform me of the results of the DNA test, so when I receive those, we'll continue this discussion. For now, let's go onto the next case."

chapter 7

Jackson Square,
French Quarter, New Orleans, Louisiana

Ted Wallace jerked on the right rein, forcing the mule to turn too quickly onto the next road of the tour. The back wheel of the carriage popped up onto the sidewalk then slammed back onto the road. "Sorry, folks—pothole!"

"I think our tour guide is drunk, honey," whispered the gray-haired lady to her husband.

The husband leaned closer to his wife. "I think so, too, dear, but don't say anything," he warned. "I don't want him to get belligerent. Let's go straight to the manager and complain after the tour. Maybe we can even get our money back."

The wife checked her watch. "It's late, past closing, so I bet we'll have to call the manager tomorrow."

The old man nodded.

Wallace leaned to the left and passed gas, which unintentionally reverberated off the wooden seat at a few decibels above that of a loud belch.

The lady's eyes flew wide open, and she covered her nose and frowned.

"Oops!" Wallace belted out. "Looks like some of the local wildlife has hitched a ride! That was the notorious skunk toad. Ya can tell by the stink just after it croaks!" he hiccupped.

The elderly man just stared at the carriage floor and shook his head.

Wallace turned onto Decatur Street, then realized he'd just missed his last tour stop, the famous Tujague's Restaurant. He shrugged his shoulders and let the mule trot on by. "Back behind ya is Tujague's. I recommend their Sazerac whiskey," Wallace belted out. "'Nuff about that place!" He snapped the leather reins, causing the mule to quicken its pace.

The elderly couple jerked their heads back to see the restaurant then whispered angrily to each other.

Wallace spotted the carriage tour drop-off point in front of Jackson Square. As the mule trotted up to it, Wallace pulled on the reins and the carriage stopped. The elderly couple disembarked as quickly as they could and immediately rushed off, purposely ignoring the tour guide.

"Thanks for riding with Carriage Tours!" he screamed after them. "Ya couple a' old farts," he mumbled under his breath as he reached into his coat pocket and pulled out a flask. "Time for a nip of Tujague's Sazerac."

As Wallace took a chug from his flask, the mule went wild, causing the carriage to buck and rock. "Whoa, whoa, Scout. What's got ya spooked?" The night was cloudy and dark, and the streetlights created deep shadows. He glanced around but saw no one near the mule. As a matter of fact, the area was unusually empty. His carriage was the last to return, and the ticket office was closed.

Crack!

He quickly glanced over for the source of the noise, which seemed to be coming from a group of a dozen or so trees in Jackson Square. His mule bobbed its head and snorted.

Wallace stared into the darkness of the trees and bushes. He could feel eyes on him, and the hair on the back of his neck rose. He spotted a shadow moving closer, then it stopped in the tree line next to the sidewalk. His mule raised and lowered its head nervously. At that moment, Wallace noticed a pedestrian walking toward the square from behind him. He quickly recognized her as one of the local sex workers and raised his hand to warn her.

As she walked between the carriage and Jackson Square, she purposely moved away from the carriage to avoid the restless mule and the unwanted attentions of its driver.

Before Wallace could utter a word, something huge leaped at her, attacked the back of her neck, and plucked her from the ground. She screamed as the thing pulled her into the darkness.

Everything happened so fast. Wallace shook his head in sober disbelief. "What the . . ." he muttered then fell silent as he heard a deep growl. The woman's screams abruptly stopped. Seconds later, he heard a loud, deep howl followed by a shriek. The blood in his face drained from fear, and he sat motionless, his jaw hanging.

The agitated mule reared onto its back legs then bolted forward.

Wallace snapped the reins with no intentions of controlling the mule as they fled wildly from the scene.

Thirty minutes later, the tour guide, his manager, Bob Sackett, and a dozen police officers crowded the entrance to Jackson Square. Wallace pointed to the location where he'd seen the attack. "Right there! Someone, or something, grabbed her right there and pulled her into the trees! There was all sorts of screaming and howling . . . I couldn't tell what was what."

Police Sergeant Scranton watched his officers scour the area. "Check out every inch of the place!" he yelled then turned to face the tour guide. "You said you recognized the woman you saw getting attacked?"

Wallace nodded. "Yeah, she was one of the local ladies of the night. A nasty piece of work. Don't know her name though."

A police officer approached from the trees. "Sarge, nothing so far. No marks, no blood; nothing."

Scranton nodded. "Thanks. Keep on searching." He called to another nearby police officer and put his hand on the tour guide's shoulder. "Could you take Mr. Wallace and get his statement? I'd like to speak to the manager privately."

"Sure thing, Sarge," the officer replied then waved to the tour guide. "Follow me, sir."

Wallace obediently followed the police officer. "I wasn't seein' things. My mule was goin' crazy."

Once the tour guide was out of earshot, Scranton turned to Sackett. "Your man there smells like a gin factory."

The manager shook his head. "I've been getting a lot of complaints," he replied. "Too bad ol' Ted's the owner's cousin, or I'd have fired him months ago." He paused, staring into the trees. "Something certainly did ruffle his feathers, but if you don't find anything, I wouldn't be surprised. He's been known to stretch the truth."

Scranton nodded. "My thoughts exactly. We'll stay here for a while and keep on looking, and we'll speak with the other local ladies to see if any of them haven't come back from a call." He nodded to Sackett. "Thanks for all your help. If anything comes up, I'll be in touch."

Two blocks away, three college-aged women stumbled down the sidewalk after a festive evening on Bourbon Street. As they neared the entrance to an alley, the tallest of the women pointed at something on the sidewalk. "What's that?"

"What's what?" the ponytailed redhead asked.

The tall woman pointed at a dark fluid flowing from the alley into the drain. "That!"

The three women bent down, inspecting it.

"It looks like blood!" the redhead exclaimed. All three stared into the alley, but even in the relative darkness they could see the first thirty feet of the alley was empty.

"There's a huge puddle just inside the alleyway," the stout, freckle-faced woman stated. She glanced around and realized they were the only ones in the area, so she pulled the other two women away from the gruesome sight. "Let's get outta here."

chapter 8

FBI Lab, Quantico, Virginia

Assistant Director Peters opened the glass doors and entered the document lab. He spotted Jack Stride huddled with a number of document analysts and technicians around a cloth-covered aluminum lab table, staring at what appeared to be . . . garbage. High-tech equipment and computer consoles filled the room around them. He approached Stride with a slight grin. "Watch out, rumors are circulating that analyzing documents is a trashy business," he joked.

Stride glanced at Peters, completely oblivious to the joke. "Oh, hi, sir. Not only are we analyzing any items with writing, we're also identifying any possible DNA sources. This trash was collected near the crime scene."

"Isn't this the job of the local detectives and their forensics lab? Didn't they do this already?" Peters asked.

"They did look at it," Stride answered. "When they asked us to review the case, we thought it prudent to inspect this again. They didn't find anything, but something in here just might break the case." Stride stood straight. "Is there anything you need, sir?"

Peters nodded. "Yes, actually," he replied then glanced around the room. "Have you seen Dr. Dunham?"

Stride pointed toward the door. "Heather found him. He's been hiding out in the conference room down the hall all morning," Stride answered. "He's reviewing the formerly classified Filipino massacre case."

Peters started for the door. "Great, that's actually why I'm looking for him. Thanks, Jack." He walked down the hall, peeked in the door's small window, and spotted Dunham at a large table reviewing the file. Photos and documents were strewn across the table, and boxes of documents were at his feet.

Dunham glanced up and spotted Peters staring at him, raised his eyebrows, and waved him in.

"I finally found you, Edward," Peters said, handing Dunham his smart phone. "Here, you left this in your office."

Dunham took the phone. "Thanks."

"I wanted to know if you've found anything new on the big case."

Dunham gestured toward the documents and photos. "I believe I have." He grabbed a file. "The original Naval intelligence investigators were quite thorough, considering the crime scene was in a jungle outside of a remote village in a foreign country, and it predated DNA analysis."

"So, you believe you found something in this huge pile of evidence?"

Dunham shook his head. "Actually, no." He paused. "It's not what's here that's revealing, it's what's *not* in here. Albeit unsolved, their best guess is that an aggressive jungle people called the Negritos attacked and murdered the villagers out of vengeance for stealing some pigs. The US sailors were just in the way. Do you recall the NCIS director telling us about local intel in the field?"

Peters nodded.

"That's code for Special Forces, which means it was they who assessed the Communist threat in the area."

"Yes, he certainly did say—or partly say—'Special Forces.'"

"Nowhere in here are the Special Forces mentioned." He glanced up at Peters. "Also, the warship didn't pick up the spy plane air crew. Special Agent Turner specifically said they were brought back to the ship, yet nowhere is this fact recorded." He paused. "They were rescued, most likely by these same Special Forces—a mission they're specially trained for."

Peters nodded slowly.

"That means Special Forces made first contact," Dunham explained, "and the Special Forces unit operating in that particular area in the 1980s was SEAL Team Six."

"Wow, the Navy SEALs . . ."

"These are clear discrepancies."

Peters placed his palm on his forehead. "Your 'Spidey senses' proved true, Edward."

Dunham shook his head. "I understand the incentive for the Navy to conceal classified SEAL team activities, but why would they alter the sequence of events from an investigation already classified—something already protected from the press? It's not like they knew a US president was going to declassify it decades later."

"Strange," Peters commented and pursed his lips. "Then again, I'm sure the general policy for the super-secret Special Forces is to disappear from the record. If the only thing the Navy SEALs did was pick up the air crew, make contact with the villagers, and assess any Communist threats—events not pertinent to the massacre three full days later—I can see why they're omitted from the story."

Dunham considered for a moment. "Still, if they expect me to unravel this mystery, I need to know everything. The NCIS director and Special Agent Turner clearly know about their involvement. It may be a dead end, but," Dunham grinned, "I just have to know."

"Ha!" Peters laughed. "That relentlessness for the facts is why you're so good at your job, Edward."

Dunham grinned. "I'll set up a meeting with Special Agent Turner."

Jack Stride burst into the room with Heather Kennedy in tow. He was beaming from ear to ear. "Dr. Dunham, Dr. Dunham! We nailed it! It was . . ." He stopped and lost his smile, immediately realizing he'd interrupted a meeting between his two bosses. "Oh, I'm sorry, should we come back?"

Dunham shook his head. "No, we just finished. What's up?"

Stride grinned and continued, "Heather just brought this to me." He handed over a sheet of paper with email correspondence on it. "You know we've been working the Big Rapids case where the mother was found dead in her first-floor apartment. Remember the prime suspect was the adult son?"

Dunham nodded. "You disagreed with the conclusion of the local detectives."

"That's right," Stride replied. "We directed them to investigate an Alvin Fresco, a neighbor who fit our criminal offender profile," he glanced over at Heather, "and we just got word Fresco was apprehended. He gave a full confession!"

"That's great!" Peters commended the duo.

"Thank you, sir," Stride replied.

"Yes, outstanding!" Dunham added.

"And it goes without saying—we couldn't have done it without Heather."

Heather gave a small grin. "Thank you, Jack."

"So, Heather," Peters began, "Jack told me you found Dr. Dunham hiding in this room. How is it that you always know where everyone is? Do you have some kind of psychic ability that you're not telling us?"

Heather's grin widened. "Some things, sir, are best left unsaid." She turned to Dunham. "Dr. Dunham, Special Agent Turner has requested a meeting with you, specifically at the zoo close to your home, apparently for your convenience. I put the details on your calendar."

Dunham smiled. "Thank you, Heather."

She nodded, turned, and left the room.

"Somehow, she manages to perform lab duties flawlessly and still find time to use that type A personality of hers to keep us organized and on the ball. If it weren't for Heather having the least tenure here, she'd be the boss of all of us," Peters said.

Dunham glanced over at Stride, then back at Peters. "We've got a great team, sir. What can I say?"

chapter 9

Tujague's Restaurant,
The French Quarter, New Orleans, Louisiana

Rob, Sarah, Uncle Gary, and Aunt Fran approached Tujague's Restaurant from Jackson Square. Rob glanced over at Uncle Gary and realized he was limping. "Mr. Smith, what happened?"

"He pissed off his personal trainer," Aunt Fran replied.

"She tried to kill me!" Uncle Gary snarled. "And I didn't deserve it."

Aunt Fran waved her finger at him. "Oh yes you did, hon!"

"What did he do, Aunt Fran?" Sarah asked.

"She was busting our asses because Gary decided to be lazy—and he had the guts to say to her, 'Aren't I your boss? Don't you work for me?'" Aunt Fran lifted both hands in the air, grinning slightly. "That's all she had to hear. Next thing you know, both of us were swimming in a puddle of sweat!"

Uncle Gary snickered. "All day, I run a company, stand up to high-powered commissioners, mayors, and CEOs, but when it comes to my half-pint personal trainer, I'm a scared puppy." He shook his head and smirked. "And she's all of four feet and eleven inches tall!"

Sarah laughed. "Too funny, Uncle Gary!"

"Admit it, Gary—she could kick both our butts." Aunt Fran glanced over at Sarah. "She's a black belt in judo."

"Hey, sometimes fear is healthy," Uncle Gary joked.

Rob indicated the restaurant before them. "So, this is the famous Tujague's. And you said it's the second-oldest restaurant in New Orleans?"

"That's right," Uncle Gary answered and pointed to the restaurant's sign. "Opened its doors for business in 1856. Best place around for authentic Cajun and Creole cuisine."

Sarah eyed the vintage storefront. "Certainly does look authentic."

Uncle Gary nodded. "What a perfect end to a full day of shopping at the French Market."

"I'd have liked to have spent a few more hours at the French Market," Aunt Fran interrupted, grinning.

"I'm with you," Sarah agreed, "but I am hungry."

Uncle Gary brushed his hands forward. "I've had my fill of shopping, ladies, so now it's time to fill up on crab gnocchi." He grinned as he faced Rob. "And the blackened catch of the day for an entrée is a must."

"Rob, you don't have to get a menu," Aunt Fran teased. "Gary has it memorized." She sighed. "I have to admit, I love this place. My weakness is the hot loaf in a bag."

They entered the crowded restaurant, and Sarah stopped, glanced around the room, and beamed. "I love the ambiance." The restaurant had what she thought were its original but refinished floors, walls, and ceilings. The walls were lined with dozens of framed photos of celebrity patrons. The room was filled with square tables covered with white tablecloths and surrounded by wooden chairs. Each table had a set of white china and a glass pitcher of water. "It's like they tried to keep the nineteenth-century look."

Rob nodded. "Check out the bar." The bar ran along one full wall, and behind it was a large mirror surrounded by Greek-style pillars that reached to the ceiling. Every barstool was occupied. Two bartenders were rushing back and forth filling drinks.

Uncle Gary waved to a bartender, who waved back. "Their Sazerac whiskey is outstanding."

"They take good care of us here. They usually find us a table close to the bar." Aunt Fran turned to Rob. "And when we get seated, I'll be surprised if you don't see a bottle of Sazerac waiting for us."

Gary said to Fran, "We do spend a lot of money here."

They were quickly seated, and just as Aunt Fran predicted, a bottle of whiskey was waiting for Uncle Gary. She merely glanced over at Rob and grinned. In less than five minutes, the manager found his way to their table and greeted

Fran and Gary, then left as quickly as he came. A few minutes later, the waitress brought their drinks and took down their order.

"I'm telling you, there's a Rougarou in Jackson Square!" a drunken man bellowed, slurring his words to the bartender and two others seated at the bar.

Patrons shook their heads and smirked, and some even belted out in laughter.

Rob overheard the drunken man's comments and quickly turned his head toward him.

"Have another whiskey, Wally!" one of the other drunken patrons replied.

"This is a no-shitter, Al!" the man yelled. "I was sitting in my carriage last night, the last tour of the evening, and I saw a Rougarou attack a prostitute walking by and drag her into the trees!"

"So, why didn't the police find anything?" the bartender retorted. "If something happened, there'd be some evidence."

The drunken man pointed his shaky finger at the bartender. "How the hell should I know?" He paused and slipped, nearly falling off his stool. "All I remember is this thing howling then screeching." He gestured with his drinking hand, unintentionally spilling some of his drink on the man sitting next to him. He leaned forward. "I crapped my pants," he said as the man angrily wiped the drink off himself. "Oh, sorry, Al." The drunken man glanced back at the bartender. "My mule shot down the street, droppin' its load a' crap too!"

Rob leaned toward Sarah, and the two whispered while the older adults chatted with another familiar server who'd stopped by to greet the regulars. "Sarah, do you remember in class when Jared said the Foliage Park killer might be a Rougarou?"

"Yeah, but I think he was kidding, Rob."

"I know," Rob replied. He gestured over his shoulder toward the drunk man at the bar. "But this guy claims a Rougarou attacked a sex worker here in Jackson Square last night." He raised his palm. "I'm not saying I believe the guy witnessed a fictional beast out of Cajun folklore, but it's what he said he heard that has me thinking. It's too coincidental . . . kind of an offender signature."

"What is?" Sarah asked.

Rob grasped Sarah's hand. "He said the creature howled then screeched after the woman was attacked. That's exactly what the witnesses said at Foliage Park!"

Sarah glanced toward the man at the bar. "OK, but if it's true, why haven't we heard about it in the news? The Foliage Park attack certainly made headlines."

Rob thought for a moment. "Well, if I'm right that a guy's using a wolf-dog hybrid as his murder weapon, maybe he's also disposing of the bodies in order to stay under the police radar."

"If you think about it," Sarah added, "the German shepherd attacked the animal in the woods, which actually gave the child molester the opportunity to get away, even if he fell dead in the girl's backyard. If there was a human in control of the animal, maybe his original intention was to take the body."

Rob nodded toward the drunk man. "And this guy's saying a sex worker was attacked—another type of person 'no one would miss,'" he emphasized with air quotes.

Rob glanced at the drunk man then back at Sarah. "If this is the case, we may have a serial offender in New Orleans!"

"Serial offender in New Orleans?" Aunt Fran repeated. "What are you two whispering about?"

"Sorry, Aunt Fran," Sarah replied. "In our class, we discussed the Foliage Park murder. You know, the one that's been in the news lately."

Uncle Gary nodded. "That's right; the dead child molester. Not too sad to see him go."

Sarah held up her hand and pointed to the drunk man at the bar so only her table could see. "Rob overheard that guy say that last night he witnessed an eerily similar attack just next door at Jackson Square, and since it wasn't in the news, maybe we have an elusive serial killer on our hands stashing the bodies somewhere."

"That's if this guy's recollections are accurate," Rob added.

"That's a big if," Aunt Fran commented. "Looks like he's trashed."

Rob grinned. "True. In the next few days, we're supposed to select an actual case to investigate for our class assignment." He looked at Sarah. "Any problem with investigating this one, partner?"

"Sounds good to me," Sarah responded. "We'll ask our other partner tomorrow."

Rob placed a large cloth napkin on his chest and stuffed the corner of it down the neckline of his shirt.

"What're you doing?" Aunt Fran asked.

Rob replied, grinning: "I'm about to ask that drunk guy a few questions, but I don't want him to spill his drink on my shirt."

* * *

Sydney and Walda Besthoff Sculpture Garden
New Orleans Museum of Art, Louisiana

"Hey, don't drink it all!" a ragged-looking bald man blurted out at the short, scruffy man who was sharing the park bench with him. He shook his head when his drinking buddy ignored him and casually swigged from the bottle of cheap whiskey. The man glanced at the entrance to the sculpture garden to their left then stared into the woods behind them. The moss-laden oak trees were faintly illuminated by the dull streetlight, which gave the forest an eerie presence.

The short man lowered the whiskey bottle. "All right, all right," he replied. "Here ya go." He handed the bottle to his companion, who took a quick drink. The short man whipped his head around at a noise coming from the darkness of the oak trees. He stared into the woods, but seconds later he shook his head. "Gettin' jumpy in my old age."

The bald man handed him the bottle then noticed a set of headlights coming up the entrance toward the art museum. As the vehicle neared a streetlight, he spotted the police lights on the roof and jumped off the bench. "Cops! Let's get into the garden!"

The short man leaped off the bench and followed the bald man through the entrance of the garden and into the darkness.

The police car moved slowly along the perimeter road that hugged the art museum. The police officer in the passenger seat turned on the car's powerful spotlight and aimed it into the trees and magnolia groves of the surrounding sculpture garden.

"Admit it, Trevor," the driver said, "you're lighting up the woods hoping to get a peek at a couple of college kids doing the nasty." He smirked.

Trevor stared into the sections of the garden lit up by his spotlight. "I resemble that remark," he replied jokingly. Just as the car reached the entrance to the sculpture garden, his spotlight illuminated a man in a t-shirt and jeans staring back at him. The man's intense glare startled him momentarily, and Trevor fumbled the spotlight handle, losing sight of man. When he regained control and shined the light back in the same direction, the man was gone. "Stop, Art! I saw someone!"

Art parked the police car and turned on his flashers. Both officers hopped out and ran into the wooded garden with their flashlights illuminating the area. "Where'd you see him?"

"Over here." Trevor scanned the area. "All right, come on out! We saw you!" They nodded a silent agreement to split up and cover more ground.

A few minutes later, Art flashed his light onto Trevor. "Ahh, he's gone. Let's go." He started for the car.

Trevor glanced around one more time before giving up and following his partner.

The two homeless men watched the police from behind a group of large pines on the other side of the pedestrian bridge and small lagoon. "Whew! That was close," the bald man commented and watched as the police car drove away. "How the hell did they see us from their car?" he asked. "We were way back here, and it's dark as hell." He glanced over at the short man. "I can't even see your face."

At that moment, a loud, deep growl emanated from the magnolia groves just ten feet behind them.

The two men spun around.

"Shit!" the bald man yelled. "Let's get outta here!" They bolted across the pedestrian bridge toward the lighted entrance to the garden.

The short man was hit from the back with such force that his body shot forward, colliding with his buddy, and both fell to the ground.

"Ahhh!" the bald man shouted breathlessly as he hit the ground and rolled over. Ambient light fell upon a huge growling creature attacking his friend, and the bald man screamed.

His friend screamed, too, but abruptly stopped.

The bald man tried to gain his feet, but the animal turned and pounced on him. He roared out in pain, but his cry was cut short as well.

chapter 10

Dunham presented his season pass to the ticket lady at the front entrance.

"Enjoy your day at the National Zoo," she said as she scanned and returned Dunham's pass.

He nodded. "Thank you." He then entered and walked straight to the nearby picnic pavilion and spotted Special Agent Turner waving to him from one of the tables.

Turner stood and shook Dunham's hand. "Nice seeing you again, Dr. Dunham." He handed over a folder. "Here's the file of my own investigation fifteen years after the incident." Both men sat. "I believe I was very thorough, although nothing came of it." He paused as Dunham thumbed through the file. "We certainly appreciate you reviewing this case for us."

Dunham gave a slight grin then scanned the area. "So, why did you ask to meet here? You could have easily given this to me at your office."

Turner grinned and also glanced around. "Why, you don't like the zoo?"

"Of course, I'm actually a member. Although my wife and I rarely have the time to visit, we like to contribute."

"Well, I do have a reason," Turner began. "You see, the director and I weren't entirely forthcoming at our first meeting."

Dunham eyed him over his glasses, wondering if he was going to admit to the Special Forces involvement. "A sensitive information issue?"

Turner waved his hand. "No, no, like Director Allen said, the case has been declassified." He paused. "It's just that he doesn't want you to think we take pseudoscience seriously."

Dunham, slightly caught off guard, said, "What?" in a rather high voice.

Turner glanced around again. "There actually was an eyewitness to the village attack in the Philippines back in 1989—and she works here."

"Oh?"

Turner nodded. "She's Filipino and lived in the village as a teenager at the time of the attack. She later met an American serviceman, they married, and she followed him here to DC." He paused and leaned forward. "Her testimony is right out of a horror novel, with the killer being a nightmarish monster—but, contrary to the director's opinion, I believe you need to listen to her and glean the kernels of truth from her story."

"How interesting."

Turner shrugged. "Her account certainly does fit the evidence."

Dunham nodded and surveyed the area, wondering if she were close by. "Sounds good . . . where is she?"

Turner pointed down the sidewalk past the Big Cats exhibit. "She'll be here on her lunch hour, which is in a few minutes." He opened his copy of the file. "In the meantime, I'd like to review the case with you." He pointed at the folder he had given to Dunham. "That's yours to take with you."

Dunham reopened his file. "Excellent," he said then paused. "So, whatever became of Petty Officer Castle after the incident?"

"I asked myself that same question when I began my reinvestigation around 2004. I wanted to speak with Joseph Castle personally, so I looked into it. Just after the Philippine incident, his commanding officer believed he needed to serve the rest of his orders off the ship, so he sent him back to command headquarters in San Diego." Turner thought for a moment. "His enlistment ended in 1990, and he opted not to reenlist. He went back to Monroe, Louisiana. He lived there throughout most of the 1990s, but then he and his entire extended family left Monroe and moved south to Lafayette, Louisiana, where the family still resides to this day."

"Kind of strange," Dunham commented.

Turner nodded. "I thought so, too, so when I was in Lafayette looking for Castle, I asked a relative why the entire family up and moved. He said they wanted to get back to their old family roots in Lafayette. Even though the family still lives there, apparently in 2000, Joseph Castle moved to Baton Rouge, Louisiana." He shook his head. "I never could find him."

Dunham studied the graphic aftermath photos resulting from the attack. "What a tragedy. Absolutely no concern for the sanctity of human life." He shuffled through the photos. "These seem to be efficient, opportunistic murders."

"What are you thinking?" Turner asked.

Dunham popped his head up then examined the photos again. "Not sure yet," he lied, aware that Turner was still holding back information; but, because he now had the opportunity to speak with a witness, he opted not to answer fully.

"Any thoughts?"

Dunham nodded. "There are no signs of organization within the chaos. Warring tribal groups have an agenda, a message of complete domination. In order to pacify any future threats, it's common for the victors to leave a calling card, maybe display their brutality, such as scalping or a field of impaled bodies." He shook his head. "I don't see organization in this case. The carnage seems haphazard, like animalistic rage with one agenda—kill and kill quickly."

"Interesting."

Dunham glanced over at Turner. "I noticed that the first NCIS investigation reported no definitive evidence of warring factions even though that's their conclusion?"

Turner nodded. "I thought it strange, too, but since I found nothing to conclusively contradict their findings, I was forced to officially support the earlier conclusion." He shook his head. "I even asked the eyewitness about this—the one you're about to meet—and she said their neighbors loved the villagers. Even the local Communist groups had a warm relationship with them." He pointed his finger in the air. "Although the villagers were afraid of the Negritos, the jungle people. She said they could be this ruthless but is convinced they weren't involved."

Dunham nodded. "I've heard of the Negritos. They possess ancient DNA and were the first wave of human beings out of Africa, populating Southeast Asia tens of thousands of years ago. The villagers likely came from the later Mongoloid Polynesian expansion." He eyed Turner. "They're also known to have worked hand in hand with US Special Forces operating in the jungles."

Turner nodded. "Exactly. Our witness says she's Tagalog. Now, the Navy knew of the Negritos' reputation, so they certainly did investigate this angle."

He shook his head. "No physical evidence pointed to them either, but they made the top of the 'warring group' list."

Dunham stared at the case file. "So, the investigators concluded that our sailors were most likely caught in the middle of jungle warfare between local ethnic groups—specifically the Tagalog versus the Negritos."

"It was the best conclusion they could come up with that somewhat fits the evidence." Turner explained. "As you can see on the official report, they concluded that the Negritos just plain lied, and since there's no evidence to press the issue, they decided to close the case without further action."

"Their conclusion seems peculiar," Dunham added.

Turner waved to a middle-aged Filipino woman approaching them. As he stood, he quickly whispered to Dunham, "Just wait until you hear the eyewitness's account." He gently shook the woman's hand. "Hi, Malaya, thank you for meeting us on your lunch break." He faced Dunham, who was rising from his seat. "This is Dr. Dunham, the man I spoke to you about. And, Dr. Dunham, this is Malaya Santos."

"Pleasure to meet you, Mrs. Santos."

"Nice to meet you, too, Dr. Dunham. Malaya is fine," she replied in Filipino-accented English.

All three sat at the table. "We'll be brief, Malaya, so we don't take up all of your lunch break," Turner explained. "As I told you over the phone, we're reinvestigating the terrible massacre that took place in your village years ago, and Dr. Dunham has offered to help. I felt it was necessary for him to hear your account of the events."

Malaya frowned slightly. "I understand."

"If it's too difficult to talk about," Dunham responded, "we can stop at any time."

Malaya nodded. "I'll be fine."

"Who did this?" Dunham asked in a kindly tone.

Malaya stared at Dunham momentarily. "It was the Aswang."

Dunham glanced over at Turner, confused, then back to the eyewitness.

Malaya answered, "Aswang are Filipino monsters that have been in our folklore for many generations. They are shapeshifters—human by day and creature by night. There are many versions, but the villagers from where I was raised believe the Aswang is something like a mix between an animal and a ghoul."

"Did you see this Aswang?" Dunham asked.

"Yes, but quickly; I mostly heard it." She frowned again. "My father, mother, and I were eating dinner in our small home. We heard everyone screaming outside. I glanced out our front door, and there were people running. I saw something flash by. It was huge and running on all fours, chasing them."

"Did you see what it looked like?" Dunham asked.

Malaya shrugged her shoulders. "It was fast, so I didn't get a good look at it, but I could tell it wasn't human." She paused. "My father rushed to the door and watched. Then he ran back into the house, grabbed me, and threw me into a small hidden closet." She dropped her head and paused. "I heard something monstrous burst into our home and listened as it killed my parents. The growl was deeper and louder than a man could make. It murdered them within seconds, then it left. By the time I heard the helicopter, no one was screaming. I wouldn't leave my hiding spot until someone found me."

Turner added, "Malaya's account of events has not changed since her first interview in 1989."

Dunham nodded to Turner then said, "Malaya, it is perfectly clear that you are very lucky to be alive."

Malaya smiled. "It sounds incredible, Dr. Dunham, but that's what I saw . . . and heard."

"Oh, I don't doubt you for a minute." Dunham paused. "Did you hear any gunfire?" At this question, he sensed Turner's calm demeanor change to concern.

Malaya hesitated. "I was never asked that question before." She stared into the air, remembering. "Yes, yes, I believe I did. Like a machine gun."

Dunham smiled. "You had stated in your interview that you believed the Negritos could be that ruthless. Why are you convinced it wasn't them? Is it possible that they used large dogs to attack your village?"

"Oh, the Negritos loved us," Malaya explained. "They even made it clear to the Communists in the valley not to bother us. Besides, their hunting dogs are small and fast—perfect for hunting in the thick jungles. Their whole life revolves around the hunt, and this is how they feed their families. Large dogs would be a hindrance." She paused. "And they eat too much."

Turner slipped a photo to Dunham. "Here's a photo of the local Negritos and their hunting dogs. These dogs appear to weigh about thirty to forty pounds."

Dunham studied the photo and nodded. "Malaya, were there any Negritos in the village that day?"

"Yes, there were," she answered. "Three of them carrying machetes."

"Machetes?" Dunham raised an eyebrow.

"I know what you're thinking, Dr. Dunham," Malaya began. "That these machetes may have been the weapons used to kill my people, but Negritos always used machetes to get around the jungle. It was no surprise for them to carry them that day."

Dunham nodded. "Do you remember what they were doing, who they were with?"

Malaya thought for a moment. "They were walking with US soldiers."

"You mean sailors, like the ones from the ship?" Dunham asked.

She shook her head. "No, soldiers in green camouflage uniforms with guns. They weren't very helpful and just walked around looking scary. I remember because I was afraid, and my father said I didn't have to worry about them. They were Americans."

"It's been a long time since the incident, Malaya," Dunham pointed out, "so are you sure you saw these soldiers on the day of the murders?"

Malaya nodded. "I'm very sure because the soldiers never left the village after they first came to our elders. It was the three Negritos who showed up on that horrible day."

Dunham glanced at Turner before continuing, "Malaya, what else should we be looking into? What should our next step be in the investigation?"

"There's nothing you can do," she answered. "No one can catch the Aswang."

Dunham smiled. "You've been very helpful. I believe that's all I need."

"Thank you so much, Malaya," Turner added. "We've taken up enough of your time. May we contact you if we need to follow up with anything?'

Malaya got up from her seat and smiled. "Of course." She turned to Dunham. "It was nice to meet you, Dr. Dunham."

"You, too, Malaya," Dunham replied and watched her leave. He turned and glared at Turner. "Special Agent Turner, your boss specifically stated that Special Forces made first contact with the Filipino villagers, yet the official report—and," he pointed at the file on the table, "your own investigation states that Navy personnel from the US warship made first contact." He gestured to the documents spread across the table. "Curiously, there is absolutely no mention of Special Forces involvement anywhere," he pointed toward Malaya, "yet she just corroborated your boss—not the official reports."

Turner stared back at Dunham, paused, glanced around, then leaned forward. "It was definitely not my idea to withhold this information from you, Dr.

Dunham. I also noticed this discrepancy during my reinvestigation, but when I approached the Navy SEALs, they closed the door right in my face. On that very day, the director was waiting for me in my office and told me about the Special Forces' initial involvement, but then he ordered me to stop that line of investigation." Turner raised his hands in surrender. "My boss assured me that the SEALs were not around during the massacre, so I decided not to push it."

Dunham stared at Turner then shook his head. "Malaya witnessed the Negritos accompanying the Navy SEALs," he jabbed his finger at the file, "on the day of the massacre." He paused. "If we accept the official conclusion that the Negritos murdered the villagers, then by extension, it is likely our own Navy SEAL team participated in the massacre."

"None of the photos show any evidence of Negritos or Navy SEALs. All the bodies are of villagers or sailors." Turner shook his head. "I knew they were there at first, but I automatically assumed they left the day the ship arrived."

Dunham sighed. "Special Agent Turner, the author that the Navy is so worried about believes there was a US military cover-up. Not only does it look like he's right, but the reason for the cover-up is worse than the author believes."

"Yeah . . . it's not good," Turner replied.

Dunham grinned. "Now, the easy answer is that the Negritos did not murder these people, thus, the SEALs were not involved, but this means I must publicly reject the official conclusion."

"I understand," Turner said.

"I do need to investigate any possible Special Forces involvement though," Dunham continued.

Turner shook his head. "There's no way the Navy SEALs will reveal their secrets, and they certainly have the power to influence my director."

"Well," Dunham began, "it looks like it's time to speak to the vice president directly."

Turner eyed Dunham and grinned. "If there's some authority who can force this issue, it's the White House." He paused. "Dr. Dunham, did you suspect something like this at our very first meeting? Is that why you asked if you could contact him directly?"

"The thought did cross my mind."

Turner shook his head, beaming. "Dr. Dunham, you certainly are the Watchmaker."

chapter 11

**Thursday Evening Vidocq Dinner Event,
the French Quarter, New Orleans, Louisiana**

Rob held Sarah's hand on the balcony of Crescent City Brewhouse as they watched the high volume of tourists strolling through the French Quarter. The warm evening and Jazz music, combined with the smells of famed Louisiana cuisine, made for a romantic ambiance. He noticed Jared standing next to a few other students on the balcony, listening to the music. "Jared, great idea to have our class's evening get-together here. Dinner was awesome and the atmosphere is amazing," Rob called out.

"Great view too," Sarah added.

"Well, if you're in New Orleans and haven't visited the French Quarter, you really have missed the heartbeat of the city. After dinner, Dr. Taylor wants to walk Bourbon Street with everyone and visit a few more places," Jared answered.

Sarah glanced over at Rob. "Sounds great." She spotted Dr. Taylor seated at a balcony table, deep in conversation with three other classmates. "Looks like he's not ready to go yet."

Lacy Gonzalez and Cedric Brown joined Rob, Sarah, and Jared.

"Hi, guys," Lacy said. "Hey, Jared, did this area get devastated by Hurricane Katrina?"

Jared shook his head. "Not as bad as north of here near Lake Pontchartrain, only one foot above sea level." He pointed at the street. "Being the oldest part of a port city along the Mississippi, the French Quarter sits on the high grounds of the riverbank."

"Makes sense," Lacy replied.

Jared glanced at Lacy's wine glass and lifted his pint. "Lacy, we're in a brewhouse with some of the best craft beers New Orleans has to offer. You must partake."

Lacy grinned and sipped from her glass. "I'm a wine lover, sorry."

Cedric raised his beer and laughed. "Lacy's a great class partner. She knows everything, but I have issues with her taste in drink!"

Lacy grinned and shrugged her shoulders. "I do have to say though, Jared, the food here is excellent and the Jazz music is awesome!"

Rob addressed Cedric. "Have you and Lacy selected a case yet?"

Lacy nodded. "An unsolved rape case in San Antonio. There's been twelve violent rapes in the last five years. Cedric's mentor teaches at the University of Texas at San Antonio and suggested it."

"Yeah," Cedric continued, "he's been assisting the San Antonio Police Department. He's a criminal profiler by profession. Apparently, he's in line for membership in the Vidocq Society."

"Who's the third in your group?" Sarah asked.

Cedric turned and pointed to a short, thin student with a huge head of red curly hair. "None other than Sebastian!"

Sebastian heard Cedric call his name and glanced their way.

"Come on over here!"

"Sebastian's a hoot," Lacy added as Cedric waved him over.

"Oh yeah, Sebastian," Jared remembered, "from LA. He's got an encyclopedic knowledge of UFOs and conspiracy theories. He's got me convinced my parents are aliens from Mars."

Sebastian crossed the balcony to join them. "From *Alpha proxima*, Jared. It's the closest star system to our sun at four-point-two light-years away. Although it would take our Space Shuttle over a hundred thousand years to get there, the 'Alpha-baters—'" he glanced over at Rob and Sarah, "that's what they like to call themselves—the Alpha-baters bend space-time and make the trip in no time." He glanced around the group. "I apologize, guys; I hate being so brilliant."

Rob and Sarah laughed. "No problem, Sebastian," Rob replied.

Jared grabbed tiny Sebastian around his shoulders with one arm, squeezing him. "My bad, Brother Sebastian, and let me guess, the captain of the Alpha-baters' spaceship is referred to as the . . . 'Master-bater'!"

Sebastian shook his head. "I walked into that one, didn't I?"

Jared laughed and replied, "Greater men have done the same."

Sebastian snickered and faced Cedric. "How can I help you, partner? Needing a wingman? Have your eye on a few babes?"

"Not tonight, Sebastian," Cedric answered. "Rob, Sarah, and Jared asked Lacy and I who our partner is, so I called you over."

Sebastian lifted his arms and posed, clenching his fists and flexing his small frame, then he kissed his unimpressive biceps. "Yes, the sun shines on Cedric and Lacy, blessed by the presence of my awesomeness."

"He's not too bad at criminal investigations either," Lacy explained.

Cedric turned to the other trio of student investigators. "I hear y'all are looking into the animal mutilation case we discussed in class a couple days ago."

Rob nodded. "We are. Even though on the surface it doesn't look like a homicide, a few things just aren't adding up."

"Rob and Sarah convinced me," Jared added. "There may have been another similar attack a few days ago just a few blocks east of here."

"Are the police aware of it?" Lacy asked.

Rob shook his head. "It doesn't look like it, but Dr. Taylor plans on setting us up with the detectives in charge of the Foliage Park incident."

"Even if they don't believe there's a connection," Sarah interrupted, "therefore, not a serial homicide case, we're going to tell them our goal is only to *eliminate* that possibility."

"A serial killer using an animal to do his murderous bidding," Rob added.

"Jared's already figured your case out," Sebastian interrupted. "The Rougarou! This part of Cajun folklore's endured for hundreds of years. Proof, really."

Jared pointed his finger at Sebastian. "Thanks for the support, m'man." He presented his fist.

Sebastian awkwardly tapped Jared's fist with his own. "Nature calls! I'll be right back." He rushed toward the bathroom.

"I don't think Sebastian realized you were just joking in class about the Rougarou, Jared," Sarah surmised.

Jared turned to Sarah, pretending to be appalled. "We Alpha-baters never jest."

Dr. Taylor approached and greeted the group then turned toward Rob, Sarah, and Jared. "Team Watchmaker, I got ahold of Detective Bakula. He and his partner gave the OK and said the three of you can come to the station tomorrow around one p.m." He shook a couple of pills into his hand, tossed them back, and swallowed.

"Excellent, thanks, Dr. Taylor," Rob replied. "Are you OK?"

Dr. Taylor nodded. "Oh, yes," he said. "I just have to take these pills for my heartburn after I eat something I'm not really supposed to. And tonight, I did just that—but it was worth it."

"That reminds me of a joke!" Jared blurted out, beaming.

Half the students groaned in unison, then all laughed.

"Go ahead, Jared," Dr. Taylor replied, "get it off your chest."

"So, Charmaine noticed Hector Two-tones moping on the docks," Jared began. "He was just staring down at the water and seemed real miserable. She went out to see him and asked, 'Hector! What's the matter? You've been glum for two days now.'

"'I got some bad news, Charmaine,' Hector replied.

"'What's the bad news?' she asked.

"'Well, I only got forty-eight more days to live,' Hector answered.

"'You mean to tell me that fool doctor told you this?' Charmaine asked.

"'Kinda,' Hector responded. 'Look here.' He pulled out a small medicine bottle from his pocket. 'He said I have to take one of these pills every day for the rest of my life!'

"'OK, so what?' Charmaine replied.

"'So what!' Hector yelled. 'Count 'em. There's only forty-eight pills left in the bottle!'"

Everyone either laughed or shook their head, grinning.

"I actually like that one, Jared!" Dr. Taylor commented, then he glanced around the balcony at the class. "Is everyone ready to walk Bourbon Street?"

At that, they all left the brewhouse and followed Jared and Dr. Taylor down Bourbon Street. The streets were crowded with tourists, but everyone managed to stay together.

Jared turned around, faced the group, and pointed up at a balcony. "See the shape of the buildings with the second- and third-floor balconies? The French Quarter was actually built during the Spanish rule, so you're seeing Spanish architecture."

"How cool is that!" Sarah blurted out. "But, New Orleans is a French word. Weren't they here first?"

Jared nodded. "Yeah, but during Spanish rule in the late1700s, a couple of fires destroyed the original French layout, so the Spanish rebuilt it."

They walked by a Voodoo shop and Sarah leaned closer to Rob. "I don't know much about Voodoo, but the idea of poking a needle in a doll and someone really feeling it kinda creeps me out."

"No one would dare do that to you, Sarah," Rob joked and hugged her tight.

"Apparently, that's a myth about Voodoo dolls propagated by Hollywood," Jared replied.

"How does Voodoo connect with Cajuns?" Cedric asked Jared.

"It doesn't," Jared replied. "It connects with Creoles." He paused. "Voodoo in New Orleans finds its origins with the African slave trade. Other places in the New World kept slaves disorganized, and within a generation or so, their African heritage was lost. New Orleans was different. Here, slaves were given a bit of autonomy, which allowed them to pass on some of their roots to the next generation. African shaman religions were then morphed by the Louisiana-born descendants into Creole Voodoo—a kind of Africanized New World religion."

"So, Cajuns and Creoles are different?" Cedric asked.

Jared nodded. "Today, the term Creole represents a melting pot of locals of French, Spanish, and African descent, but it was first used to refer to Louisiana-born slaves from Africa. Creole Voodoo was specifically from the African line. Now, most of us Cajuns consider ourselves Acadians from the northeast coast of pre-Canada. Acadia was part of New France, colonized by the French in the seventeenth century but taken over by the British. After the French and Indian War, around 1763, the Brits kicked us out, so we settled in Louisiana."

"No wonder this place is rich in cuisine and music," Rob commented. "It's diverse in history."

chapter 12

JR's Quality Auto, New Orleans, Louisiana

Joe "JR" Rastelli, sat at his desk counting cash. He stacked a small pile of bills, placed them in an envelope, then peeked out into the auto garage from his tiny office and eyed one of a dozen auto workers and mechanics. JR raised the envelope. "Charlie Hastings! Your week's pay!"

Hastings, working under a car positioned on a lift, turned, tossed a wrench onto his tool cart, and headed for JR's office.

JR placed the envelope on the corner of his desk, searched for his bottle of Coke, then turned and glared at the other man in his office, reclining in a chair, reading a newspaper, and holding onto a bottle. "Jeb, did you take my Coke?"

Jeb didn't lift his eyes from the paper as he took a swig. "Sorry, boss, I was thirsty."

JR shook his head, reached into his small refrigerator, and grabbed another bottle.

Hastings stuck his head into JR's office and grabbed his cash from the corner of the desk. Ignoring JR and Jeb, he stuffed the envelope into his pocket and went back to work under the car.

Jeb glanced over his newspaper at Hastings then stared at the newspaper again. "That Hastings is one strange cookie; never talks." He paused. "And he stinks like a wet dog."

JR glanced over at Jeb, eyed Hastings, then started counting another stack of cash on his desk. "Never gives me any problems, always on time for work, and doesn't mind being paid in cash. I save a boatload of money that way. He can stink like beaver ass for all I care."

"Just sayin', boss," Jeb replied. "Y'all can be good with him, but to be honest, I'm scared shitless of the guy. I swear I saw him pick up the front end of Chevy Aveo all by himself. Heaves those tire rims like they're Frisbees."

"I bet he throws a mean Frisbee too. His poor dog's probably got to run a mile to catch one."

Jeb raised an eyebrow. "How'd you know he's got a dog?"

"He came in one time to pick up his check and he had scratch marks on his arms. Said it was from his dog."

Jeb nodded. "That explains the wet dog stink."

Ding, ding, ding rang the service bell.

JR popped his head up and spotted an older lady and young girl at the counter out front. "Back to work, Jeb. You have a customer."

"I heard it," Jeb grumbled, dropped the paper, and slowly pulled himself out of the chair, carrying JR's Coke with him.

"Gramma, why does everyone call you Gro Mambo Boutte?" the nine-year-old girl asked as they waited for the auto shop attendant.

Gramma Boutte's eyes opened wide. Then, she glanced around to see if anyone heard Nina's question. She bent down. "Don't say Gro Mambo in public again, child," she whispered. "That's just for our family and our people to hear."

"Why?" Nina asked.

"'Gro Mambo means high priestess in our Voodoo faith, honey," Gramma Boutte said. "We're Creole. Most people don't understand that Voodoo is a good and pure religion." She shook her head. "They believe it's devil worshipping, and they're afraid I'll cast an evil spell on them—or they think I'll poke needles in a doll or something." She hugged her granddaughter. "I would never do that."

Nina shrugged her shoulders and tapped on her tablet.

"Who told you that anyway, Nina?" Gramma Boutte asked.

"Momma mostly," Nina replied. "She said I'm going to be one, too, when I grow up."

Gramma Boutte frowned. "You are, indeed, princess, but your momma talks too much." She leaned to her granddaughter's ear and said, "We have the gift of second sight, but you have to keep it a secret."

"If our religion's a secret, then why do we have a Voodoo store?" Nina asked.

Gramma Boutte grinned. "We need to make a livin', don't we? Tourists love it, and it's good business, but what we sell and what we practice and believe are two different things."

Jeb walked in from the back through a set of large, wide-open double doors. "What can we do for you, ma'am?"

Gramma Boutte put her hands on her hips. "My car's smokin' under the hood somethin' awful. Can you fix it?"

Jeb grinned and started typing on the computer. "Every time, ma'am." He typed again and moved his computer mouse then stared at the monitor. "I'll need some information from you first, once I get on the right page. Computer's been slow today."

Gramma Boutte nodded in approval then turned her head and casually glanced through the double doors into the auto garage. Just then, a man in the garage walked into her field of view. Her eyes flashed wide open, and her jaw dropped. She froze in fear.

The man in the garage stopped abruptly then jerked his head toward the customer area, making eye contact with the old lady. His demeanor changed immediately from calmness to limitless rage. He glared at her and bared his teeth.

Gramma Boutte raised her hand and whispered a chant.

The man dropped to his knees, shut his eyes, and brought his hands up to his ears, gritting his teeth in pain. He then bolted back into the garage and out of sight. She grabbed her granddaughter's arm. "Come, child, we're leaving," she said as they rushed out of the auto shop.

Jeb glanced up to see the old lady and young girl running out of the shop. "Wait! Where are you going? I thought your car was smoking?" He watched them get into their car and speed out onto the street. Smoke followed them.

The angry man approached Jeb. "Who was that lady?"

Jeb glanced up. "Oh, Hastings," he said, staring down the road. "Don't know. Strangest thing—she wanted us to look at her car, but when I was about to get her info, she ran outta here."

Hastings hurried to the front window and stared out onto the street. He frowned then walked back into the garage.

chapter 13

Office of the Chief Medical Examiner,
Manassas, Virginia

Dunham stared out the front window of his car at Highway 95's atrocious morning traffic. He frowned and glanced at his watch. *Not like I didn't expect to be stuck in traffic around DC,* he thought to himself. *There must be an accident ahead.*

His iPhone rang, and he answered it on speaker. "Dr. Dunham."

"Hi, Dr. Dunham, it's Heather . . . you're supposed to be driving right now—why are you answering your phone on the road?" she admonished jokingly.

Dunham snickered. "Hey, I'm moving at the breathtaking speed of zero miles per hour at the moment, so technically, I'm answering from a parked car. What's up?"

"You must be on the 95," Heather surmised. "News traffic is reporting an accident."

"Don't I know it!"

"The chief medical examiner from Manassas called again. He's asking if you could come and take a look at a medicolegal death case this morning."

Dunham nodded, grinning. "Ahh, Dr. Greeley."

"Why are you always helping that old man out? He should've retired ten years ago. He must be in his seventies."

Traffic began to move slowly.

"I agree, but Dr. Greeley's a good man, Heather. Besides, he took me under his wing years ago when I was a nascent researcher." Dunham knew Greeley's memory was slipping in his old age, which was the real reason why he wanted to help him. He spotted the Manassas exit across the congested highway. "Looks like I'll be late for work anyway, so why not make the most of my time and help Dr. Greeley out." He pulled to the right then onto the exit. "Could you call him for me and tell him I'm on my way?"

"Will do, but I'll have to scream into the phone. I think he's legally deaf," Heather replied. "I'll see you back at the office this afternoon."

When Dr. Dunham found Dr. Greeley in the Virginia Department of Health building, the latter was examining the body of a deceased stocky middle-aged female. A white sheet covered most of the body. "Hi, Dr. Greeley!" Dunham shouted to the man whose frail frame was bent over the corpse, his wire-rimmed glasses and thinning gray hair mere inches from his patient.

Greeley slowly raised his head. "Oh, hello, Edward. It's great you could come." He crossed over to Dunham, shook his hand, then walked over to an old wooden table with documents and photos spread out. "Here's the case file I called about. The detective in charge brought it to me yesterday, although the body's been here for two days."

Dunham sat down, opened the folder, and began to read. He glanced up at the body. "Is that the deceased?"

Greeley cupped his hand to his ear. "What?"

Dunham grinned, pointed to the body, and yelled, "Is that the deceased?"

"Oh, yes, it is." Greeley pulled his hearing aid out of his pocket and put it in. "She was a nurse named Dara Truskie—strange name." He paused. "She was in her late thirties and had a history of excellent health. She was found dead in her bed by her female partner and roommate Cindy Meierer. The detectives said there was no evidence of foul play." He pointed to a document. "I've yet to find a cause of death, other than she just stopped breathing."

"Hmmm." Dunham found the preliminary toxicology report and reviewed it. "The initial test showed no evidence of suspicious drugs in her system, yet there is a relatively high level of ethyl alcohol. Apparently, she was drinking the night before."

Greeley nodded. "Witnesses told Detective Brown she had a party that evening, a party with over a dozen of their girlfriends. Meierer, another nurse, was not at the party because she was working third shift. According to a couple of the friends in attendance, the deceased strangely became romantic with her roommate's ex-partner." He pointed at a name in the report. "Her name was Anne Hessler."

Dunham popped his head up. "So, Detective Brown is considering a possible homicide? A love triangle?"

Greeley nodded. "What surprised the witnesses is, before the party, Truskie and Hessler hated each other because of their shared interest in Meierer. They were surprised Hessler even showed up to the party. She knew damn well the roommate wasn't going to be there."

Dunham read the report. "So, the witnesses claimed Hessler, our possible suspect, was the last to leave."

"That's right."

"Let me get this right . . . Detective Brown suspects that Anne Hessler faked interest in Truskie to get her alone and to put her in a vulnerable state in order to murder her?" Dunham stared at the ceiling in thought. "But his hands are tied until we can find a cause of death."

Greeley nodded. "That's about it."

Dunham stood. "May I inspect the body?"

"Of course," Greeley said as he led the way to the exam table.

"Do you mind if we first turn the body over?" Dunham asked.

"It's best if you help me," Greeley responded. "I'm feeling my age."

Dunham's phone buzzed in his pocket. "One moment," he said, holding up his index finger. He quickly glanced at the text message. From Peters, it stated: 'Meeting set up with the VP in the video conference room at 3:00pm! Turner will be here.' Dunham texted back: 'I'll be back in an hour.' He looked up and smiled at Greeley as he slipped his phone back into his pocket. "Sorry, of course I'll help."

"Get a good grip," Greeley directed.

Dunham helped turn the body then grabbed a light and magnifying glass. He slowly studied the subject, spending additional time wherever he spotted a skin wrinkle, tuck, or fold, especially around the buttocks. He glanced up at Greeley. "I believe I found it."

Greeley learned forward. "Found what?"

"Because our prime suspect is a medical professional," Dunham began, "my suspicion is that our victim received a lethal dose of a drug not usually tested for with normal toxicology tests." He pointed to a small pinprick inside the fold of the buttocks.

"My hunch is the offender gave the victim a high dose of Propofol."

Greeley beamed. "That's right! High doses of that sedative *are* a powerful anti-breathing drug! We can easily test for Propofol."

Dunham nodded. "If this small pinprick is where the drug was dispensed, she received an intravenous injection with a tiny pediatric butterfly needle—the kind that comes with a syringe cap."

"What are you getting at?"

"There was a recent case of a nurse using a butterfly needle to murder someone, and they discovered the syringe cap. Since nurses often grip the caps with their mouths, they tested for the offender's DNA on the cap and found it. My recommendation is to check the trash containers along the paths from the victim's residence to the suspect's. Maybe you'll get lucky."

Greeley shook his head. "Why didn't I think of this? I need to keep up on the recent cases, like you do, Edward. And thank you; I will pass this onto the detectives."

Although this was an unusual case, and may have slipped by many medical examiners, Dunham knew darn well that Greeley would have easily figured this out back in his prime. "Could you contact me if this lead proves fruitful?"

"I certainly will, Edward. You keep this up, young man, you just might get noticed some day."

Dunham grinned, aware that the elderly Greeley still mentally lived in the 1980s and had no idea that his protégé was now considered an authority. "Thank you, Dr. Greeley. Take care."

* * *

FBI Lab Video Conference Room, 2:50 p.m.
Quantico, Virginia

Dr. Dunham, Assistant Director Peters, and Special Agent Turner sat in the video conference room. Along one wall was a large screen displaying the video feed to the White House. On the screen were two men in suits, apparently Secret Service agents, standing with their hands crossed in front of them.

"Hello, gentlemen," Peters greeted the men on the screen. "We're all here."

One of the men nodded. "Hello, Assistant Director Peters, the vice president will be here shortly. You will have ten minutes with him."

"Thank you," Peters replied as the trio waited for the guest of honor.

Minutes later, Dunham watched a door behind the agents open, and the vice president and three other men entered the room. Peters stood, so Dunham and Turner followed suit.

The vice president approached his seat. "Please, please, everyone take a seat." When everyone was settled, the vice president began the meeting. "What can I do for you, Dr. Dunham?"

"Hello, Mr. Vice President. I apologize, but your assistance is unavoidable. I'm sure you're aware that when the spy plane crashed off the coast of the Philippines a few days before the massacre, Special Forces were sent in to collect the aircrew. They were also the first to make contact with the Filipino villagers in order to secure the area and ensure there was no threat to the subsequent salvage operations."

The vice president nodded. "Yes, I was aware of this."

Dunham glanced over at Turner. "I've been asked to investigate this case in order to combat soon-to-be published misinformation about it being a military cover-up," he paused, "but my conclusions will demonstrate this very thing."

The vice president sat up in his chair. "Oh?"

Dunham took a deep breath. "The official report makes no mention of Special Forces being involved," he raised his finger, "and it specifically states that the ship's personnel made first contact. A clear case of misinformation."

The vice president relaxed and grinned. "This shouldn't be an issue, Dr. Dunham. It's always been standard policy and past practice to remove any mention of Special Forces involvement for national security reasons. Besides, they were long gone by the time the massacre occurred. By all means, go ahead and report the discrepancy and the reason for it—not referring to it as a cover-up, of course. The fact that Special Forces made a threat assessment of the area should negate any damage done by the author's claim."

"There's more," Dunham said bluntly.

"Oh?"

"The conclusion of the official report stated the Negritos attacked the villagers and sailors." Dunham paused. "When speaking to the only living witness and survivor of the massacre, a young female Filipino villager, she specifically remembers the Navy SEALs never leaving the village." He paused again. "They were accompanied by three machete-wielding Negritos . . . on the day of the massacre."

The vice president raised his eyebrows in surprise. "Go on."

Dunham leaned forward. "We have the Navy concluding that the Negritos did it, yet we also have the Navy SEALs accompanying the Negritos on that very day." He glanced at Peters and Turner then looked back to Vice President LaRue. "Many readers may believe the Navy's official conclusion as proof that their own Special Forces coordinated the massacre." He paused. "I can see conspiracy theorists claiming the US government did this in order to eliminate all witnesses to some highly classified event."

The vice president remained silent then glanced over at one of the men who'd followed him into the conference room.

"Mr. Vice President," Dunham said, "I'm convinced our own Special Forces would not have been involved with the massacre, but I need to know the whole story in order to discover who killed your nephew and the others. I just might be able to figure it out . . . but only if I have the complete picture."

The vice president nodded to the other man, who nodded back. He turned back to Dunham with a big smile. "Dr. Dunham, I should not be surprised you figured out the Special Forces involvement, and I apologize for not authorizing you full disclosure." He stood, which prompted everyone to stand. "You'll have your request." He turned and left the conference room, his entourage in tow.

Turner leaned over to Dunham. "Excellent job convincing the vice president, Edward."

"I figured if he honestly wants to know how his nephew was killed, he'll help."

"Hopefully, this'll give you a lead," Peters added.

chapter 14

Detective Bakula's lips twisted as he took a sip of his stale coffee and stared at the computer screen on his desk. He glanced to his right at his partner, Detective Oglesby, completely reclined in his desk chair, texting. "Oges, you workin' hard or hardly workin'?"

Oglesby continued to text. "Don't get grumpy with me. You're just pissed because your Buffalo Bisons lost again. Not my fault they suck at baseball."

"Hmm, head and shoulders above the New Orleans Zephyrs." Bakula paused. "What the hell is a zephyr anyway?"

"Look it up in an encyclopedia." Oglesby glanced up from his phone. "So, when are these kids coming in? I hope I don't have to wipe their noses."

Bakula shook his head. "They're college students, dumb ass. Probably smarter than the two of us combined."

Oglesby looked back at his phone, still reclined with his feet on his desk. "I'm too busy for this kinda shit." He eyed Bakula again. "So, they're supposed to help us out on one of our active cases? Is that legal?"

"As long as it's been approved by the Brass," Bakula replied then shook his head. "Oges, you're not seeing the bigger picture here. They're coming because of the Vidocq Society. It's a chance to make connections with the top people in the field—the movers and shakers. If you're in with the Vidocq Society, your career automatically goes into high gear."

"Not interested, Bak. I'm retiring in a few years, and phase two of my life begins in an entirely different field."

Bakula grinned. "A couple of these students are buddies with the Watchmaker, and he'll be helping them out with the case."

Oglesby's head snapped up, and his eyes widened at that. "Why didn't you tell me? Now, *that* I'm interested in. Is he coming in with them today?"

"No, but eventually he might."

Oglesby sat back in his chair. "I wonder why they call him 'the Watchmaker.'"

Bakula shrugged his shoulders. "Not sure, but I bet it has something to do with how good he is."

"It'd be kinda cool to have a nickname."

"You do have one," Bakula answered. "They call you 'Shade' because you're always overshadowed by . . . my awesomeness." He snickered.

"Ha!" Oglesby blurted out. "Not even on your best day, my friend." He glanced over at the front desk and noticed three young people being escorted in their direction. "Bak, I think they're here."

Bakula sat up and spotted the trio. "I think you're right."

"Detective Bakula," the approaching officer said hurriedly. "Here are the guests you were waiting for."

"Thanks, Officer Crane," Bakula replied then faced the three visitors. "Rob, Sarah, and Jared, right?"

Rob smiled and shook Bakula's hand. "Yes, hi, I am Rob Faulks, and this is Sarah Blaine and Jared Dugas."

After introductions and handshakes all around, Bakula pointed to three empty seats. "Please." As all parties sat, Bakula began: "Your instructor, Dr. Taylor, contacted me and said the three of you have asked to assist in an investigation that's assigned to Detective Oglesby and me."

"That's right, sir," Rob answered and glanced over at Sarah and Jared. "We certainly appreciate you allowing this, and with all the man-hours we plan on putting in, hopefully we can find something helpful."

"The FBI forensic scientist, Dr. Edward Dunham, will be giving us some direction too," Sarah added.

Bakula nodded. "That's right. Dr. Taylor informed us of this. How exciting. By your accents, I notice you're not from the area. If you need any assistance getting around—"

"We should be fine," Rob interrupted then glanced over at Jared.

Jared nodded. "How y'all doin'?"

Oglesby smiled in recognition of Jared's Cajun accent. "Well, we can start by letting you know which cases we're dealing with at the moment."

"We've put a lot of thought into this, Detective," Rob said, "and we've already chosen a case. We'd like to assist you with the Foliage Park attack."

Bakula and Oglesby eyed each other. "There's really not much left to investigate," Bakula said to Rob. "Are you aware that the DNA results are in?"

Rob glanced at Sarah. "No, what were the results?"

"Canine," Bakula answered, "and only one donor, meaning an individual attacker and not a pack."

"Could they tell if it was a dog or a wolf?" Jared asked.

Bakula shook his head. "Not really; the report stated that the DNA evidence was consistent with the domesticated dog/gray wolf line. It also stated the results are inconsistent with the coyote or fox line."

"The report even states that the results were consistent with the donor being a wolf-dog hybrid," Oglesby interrupted.

"This would explain why it got away without being seen in an urban area," Bakula added. "Wolves are so elusive, and dogs are comfortable around humans in urban areas."

"We read that you used the opinion of an animal attack expert," Rob said. "Are they the one who made this conclusion?"

Oglesby shook his head. "No, actually; the expert wasn't too fond of the idea, but we went with it anyway since that's what the report said."

"I can see why the expert was skeptical," Sarah interrupted. "The animal's either shy and elusive around humans or it's not—not both."

Bakula shrugged his shoulders. "Regardless, it's clear that it was an animal attack and not a homicide. To be honest, we were about to close the case."

"Before you do that," Rob said, "do you mind if we investigate it further? We would like to eliminate the possibility that the animal was controlled by a handler."

"A homicide . . . via pet?" Oglesby asked.

Rob shrugged. "Maybe multiple homicides by the same hand."

Bakula's ears perked. "A murder spree?"

"Three points," Rob began. "First, no one witnessed a large animal leaving the scene, which could be explained by a handler retrieving it in the woods then hiding it in a van or something. Second, it seems suspicious that a child molester, who was hidden in the woods just feet away from a young girl—possibly about to kidnap her—is murdered at that very moment."

Rob glanced back at Sarah and Jared, then to Bakula. "Lastly," he said, "when Sarah and I were eating dinner at Tujague's Restaurant near Jackson Square, we overheard a carriage tour driver talking about witnessing some kind of huge animal attacking a sex worker."

Bakula glanced over at Oglesby, totally confused.

Oglesby nodded. "Yeah, the drunk guy, remember?" he said, then he eyed Rob. "We had four units on the scene within a half hour, and they searched the entire area inside the square and out, but they came up with nothing, not one drop of blood. I'm not sure you should put too much weight on what that guy said. He was reported to be half in the bag."

Rob nodded. "Yes, it sounds farfetched, but we'd still like to eliminate this possibility. The witnesses at the Foliage Park attack stated the animal howled then shrieked—an unusual combination—and that's exactly the noise this guy said the animal in Jackson Square made."

"Also," Jared chimed in, "if it was a serial murderer trying to hide his tracks, both victims, assuming the sex worker was a victim, were 'unwanted' members of society. It could be a victimology pattern."

"And remember, our goal is only to try and eliminate these possibilities," Sarah added, "not to try and prove them."

Bakula turned and faced Oglesby, then nodded to him. "If that's the case you want, it's OK with us. We won't close it yet, and we'll give you access to the file. And don't hesitate to ask for our assistance."

"Thank you, sir," Rob replied.

"How much time will you need?" Bakula asked.

Rob glanced at Sarah and Jared. "Well, the class only goes for a few more weeks, so just that."

Oglesby grinned. "You do realize that if you're right, we have to start a full-blown task force."

"Oh, the mayor's gonna love to spend that kind of money!" Bakula joked.

Rob, Sarah, and Jared stood. "Thanks again for everything, gentlemen," Sarah said. They shook the detectives' hands and left the building.

"Let's go eat," Jared suggested as they walked to Rob's car.

Rob and Sarah nodded to each other. "We're in. Any recommendations?"

"I know of a nice sub shop next to campus," Jared answered.

Twenty minutes later, Rob, Sarah, and Jared were eating in a booth at the sub shop. Rob glanced up and saw Sebastian walking through the dining area with a sub and a drink and waved him over. "Hey, Sebastian! Come join us."

Sebastian changed direction mid-stride and headed their way. "Hi, guys, don't mind if I do," he said, sliding in the booth next to Jared.

"We're discussing our case," Sarah said, "so I hope you don't get bored."

Sebastian took a sip of his drink. "Not in the least, my friends. You may need my expertise anyway."

"We're working on our 'Foliage Park Serial Killer Using a Wolf-dog Hybrid as a Murder Weapon' theory," Rob explained. "We have a few small leads, but we're hitting dead ends."

"One big hurdle," Jared said through a mouthful of bread, meat, and cheese, "is that I can't find any other case with someone using a dog or wolf-dog hybrid as a murder weapon."

"You're looking in the wrong place," Sebastian interrupted then took a bite of his own sub. "I know of another case, and it was a nasty one at that, but I can see why you've never heard of it. It's only popular within the cryptozoology community."

"Do tell!" Sarah exclaimed.

"The Beast of Gévaudan," Sebastian proclaimed.

"Is that in France?" Jared asked.

"That's right," Sebastian replied. "There was a series of wolf attacks in the Gévaudan countryside of France from 1764 to 1767. It's the foothills of the Alps. Some say the beast attacked over two hundred commoners, mostly women and children tending livestock in the fields. And over a hundred of the attacks ended in death—all in a sixty-square-mile area."

"I've never heard of this," Sarah replied.

Sebastian nodded. "Eyewitness accounts varied, but many experts today believe it was a wolf-dog hybrid that had reddish hair, a long tail, and massive jaws."

"And this was a case of someone controlling the beast?" Rob asked.

"One well-accepted theory goes that way since it killed so many, and it seemed to disappear when the hunters arrived with their bloodhounds. To re-inforce this theory, a local hunter quickly and almost effortlessly dispatched the creature when the king's chosen experts couldn't do it. It was later discovered that this hunter owned a huge red mastiff, possibly siring the creature by breeding it with an Asian gray wolf."

"How do you know so much about this, Sebastian?" Sarah asked.

"As I said in class, cryptozoology is my thing, along with ufology and paranormal investigations."

Rob fingered his straw. "Hey, if this was a court of law, we now have legal precedent."

"But is it persuasive precedent?" Sarah asked.

"Don't be so picky, Sarah," Jared joked. "We need all the support we can find—even the sketchy eighteenth-century kind."

"Let's research the Beast of Gévaudan a bit more," Rob answered. "Maybe something from those French murders will help us find a pattern in these. Sebastian, could you recommend the best websites for researching?"

"Of course."

Sarah patted Sebastian on the hand. "I guess you did help us out, Sebastian! You're an honorary member of Team Watchmaker."

"Does that mean I get to *meet* the Watchmaker?" Sebastian asked.

"Hey!" Jared yelled. "Get in line." He leaned closer to Rob. "Sebastian brings up a good point, Rob. You have to figure out how we can get Dr. Dunham to visit New Orleans."

Rob turned to Sarah and smiled. "Not sure, but we can try."

chapter 15

The Beast,
Province of Gévaudan, France,
Fall 1764

As local administrator to both the king and the church, Etienne Lafont knew that he, more than any other nobleman, was best suited to take charge of the immediate crisis—literally a monstrous calamity. He rushed through the small village, and as he passed an elderly man, he quickly nodded and touched his cocked three-sided beaver felt hat. "Good day, sir."

The man nodded back but maintained his frown.

Lafont continued to make his way to the inn feeling more anxious than he'd felt in years. Peasant tenants, mostly women and adolescent children old enough to lead livestock to pasture, were being attacked in the fields and killed by a ravenous wolflike creature nicknamed 'the Beast.' These poor souls were found with their throats ripped out, some partially eaten. He knew full well singleton wolf attacks were not unusual in this rugged, low mountainous region of France, riddled with rocky outcrops, small patches of forests, moors, and marshlands. It was a perfect environment for quick surprise attacks on prey in the small fields.

"G'day, monsieur," a young female villager greeted Lafont as he walked by.

Lafont gave her a courteous smile and touched the front of his hat but rushed past her at a deliberate pace. Beginning this summer, wolf attacks took on a completely different pattern. They not only increased in frequency but were much more brazen, and with a focus more on the peasants than the livestock. Witnesses warned of an unusually large wolflike creature with huge teeth and a long tail prowling the area. Seven violent deaths occurred throughout the summer, and this fall had already seen four attacks, with one woman completely decapitated just feet away from her front door.

Lafont spotted the village inn ahead. As he entered, he took off his hat and acknowledged the innkeeper behind the bar.

"Evening, Etienne," the innkeeper greeted then pointed to the back of the large room. "The marquis and the council are waiting."

Lafont nodded and rushed to the committee of six councilmen seated behind a long table, shoulder to shoulder, conversing in low tones. All were *seigneurs*, noble landowners who basically owned everything—and a significant portion of their wealth was in jeopardy from these disruptive attacks. The current marquis, an appointee of the king, was responsible for the protection of the region from foreign armies. Jean-Joseph d'Archer sat to the middle right. The marquis was the highest royal official in the region, subordinate only to the governor, a duke. While most of the councilmen were elderly, the marquis was in his early thirties. He was kind but very politically astute.

D'Archer noticed Lafont. "Good evening, Etienne."

Lafont bowed to d'Archer, with whom he had an excellent relationship. "Marquis." Lafont then eyed the man sitting to his left, Jean-Francois Charles de La Molette, the 'retired' Marquis de Morangiès, the wealthiest and most influential of the nobles. He was a recluse, and rarely did he leave his chalet castle, but today was different. Lafont knew the Marquis de Morangiès had grave concerns about the Beast.

Lafont bowed. "Monsieur."

The Marquis de Morangiès returned a head bow then raised his finger. "Etienne, good, you've made it. As you are aware, this mountainous province has little tillable land, so our cattle and sheep are our lives. If our shepherds and handlers don't lead the animals to pasture for fear of being attacked by the Beast, we lose revenue and are forced to default on our lands and properties." He gestured toward the others at the table. "Ultimately, our workers and their families will starve."

Lafont stared back at the councilmen. "Which is why I've been warning you for months to have everyone escorted by the men through these valleys."

The Marquis de Morangiès shook his head. "Our able-bodied men need to be tilling the furrows of our precious fields, Etienne. We can't afford to buy food from the neighboring provinces."

"I understand, but it's the only chance these defenseless women and children have."

The marquis's son, Comte de Morangiès, sat to his left. As the local count, he reported directly to the Marquis d'Archer. He raised his hands in frustration. "The men even fear the Beast, Etienne. How can they effectively arm themselves against this monstrous creature when it's illegal for them to carry firearms?"

Lafont nodded. "I've been pressing the provincial intendant to temporarily approve the use of firearms for protection, but my request has been rejected." Lafont glanced over at d'Archer. "I even asked the governor to intercede, but he agreed with the intendant."

D'Archer nodded. "I can understand Versailles's reticence. The recent defeat at the hands of the English has our government insecure about rising internal dangers. Neither wants to explain to His Majesty's advisors why they armed angry peasants."

"Thus, I am here to ask this council to finance the production of long staffs fitted with bayonets to arm hunting parties." Lafont paused. "Also, with some training, women and older children should be able to use these to fend off an attack from the Beast as they lead the livestock to pasture, leaving enough men to tend to the fields."

The council members glanced around the table; some nodded.

At that moment, the front door burst open. Lafont turned and smiled at Captain Jean-Baptiste Duhamel, commander of the governor's military unit assigned to Gévaudan. He tucked his hat under his arm and hurriedly approached them with four soldiers in tow. Lafont faced the council again. "Correspondence with the governor was not a complete failure, though, gentlemen." He pointed to Duhamel. "His military commandant has ordered Captain Duhamel to take charge and reinforce our permanent hunting parties. He, along with fifty armed dragoon horsemen, should be more than a match for the Beast."

One of the council members glanced around at the other members then faced Lafont and said, "Soldiers certainly have the needed courage for a job like this, but will they be up to the task of hunting?"

"Yes, indeed," the captain answered confidently. He placed his hand on Lafont's shoulder. "Your royal subdelegate here, Monsieur Lafont, was given orders to recruit your huntsmen to complement my elite dragoons in their saddles. They and their hounds will discover in which patch of woods this man-eating wolf, or wolf pack, temporarily resides, and we will dispatch it."

Lafont nodded. "Each huntsman will be compensated twenty sous per day in order to offset their loss of a day's wage working in the fields." He eyed the captain. "I've been assured that your first group of huntsmen will be waiting for you tomorrow morning in the village common."

"Excellent!" Duhamel belted out. He faced the council members, clicked his heels, and gave a short head bow. "Gentlemen," he said in farewell as he donned his hat, turned, and rushed out of the inn, followed closely by his subordinates.

Lafont watched the council members huddle around each other and converse privately, occasionally glancing up at him.

The Marquis de Morangiès nodded to the others then addressed Lafont: "We've agreed to finance the production of your weapons, Etienne."

Lafont smiled and gave a head bow.

"Hopefully, Captain Duhamel will have . . ." the Marquis de Morangiès paused," dispatched the Beast before we arm the entire province."

"Thank you, gentlemen," Lafont replied. "I will keep you informed as best I can." He pulled his hat low over his forehead and quickly left the building.

* * *

Two months later, at dusk, the Woods of Chazaux, near Saint-Denis, France

Two of Captain Duhamel's dragoon soldiers, John Fenwick and George Wade, positioned their horses near the tree line close to what seemed to be a path into the thick woods. Fenwick glanced up at cold, pelting snow and uncocked the wide brim of his hat, losing its triangular shape but better protecting his face from the elements. He repositioned his musket under his cloak. "The gunpowder is getting wet from the snow. We may only get a single shot at the Beast if it truly has harbored itself in these woods, and I would hate for a misfire."

Wade shook his head in dismay. "This is the sixth day we've had to endure this freezing weather. I tell you, the Beast is still south of here." He shook his head again. "The captain is putting too much pressure on himself, and as a result, he's making callous decisions. I warned him of the dangers of baiting this creature with the cadavers of its victims. He's even lost favor with the landowners."

Fenwick nodded as he spotted a huntsman walking out of the woods. "Agreed. I overheard Count Morangiès screaming about this kind of treatment of the dead."

"Anger from the locals is temporary," Wade replied. "Everyone is just frustrated that the Beast continues its murderous rampage. Once we shoot the Beast, all will be well."

The huntsman approached the dragoons. "Nothing so far, I did see—"

At that very moment, an enormous wolflike creature leaped out of the woods with lightning speed and gripped the huntsman by the throat, knocking him off his feet. As the man fell to the ground, the creature shook its massive head, instantly snapping the man's neck.

The horses immediately reared, and both horsemen tried desperately to pull out their muskets from their cloaks while remaining in their saddles.

The creature saw the movement and lunged for the closest horseman. It hit Fenwick broadside, and the Beast's weight carried the man backward off his horse. It gave a snarl to the remaining human, turned, and bolted away.

Before Wade could aim and fire his musket, the creature vanished over the ridge and into the adjoining valley.

Captain Duhamel sat on a tree stump with his musket in his lap, facing a patch of marshland in a deep ravine, his horse tied up next to him. He was sitting behind a large felled tree, which he planned on using to support his musket as he fired it. He'd purposely positioned himself in the adjoining valley near the woods just in case the Beast successfully evaded his dragoon horsemen and huntsmen. *If the Beast is in those woods*, he thought to himself, *it'll attempt an escape through this valley.* At that moment, he noticed a dark object streak into the valley from over the ridge. He was staring at the largest wolf he'd ever seen and realized his strategy had worked. It must be the Beast!

The captain propped his musket onto the tree trunk and aimed it at the running creature. "Come on, stop in the ravine," he whispered. The creature did just that; it ran into the marsh and stopped. Its side was exposed for a perfect shot. Blood and adrenaline pumped through Duhamel's veins, but he still managed to keep his musket steady for a shot. Just as he was about to pull the trigger, the creature leaped forward. Two of his dragoons galloped into the valley from over the ridge, intent on chasing the creature.

The Beast raced through the ravine at amazing speed.

The captain aimed his musket and shot, but the musket ball missed its target, landing harmlessly behind the running animal.

The Beast streaked over the ridge and out of the valley.

"Damn!" Duhamel yelled furiously and kicked the tree. He had a shot at killing the very creature that had managed to elude him for so long, and his own horsemen unintentionally ruined the opportunity. He knew darn well another chance like this may never come. Duhamel watched the two horsemen follow the Beast's trail.

Within a few minutes, over a dozen dragoons rode up to Captain Duhamel. "Did you see the Beast, sir?" the lead rider asked. "We heard the shot, then we followed a wolf trail to this valley."

The captain nodded as he placed his foot into his horse's stirrup and mounted. "It was the biggest and fastest wolf I've ever seen, Sergeant. It must be the Beast. I spotted it running from the woods into this ravine. Before I could get off a kill shot, two of our soldiers spooked it. They're following its trail in the snow as we speak."

"That was Beaumont and Duval, sir," the sergeant replied then pointed at the woods behind him. "The huntsman who accompanied them is lying dead with a gaping flesh wound to the throat. It seems they were following it after it exited the woods and attacked the huntsman."

"Leave a couple of soldiers near the huntsman's body," the captain directed. "Maybe it'll return for a meal. Have the rest of your men follow me, and we'll track it through the snow." He knew they had a very low chance of catching up to an animal with that much speed and endurance, but he hoped maybe fortune would favor them tonight.

chapter 16

Drake Brackston,
NCIS Headquarters, Quantico, Virginia

Upon receiving word from Assistant Director Peters that a representative of the Navy SEALs had walked into Special Agent Turner's office unannounced, Dr. Dunham drove immediately to NCIS Headquarters.

Twenty minutes later, he was approaching Turner's office door. He knocked, walked in, and spotted Turner at his office table to the left of his desk. He was seated with a powerfully built middle-aged man with short dark hair and a strong jawline, who was wearing a tailored suit.

"Welcome, Dr. Dunham," Turner said.

As Dunham joined them, the man kept eye contact with him, neither smiling nor frowning, just maintaining a calm poker face. This man exuded confidence.

Special Forces team member for sure, Dunham thought.

"Dr. Dunham," Turner began, "I'd like you to meet Drake Brackston, former member of SEAL Team Six, currently assigned with the CIA's Special Activities Division."

"How do you do, Mr. Brackston?" Dunham replied, shaking the offered hand.

"Mr. Brackston wanted to wait until you arrived before he got into any details."

"My superiors have ordered me to answer every one of your questions regarding the events surrounding the spy plane crash in the late 1980s off the Luzon coast of the Philippines."

"Mr. Brackston was one of the SEAL team members in the village on that fateful day," Turner added.

Dunham sat straighter his chair. "Our Filipino survivor said she saw two SEAL team members just before the massacre."

Brackston nodded. "That was me and Petty Officer Beals—died in '02." He paused. "We had overlapping missions . . . the one you're aware of, involving the crashed spy plane, and another involving a Soviet double agent extraction. The entire team participated in the first mission, then Beals and I stayed behind to accomplish the extraction."

Dunham glanced over at Turner but remained silent.

"You see, the USS *Ouellette* had been in the Sea of Japan, just off the Soviet coast near their port city of Vladivostok," Brackston explained, "and in the night, the double agent was sneaked onboard. He then blended in with the ship's company by impersonating a sailor. The plan was, the day before the ship was to pull into port at Subic Bay, Philippines, for liberty, their helicopter would fly the double agent off to Cubi Point Naval Air Station, where we'd collect him."

"But things changed when the spy plane crashed," Dunham interrupted.

Brackston nodded. "Precisely. The *Ouellette* was the closest ship to the crash site, so they were redirected to the scene to take control of the waters. My superiors decided to combine the two missions—have the entire team secure the beach and surrounding areas, then leave two of us behind to receive the double agent for extraction. Since the Negritos were our jungle escorts, we had to wait for their arrival, which meant leaving on the third day after the ship's arrival."

"Which coincidentally corresponded with the massacre," Dunham added.

Brackston nodded.

"Were you there?" Turner asked. "Did you see anything?"

"Do you mean were we in the village at the time of the massacre?" He shook his head. "No, but we were close enough to hear the chaos in the village." He sat back in his chair. "Once our escorts arrived, Beals and I grabbed the double agent then left the village along a jungle trail. Just a few minutes after we left, we heard loud noises and screams coming from the village. We continued through the jungle and never looked back."

"If you heard the screams, why didn't you go back and help?" Turner asked.

Brackston turned his head and stared at Turner with his poker face, showing no anger or remorse. "Special Agent Turner," he said, lifting his phone. "If I received orders right now to eliminate everyone in this room, I would do it without question and without emotion. The reason Special Forces has such a high success rate is because we never question our orders, and we follow them with ruthless efficiency. Exercising value judgments, such as 'doing the right thing,' impedes mission effectiveness. The chaos in the village was a threat to the success of our extraction mission. This man had information vital to the downfall of the Soviet Union." He paused. "Besides, our Negrito escorts wouldn't let us. These jungle fighters had fear in their eyes. I'd never seen them afraid of anything before this."

"What do you think their concern was?" Dunham asked.

Brackston shook his head. "Not sure, but they kept on saying some foreign word over and over."

Dunham glanced over at Turner then back at Brackston. "Aswang?"

Brackston paused then shrugged his shoulders. "Sounds right, but that was years ago, so it could've been anything. Anyway, as we exited along the path, Beals and I heard someone or something following us, streaking through the jungle, just beyond view. It had to be eliminated, so we moved everyone just off the path near the protection of a fallen tree and aimed our weapons in the direction of the movements and sounds. I took a shot and heard a scream—although the scream sounded more like an animal than a man. We quickly exited the area, but before we did, I turned back, and I swear I saw the asshole watching us from between the trees."

Dunham and Turner glanced at each other. "Asshole?" Dunham asked.

Brackston nodded. "One of the sailors, the big mouth that the other sailors hated. If we had to stay in the village one more day, I would've taken him into the jungle and given him a lesson on courtesy."

Turner searched through his file, pulled out photos of the eight sailors, and presented them to Brackston. "Which one?"

Brackston stared at the photos and pointed to one. "That one, I think. It's been a while."

Turner said, "Petty Officer Castle."

Dunham nodded. "That makes sense. He was found unconscious just outside the village."

"Unconscious my ass," Brackston blurted out.

"Did you see or hear anything else?" Turner asked.

Brackston shook his head. "That was it. Once we left, our connection with the village was done."

Turner glanced over at Dunham. "I have nothing else. How about you, Dr. Dunham?"

Dunham shook his head and stood. "Well, thank you, Mr. Brackston. You've cleared up all my questions."

Brackston nodded, shook hands with both men, then walked out of the room without another word.

Turner stared at the door Brackston had left open. "I believe he *would* have killed us without blinking an eye."

Dunham nodded. "Most serial offenders do not have the ability to sympathize or even empathize and, therefore, have no need to repress emotions after they kill. Many soldiers coming back from combat have major psychological issues, since they do sympathize and, thus, have repressed these emotions only to have them pop up later." He paused. "I believe Mr. Brackston has repressed nothing from his past, and his apparent sociopathy, or even psychopathy, lends well to him being so cold and calculating."

"I believe you're right." Turner switched gears. "Well, it looks like the Special Forces involvement in the massacre is a dead end, thankfully. Now what?"

Dunham glanced at Turner. "A priest recently told me that I must first follow my gut and trust those instincts, and actually, because I once ignored his advice, a woman almost lost her life. With the evidence so limited and even contradictory in this case, my gut is telling me to locate and speak with Joseph Castle. Brackston saw him fully conscious. I believe Castle saw something and, for whatever reason, he's refusing to say."

Turner nodded. "I hope you have better luck finding him."

Dunham grinned then leafed through the folder. "Do we have a DNA sample on Castle? If he's hiding in plain sight, I may need it."

Turner shook his head. "We now get DNA samples from every military service member, but not back then. We do have his dental records, though, so those could be used for identification."

"OK, dental records will help," Dunham replied. "I'll see if I can get a DNA sample from a close relative."

"Ha!" Turner blurted out. "Excuse the skepticism, but this family is very suspicious of outsiders."

"Any suggestions?" Dunham asked.

Turner thought. "Cousin Freddie," he answered. "He was the family member who told me that Joseph Castle left for Baton Rouge in 2000. When I spoke with him, I got the feeling that he disliked his cousin Joseph."

Dunham closed his file. "Well, Special Agent Turner, I believe I have enough to get started." They stood and shook hands. "I apologize in advance for not finding anything. A dead end just might be inevitable."

"No problem," Turner replied. "Anything will help. You have my number, Dr. Dunham, so, if you need anything, text or call me."

"I certainly will," Dunham replied, "and I'll keep you in the loop."

chapter 17

Abandoned Six Flags Amusement Park,
New Orleans, Louisiana

A thin man with short, sandy-colored hair pulled his van up to the amusement park and parked it next to the fence in a small driveway blocked from view by a garage. He glanced around and saw no one in view.

A dark-haired, rough-skinned lady, dressed in a well-worn short skirt paired with high heels, peeked out the passenger side window at the abandoned park. "We're gonna do a trick in here?" She shook her head. "Hmph, this'll be a first. Well, let's get this shit over with, but you gotta pay up front."

The man reached into his pocket, pulled out some cash, counted it, then handed it to her.

She grabbed it, quickly re-counted the bills, and opened her bag just wide enough for him to see her old thirty-eight caliber handgun. She stuffed the money inside her handbag. "Let's go."

They exited the van, and the man walked over to some thick brush, put on work gloves, then pulled out a large wooden crate exposing an opening in the fence. He slipped into the amusement park and held the opening for the woman to follow him. After she entered, he led her down a short path through overgrown weeds. He pointed to a building covered in graffiti, which butted up against a large, rusted rollercoaster. "In there," he said.

The lady stared up at the rollercoaster as she followed him to the building. "What a waste."

They approached the building, stopped at the padlocked door, and the man quickly scanned the area. He pulled out a key, opened the lock, and shoved the creaky door inward.

She entered first, walking into a nasty-looking room with a single bed in the corner. She glared at the man, who was padlocking the door from the inside. "This shithole?" she asked, noticing a second, larger back room. "I hope ya got somethin' better in there."

The man pointed to the bed. "Sit down and shut up."

"Don't expect to kiss me with that mouth, prick." She approached the bed and sat. As she took off her high heels, she watched the man walk into the other room. She reached into her bag and pulled out a cigarette and lighter as she listened to him making a lot of clanging noise back there. "Don't have all day!" She took a big puff.

The woman glanced around, getting even more irritated. The clanging noise stopped, so she leaned over and peeked into the back room. "Let's go!"

A deep growl emanated from the direction the man had gone.

"What the . . .?" She shot up from the bed and backed up to the door, staring at the entrance to the back room. A massive dog—no, wolf—came into view, and was glaring right at her.

The animal growled again, dropped its head, and gnashed its teeth.

She quickly turned and tried to open the door, but the padlock precluded her escape. She whirled around and faced the animal, which was now halfway across the room, stalking slowly toward her. She screamed at the top of her lungs and scrambled through her bag for her gun.

Outside, three high school-aged boys strolled through the abandoned amusement park, each holding onto cans of spray paint. The shortest, stockiest boy pointed up at the rusted roller coaster. "Hey, I used to ride this thing when I was a kid."

The tallest boy glanced over at him. "Bullshit, you don't remember that far back. Pot's got to your head."

"I remember riding it too," the redhaired boy added.

The tall boy walked up to a section at the base of the metal coaster, next to a small building, and shook his can of spray paint. "Well then, let's memorialize it for you two," he said as he pointed the can and started to spray.

The other two boys joined in.

A high-pitched feminine scream came from within the building, followed by a loud, animalistic growl, and all three boys froze. "What the hell?" The short boy stared at the building, his eyes wide open.

"What's going on?" the tall boy asked.

"I don't know, but it's not good," the redhaired boy replied.

"Let's get the hell outta here!" the short boy bellowed, and all three bolted.

The noise in the building stopped abruptly, and silence returned.

chapter 18

Uncle Gary's Bat Cave
New Orleans, Louisiana

Sarah approached her aunt and uncle's front door, Rob and Jared following on her heels.

As she made her way through the main living room, she quickly realized Jared was no longer with them. She turned around and spotted him standing in the foyer, staring at the interior with his eyes wide open and jaw hanging. She giggled, remembering Rob's identical response to seeing this gorgeous mansion.

"Wow!" Jared muttered then shifted his stare from the black-and-white tile floor to the massive crystal chandelier looming over the living room. "This is my kind of place!" His eyes swept over the large spiral staircase rising up to a beautiful second-floor landing filled with furniture. He pointed at it and said, "We have to work up there!"

"I hope the ambiance isn't too Spartan for your tastes, Jared," Sarah replied jokingly.

Jared grinned, then he spotted the large fireplace with the fancy mantelpiece under a highly adorned mirror. "No, no, this'll do. Can't think of a better place to work on our investigative assignment." His eyes flew to Sarah. "This is probably a silly question, but do they have Wi-Fi?"

Sarah nodded. "On steroids. They have a wireless distribution system that covers their home, the garage, the outbuildings, the pool area, the gazebo, all over the entire grounds."

Jared glanced over at Rob. "I could get used to this."

"Right!" Rob agreed.

Sarah pointed at an adjacent room. "Actually, Jared, let's work in the family room, which is just past the dining room" she said as she led the way. She pointed to a huge U-shaped, soft, white-leather couch circling an oak-and-glass coffee table. "Get comfortable. My aunt and uncle will be here soon. Saturday is their big food shopping day."

Rob and Jared pulled out their laptops. Rob raised both index fingers. "So, I asked for us to get together and brainstorm on what we should do next in our investigation of the Foliage Park incident."

Sarah hurried behind the massive bar and opened a large refrigerator. "Soda, anyone? They've got everything."

"I'll take a Coke or Pepsi," Jared replied. "Thanks."

Rob glanced up. "Sure, thanks, Sarah. I'll take a Diet Dr. Pepper."

"So, we're working under the premise that the Foliage Park mutilation was a homicide, perpetrated by a possible serial killer using a wolf-dog hybrid as his murder weapon," Jared summarized.

Rob nodded and continued, "And we can use that as a premise because our goal is to eliminate it as a possibility."

Sarah handed Rob and Jared their drinks and sat down with hers. "That means we should be looking for two things: supporting evidence and conflicting evidence."

"Yes," Rob began then started counting off. "First, evidence to the affirmative. We have DNA evidence that the killer at Foliage Park was a type of canine." He raised a second finger. "Second, the killer must have been big enough to mutilate a man and fight off a German shepherd, yet no one saw any creature come or go—highly suggestive of a human in control of the animal and concealing it." He lifted a third finger. "Days later, we have a possible eyewitness account of a sex worker being attacked by a large animal eerily similar to the Foliage Park animal."

"As yet unfounded," Jared interrupted.

Rob nodded. "Note taken," he replied then put up a fourth finger. "Lastly, we have a precedent case in France in the eighteenth century where a serial killer used a wolf-dog hybrid to do his murderous bidding."

"Possibly," Jared interjected again.

"Don't rain on my parade, Jared." Rob smirked. "I'm trying to make a case here."

"Evidence to the contrary for a serial killer," Sarah began. "All of the evidence to the affirmative is circumstantial and refutable and we have absolutely no hard evidence linking anything."

Jared grinned. "It's Sarah who just rained on your parade, Rob; not me."

Rob shook his head. "Yeah, she has a way of keeping my feet grounded in facts. Not a lot to go on, is it?"

Sarah took a sip. "I still think you're onto something, Rob. I say the answer will be found in linking. If we find other cases with similar offender signatures, we may discover a linking pattern."

"Agreed," Rob replied.

"Maybe we should search missing persons cases too," Jared suggested.

Rob nodded then turned his head in the direction of the front door as he heard it open.

Aunt Fran and Uncle Gary had returned. Uncle Gary peeked into the family room, two large pizza boxes in his hands. "Hi, guys, we brought some pizza for you. We bought a ton of food, which is in the back of the van, so we decided to bribe you into helping us bring it in to the house."

Rob jumped out of his seat. "Absolutely!"

"Aunt Fran, Uncle Gary," Sarah began and pointed to Jared, "this is our partner-in-crime-solving, Jared Dugas."

Jared hurried toward Aunt Fran and Uncle Gary.

"Jared is the only one in our class from the area," Sarah explained.

"Nice to meet you," Jared greeted them and shook their hands.

"Nice to meet you, Jared," Uncle Gary returned.

"Hi, Jared," Aunt Fran called on her way to the kitchen. "I hope you're hungry."

Jared patted his relatively large stomach. "I'm always ready to eat."

"And tell a joke!" Rob yelled.

Jared grinned then eyed Fran and Gary. "So, Hector Two-tones was lying in bed one night with his wife, Mary," he began.

"Look what you started, Rob!"

Uncle Gary grinned at Sarah's admonishment. "I love a good joke! Keep going, Jared."

Jared grinned and cleared his throat. "Hector Two-tones looked over at his wife and said, 'Mary, if I died, would you get married again?' Mary thought for a moment. 'I guess so, the kids need a dad don't they?' Hector Two-tones was silent for a bit. 'Mary, would ya sleep in the same bed with him?' Mary shrugged her shoulders. 'Well, there's only one master bed, so yeah.' He thought again. 'Would you make love to him, Mary?' Mary looked up at the ceiling and nodded. 'I guess so, since he's my husband.' Hector two-tones looked out the window. 'Mary, would you give him my pick-up truck?' Mary shook her head. 'Naw, I wouldn't. Besides, he doesn't know how to drive a stick shift.'"

Everyone laughed.

"No more tonight, Jared!" Sarah blurted out in jest.

Jared snickered. "I won't, just for you, Sarah."

Aunt Fran placed her hands on her hips. "So, we need some hands to bring in the food, and then let's eat!"

Fifteen minutes later, everyone was seated around the dining room table, tucking into the two large pizzas.

"Aunt Fran and Uncle Gary, may I move in with you? I believe it's legal to adopt a poor college student in the state of Louisiana," Jared pleaded.

"You're welcome at any time, Jared," Aunt Fran commented then glanced around at everyone. "So, how's your investigation going?"

Rob nodded. "OK. We were about to figure out our next step."

"Basically," Sarah added, "we need to find more evidence that we're dealing with a serial killer in New Orleans—as in, investigate recent unsolved cases, possibly discovering a linking pattern."

"I think it's time to go online and see what we can find," Jared recommended.

"I have a better idea," Uncle Gary interjected.

Rob stopped chewing. "Oh?"

"I have a," Uncle Gary paused, "basement office."

"Basement office!" Aunt Fran interrupted. "It's the bat cave!"

"Bat cave?" Sarah asked. "I didn't know you had a bat cave."

"Gary's a survivalist at heart," Aunt Fran explained, "so he set up a control center just in case the government collapses and everyone has to fend for themselves."

Gary waved off Fran's comment. "Don't mind her. I've loaded it up with top-of-the-line hi-tech gadgets and computer consoles." He grinned. "You name it, it's in there! I can control my security cameras, doors, lights, locks, speakers, drones, everything from there."

"Drones?" Rob asked.

"How else am I going to drop my canisters of pepper spray from a safe distance?"

Jared glanced over at Aunt Fran. "How cool is that!"

"Now you're just showing off, Gary," Aunt Fran commented.

Uncle Gary shrugged his shoulders. "OK, OK, back to you and your investigation. Not only are these computer consoles control stations, they also give you access to the internet—" he grinned again, "and other databases not available to the public. In your case, there's a link to the New Orleans newspapers and even obituary records."

"I'd love to see that, Mr. Smith," Rob said.

"That settles it. After dinner, I'll take you down there, and you can use the consoles."

As promised, Uncle Gary escorted Rob, Sarah, and Jared to the basement. They walked by a number of pallets loaded with bottled water, freeze-dried and canned goods, and other pallets with covers on them.

"What's under those tarps, Uncle Gary?" Sarah asked.

"Anything and everything you would need in a survival situation," Uncle Gary stated then pointed to the door ahead of them. "Here's my bat cave."

When Uncle Gary turned on the lights, they saw a room filled with electronic equipment and computers.

"Wow! Nice place," Sarah commented.

"I told you. The computer consoles should be ready to go. I have them set to turn on when I flip the light switch."

Jared sat at a console. "Thank you, Mr. Smith."

Uncle Gary walked to the door and tapped above the light switch. "When you leave, just turn the switch off." He pointed to the massive metal door to a safe, situated on the far wall. "That's where I keep my high-value survival items," he said, flashing a big grin as he left.

"I think your uncle is expecting a zombie apocalypse, Sarah," Jared joked.

Rob glanced over at Jared. "What? You don't believe there could be one?" he asked facetiously.

"Hey, this is New Orleans," Jared replied. "If there is going to be a zombie apocalypse, it'll start here, in Voodoo country."

"All right! Time to get started," Sarah commented and sat at a third computer console. "I'll take the depressing job of searching through local obituaries."

"The first one who finds anything gets a dollar!" Jared yelled.

Rob grinned. "You're on!"

All three went to work in earnest, discussed each other's possible hits, quickly discounted them, then continued the search.

After nearly two hours, Jared left his seat and began to pace back and forth behind Rob and Sarah. "I thought this was going to be easier," he commented and shook his head. "Maybe this means there is no serial killer."

Rob shrugged. "Could be, but I'm not yet ready to give up. Maybe it's a case of a serial killer selecting victims no one cares about in order to stay under the police's radar. Some say that's why Jack the Ripper selected prostitutes from the poorest area of London."

"OK," Sarah replied, "I'll narrow my search to undesirables living on the fringes of society—like sex workers, convicts, homeless people . . ."

"There's leftover pizza up there, isn't there?" Jared asked.

"I could go for another slice too," Rob replied.

"Hey, check this out," Sarah interrupted. "I found a website called *The Plight of New Orleans Homeless*. This lady ran a soup kitchen downtown."

Jared walked behind Sarah and looked at her monitor. "What about her?"

"Well, she spends an awful lot of time writing about how the homeless are ignored," Sarah explained and pointed at the screen, "but then down here, she says, 'Now, some of the homeless are afraid to go in certain areas because of some kind of hairy monster.'"

Rob's head popped up, and he shot over to Sarah's computer.

"She doesn't believe them," Sarah continued, "because she thinks it's just their way of getting people to hear their cries."

"Or they're really telling the truth," Rob commented then paused. "I'm getting that gut feeling again." He glanced over at Jared. "It wouldn't hurt to visit this soup kitchen and ask her a few questions. It's our only lead."

"Let's do it," Jared replied. "How about we discuss it over another slice of pizza!" He and Rob started for the door.

"Ahem," Sarah interrupted, her right palm open. "Don't the two of you owe me a dollar?"

chapter 19

Château de Versailles,
France,
January 1765

King Louis XV sat at a long, marble-topped table in his antechamber. He shifted his weight, sinking into a cushioned red velvet seat. His legal administrator stood at his side and placed another parchment in front of him. The king quickly read the document, and just as he was about to sign it, he noticed one of his royal secretaries entering the room.

"Your advisors are here, Your Excellency. Ministers Comte de Saint-Florentin and Controller-General Charles-Francois L'Averdy."

The king signed the parchment then said, "Send them in."

The secretary made a deep bow, turned on his heel, and hurried from the room.

Moments later, the two ministers entered. "You sent for us, Your Excellency?"

"Yes, Saint-Florentin," the king answered as he scanned the next parchment that was placed in front of him. "Rumor has it that a ferocious wolf has been terrorizing the peasantry in the mountain provinces around Gévaudan since last summer," he raised his eyes to the legal administrator and handed him the parchment, "and the hunting parties have tried in vain to kill it?" The king shifted his gaze to Saint-Florentin. "Is this true?"

Saint-Florentin bowed. "Yes, Your Excellency. The provincial governor and your intendant have been sending us weekly updates. They wanted to resolve the issue at their level by using local huntsmen and the military garrison stationed in the region." He paused. "The hunt has not been fruitful, so the Council of Ministers planned on informing you about the details next week at our January meeting."

The king narrowed his eyes into a glare. "Why was I not informed of this earlier?"

Saint-Florentin paused and sneaked a glance at L'Averdy, aware that the king had been depressed and quite irrational ever since the defeat of his military by the English two years ago. News of an unstoppable wolf or wolf pack mutilating dozens, maybe even a hundred villagers and laborers in the heart of his country just might put him over the edge.

"Well?" the king demanded.

Saint-Florentin bowed. "When the local authorities first informed us last fall, Your Excellency, we were led to believe the attacks were normal—the usual wolf attacks in these rural mountainous regions, from a rabid wolf soon to die of the disease." He glanced at L'Averdy again. "The council fully expected the attacks to wane, but it was only a few weeks ago that we received word they are continuing."

The king gave all of the documents to the administrator and shooed him away. He watched the administrator leave the room. "My sources also tell me that the reason why this beast has not been killed is because it's—it's a werewolf."

"Superstitious nonsense from the mouths of ignorant peasants, Your Excellency," L'Averdy responded. "The creature is obviously a large wolf or maybe a whole wolf pack." He paused and grinned. "These sorrowful attacks may be to your advantage."

The king glared at L'Averdy. "Oh? How so?"

"The Beast—the name the locals have given this animal—has unintentionally provided us with an excellent opportunity to show the people of France that His Majesty is their savior." He gazed back at the king. "We shall inform the newspapers that upon hearing about the murderous rampages of the Beast, their king and protector immediately dispatched the greatest wolf hunter in France to rid them of this evil."

The king stared up at the ceiling for a moment then beamed. "This is genius!" He eyed Saint-Florentin. "Do we have such a hunter?"

Saint-Florentin bowed his head. "Sir Martin Denneval, a Norman. He is reputed to have killed over twelve hundred wolves in his career. He's a bit pompous amongst the commoners, but he's excellent. One lone wolf will be no match for a huntsman of his caliber."

The king paused then glanced over at the two ministers. "Handle the details and make it so!" he commanded, eyeing L'Averdy, the controller of his purse strings. "Regardless of the cost." He waved the back of his hand at the ministers, directing them to leave. "Inform the rest of the royal court of my decision."

The two ministers gave a deep bow then hurried from the room.

* * *

The Village of Malzieu,
Gévaudan Province, France,
February 1765

Lafont and Count Morangiès dismounted their horses outside the high-end Le Malzieu-Ville Hotel. "So, this is where the celebrated wolf hunter, Sir Martin Denneval, and his son are staying." Lafont paused. "He certainly enjoys his luxuries."

Morangiès glanced around. "It's apparent he's had a successful hunting career."

"All the better for us," Morangiès added as they walked up to the front door, removing their hats as they entered.

Lafont noticed a large crowd near the back of the dining area giving their undivided attention to two men holding glasses of wine, one elderly and one a generation younger. The crowd blurted out in laugher after the elderly man made a comment. Lafont turned to Morangiès. "I believe we've found Monsieur Denneval."

"Entertaining his audience, I believe, with his past exploits," Morangiès replied.

"No wolf has escaped me yet!" Denneval yelled then glanced over at the younger man. "My son here, Jean-Francois, has told me I've eliminated over twelve hundred wolves in Normandy alone."

"My father may be in his sixties," Jean-Francois interrupted, "but he's retained the energy of his youth and has even led his hounds—reins in hand—sixty leagues before dispatching his prey!"

"Oh, don't make me out as a fool, my fine friends," Denneval added, scanning the crowd. "Yes, I still participate in hunts, as I shall with this Beast, but my age has forced a more sedentary role," he slapped his son on the back, "and I have indeed passed the reins onto my strapping young son!"

The crowd laughed.

"Monsieur Denneval!" Lafont called out.

Denneval spotted Lafont. "Yes? Do you have a question?"

"It is quite an honor to finally meet you," Lafont began. "I am your point of contact, Etienne Lafont, subdelegate to His Majesty's Intendant Saint-Priest and Syndic to the Bishop." He pointed to Morangiès. "This is the Comte de Morangiès."

Denneval waved to the crowd as he approached Lafont and Morangiès. "All good things must come to an end, everyone!" He faced Lafont and gave a bow as the crowd dispersed behind him. "Thank you for meeting me here, messieurs. Monsieur Lafont, as syndic, you are well aware that if the bishop invites you to dine with him, you accept, which is where my son and I will be tonight."

"Completely understandable," Lafont replied. He noticed Denneval's son approaching.

"This is my son, Jean-Francois," Denneval introduced. They greeted each other and settled at a table.

"I'm sure you want to meet Captain Duhamel, but he is currently tracking the Beast not far from here." Lafont paused. "Last night, we had another gruesome attack, and two young women were found mutilated."

"I am not interested in meeting this failure," Denneval replied smugly. "As a matter of fact, I insist you inform him that his services are no longer needed."

Lafont paused, taken aback by Denneval's abrasive response about the captain, a man he respected. He noticed the frown marring Morangiès's features; clearly he was irritated by Denneval's remarks as well.

"We do not have the authority to dismiss Captain Duhamel, monsieur," Lafont said to Denneval. "This must come from the military commandant of the province, or the governor himself."

Denneval shook his head. "Unacceptable."

"I will pass on your demand, but don't you think you need to at least discuss with the captain? He has many lessons learned."

"Useless to me," Denneval dismissed. "I've read all of the reports coming into Versailles, and that's all I need. It's my own expertise and experience in wolf hunting that will lead to success." He closed his eyes smugly. "Recently, in Soissons, I quickly dispatched a massive creature, very similar to your Beast but even more ferocious." He pointed his finger. "What I do need are my hounds, yet it might take a few weeks for them to arrive." He shook his head and frowned. "I had to personally fund their transport."

"I am surprised they did not give financial assistance," Lafont replied.

"No matter; I will merely charge Versailles a higher price for my services." He glanced around the room. "Once I have my hounds, expect a resolution to your problem within two weeks."

Morangiès rolled his eyes as he said, "Monsieur Denneval, Soissons has a completely different terrain than we have here in Gévaudan—here it is much rougher, especially in the winter."

"The terrain is not the problem, Seigneur Morangiès; the problem is the captain. Word has come to me that he stages simultaneous large, noisy hunts. The Beast hears them coming from leagues away. Your captain is clearly no huntsman."

"We have come very close to killing the Beast," Lafont retorted.

Denneval paused, glaring at Lafont. "I am aware of the dismal failure of the coordinated hunt the captain led last week. I hear there were over twenty thousand capable men involved, yet the Beast slipped away with ease. I hear the captain did snare peasant workers in his metal traps though."

"The fault of a local village noble," Morangiès blurted out. "The defiant bastard ordered his commoners to stay indoors at the very location the Beast was spotted escaping."

Denneval drank from his stein, unimpressed with Morangiès's comment. "His fault was relying upon locals. Once my six large hounds get on this creature's scent, they will be relentless and run it to exhaustion, only breaking off the chase after a well-placed shot from my musket." He stood, followed by his son. "If you'll excuse me, gentlemen, we must prepare for our visit with the bishop."

Lafont and Morangiès gained their feet. "Certainly," Lafont answered. "Until our next meeting."

Lafont and Morangiès donned their hats and headed for the front door.

Denneval stared at them as they exited the hotel. "Jean-Francois, I hope our hounds come soon. I fear we have a rabid wolf on our hands. We need to hunt it down before it dies of the disease, else much-deserved fame and notoriety may slip through our fingers."

Jean-Francois nodded. "Shall I inform our point of contact when the hounds arrive?"

"No," Denneval blurted out quickly. "Tell them nothing. Let them seek us out for updates on our progress. I hear this local administrator, Lafont, and the seignior for that matter, are 'quick with the quill,' and I would like to control any information about our progress that Versailles receives."

"I foresee difficulties," Lafont commented as the pair mounted their horses. "The captain will not take this lightly."

"What arrogance," Morangiès replied. "If it wasn't for our people being slaughtered by this creature, I would pray for Denneval's failure." He paused. "I hope Versailles knows what they're doing."

chapter 20

Lafayette Police Department,
Lafayette, Louisiana

Major Ted Simon, commander of the Criminal Investigative Division for the Lafayette Parish Sheriff's Office, knocked on the door of Major Joseph Mowins, commander of CID for the City of Lafayette Police Department. "Joe, is he here, yet?" Simon asked as he strode into the room. He wore a brown tweed sports coat.

Mowins looked up from his computer and noticed that Simon seemed unusually upbeat. He glanced over at an empty seat in his office. "No, come on in, Ted, and take a seat. He should be here any minute," he replied, straightening his blue sports coat.

Simon dropped into the chair. "How cool is this? We finally get to meet the Watchmaker face to face!"

Mowins grinned. "Isn't it? Now, on the phone, Dr. Dunham thanked us in advance for our assistance, and to reciprocate, he's offered to assist us in any investigation. I say we should take him up on his offer. Any thoughts on which one?"

Simon nodded. "How about those unsolved serial murders from a few years back? They stopped, but I'd love to nail the guy."

"I was thinking about those, too, especially since the Watchmaker is a serial killer expert." Mowins paused. "But, we only have him for an hour or so before you escort him to the Castle residence. I was thinking of the all-too-public Stanley murder."

"The Stanley murder?" Simon repeated then sat back in his chair and glanced up at the ceiling, pondering.

Mowins leaned forward over his desk. "We're about to stick our necks out and arrest the daughter of a prominent Lafayette multimillionaire businessman for murder. We only have one piece of evidence—albeit a solid piece—but it's still only one connection to the murder. I'd like to reinforce our case."

Simon grinned. "I like how you're thinking, Joe, especially since the murder occurred in my jurisdiction. The pie will be on my face if the trial goes south."

Mowins's secretary popped her head in. "Sir, Dr. Dunham is here to see y'all."

Simon and Mowins immediately leaped from their seats. "Thank you, Tonya," Mowins replied as he and Simon rushed out of his office straight to the front desk.

Dunham scanned the detective division office space and realized that, within the last two minutes, while introducing himself to the secretary, the loud, busy group of detectives had stopped conversing or working and were staring at him. He spotted two men approaching him with the secretary.

Simon reached Dunham first and shook his hand. "Dr. Dunham," he greeted. "It's great to finally meet you. Major Ted Simon, CID Commander."

"How do you do, Major?"

"This is Major Joe Mowins, my CID commander counterpart for the Lafayette Parish Sheriff's Office."

Mowins shook Dunham's hand. "Pleasure, Dr. Dunham. Ted and I work hand-in-hand with all the major cases being investigated, especially since the drastic budget cuts went into effect."

Mowins noticed the rest of the detective division staring at them. "Well!" he blurted out, "since all y'all aren't working anyway, get your asses over here and introduce yourselves!" He faced Dunham. "Excuse the interest in you, Dr. Dunham. Our annual divisional training two weeks ago involved the case studies of your Cincinnati and Niagara Falls serial murder investigations. Everyone's fully aware of your record of success."

Dunham blushed, then nodded. "It's great you used those, Major. Both were classic cases of success not by just me but through teamwork."

The other detectives approached Dunham and greeted him, one by one.

A few moments later, Simon raised his hand, catching Dunham's eye. "So, the plan, Dr. Dunham, is to have Major Mowins be your escort to the Castle residence, since it's in his jurisdiction."

Dunham nodded to Mowins. "I certainly appreciate this, Major," then he glanced around at everyone, "but before you help me out, I was serious about offering my services."

Mowins nodded and glanced around the room. "Detective Dabadie, fetch the Stanley murder case file and meet us in the conference room."

Dabadie nodded and rushed away with another detective.

"Thank you, Dr. Dunham. We certainly would like you to take a look at a high-profile case, which has received the approval of the district attorney for an arrest," Mowins explained then pointed to a large office space. "How about we make our way to the conference room?" He glanced at the other detectives. "And yes, if anyone would like to sit in on this, y'all are welcome."

Everyone made their way into the conference room and settled in. Detective Dabadie placed a folder before Dunham. "Here's the Stanley case file, Dr. Dunham—coffee?"

Dunham opened the file. "Thank you, and yes; cream, please."

"Let me quickly summarize the case as you peruse it," Simon began. "Charles Stanley, the husband of Janice Stanley, was found dead with a 9-millimeter bullet wound to the head; entry wound in the back and exit wound in the front." He paused. "Janice Stanley is the daughter of Lafayette multimillionaire and businessman Donald Dafoe."

Dunham nodded. "I see why this is a high-profile case."

Simon smirked and continued: "Burn marks around the entry wound indicate the barrel was only an inch away from his head. The wife states she was sleeping on the recliner in the living room because of her injured back. She woke up in the morning, went into the bedroom, and claims she found her husband in a pool of blood with a pillow over his head. She stated she immediately called 9-1-1. The bedroom window screen was up, and she stated they always had the screen down to keep the insects out, suggesting someone entered the home through the window, shot the victim, burglarized the house, then exited back out the window into the backyard."

"Did you collect any latent evidence on or around the window?" Dunham asked.

Simon shook his head. "We conducted a search but found nothing—and curiously, there was no evidence discovered outside the window either."

Dunham scanned a page in the file. "You said theft was involved?"

"Yes," Simon answered, "the jewelry box was stolen along with a small safe. According to the wife, the jewelry box contained at least ten thousand dollars in jewelry, and the safe held a few hundred dollars in cash."

Dunham glanced up at Simon and Mowins. "Did you find the murder weapon?"

"Nope," Mowins replied, "we conducted the usual search—presuming the perp to be an acquaintance, family, or friend—so the first person we focused upon was his wife, Janice." He paused. "And we didn't have to look any further."

"Interesting," Dunham commented.

"The key piece of evidence contradicts her story," Mowins explained. "We sprayed her nightgown with luminol, and six tiny spots glowed blue, revealing minute particles of blood. The tiny spots are consistent with blood spatter resulting from a gunshot wound to the head, with most of the splatter hitting the pillow. She claimed she was in the living room at the time of the murder." He shook his head. "But, facts don't lie."

Dunham searched through the file. "Where is the forensic report? Oh, here it is." He read the report then glanced up at the officers. "Is this report complete?"

"Yes, sir," another detective said, sitting to the left of Mowins. "Every bit of forensic testing is in that file."

Mowins pointed to a photo of the bathroom. "We then noticed the adjoining bathroom was unusually clean, and a bottle of bleach cleaning spray was left out."

Dunham shot a look at Mowins. "Bleach?"

"Yes. Multiple towels were hanging off the shower door to dry, suggesting to us that she attempted to wash away latent evidence."

"Any evidence of blood in the drain?" Dunham asked.

Mowins shook his head. "Nope, nothing, but if there wasn't a whole lot of blood to clean up, it might have been missed. Janice Stanley admitted to cleaning the bathroom, but she claimed she did so just before bed."

"We then looked at motive," Simon interrupted, "and we discovered her husband was having an affair for the past year. According to his girlfriend, he was planning on divorcing his wife. What's also suspicious is the husband upped his life insurance, only a month prior, to 1.2 million dollars—and Janice's signature's on it. She was fully aware that she was the beneficiary." He paused and raised three fingers. "We now have motive, opportunity, and a huge piece of incriminating evidence."

"Of course, she claims she didn't know of the affair," Mowins added.

Simon eyed Dunham. "With her father's money, we know she'll have a high-powered defense team, so we would love to have you look over the case to see if there are any holes. Maybe you can find something we didn't."

Dunham read the file, flipped through the photos and reports, then continued reading.

Everyone else in the room sat silently, staring at him.

A few minutes later, Dunham's head popped up. "I see she has no arrest record and no history of violence." He closed the file and sat back. "I'm glad I got to look at this case because I believe Janice Stanley is innocent."

The detectives sat up and eyed each other, taken by surprise.

Simon raised his finger. "But the evidence clearly shows blood spatter marks on Janice Stanley's nightgown, the very gown she was wearing that night!"

Dunham shook his head. "It's true that facts don't lie, but sometimes interpreting facts can be less than perfect." He paused. "She has no blood spatter stains on her nightgown."

Mowins frowned, glanced at Simon, then at Dunham. "What do you mean?"

Dunham nodded. "Remember that luminol certainly does exhibit chemiluminescence of a blue glow for thirty seconds when in contact with blood, but it also does so for any compound containing an oxidizing agent. The oxidizing agent in blood is iron. Substances with the oxidizing agent copper also glow blue; hydrogen peroxide does, too, as well as fecal matter—and even horseradish." He pointed his finger. "But in this case, she was exposed that very night to bleach, a substance that gives off a blue glow, just as blood does." He paused. "Now, I do recommend you confirm this by testing for bleach, but I'm quite confident."

The detectives glanced at each other, dumbfounded.

"Also," Dunham continued, "in cases with an emotion-based motive, as you're arguing this is, there is generally evidence of anger expressed within the act of murder, such as multiple rounds fired into the victim, bruising to the face, destruction of the surroundings." He paused. "In other words, excessive violence." He shook his head. "I see evidence of a methodical crime perpetrated with unusual precision by a very experienced offender." He pointed to a photo of the victim. "One kill shot to the back of the head, no destruction of the surroundings, extraction of only the highest-valued possessions, and leaving little if no evidence of their entry and exit."

Simon raised his hands in the air. "So, we're back to the drawing board."

Mowins streaked his fingers through his hair. "At least we didn't embarrass ourselves and aim to convict an innocent person–an heiress, at that."

"There's good news," Dunham interrupted. "I see a number of possible leads. First, this offender has clearly done this before, which means he most likely has a record. Second, I believe we're dealing with a male psychopath guided by thrill-seeking. Not only does the offender enjoy the theft, he takes pride in his efficiency—even in the act of murder."

"But, as you say," Simon interrupted, "someone like this certainly didn't leave behind latent evidence."

Dunham nodded. "In the home, but," he paused and pulled out a photo, "it's my opinion our offender didn't exit through the window. Someone this efficient would have closed the screen behind him. I see the screen being left up as a ploy to mislead the investigation. And 'acts of misleading' can be an offender's calling card." He sat back in his seat. "I say he was brazen enough to walk out the front door, and if he did, we may have this recorded."

Simon sat up straight. "What do you mean?"

Dunham searched through the file and pulled out a map of the victim's neighborhood. "I see the Stanleys' home is in a wealthy suburb and is situated near this intersection." He glanced up at the detectives. "Are these intersections equipped with cameras?"

Mowins beamed. "They are, and I see where you're going with this. Review the photos just after the time of death."

"Exactly," Dunham replied, "but also, since he seems to have cased the Stanley home, check out images for the week prior. We might get lucky." He glanced at the detectives around the table. "Please keep me informed if anything breaks."

Simon and Mowins stood, which prompted everyone to do the same. Simon shook Dunham's hand. "You're a lifesaver, Dr. Dunham, and we certainly will."

"Thank you, Dr. Dunham," another detective said, collected the case file, and started for the door. "Time to go to work." He and the other detectives left the room, leaving Dunham, Simon, and Mowins alone.

"Well, are you ready to go?" Mowins asked.

Dunham nodded. "Sure am."

* * *

In the Bayou,
Lafayette, Louisiana

"We're almost there, Dr. Dunham," Mowins announced then glanced up at the rearview mirror.

Dunham watched the cypress trees flash by the passenger-side window of the unmarked car. "The Castle family certainly lives in the boondocks."

Mowins grinned. "It's a hard life back in the bayou, for sure. It's been my experience that they don't take a liking to strangers, so don't expect much."

"I've been warned."

"It's probably because the only time strangers come into these parts," Mowins surmised, "is to take something from them."

Mowins pointed to a rundown home near the edge of a wooded area. "There are four Castle families, all related to each other. That's the home of Joseph Castle's mother and brother, Jeremiah."

Dunham stared at the home. "So, Joseph Castle's father passed away?"

Mowins nodded. "A few years back, here in Lafayette, maybe fifteen years ago." He slowed down and pulled onto a long dirt road that led into the thick cypress trees. "This is Freddie's driveway. As you can see, he lives even deeper in the woods."

After a few moments, they drove into a clearing, revealing another rundown home. Two chained hounds were barking incessantly.

"This is it," Mowins declared. He pulled up near the house, and the two exited the car.

Mowins glanced over at the barn. "Doesn't look like anyone is home. I'll take a walk behind the barn and check the field while you knock on the front door."

Dunham nodded. "Sounds good." They separated, and Dunham made his way to the front porch. *If anyone's home,* he thought, *they certainly know we're here, with these hounds announcing our arrival.* Before walking up to the front door, he decided to see if anyone was behind the house, near the woods. As he walked past the porch, he heard a branch crack to his right, and in his peripheral vision, he caught sight of a stocky young man.

The man rushed at him in a full run.

He spotted a second solid young man to his left.

The second man rushed at Dunham from the opposite direction.

In pure aikido fashion, Dunham paused for a moment, and when both were almost upon him, he advanced toward the closest one and blended with his attack like a bull attacking a matador.

This caught the attacker off guard. The young man tried to grip him with both hands, but his momentum carried his body past Dunham.

At that moment, Dunham grabbed the attacker by his elbows and twisted him like he was turning the steering wheel of a car, which caused the young man's head to drop and his feet to lift off the ground. Dunham then redirected the flying young man into the other attacker, causing a forceful collision between the two.

Both attackers groaned upon impact and lay crumpled on the ground, aching in pain.

An older man on the front porch glared at the two attackers. "What in Sam Hill are you two idiots doing?"

At that moment, Mowins rushed up to the two collapsed young men, his handgun aimed at them. "Sheriff's department! Face down! Hands behind your heads!"

Both slowly moved into position, groaning.

Mowins glanced up at Dunham as he straddled one of the young men and secured his wrists. "Are you OK, Dr. Dunham?"

Dunham brushed himself off. "I believe so."

Mowins cuffed the second young man. "I see you met Freddie Junior and Tucker."

"I think I made out better than they did, Major," Dunham replied then faced the middle-aged man on the porch.

"Apologize about my boys, stranger," the man said. "We just had somethin' stolen off our property," he glared at his sons again, "and they're too stupid to know someone in a suit wouldn't be stealing equipment."

"Sorry, Pa," one of the young men apologized then moaned.

Mowins nodded to the man on the porch. "How ya doing, Freddie?"

Freddie nodded back. "Detective." He paused. "I do somethin' wrong?"

"Not at all," Mowins replied then glanced at Dunham. "We're hoping you'll help us. I want to introduce you to Dr. Edward Dunham, special agent for the FBI."

Freddie eyed Dunham suspiciously and nodded to him.

"Hi, Mr. Castle," Dunham said. "Your assistance would be greatly appreciated. I'm following up with Special Agent Turner's investigation. He was here a few years back. Do you remember him? He worked for the Navy?"

Freddie eyed Dunham. "Yup, he was lookin' for Joey."

"Yes," Dunham continued. "He told me that, in 2000, Joseph Castle moved away from here to live in Baton Rouge."

Freddie nodded. "About right, but he hasn't been back since. Not welcomed, really. Don't know where he is now."

"Do you mind if I ask why he moved away from the family?"

Freddie frowned, remained silent for a moment, then nodded. "He's a bad egg, and ever since he came back from the Navy, he was worse."

"I'd like to find him and ask him about some events he experienced while in the Navy, Mr. Castle," Dunham explained.

"Don't think you'll find the bastard. He's probably changed his name."

Dunham glanced over at Mowins, then back at Freddie. "I'd like to take advantage of modern technology, Mr. Castle. It'll require a sample of your DNA." He gestured at the two sons. "Or a sample from Freddie Junior or Tucker. Of course, I'll forget their assault on a federal law enforcement officer."

"Seein' my two bullheaded sons get what was comin' to 'em was the highlight of my day, Mr. FBI Agent." He grinned. "How about gettin' a sample from Freddie Junior here—and I hope it hurts!"

Dunham chuckled as Mowins released the two young men.

Freddie turned toward his front door. "Everybody come on inside."

Twenty minutes later, Dunham and Mowins were in the unmarked police car on their way back to Lafayette. "Thank you for all the help, Major. I couldn't have done it without you."

Mowins grinned. "Everything went better than I expected." He glanced over at Dunham. "Other than his sons attacking you."

Dunham laughed. "Apparently, we had to get the ice broken!"

"I saw the whole thing as I was coming back from the barn. You're full of surprises, Dr. Dunham. Are you a martial artist or something?"

"Well," Dunham responded, grinning slightly. "I never thought I was a martial artist, but I have been practicing aikido pretty consistently lately, so apparently, yes. Friends of mine in Buffalo and Boston are senior instructors in a very effective style of aikido."

"I can tell."

Dunham grinned. "Both of these instructors got me into it. Luckily, there's a sister dojo just forty minutes away from my home in Virginia, so I've been keeping up on it. It actually saved my butt last year."

"Well, next time you come into town, instead of asking you for a class on serial offenders, maybe we should be taking some aikido lessons!"

"Ha!" Dunham blurted out. "How about both?"

"What's your next step in the investigation?"

Dunham stared out the passenger window. "Keep on searching for Joseph Castle, wherever he may be. If he is living under an alias, I may have a tough road ahead of me, and the DNA test will only help once I have a few candidates to compare it with." He glanced at Mowins. "His post-Navy residence pattern suggests he's most comfortable in the South, specifically Louisiana, which greatly reduces my search area."

Mowins shook his head. "Still an awfully big area, but at least it seems you can cross off Lafayette."

"Hey, it's a start," Dunham answered. "His last-known location was Baton Rouge, so hopefully I can pick up his trail there."

"Louisiana State Police Headquarters is out of Baton Rouge. They may be able to assist you."

"Thanks," Dunham replied. "Once I process this DNA sample back at the FBI lab, I'll do just that."

"Also," Mowins began, "there are awesome state databases and archives at the Louisiana Public Library in New Orleans. It helped us out on a few investigations."

Dunham grinned. "Major, you've been an excellent resource. This is great."

"Just giving you some incentive to keep Lafayette on your mind, Dr. Dunham, and we certainly do appreciate your help on the Stanley case."

chapter 21

The Plight of the Homeless

Sarah waited for her crime-solving partners on the street in front of her aunt and uncle's mansion. She watched as a small, light-blue car approached. As it stopped before her, she spotted Jared behind the wheel, Sebastian in the passenger seat, and Rob in the back seat. "Hi, guys." She slid into the back and kissed Rob.

Jared stepped on the accelerator, and the car started off down the street.

Sebastian stared at the mansion as they passed. "Nice place, Sarah. Take out a lot of loans for this?"

"Thanks, Sebastian. It's my aunt and uncle's. I didn't know you were coming with us to the homeless shelter."

He turned around, facing Sarah. "Cedric and Lacy are out on a date, and I was a fifth wheel—so to speak."

"Classroom romance," Jared interrupted. "Love is in the air." He shot a quick glance at Sarah. "I saw Sebastian doing the loner thing at the hotel, so I forced him to come."

"Well, you're an honorary member of the Watchmaker Society," Sarah added, "so you have a home with us. How's your case going?"

"Well, there's been an arrest in our San Antonio serial rapist case. The DNA results found a match, so it seems contribution from us is no longer needed. That means my partners have time to go on a date."

"So, you don't mind helping us on our case tonight?" Sarah asked.

"Of course not," Sebastian answered then made a karate chop motion with his skinny arms. "The way I see it, you three are headed to an unsafe neighborhood, and you'll need some serious muscle! Consider me on the job—a hundred and twenty pounds of protection."

"And a registered lethal weapon you are, Brother Sebastian!" Jared said, chuckling.

"That's right, Jared m'man," Sebastian joked back. "Dynamite comes in small packages, and my muscle density is on par with nonhuman primates; four times that of man." He glanced over at Sarah. "Hey, maybe my nickname should be 'Four X.'"

"Only other geeks, like us, would get that, Sebastian," Rob replied.

Sebastian lost his smile. "On a serious note, this area we're going to is known throughout the paranormal community as vampire hunting grounds." He pulled out a baggie containing a large clove of garlic and lifted it in the air. "Always be prepared, my friends."

"I wondered what that smell was," Rob commented. "I just thought you forgot to brush your teeth."

Sebastian put the garlic back into his pocket. "I chose nonlethal vamp defense tonight since these bloodsuckers keep the zombies in check. Too many dead vampires might cause a shift in the balance of power, and we'd probably have a zombie apocalypse on our hands."

"I'm with ya, Four X," Jared replied. "I'll take some of that garlic."

"I brought enough for all of us."

Rob smirked and glanced over at Sarah, who was shaking her head and grinning.

Fifteen minutes later, Jared pulled his car up next to the emergency housing and parked in the street. "Looks like this is the place, team."

Rob tapped Jared on the shoulder. "Thanks for driving."

"It had to be my ol' car. Your new rental would've been a prime target in this rundown neighborhood. Now, we blend in."

"Your car's not that bad," Sarah complimented. "I've seen lots of rust buckets worse than yours."

"No salted roads in winter for the win, I guess. Well, are we ready to go in?" Jared asked.

All four exited the car, and Rob led the way. They entered the building, where the dinner tables were full of people eating.

"Pretty full," Rob commented.

"Well, it's a little late, but it's still near the dinner hour," Sarah answered.

Rob spotted a lady in the back of the kitchen who seemed to be in charge. "Maybe that's her." They walked over to the large counter that opened into the kitchen.

The older lady noticed their approach, so she met them at the counter. "Are y'all here to volunteer?"

"I'm sorry, no; perhaps another time," Rob answered. "We're looking for Marion Thibodeaux."

The lady frowned and stared at them suspiciously. "What fer?"

"Well, we're forensic students at Loyola, assisting the New Orleans Police Department on an investigation, and we noticed on her *Plight of New Orleans Homeless* website a concern she had about something scaring the homeless people on the streets. This might be connected to our case."

The lady continued to stare at them suspiciously, then she dropped a rag and started to walk away. "I'm Marion; follow me."

Rob, Sarah, Sebastian, and Jared glanced at each other then followed Marion.

She took them to an open table in the main room and pointed to the seats as she sat.

Rob sat next to her as the rest took their seats. "Thank you, Mrs. Thibodeaux."

"Call me Marion, everyone does."

Rob nodded. "OK, Marion." He paused and glanced over at the others. "My name is Rob, and this is Sarah, Sebastian, and Jared."

All three said, "Hi," but Marion just nodded back to them.

"Well," Rob began, "as I was saying, we noticed that you stated that some of the homeless are unusually afraid and are talking about some hairy creature lurking in the darkness, stalking them."

"Probably nothin' to those stories," Marion answered bluntly. "Lots of 'em make up stories all the time. It passes the time." She glanced over at some of the people eating soup. "Although, it is true I haven't seen a few of the regulars."

"You are probably correct that it's nothing," Rob agreed, "but just recently there was a man in Foliage Park who was killed by a large canine. It's still on the loose, and we'd like to eliminate the possibility that this is the creature the homeless are talking about."

Marion stared at them. "You'll want to talk to Crazy Harry, one of my regulars." She paused. "He claims he saw it kill another homeless man."

"Where might we find him?" Rob asked.

Marion glanced around the room. "He was just here, eating, but he usually hangs out two blocks down and to the left near the levee. Ya can't miss it. Lots of trees and places for the lot of them to sleep off their stupor. You'll see lots of folks there, so just ask any of them where Crazy Harry is, and they'll tell ya." She paused. "Fer money, of course."

"Of course," Rob repeated. "Thank you, Marion." The students stood to leave.

"Be careful," Marion warned then glanced out the window at the low sun. "It's not the safest place to be at night. Best to keep yer car parked here."

All four nodded to Marion then walked out of the shelter and turned left down the street.

Rob pointed. "I see the entrance to the levee area."

"Remind me again why we're walking in an unfamiliar, sketchy neighborhood at sunset?" Sarah asked.

Sebastian glanced around, shaking, his eyes wide open. "I hope you guys know I was kidding about being a lethal weapon. I actually break easily."

"We'll be fine," Jared stated confidently. "I volunteer on occasions a few blocks down from here. This neighborhood is not known for a ton of violent crime; it's just old and dirty. As long as we stick together and leave before it's fully dark, all will be good."

"Well, let's find Crazy Harry then," Rob replied.

They neared the entrance to the levee area and spotted an old man rummaging through the trash. Jared approached and handed him two dollars. "How y'all doin'? Would you happen to know where Crazy Harry is?"

The man took the two dollars and pocketed it. "Much obliged, fine sir," he said then pointed to an old man in ragged clothes rummaging through a second trash can. "That's him."

"Thanks," Jared replied.

Crazy Harry turned and eyed the four. "Lookin' to preach to me er somethin'? It'll cost ya five bucks."

"Not tonight, Harry," Jared responded.

Crazy Harry jerked his head back, surprised at this young man knowing his name. "Who er you?"

"My name is Jared; this is Rob, Sarah, and Sebastian. We're helping out the New Orleans Police Department on a case involving a large, hairy, dog-like creature attacking people, and we heard you witnessed an attack."

"Sure did," Crazy Harry replied and held out his hand.

Jared gave him two dollars.

The disheveled man pocketed the money then pointed toward the sparsely wooded area near the massive levee. "Just there, but I don't go over there anymore."

"Could you show us the location?" Rob asked.

"That'll cost ya five bucks."

Rob already had the five-dollar bill tucked away in his palm and quickly handed it to their informant.

He pocketed it and led the four toward the desolate area.

Sarah glanced up at the near-setting sun and grabbed Rob's arm for comfort.

To her surprise, Sebastian grasped Sarah's other arm and pulled out his garlic.

Rob grinned at Sebastian.

"The creature was bigger 'en any wolf er dog I ever seen," Crazy Harry explained. "It was the Rougarou."

Sebastian made eye contact with Jared, and both grinned. "You called it," Sebastian whispered.

"I told you so," Jared mouthed back.

Sebastian turned and glanced around at the coming darkness nervously, suddenly aware that the creature might be in the area. He stared at his garlic and pocketed it, frowning. "Wrong defense. I need wolfsbane," he muttered.

"Did the creature make a screeching noise?" Rob asked.

Crazy Harry stopped abruptly and stared at Rob. "Why, have you seen it too? This first thing it did was screech."

"No, I haven't, but others have said it did."

They walked around a couple of trees, and Crazy Harry stopped and pointed at the bottom of a tree trunk. "It killed Ol' Danny right there. You can still see his blood."

Rob approached the spot and inspected the large bloodstains, pulled out his iPhone, and used the flashlight to illuminate the darkened area.

Crazy Harry glanced up at Jared. "After it killed him, it picked him up in its jaws and ran away as if Ol' Danny didn't weigh a thing."

Sebastian grabbed Sarah's arm again, staring nervously into the twilight.

Rob turned and faced everyone. "It certainly is blood, guys, and lots of it. I think we're legally obligated to call this in."

"Or just get the hell outta here!" Sebastian suggested half-seriously.

Sarah nodded and pulled out her phone. "I'll call Detective Bakula." She quickly searched her contacts, pressed his name, and put the phone to her ear.

Crazy Harry backed up slowly, shaking his head. "You didn't say anything about cops." He turned and ran down the levee and into the darkness.

Jared elbowed Rob and snickered. "Hey, Sebastian, go chase him down and bring him back."

Sebastian looked west at the setting sun then toward the direction where Crazy Harry ran off. "Sorry, I left my silver bullets at home."

"OK, we'll stay right here," Sarah replied over the phone, hung up, then said to everyone, "Detective Bakula and his partner are downtown and should be here in five minutes."

"Great," Rob replied then walked over to a concrete block and sat on it. "Might as well make ourselves comfortable."

Sarah sat next to Rob while Jared and Sebastian leaned on another concrete block. "I'd love to be in the forensic lab and observe them analyzing this blood."

"I'm sure Dr. Taylor could make that happen," Jared replied.

Rob faced everyone and raised his finger. "This guy's a collector."

The three stared at him.

"The killer has the animal collect their bodies." Rob gestured to Sarah. "Sarah pointed out that the Foliage Park child molester probably would've been collected, too, but the German shepherd didn't allow it."

"Makes sense to me," Sarah responded, "but hey, you're preaching to the choir."

As Rob, Sarah, and Jared continued their discussion, Sebastian turned his head and stared into an area of darkness within a few trees. He thought he caught a glimpse of something moving, so he took a slow step toward the trees. He stopped, turned, and faced the group again.

Snap.

Sebastian jerked around, scanning the location he heard the noise coming from—the same dark area within the trees. "What the . . .? Did you hear that?"

"Hear what?" Rob asked.

Crack. Shuffle, shuffle.

Sebastian jumped back toward the group.

Rob, Sarah, and Jared stood immediately.

Sebastian pointed into the trees. "Something's right there!"

Jared stood next to the Sebastian and stared into the darkness.

A soft but deep growl emanated from the trees.

Everyone froze in fear, immediately connecting this dog-like growl to the reason why they were here.

"Let's back up slowly to the road," Rob ordered.

"I knew we shouldn't have come," Sebastian commented.

At that moment, a flashing unmarked police car drove up to them at a high rate of speed and stopped just feet away. The car's headlights illuminated the entire patch of trees.

Rob stared into the trees and saw nothing. Whatever was in there had vanished.

Detectives Bakula and Oglesby jumped out of their car and approached them. Bakula noticed their frozen, wide-eyed stare. "What? Are you kids all right? It looks like you've seen a ghost."

"No, we're fine," Jared blurted out and quickly glanced at the others. "We're just freaked out by being here at night."

Rob also thought it prudent to keep quiet about what they believed they'd heard—at least for now. He pointed to the bloodied area. "It's over here, Detectives. Your headlights should be lighting it up nicely."

Bakula and Oglesby knelt down at the bloodied area and studied it.

"A homeless man named Crazy Harry showed it to us," Rob explained. "We heard from the lady who runs the shelter two blocks away that Crazy Harry claimed to have witnessed Ol' Danny get killed here."

"He took off once he heard me call you," Sarah interrupted.

"Yeah, well, Crazy Harry's been in and out of jail," Oglesby explained, "so I'm not surprised he bolted." He glanced at Bakula. "Looks like blood to me, partner. We'll need to treat it as a crime scene. I'll call it in." Oglesby walked toward their vehicle.

"Thanks, Oges," Bakula replied then turned and faced Rob and his friends. "Which direction did Crazy Harry run off to?"

Rob pointed down the levee. "That way."

"We'll find him," Bakula said. "Did he tell you who attacked Ol' Danny?"

"He said he saw the Rougarou kill Ol' Danny," Sebastian blurted out, "then carry his body away like it was a rag doll."

Bakula did a double take at Sebastian. "Hang on, who are you?"

Rob made the requisite introduction, and Sebastian greeted the detective.

Bakula flipped open his notepad and clicked his pen. "Crazy Harry said a Rougarou killed Ol' Danny?"

"Yes," Rob answered, "which is actually why we interviewed him."

"I was going to ask how y'all ended up here," Bakula admitted.

Rob nodded and glanced over at Sarah. "Sarah read on a website that homeless people, like Crazy Harry, were telling the shelter manager that some kind of large animal was stalking them."

"Ahh," Bakula interrupted, "so, you were investigating the Foliage Park case, the man-killing canine connection/serial killer theory."

"Yes."

Bakula nodded then glanced over at the bloodstains. "If the blood proves to be human, then you four just might be onto something—although probably not enough to begin an all-out serial killer task force."

Detective Oglesby approached them.

"Curiously," Rob began, "it was the idea of a serial offender killing people on the outskirts of society in order to fly under the police radar that led us here."

Bakula raised his hand. "Hey, I'm not trying to tell you kids to stop your investigation—actually I'm encouraging it—but there's more work to be done here." He paused. "Is there anything else Crazy Harry said or anything else I should know?"

"Yes," Sarah blurted out then glared at Rob and Jared.

Bakula waited for a moment, his eyebrows raised. "What?"

"Rob and Jared don't want to sound crazy, but I will," Sarah exclaimed. "The reason why we looked like scared chickens when you got here is because," she pointed into the patch of trees, now well lit, "we heard some kind of deep growl right there!" She paused. "And yes, all of us were thinking that whatever killed Ol' Danny, and probably killed the child molester in Foliage Park, could easily have been what made that growl!"

Bakula stared at them silently.

"It vanished when it saw your car streak up to us," Jared explained.

Bakula turned and stared into the trees. "There's something or someone wreaking havoc around these parts, so we believe you, and I'm glad you spoke up."

Oglesby started walking back to their vehicle. "I'll call the K-9 unit."

"Call in a few more units too," Bakula directed, turning his head at the sound of police sirens, then he eyed the four students. "You're most welcome to stay and watch how we treat a new crime scene, if you'd like. I'm sure your class would love to hear about it."

Rob, Sarah, Sebastian, and Jared turned to each other and nodded, all grinning.

"We'd love to," Rob answered.

Three blocks down, Crazy Harry sat in the near darkness on a concrete block at a dead-end street that butted up to the levee. He drank from his whiskey bottle, listening to the police sirens and watching the vehicles streak by. He took another swig then realized he wasn't alone.

A man thirty feet away from Crazy Harry stood under a building entranceway, glaring at him.

"What er you lookin' at?" Crazy Harry barked then belched.

The man didn't reply; he just continued to stare at him as if he hated his guts.

Feeling uneasy, Crazy Harry got up and left the area, glancing back a couple of times, ensuring the man wasn't following him—and he wasn't.

The man just stayed in the doorway entrance and stared.

After he walked a few hundred yards, Crazy Harry stepped into an alley and made his way back toward the levee. He spotted a secluded location near a small broken piece of concrete and sat on it. The area was quite dark with the only ambient light coming from a corroded old lamp situated above the entrance to a small abandoned concrete shed, but he liked it that way, especially when unwanted types might be following him.

After a moment, he stood and began to urinate on a tree, staring down so he didn't accidentally spray his boots. He casually gazed up and noticed a large shape at the other end of the old shed, barely visible in the dull light. He squinted, staring at it. To his surprise, the large shape moved toward him, right into the lamplight, and stopped. He gasped, recognizing it was a massive, dark-haired dog or wolf with glowing red eyes locked on him!

The creature growled then advanced slowly toward Crazy Harry.

Crazy Harry moved quickly backward but tripped and fell to the ground. He got up, turned, and ran headfirst into a tree, thumping his forehead onto the trunk. He stood, dazed and drunk.

The creature leaped and pounced on him, grabbing him around the neck and quickly snapping it. Silence returned to the darkness as the monster carried Crazy Harry's lifeless body away.

chapter 22

Phone a Friend,
Vidocq Crime-Solving Course,
Loyola University, New Orleans, Louisiana

Dr. Taylor stood in the back of the classroom observing his busy students, all working cooperatively with their teammates. The room was buzzing with activity. He noticed a number of students on their cell phones speaking to law enforcement officers and forensic specialists about aspects of the real investigations. Others were analyzing photos and documents and bouncing ideas off each other. He beamed. This is exactly what he'd envisioned for the first Vidocq course: productive participation in ongoing cases. "Love it," he said quietly in satisfaction as he approached the closest table.

"Love what, Dr. Taylor?" a student in that group asked.

"The fact that you're on a hot lead," he answered, then he approached Sebastian, Cedric, and Lacy. "How's the DNA analysis going?"

Cedric's head popped up. "Actually, quite well, thanks to Lacy's microbiology background."

"I had better know this!" Lacy exclaimed.

"How did you get the results of the DNA tests so quickly, Dr. Taylor?" Sebastian asked. "They just arrested the guy."

Taylor grinned. "It's a combination of connections and the reputation of the Vidocq Society." He turned and spotted Rob with Sarah and Jared at another table. "Oh, that reminds me," he said, joining them.

Sarah glanced up. "Oh, Hi, Dr. Taylor."

Taylor nodded. "Detective Bakula called this morning. He wanted to pass onto you three the results of the bloodstains."

The group members stopped what they were doing and blinked up at Dr. Taylor.

"Human blood all right, although they have no idea who the human donor is—though they seem to think, given the area, that a homeless man is their best bet."

"Ol' Danny?" Jared replied. "Maybe they can ask the lady at the homeless shelter."

"Apparently they did, but she didn't know him well and could only give a general description."

"Did he tell you if they found Crazy Harry yet?" Rob asked.

Taylor shook his head. "They haven't, and the other problem is the bloodstains do not necessarily mean a death has occurred—*Corpus delicti*."

Jared sighed. "Meaning, with no body, it's a missing persons case first. Great." He slumped back into his chair.

Rob shook his head. "Well, Crazy Harry saw something, and it involved violence against a human. There's no reason why he would lie about who the victim was."

Sarah caught Rob's eye. "I just don't see how the police will be convinced enough to commit to a serial killer case until we find irrefutable evidence."

"How are we gonna do that?" Jared asked.

"I believe it's time to phone a friend," Taylor suggested.

"It's the perfect time!" Rob blurted out then pulled out his cell phone. "I'm calling Dr. Dunham now."

"Great idea, Dr. Taylor," Sarah complimented.

Rob tapped on Dunham's contact and put the phone to his ear. "I hope he can speak with us right now," he mumbled.

Dunham sat at his kitchen table, staring at his laptop computer screen.

His wife, Maggie, was just behind him, watering her favorite chrysanthemum then touching its soft pink flowers.

Still entranced by the text on the computer screen, Dunham felt around for the ringing phone next to his laptop. Without glancing at the caller ID, he answered, "Dr. Dunham."

"Hi, Dr. Dunham, it's Rob Faulks. Are you available to speak?"

All the students from the other tables abruptly turned in their seats toward Rob, their work forgotten for the moment at the mention of Dr. Dunham's name.

"Hi, Rob, it's great to hear from you!" Dunham replied, turning away from the laptop. "Actually, you caught me at the perfect time. I'm out of the office this morning since I flew in so late last night. What's up? Are you enjoying your Vidocq course?"

Rob glanced at everyone around the table and nodded. "Yes, very much, and it's the reason I called. This is our 'phone a friend' moment, and we were wondering if you could help us in our investigation."

"Certainly," Dunham replied, "although I don't know how much help I'll be from a phone call."

"Any assistance is welcomed," Rob reassured him. "Do you mind if I put you on speaker? I'll introduce you to everyone before I go into the investigation."

"Great," Dunham replied.

After introductions, Rob spent the next five minutes giving Dunham every detail on the case, including the screeching sound the animal made and the possibility of the offender being a serial killer.

Dunham asked a few clarification questions as Rob continued.

"Dr. Taylor is correct about Corpus delicti," Dunham explained, "however, if there is indeed a serial offender in New Orleans selecting victims from the fringe of society, he's far from being done, so we need to act now."

"*We?*" Jared mouthed to Rob, and Rob smiled in knowing excitement.

Edward Dunham glanced over at his wife. "Maggie, want to take a trip with me to New Orleans for a long weekend?"

Maggie spun around, beaming. "Of course! You know I've been wanting to go there forever!"

Dunham peeked at his watch. "Rob, you've hooked me. I'll be there Friday morning."

"Yes!" Jared blurted out, his fists in the air.

The crowd of students started whispering louder.

"Dr. Taylor, Rob," Dunham interrupted, "I'd like to have a meeting with the detectives as well."

"I'll make that happen, Dr. Dunham," Taylor replied, gazing around the room at everyone's excitement. "If time permits, any chance you could meet the class? We could convene anytime on the weekend, anywhere." He raised his eyebrows at the class and every student nodded in agreement.

"Great idea," Dunham confirmed. "I'll see everyone then."

* * *

Honey Island Swamp Tour,
Slidell, Louisiana

Lawrence and Olivia shuffled their way out of the hotel van and into the Honey Island Swamp Tour parking lot. His plump sixty-year-old body—matched by his wife's hefty midsection—made for a slow exit, bottlenecking everyone else's departure from the van.

Lawrence stopped right in front of the van's steps, glancing up at the Honey Island Swamp Tour store. "That was a twenty-minute drive from downtown New Orleans to here, Olivia!"

"I know, Lawrence," Olivia responded. "I was in the van too. Come on," she said, dragging him away from the vehicle.

The four other tourists finally exited the van, all snickering at the old couple bantering with each other.

The van driver pointed to the souvenir store. "Tickets for the swamp tours are in the store, ladies and gentlemen."

"Don't forget to use the lavatory before you go on the boat, Olivia!" Lawrence bellowed. "The tour is supposed to be two hours long!"

"You don't have to yell, Lawrence!" Olivia retorted. "You're the one with the hearing aids."

The four tourists found their way to the souvenir store, followed slowly by Lawrence and Olivia.

The shop was filled with other tourists, Cajun and swamp paraphernalia, coffee mugs, honey in containers labeled 'Honey Island Honey - $7.00,' strips of gator jerky, candy, toys, and even alligator skulls and snake skeletons.

A boy grabbed a large alligator-shaped container filled with candy and approached a tall, wide-framed man wearing a cowboy hat, expensive summer clothing, and a solid gold watch. "I want this, Dad, now."

"Hold your horses, son," the man blurted out in a heavy Texan drawl. "We're not buying anything until after the swamp tour. Then, we'll buy the half store out if you want." He glanced around, ensuring everyone in the store knew he was wealthy. He threw three bags of marshmallows on the counter in front of the cashier. "We do need to buy critter food though." He eyed the cashier. "Also, ma'am, I'd like three swamp tour tickets for myself, the wife, and my son."

Lawrence spotted the rich Texan's bags then turned to Olivia. "Don't forget to buy some marshmallows! We get to feed the alligators!"

She shook her hands, holding up two bags of marshmallows. "What do you think these are for?"

"Ten minutes until the swamp tour, everyone!" the cashier yelled. "Yer captain'll take yer tickets at the boat!"

The tourists made their way outside and toward the swamp boat, some quicker than others. The swamp boat was a large, flat-bottom boat made of aluminum. It could hold two dozen riders. Over the head of the rows of seats was a white canvas canopy flapping in the light wind, and on the stern was written the boat's moniker, the *Swamp Princess*.

The captain was standing next to the boat, wearing an earthy-colored, long-sleeved cotton shirt, a tan fishing vest, matching tan cargo shorts, and a soft, collapsible, wide-brimmed outback hat snapped on one side. "Come on over here, folks!" he called loudly.

Everyone crowded in front of the captain.

He gave a big grin. "I'll take yer tickets as you board the *Princess*." He pointed down at a small step painted to look like an alligator. "The boat is jostling around a bit, so to assist you in your embarkation, step on the—" he paused and stared at the crowd with a slight grin—"gator aide!"

Lawrence, not hearing what the captain said, noticed the other tourists laughing. "What did he say, Olivia?"

Olivia shook her head. "He said don't trip!"

Minutes later, Lawrence, Olivia, and eighteen other tourists were settled in their seats and ready to go.

The captain started the dual engines then turned and faced the tourists. "How y'all doin'? Time to introduce myself. My name is Ronnie Dupree, your captain for this boat tour. I'm a full-blooded Cajun 'redneck' and have lived in these swamps all my life."

Lawrence leaned over to Olivia. "Did he say his neck was red? Sunburn?"

"Never mind, Lawrence," Olivia replied, glaring at him. "Just get your marshmallows ready."

Dupree pointed at the swamps. "The Honey Island Swamp gets its name cuz of all the honeybees that used to inhabit a stretch of island. The swamp is considered a marshland and one of the least-altered river swamps in the United States, and it's over on hundred forty square miles of pristine swampland habitats."

"Should I open the bag now, Olivia?" Lawrence asked.

"No, not yet, Lawrence," Olivia answered then filched a couple of marshmallows from her own bag and popped them into her mouth.

Dupree walked to his pilot seat. "Luckily, it's summer, so standby for some gator sightings."

Two assistants on the dock released the boat from its ties and pushed the vessel out.

Dupree shifted gears and set off into the swamp. "Watch yourselves, now, we're off." He turned a corner in the first bayou channel. "You're about to see lots of Honey Island swamp critters—alligators, maybe black bear, raccoons, owls," he turned and eyed the tourists, "and nutria, which are huge river rats."

"Yuck!" blurted out a young female tourist.

Dupree grinned. "There's wild boar, turtles, and possibly a poisonous moccasin snake or two." He turned around and faced the crowd. "Now, these snakes are as scared of you as you are of them, so if one falls on your head from the canopy, just throw him back in the swamp!"

The crowd laughed nervously, though most glanced up at the looming cypress trees, scanning the branches for snakes.

Dupree pointed at a rundown shack on the banks. "We have a few Cajun 'neighbors' in the swamps here on the Pearl River, too, and we even have a Cajun village, so don't be surprised if you see a few folks huntin' and fishin'."

Lawrence spotted Olivia's marshmallow bag. "Olivia, your marshmallow bag's half empty! Where'd they go?"

Olivia stared out into the swamp, swallowing. "Shut up, Lawrence."

Dupree pointed up into the tree canopy. "If you look up, you see the canopy of bald cypress trees, and do you see all that moss draping over most of it?"

Most of the tourists nodded.

"That's Spanish moss, which gets its nutrients from the air, so other than shrouding the trees, they don't hurt 'em much."

"Makes it look a little scary," the Texan commented, "as if we're gonna see zombies popping up everywhere."

Dupree nodded. "You can see why Hollywood loves to make films in the swamps."

After about fifteen minutes of traveling through the swamp channels and pointing out flora and fauna of interest, Dupree slowed the boat down and placed it near a mound of dry land. "Folks, this land jutting out of the water is called a hummock, and as you can see, there are loads of them in the bayou. They tend to stay dry throughout the year."

He pointed at some cypress trees growing in the water. "These trees growing in the water are called mangroves."

"What are these plants that are covering the water?" a tourist asked.

Dupree nodded. "Notice how these plants nearly cover the entire surface? They're mostly hyacinths and water lilies." He spotted some water lilies moving and grinned. "And the real reason I stopped at this hummock." He pointed at the moving lilies. "Here they come, wild pigs! Git your marshmallows ready, but don't use 'em all up. We have a few stops."

Over a half-dozen dark-haired wild boars swam up to the boat, all grunting and begging.

The tourists threw dozens of marshmallows in front of the boars.

"Throw a couple of marshmallows in, son," the Texan directed.

The boy grabbed a large handful of marshmallows and tossed them in.

A couple marshmallows dropped in the water near the boat and a boar swam up to them.

The boy reached over to touch it.

"Wild pigs have been known to eat fingers!" Dupree warned.

The rich Texan grabbed his son by the scruff of the neck and jerked him back. "Keep your hands in, son."

After a few minutes, Dupree steered the party out of the area and made his way through the swamp. He continued giving details about the plants and wildlife they encountered, and he even gave a running narrative about the people living in the swamps. He pointed forward. "Here we go. Time to feed the gators."

"Finally!" a tourist blurted out.

"Safety tip! Everyone keep your hands inside the boat." Dupree turned and stared at the boy from Texas with a devilish grin. "I don't want to have to give anyone the nickname 'Gator Bait'!"

"Ha!" the rich Texan belted out laughing. "My boy's new nickname!" He slapped his son on the back. "Grab some marshmallows, Gator Bait."

As Dupree idled the engines and stopped the boat, six or seven alligators slowly swam out of hiding and glided toward them. "As you can see, folks, these gators are used to us feeding them, but they ain't tame, so be careful." He pulled out a stick with a piece of uncooked chicken on it and placed it in front of the largest alligator. It leaped out of the water and nabbed the chicken.

"Wow!" roared a number of tourists. Everyone applauded.

"That one is probably a thirteen-footer, easily capable of giving you a dead roll. Throw in a few marshmallows."

Tourists followed orders, causing a slight frenzy of activity with the alligators as they ate the sweet treats.

After a few minutes, Dupree turned up the engines and continued the tour. "Keep an eye out for anything tall and hairy with yellow eyes and walking about on two legs, folks!" Dupree instructed. "This is where some locals saw the Honey Island Swamp Monster a few years back."

"How cool!" one of the tourists exclaimed.

"There's even a short video clip of the monster, shot by a man named Harlan Ford, a retired air traffic controller," Dupree continued. "Apparently, he had his first sighting in 1963 and was obsessed with finding it ever since."

"I remember watching a show on the Honey Island Swamp Monster," the rich Texan interjected.

"Local legend has it that there was a train crash in the area," Dupree explained, "and a group of chimpanzees escaped and some interbred with a few alligators."

A few tourists laughed.

Dupree shook his head. "That's a genetic impossibility, but at the time, no one knew that, so the legend grew. If it is true, then they saw something different. My guess is it was the southern Bigfoot—what locals call the skunk ape. Others say they probably saw a huge black bear standing on its feet or something."

"It's Bigfoot, all right," the Texan belted out confidently.

Dupree pointed forward. "The water channel's narrowing a bit."

Olivia noticed it getting darker and realized the moss-draped tree canopy now covered their heads. It made her feel a little uneasy.

"We've been out here an hour and a half, Olivia!" Lawrence announced, looking at his watch and rubbing his lower stomach.

"You're gonna have to hold it, Lawrence!"

Dupree turned around. "This is as deep as we're going into the swamps, folks, and as you can see, no one lives this far in." He pointed into a channel overgrown with foliage. "Lately, the locals have been reporting sightings of a large hairy creature just down there a bit. They've even found a couple of half-eaten gators. Some say the Honey Island Swamp monster has returned."

"Can we check it out? Is it safe?" a tourist asked.

"Yeah, let's do it!" the rich Texan agreed.

Dupree raised his hand as a number of other tourists joined in. "Well, it's not too far in . . . just a few minutes," he shook his head, "but it's not part of the tour. The boss'll have my butt."

The rich Texan pulled out a hundred-dollar bill, raised it high, clearly show-ing off, then placed it into Dupree's tip jar. "Aww, c'mon, Captain. It's only just a few minutes in, right?"

Dupree stared at the hefty tip for a moment then glanced at the tourists. "Promise not to tell the boss?"

"No!" Some yelled in unison.

He turned the boat toward the wild channel.

The crowd applauded. One tourist slapped the rich Texan on the back.

Dupree slowly maneuvered the boat in the narrow channel, ensuring the awning made it through the cypress canopy. He gazed into the water. "Lots of snakes within the hyacinths here, so definitely keep your hands in."

"Ya hear that, Gator Bait!" the rich Texan belted at his son.

The thick cypress forest and Spanish moss blocked so much sunlight that a few spots were quite dark. As they made their way around the bends, Dupree talked about how the locals hunted and fished the area. On the port side of the boat was the bank of a long hummock raised a few feet above the water line. Suddenly, he pointed forward in the water and to the right. "There! There's a poi-sonous moccasin." Everyone leaned forward and watched the swimming snake.

Olivia turned around to sneak another marshmallow then happened to glance up between some mangroves. She spotted a scruffy-looking man about forty yards away, knee-deep in water, dropping a burlap bag into the water.

The man then closed a metal-wired door over the top of it. As he closed it, he glanced up and saw her watching him. He stopped moving and just glared at Olivia.

Uneasiness settled over her. She gasped.

The man abruptly moved toward the boat, hiding behind large cypress trees as he made his way closer, maintaining eye contact with Olivia. He then pulled out a large machete-like blade.

Her uneasiness turned into all-out fear. Olivia turned back toward the tour guide and waved wordlessly, but he was still discussing the snake with the other tourists. Even Lawrence, seated right next to her, was oblivious to their predica-ment. She whirled around again to see if the man was still behind the large cypress tree, and to her shock, he was now only twenty feet away standing on the dry hummock.

He was glaring at her, machete in hand.

Olivia knew he could be on the boat in one leap, but in her terror, she sat frozen.

At that moment, the captain pulled the boat forward and casually drove off, completely unaware of what was happening behind him.

The forward motion of the boat caused Olivia to glance away from the menacing man. She dropped her head and covered her eyes with her hands.

The boat turned right into the open waters, well away from the bank.

Lawrence turned and noticed Olivia sweating profusely with her hands over her eyes. "You've been scared of snakes all your life, but the creature was all the way out in the water!"

Olivia glanced back at the hummock, but the man was nowhere to be seen. She slowly turned toward Lawrence but remained silent.

chapter 23

Young Simon walked along a mountain path, trailing behind the last of the dozen tan-colored cattle. The staff he held was unusually large, and the end was sharpened to a point. Being a year younger than his fourteen-year-old brother, Baptiste, he had to trail the herd while Baptiste led the way to the mountain field. He stared into the woods. "Do you think Father is right, Baptiste? The Beast is far south of us?"

Baptiste whipped the lead bull to quicken its pace. "I do, brother, but just in case, don't stray too far from the trailing bull. These Aubracs can handle a lone wolf."

Simon stared into the woods again, held his staff tighter, then rushed up next to the bull. "Do you think these staffs can kill the Beast?"

"I hope we don't have to find out!" Baptiste called back over his shoulder. They finally made it to the small grassy field, which was surrounded by rocky outcrops and a few patches of small woods.

Minutes later, Simon and Baptiste settled near a rocky outcrop as the cattle grazed, giving them a complete view of the field. Simon glanced at his older brother. "I overheard Father complaining to Uncle Benoit that the king's famous Norman wolf hunter fears the Beast. They say he stays indoors feasting upon local cuisine as we get slaughtered."

Baptiste leaned back on a large rock. "He's been here for months now, and he's no closer to killing the Beast than when he arrived." He grabbed a stone and threw it. "His famous hounds are nothing."

Simon scanned the wooded patches around the field. "Uncle Benoit says he's not surprised because the Beast is not a wolf—it's a werewolf."

Half the cows raised their heads and stared at the cowhands. The two bulls pawed the ground, charged at each other, then stampeded toward Simon and Baptiste.

"Now what?" Baptiste complained as he and Simon got to their feet. "They were all grazing nicely."

One of the bulls snorted as it headed straight for the boys.

Simon and Baptiste squared up to the bulls with their staffs pointed forward.

"Are they after us, Baptiste?"

"Hey!" Baptiste screamed and waved his staff at the bulls, but they kept on coming. As they were almost upon the boys, Baptiste and Simon crouched behind a big rock with their staffs pointed forward.

At the last moment, the first bull dropped its head, presenting its formidable horns, but instead of charging them, it bypassed the boys and slammed into an enormous wolflike creature only feet away.

The creature squealed and snapped at the bull, but it retreated as the second bull closed in.

The boys stared at the huge animal, stunned. Baptiste realized immediately that the bulls weren't charging them; they had been protecting them. It was a wolf, but different—much larger and with an exceptionally long tail, a reddish-gray coat covered in long curly hair, and its jaws were massive. Then it registered to Baptiste that he and his brother had been less than a second away from being torn apart by its powerful jaws.

"The Beast!" Simon screamed.

The creature ran to the left, behind a patch of woods.

The bulls stopped in front of the woods and paced back and forth, now ready for another attack.

Baptiste grabbed Simon and lifted him off the ground. "Get up! We need to get in the middle of the field with the herd!"

Simon knew exactly what his brother meant. If they were in the center of the field, the bulls would be able to defend them. They made it to the center of the field and surrounded themselves with the agitated cows.

The Beast popped up on the ridge and stared straight at Baptiste and Simon. "It's after us, Baptiste!"

"Keep your staff pointed at it just in case it gets by the bulls!"

The Beast dropped behind the ridge, and seconds later it emerged from another location then bolted with amazing speed toward the boys. The two bulls rushed it again.

Baptiste judged that the Beast was going to reach them before the bulls. He aimed his staff straight at it, but just as it reached him, it leaped for Simon. This gave Baptiste an opportunity to thrust his staff at its neck, and he made contact.

The momentum of the massive animal was so powerful it knocked him backward, but the Beast fell to the side, missing Simon.

The missed attack allowed the bulls to enter the fray, close in, and slam into the animal.

It screeched again and snapped its massive jaws but was knocked back. Once it regained its footing, the Beast retreated over the ridge.

"Back-to-back, Simon! It may come from any side!"

The Beast attacked them two more times, but thanks to their staffs and the fearless bulls, it was unsuccessful and was forced to retreat over the ridge.

After what seemed like an eternity, Baptiste realized the cattle, including the bulls, had settled down, and they went back to grazing. He took a deep breath.

"Is it gone?" Simon asked.

"I think so," Baptiste replied. "The bulls don't sense it. We need to warn Father and Uncle immediately!"

About an hour later, an elderly woman was walking to the chicken coop near the edge of a large section of woods. She noticed a young lady running by, who stopped when they made eye contact.

"Haven't you heard?" the young lady called out loudly. "The Beast is in the area! Baptiste and Simon Desmarias fought it off in the fields not even an hour ago!"

The old lady waved off the young lady defiantly. "Bah! Those two scoundrels make up stories all the time for attention, just like their father does," she replied and continued to the chicken coop.

The younger woman shook her head, taking a step forward.

The older lady noticed the chickens were squawking more than usual. *Strange*, she thought. As she rounded the corner of the coop, she spotted what was causing the chickens' distress.

Just at the edge of the tree line near the chicken coop was a massive, wolf-like monster glaring at her, saliva dripping down its jaw.

She jerked her hands up to her face and screamed.

The young lady stopped as she heard the scream and turned around just in time to see the Beast lunge at the old lady and clamp its jaws around her neck.

The attack knocked the lady off her feet and onto her back. In an instant, the Beast shook its head and decapitated the old lady.

The younger woman froze and watched as the creature mutilated the old woman.

The Beast looked up and spotted her, abruptly halting its ravenous attack. Its attention was now completely on the young lady, glaring at her.

She screamed and took a step backward. As she did, the Beast glided off of the woman and headed toward her! She turned, spotted the closest building, and rushed for it. As she neared the door, she reached for the wooden door handle. She had no idea how close the Beast was to her and felt in her bones she would be attacked before she could open the door. At that moment, someone inside the home opened the door, and she shoved the person back into the home, slammed the door behind her, then dropped the large wooden lock latch.

Crash!

Something powerful hit the door, nearly breaking the wooden plank on the latch. The young lady and the old man leaned against the door, preparing for another collision.

Lafont burst into the inn, paused before the first set of tables, and scanned the room. He spotted the wolf hunter, Denneval, seated by himself at a corner table. He took off his hat and hurried toward him.

Denneval, disheveled in appearance, was slumped over a large drink. As he hiccupped, he saw Lafont approaching. Denneval rolled his bloodshot eyes then dropped his head again.

Lafont knew the famous hunter was drowning his sorrows in drink because of his complete embarrassment at failing in his royal assignment to hunt down the Beast—but Lafont felt no sympathy for the disgraced man. For the first two months, Denneval and his son had gloated about their hunting prowess, but they and their prized hounds had been no match for the creature. In his arrogance, Denneval had ignored their advice at the onset and dismissed the difficulties of hunting with hounds in the mountainous region, especially in the winter.

"Monsieur Denneval," Lafont began, "there's been a woman mutilated just fifteen minutes' ride from here, not two hours ago. The Beast first attacked two young cow handlers, but their bulls fought it off. Then it decapitated the old woman near the village."

Denneval kept his head down then raised it enough to drink out of his stein, but he remained silent.

"What are you going to do about it?"

"I'll have my son handle it when he's done caring for the hounds."

Lafont glared at him. "This is an urgent matter, Monsieur Denneval! Didn't you promise you'd kill the Beast in two weeks?"

Denneval jerked his head from the table and scowled at Lafont. "It is impossible for my hounds to follow this creature into the dense patches of woods," he waved his hand, "and these impenetrable marsh valleys and near-vertical slopes."

"We warned you of this months ago!" Lafont retorted.

"And the ubiquity of the attacks," Denneval continued, completely ignoring Lafont's comment, as if he were speaking to himself. "The creature seems to be everywhere. It kills near one village, and mere hours later, it kills leagues away." He shot a glance at Lafont. "Might there be more than one? Did the Beast of Soissons sire two?"

"All the more reason why you and your son should be out in the field joining the hunts!" Lafont pointed out the window. "Your pikeman was overheard complaining that if you or your son had shown up at the rendezvous point of a chase, the outcome may have been different."

"A miscommunication," Denneval growled.

Lafont leaned forward, hands bracing on the table, and he stared at Denneval. "So, instead of rushing to the deadly attack, you tell your pikeman to lace the deceased with poison and hope the Beast will die from poison by feeding on her!"

"This kind of strategy has worked in the past with wolves," Denneval responded, "and I saw no reason to change. I still don't."

Lafont paused and straightened up. He turned toward the door. "Although it is your practice to keep everyone in the dark, Monsieur Denneval, it is not mine. Count Morangiès and the nobles have submitted a letter to Versailles and have formally demanded your removal." Lafont walked away without saying goodbye.

Denneval drank again from his stein. "Godforsaken place anyway."

chapter 24

Police Department Headquarters,
New Orleans, Louisiana

Dunham examined himself in the bathroom mirror, fixed his tie, then walked out into the hotel suite. He saw Maggie in the small kitchen, still in her robe, pouring herself a cup of coffee.

"Want some?" Maggie asked as she stirred some cream into her cup.

His iPhone buzzed, so he pulled it out of his pocket and read the text. "Thanks, hon—black, please." He pocketed his phone. "It looks like my meeting with the New Orleans detectives is this morning."

Maggie handed him a cup. "I thought you were meeting up with Rob and Sarah, helping on some class assignment."

"Thanks." He sipped his coffee. "I am, but they're working an actual ongoing investigation from the New Orleans Police Department, and the detectives in charge of the case insist upon helping them." He put his coffee down and donned his jacket. "Very helpful people."

She eyed her husband, grinning. "Edward, it's a chance for them to meet . . . the Watchmaker. You've told me how local police are always excited to meet you."

Dunham blushed and lifted his coffee to his lips. "You're too kind." He took another sip. "And, years ago, I learned never to disagree with you because you're usually right." He placed his mug on the table. "Regardless, I'm happy to see it happening because I think Rob is onto something—and if he is, the cooperation of the New Orleans Police Department is paramount."

"You must see some potential in Rob, taking him under your wing like you have."

He nodded. "Rob has a gift for forensics and criminal investigation—Sarah, too—which is why I recommended both of them for the Vidocq course."

"Have you accepted the Vidocq Society's offer to be a member?"

"Well, it's actually an offer for future membership," he explained. "They have a set membership limit but plan on expanding their numbers because of the unexpected demand for their assistance." He paused. "I told them I'm interested; but no, I haven't accepted anything yet."

"You'd be their biggest catch, sweetie," she complimented.

"Thanks, hon." He grabbed his cup and took another sip. "So, your plan is to shop at the French Quarter?"

Maggie beamed. "I have my whole day planned out, so . . . while you're spending your time with police business, I'll be spending your money."

"Hey," he responded, grinning, "don't you make more than I do?"

Maggie giggled. "I'll spend some of mine too." She pulled out her iPhone. "Do you remember my old college roommate and fellow anthropology professor, Dr. Angie Frazier? She's been living in New Orleans for years and is meeting me for lunch."

Dunham faced Maggie. "I remember Angie."

"She thinks she was Cajun in a prior life."

"Great," he replied. "I won't feel guilty about leaving you alone." He grabbed his briefcase and kissed her then headed for the door. "Gotta go. I'll see you this afternoon."

Maggie waved. "Have fun solving crime, dear. Text me when you can."

Twenty minutes later, Dunham entered New Orleans Police Headquarters and approached the front security desk. It was covered by two elderly police officers sitting behind the large desk. A third very young-looking police officer was standing to their side next to the metal detector.

All three noticed Dunham, which prompted the two elderly officers to leap out of their seats.

"Dr. Dunham!" one of the police officers began then reached forward and shook his hand. "It's a pleasure to finally meet you. Officer Dick Cavet." He pointed to the other elderly officer. "And this is Officer Darrel Galloway." He turned and presented the younger officer, "And fresh from the academy, Officer Jeffrey La Bouche."

Dunham smiled and shook their hands.

"Everyone's waiting for you on the fourth floor," Cavet informed him. "Just walk around the metal detector."

"Thank you."

"Better yet," Cavet pointed to his colleague, "Officer La Bouche, escort Dr. Dunham to Criminal Investigations."

As the young officer escorted the esteemed special agent, Cavet and Galloway sat back down, still staring after them. "The Watchmaker, Darrel!"

Galloway mused, "Wonder why they call him the Watchmaker anyway."

"Beats me," Cavet replied then paused. "Maybe because his investigative skills are so precise; it's like he's a fine-tuned quartz watch?"

Galloway shrugged. "Sounds good to me."

La Bouche pushed the elevator button. "Are you enjoying your stay in the Big Easy, Dr. Dunham?"

"I am, actually; and I brought my wife." The elevator door opened, and both entered. "She's got the whole weekend planned."

"I'm sure the French Quarter is on her itinerary," La Bouche predicted then eyed Dunham curiously. "By the way, I've never seen Officers Cavet and Galloway leave their seats like that for anyone—not even the chief." He paused. "You special or something?"

Dunham smirked, slightly surprised by the young officer's question. "I wouldn't say special. My last few cases did make the papers, so I'm sure that's why."

La Bouche nodded, accepting his answer, then stared straight ahead as the elevator stopped on the fourth floor. "Well, we're here. I hope all goes well."

Dunham thanked him as the elevator doors opened then turned to see a crowd of detectives, all very attentive, staring right at him.

"Holy smokes!" La Bouche muttered as he, too, noticed how excited the detectives were to see Dunham. "Those must have been pretty important cases, Dr. Dunham!"

Dunham grinned and walked out.

Bakula approached Dunham and shook his hand. "Hi, Dr. Dunham, it's great to finally meet you. Detective John Bakula."

"Nice to put a face to your voice and texts, Detective Bakula."

Bakula presented Dunham to the others. "This is Captain Cyndy DeBlanc, commander of the Criminal Investigative Division." Deblanc's dark brown hair was pinned loosely to the back of her head. She was nearly as tall as Dunham and possessed an athletic frame. She shook Dunham's hand. "It's an honor to meet you, Dr. Dunham."

"Hi, Captain, and thank you for allowing me some time with your detectives."

DeBlanc faced the crowd. "You're welcome, and as you can see by everyone insisting upon meeting you, the pleasure is all ours. You're a celebrity in these parts."

"This is my partner, Detective Harold Oglesby," Bakula continued.

Oglesby shook Dunham's hand. "It's a pleasure, Dr. Dunham."

Dunham nodded. "Hi, Detective. Nice to meet you." He then took the time to greet everyone.

Bakula placed his hand on Dunham's shoulder. "Follow me, Dr. Dunham; Oges and I reserved a conference room. Your three students are waiting for us."

"Excellent," Dunham replied. He followed the detectives to the conference room, and as he entered, he spotted Rob and Sarah. "Rob, Sarah, how are you doing?"

Rob, Sarah, and Jared stood.

"Hi, Dr. Dunham," Rob greeted. "We're doing great. Thanks for coming."

"Hi, Dr. Dunham," Sarah replied.

Rob presented Jared. "Dr. Dunham, this is Jared Dugas, our partner on this assignment."

"Oh yes," Dunham said and shook Jared's hand. "Dr. Perry at Loyola recommended you to the Vidocq class, is that right?"

Jared beamed, impressed that Dr. Dunham, himself, knew something about him. "Yes, sir; it's great to meet you."

Dunham took the center seat at the table. "Well, let's get down to business." Everyone sat.

Gesturing to Rob, Sarah, and Jared, Dunham said, "So, at the outset, the purpose of my visit was to assist you in your classroom project." He nodded to Bakula and Oglesby. "Because of the unique aspect of it being part of your investigation, maybe I can be of assistance to you as well."

Bakula grinned. "There are teaching hospitals giving up-and-coming physicians hands-on training, so why not call this a teaching police department?"

Oglesby nodded. "Hey, whatever it takes to get you on a case I'm working, I'm in." He handed Dunham two files. "Here are the case files."

Dunham glanced at Bakula then opened both files. "I recall you stating that saliva was collected off the deceased in the Foliage Park case and was confirmed to be canine, is that correct?"

"That's right," Bakula answered, "the DNA is consistent with both the gray wolf and the domesticated dog."

"How about the human bloodstains found near the levee?"

Bakula pointed at the case file Dunham was holding. "Definitely human, and so—by law—we must first consider it a missing persons investigation, entirely separate from the canine attack."

"I understand," Dunham replied, "Corpus delicti." He paused. "Have you made any headway?"

"We collected some hair follicles in a hairbrush, and we believe they are from the donor of the bloodstains," Oglesby explained. "He was a homeless person nicknamed Ol' Danny. They're being tested as we speak."

"How did you find Ol' Danny's hair?" Rob asked.

"We approached the owner of the shelter," Bakula answered, "and she surprisingly had some of his personal possessions, including the hairbrush."

"Excellent," Dunham said. "Rob, I read your explanatory email, and you, Sarah, and Jared are suggesting we may have a serial offender on our hands."

Robbed nodded.

"And you're basing this upon similarities between cases, such as the same animal screeching sound, a similar offender signature at the crime scenes, and the testimony of a transient man, who seems to match the results of bloodstains test—human blood."

"Not very solid, but yes."

"We are open to the possibility, Dr. Dunham," Bakula pointed out, "but because there is no firm evidence, as in a trail of bodies, we're at a standstill."

Rob nodded. "Which is why the thrust of our investigation is aimed at eliminating the possibility of the Foliage Park event being a homicide." He sat back and said to Dunham, "When the bloodstains were found to be human, it didn't help our cause to eliminate the possibility of murder."

Dunham stared at the files. "For argument's sake, let's assume we have a homicide on our hands. According to the manager of the shelter, the homeless are claiming they're being attacked by a canine-type of animal."

"To be fair, she does not believe their stories," Jared commented. "She thinks they're just trying to get attention."

Dunham nodded. "On the surface, the selection of victims, in this case, those hiding on the fringes of society, conforms unusually well with a serial offender attempting to satisfy his murderous agenda without being detected."

Rob, Sarah, and Jared glanced at each other, smiling.

Dunham held a finger in the air. "If true, we have an anomaly in his offender signature pattern—a red flag," he turned and faced Bakula and Oglesby, "and red flags often lead to breaks in a case."

Bakula sat up, shot a quick glance at Oglesby, then looked back at Dunham. "Absolutely."

Rob, Sarah, and Jared glanced at each other again, but this time, they had surprised looks on their faces.

Dunham nodded. "Frankie Hambone."

"The Foliage Park victim?" Oglesby interrupted. "The scumbag child molester?"

"You mean the fact that he wasn't collected like the other victims?" Sarah asked. "That's easily explained by the German shepherd fighting the animal, which gave Hambone the chance to get away," she paused, "even though he fell dead in the backyard."

Dunham shook his head. "No, that's not the anomaly," he gave Sarah a slight smile, "but very perceptive, Sarah—you're thinking."

Sarah beamed. "Thank you."

"I'm referring to victimology. Hambone doesn't fit the victim profile; 'down and out' people lost in the streets of a large city—off the grid." Dunham scanned the file. "Although a convicted child molester is certainly someone shunned by society, thus, a potential victim with no love lost by anyone . . ." he placed a document in front of Bakula.

Bakula studied the document as Oglesby read it over his shoulder. "The report says he worked as a tour guide on a popular swamp tour."

Dunham shook his head. "This is not the type of job someone attempting to stay off the grid would take."

Bakula and Oglesby glanced at each other.

"Our offender would certainly have known that those who worked with Hambone on a daily basis would report his absence, sparking an investigation," Dunham paused, "yet he still did it."

Oglesby offered, "Although our official report does not have Hambone classified as a homicide victim, we did discuss the possibility of a homicide—not at the hands of a serial killer but by someone who knew the girl. Since Hambone was attacked just before he was about to kidnap a young girl in her backyard, we considered the possibility of someone protecting the girl."

Bakula nodded. "When Rob came to us with the suggestion that a dog, or wolf-dog hybrid, was used by someone, Oges and I investigated the possibility of a vigilant family member or friend intervening before Hambone could kidnap the girl, but we came up with nothing."

Jared slapped Rob on the shoulder, grinning. "See, they were listening."

"No one in their extended family owns a big dog except for the mother," Oglesby added, "and we quickly eliminated her German shepherd killing Hambone."

Dunham shook his head. "I'm going to suggest protection of the girl was not the motive." He paused. "*If* we indeed have a serial offender on our hands," Dunham glanced at Rob, "and I believe we do."

Rob sat up straight, realizing he'd convinced Dr. Dunham, of all people, to his theory.

"Serial offenders tend not to have the capacity to sympathize, or even empathize, with a potential victim—even an innocent girl about to be molested."

Bakula grabbed his chin, taking in Dunham's comments. "I think I follow you."

Dunham leaned forward. "Normally, human beings—even those who've had a very hard life—still have a sympathy bone, especially for pretty young girls about to be victimized by a child molester. It's the very reason why child molesters must be protected in prison from violent offenders."

Oglesby nodded.

Dunham glanced around at everyone. "If we are to discover the motive of a serial offender, we need to understand what it's like to have concerns only for oneself—absolutely no regard for others." He sat back. "In view of this, one explanation for the red flag is that Mr. Hambone was killed because he was a direct threat."

Everyone remained silent, one hundred percent of their attention on Dunham.

"This serial killer has gone to great lengths to stay under the radar," Bakula interrupted, breaking the silence, "so, he may have believed Hambone was going to expose his murder spree!"

Dunham pointed his finger at Bakula. "Exactly."

Jared leaned forward, hands out. "So, you're saying the killer didn't know the girl, he knew Frankie Hambone—and Hambone knew him—or at least knew what he was up to."

Dunham nodded. "Maybe, and this might translate into a lead."

Oglesby grinned. "Now you're talking!"

Dunham leaned forward again. "We may find our offender in Hambone's world; thus, my suggestion is we begin by following the last few days of his life."

Bakula glanced over at Oglesby. "The Honey Island Swamp Tour."

Oglesby nodded. "The Honey Island Swamp Tour." He stood, pulled out his phone, and searched through his contacts then pressed one and put the phone to his ear.

Sarah turned to Bakula. "Why the Honey Island Swamp Tour?"

"That's where he worked." Bakula pointed his thumb over his shoulder at Oglesby. "Detective Oglesby went to the Honey Island swamps to inform his workmates of his passing. While there, he discovered Hambone went to Foliage Park straight from work."

Dunham smiled. "Excellent. He may have been followed by the offender straight from work."

Bakula grinned back and nodded.

"Yes, hello," Oglesby said into his cell phone. "This is Detective Oglesby from NOPD. I spoke with the owner a few weeks back. Is he available?" Oglesby eyed Bakula and nodded. "Hello, Mr. Belanger, this is Detective Oglesby again, do you have a minute?" He paused. "Thanks, I'm going to put you on speaker so the other investigators can listen in." Oglesby tapped his phone and set it on the table. "Can you hear me, Mr. Belanger?"

"Yes, Detective, what can I do for you?"

"We're putting the final touches on the investigation into the death of your former employee, Frank Hambone, so we have a couple of questions. If you could think back, when you last saw him on that fateful day, did he happen to mention having problems with anyone?"

"Sure did," Belanger answered.

Oglesby glanced over at Bakula and Dunham. "Oh, who? What happened?"

"Frankie came back from his last swamp tour complaining about some Coon-ass pointin' a machete at him while he was on the boat with tourists when he was deep in the swamp."

Sarah leaned over to Jared and whispered, "What's a 'Coon-ass'?"

"An ethnic slur meaning Cajun, probably someone living in the swamps."

"Hi, Mr. Belanger, this is Detective Bakula. Did Frankie Hambone say he knew the man?"

"Don't think he knew him. He just said he saw a guy doin' something—settin' a bear trap as I recall—and the guy took exception to Frankie starin' at him. Shouldn't have been settin' traps in the tourist channels anyway." He paused. "What? Do ya think this guy killed Frankie?"

"We don't know, Mr. Belanger. It's probably nothing," Bakula replied. "Do you mind if we stop by and discuss this further?"

"Sure, and now is the best time, actually."

"Thank you, Mr. Belanger," Oglesby replied. "We'll see you in thirty minutes." He hung up.

Everyone stood, and Bakula glanced over at Rob, Sarah, and Jared. "Sorry, guys, you won't be able to come—department regs," he turned to Dunham, "but Dr. Dunham, we'd love for you to join us."

"I certainly will," Dunham replied then glanced over at the three students. "Rob, I'll text you and hook up with you guys when we're done." He waved hastily and followed Bakula and Oglesby rushing out the door.

Jared walked to the conference room door and watched the them leave. He turned back to Rob and Sarah. "How awesome was that! He comes here to help, and in two minutes we have a huge lead." He shook his head, grinning. "I've heard the rumors about him, but to see him in action is amazing!"

"I watched him do the very same thing in Boston," Sarah replied.

Rob nodded. "And I've had the opportunity to see him do his magic in both Buffalo and Boston!"

Jared beamed. "And now New Orleans."

Rob paced back and forth. "Now that we have Dr. Dunham on our side, I'm sure the New Orleans Police Department will stay onboard. How about we go to lunch and do some brainstorming before we see Dr. Taylor. I'm sure he'll want to know everything."

"Sounds like a plan," Sarah agreed.

"Hey, maybe we'll be part of the serial killer task force!" Jared blurted out.

Rob shook his head. "Let's just have some lunch first."

chapter 25

The Trail of Bodies,
Slidell, Louisiana

Dunham followed Bakula and Oglesby into the Honey Island Swamp Tour store. He glanced around at the items on the shelves. "I think my wife, Maggie, would like to come here."

Bakula grinned. "This place has a good reputation, and the swamp tour is great too. Whenever my family or friends come visit, this is where I send them."

Oglesby pointed to the back room. "I see Mr. Belanger sitting at his desk. Follow me."

Belanger popped his head up as Oglesby knocked on the door frame. "Detective Oglesby, it's nice to see you again. Come in, come in."

Oglesby entered the office and shook Belanger's hand. "This is my partner, Detective Bakula, and this is FBI Special Agent Dr. Dunham."

Belanger shook their hands then glanced at Dunham. "This must be a big thing if the FBI's involved."

"Yes and no, Mr. Belanger," Dunham replied. "I'm here assisting in some training, so I wanted to follow Detectives Oglesby and Bakula here. Do you mind?"

Belanger shook his head. "Not at all." He faced Oglesby. "Well, after we spoke on the phone, I started digging into what Frankie was bitchin' about the day he died, and I believe I found someone who can help."

"Excellent," Oglesby replied. "Who?"

Belanger pointed outside his window at a man securing one of the flat-bottom boats. "That's one of my boat captains, Ronnie Dupree. He claims one of his tourists came up to him after the ride and told him about some swamp man threatening her with a machete."

Oglesby's eyes widened, and he shot a quick glance at Bakula and Dunham. "That certainly sounds promising."

Belanger peeked out the window and nodded. "Yup, and I see Ronnie's on his way in."

A few minutes later, Ronnie Dupree entered Belanger's office. "I'm back, boss."

"Thanks, Ronnie, here's Detective Oglesby, his partner, Detective Bakula, and FBI Agent Dunham."

Oglesby shook Dupree's hand. "We appreciate your assistance, Mr. Dupree. Your boss informed us that a tourist on your boat said someone threatened her in the swamp?"

Dupree nodded. "Yep. A chubby ol' lady named Olivia. I remember her name because her chubby ol' hubby kept on saying her name throughout the tour." He paused. "They were irritating, really."

"What did she tell you?" Bakula asked.

Dupree thought back for a moment. "Well, when we finished the tour, she came up to me. She was really shaken up, so I asked if she was OK. She told me a swamp man, hidin' in the cypress trees and holding onto a machete kept on starin' at her. She said he even came at the boat, pointing the machete at her. I didn't really pay no mind to her story since she wasn't hurt or nothin'. I figured it was probably some swamp man havin' fun scarin' the tourists," he nodded toward Belanger, "but when the boss-man talked to me today about someone Frankie saw, it clicked right away."

Dunham glanced at Belanger then at Dupree. "Mr. Dupree, is there any chance you could take us into the swamp to the location where your tourist claimed she saw this man?"

Dupree eyed Belanger, who nodded. "Sure, the *Swamp Princess* is ready to go."

All three followed Dupree onto the flat-bottom boat. Dunham leaned over to Oglesby as Dupree started up the engines and asked, "Was Frankie Hambone wearing the same clothes as Mr. Dupree?"

Oglesby looked over the boat captain's attire and nodded. "Yep, same thing—except for the vest."

Dupree kicked up the speed through the swamp channels. He turned and faced his passengers. "We usually go pretty slow around this area, but I'll cut to it and go straight to the spot." He scanned the area in front of the boat then turned back to the investigators. "I didn't want to say this in front of the boss, but the area Olivia spotted the swamp man with the machete was not along the usual swamp tour."

"Oh?" Oglesby asked.

Dupree nodded and turned forward. "Tourists are interested in the ol' stories about the Honey Island Swamp Monster from the 1970s, so I tell them about how locals have been seeing something similar even today." He turned around and faced them again. "True story." He turned back to the front. "Anyway, they usually want to visit this place, but it's not part of the swamp tour path, and the boss-man made it clear we aren't supposed to stray from the designated channels." He scanned the area around him and turned. "This time, some rich tourist gave me a hundred bucks, so I did."

"We're not interested in telling on you, Mr. Dupree," Bakula explained. "We just want to figure out who this guy is."

Dupree scanned the area and pointed at the trees in front of him. "We're coming up to the place. Notice how thick the cypresses and Spanish moss are getting. Not many come into this area, even when they're huntin' or fishin'."

Bakula, Dunham, and Oglesby looked up at the canopy then scanned the trees, trying to see beyond their shadowy trunks.

"If you spot anyone, Mr. Dupree, let us know," Bakula replied.

Dupree stopped at the bank where he had positioned the boat during the tour and where Olivia claimed to have seen the man. "This is the place." He pointed behind the boat. "She said the guy came at us from that direction, but I'm not sure exactly where since I never saw him."

Dunham scanned the area and pointed. "Do you mind taking us over in that direction? I'd like to see this bear trap. Something doesn't sound right."

Dupree backed the boat up then pulled forward slowly. "Shouldn't be a problem going in there. This boat has a very shallow profile. Going over the water lilies and hyacinths is not a problem."

Oglesby scanned the dry land nervously. "Any chance of a bear encounter?"

"Not likely," Dupree answered. "Not many black bears in these parts," he pointed down at the water lilies, "but there are poisonous water moccasins."

Bakula scanned the area, gripping his handgun. "We need to be on swamp man alert, especially if one has a machete."

"Been lookin'," Dupree answered, "but so far nothin'."

Oglesby quickly glanced down at the lilies. "Hard to see into the water."

Dupree pointed to the deck. "There are a couple of oars and staffs. Use those to search through the lilies and hyacinth leaves."

They each selected a tool or two. As the boat cleared a couple of mangroves jutting up out of the water, all eyes gazed downward, looking for the trap.

As they neared one particularly large cypress tree, Oglesby's attention was at the root area. He pointed to the water. "I see something!"

Everyone crowded Oglesby and squinted into the water.

"It looks like a metal cage just under the water line," Oglesby commented.

"I see a latch," Bakula observed.

Dupree walked over and looked down. "That ain't no trap. It's a cage made of a metal frame and wire fencing, and it looks like there's a burlap potato sack in it." He walked to the back of the boat, opened a storage bin, and pulled out a pair of leg-length rubber boots and handed them to Oglesby. "Be my guest."

Oglesby grinned. "I was just about to ask if you had a pair of these." He put them on and jumped into the swampy water at the base of the cypress tree then waded toward the cage. He glanced up at Dupree and said, "Let me know if any snakes or alligators come my way!"

"Already checked," Dupree answered, "and you're OK. I'll keep watch though."

Bakula scanned the area again then watched Oglesby.

Dupree pulled out a couple sets of work gloves and handed them to Bakula. "Here ya go, Detective."

Oglesby motioned at Bakula, who threw a pair to him. He caught them and put them on then reached down into the water and opened the front latch of the cage. He stared in the cage for a moment, then he reached in, grabbed the burlap sack, and lifted it out.

"It's filled with something," Dunham commented.

Oglesby approached the boat and heaved it on the deck.

Bakula put the other set of gloves on and grabbed the tie on the sack. "Well, let's see what's in it." He loosened the ropes, opened it, peeked in, then dropped the bag. "Ahhh!"

The bag fell to the side, and a human head rolled out.

"Oh my God!" Dupree exclaimed and backed off.

Dunham leaned over the bag, pulled out his pen, and used it to peek in. "I believe I see three decapitated human heads," he continued to stare in the bag, "in various stages of decomposition; mostly fresh."

"Holy shit!" Dupree blurted out, disgusted.

Dunham glanced up at Bakula. "Well, Detective, it seems we have discovered the trail of bodies—or, more accurately, the trail of heads." He stood and scanned the swamp. "You have a serial offender on your hands."

"Can't be!" Bakula denied, but he knew full well Dunham was right. "We would've known about a serial killer on the loose in New Orleans, right? Someone would've reported missing persons, wouldn't they?" He shook his head then grabbed his chin. "Maybe this guy's just been grave-robbing and collecting heads."

"Sorry," Dunham answered and bent down to reinspect the heads. "These are ante mortem abrasions, i.e., the victim was alive when the abrasions were inflicted upon the body, including the decapitation wound."

Bakula crouched next to Dunham.

Dunham pointed at a cut. "All the cuts and abrasions exhibit vital reactions. Notice the bruising. This doesn't happen postmortem; the heart was still pumping." He paused then nodded. "This is highly suggestive of a homicide—actually, multiple homicides," he turned and faced Bakula, "but we can confirm this. We're testing for Ol' Danny's DNA profile as we speak, so if one of these heads is a match with him, then there's no doubt."

"He's right, Bak," Oglesby commented.

"Prudence dictates we operate from this premise," Dunham said.

Bakula stared at the decapitated head literally peeking out of the bag, then he took a deep resigning breath. "OK, so we have a whole new ball game here." He scanned the woods again, ensuring they were alone. "We don't want to screw this up," he mused aloud.

Dupree said, "Detective Bakula, people have to know about this! What if he strikes again?"

Bakula put his hand up. "Slow down, Mr. Dupree. It would be foolish to sound the alarm about a serial killer on the loose, causing undue public hysteria, only to find out we have something entirely different going on. We have to let the crime scene investigators do their job." He pointed out into the cypress trees. "Right now, I need you to keep an eye out for anyone coming this way."

"Wait!" Oglesby blurted out as he stared into the cage. "I see two more bags." He reached in and pulled out the burlap bags, both darker than the first. "These have definitely been in the cage longer." He heaved them onto the boat deck.

Bakula opened both bags, and he and Dunham peeked into them. "Six decapitated heads, but these show much more decomposition."

Dunham glanced at Bakula. "Same here; six heads." He stared at the three bags. "That makes sixteen victims."

"Sixteen victims!" Bakula blurted out in disbelief.

"Judging from the extent and variability of decomposition," Dunham surmised, "the victims died at different times, suggesting a series of murders throughout the last year, maybe two."

"Maybe more," Oglesby replied, staring down into the cage. "I think I see another bag."

Bakula stared at Oglesby. "Are you kidding me?"

"Gentlemen," Dunham began, "it looks like your minor animal attack case has just ballooned into one of the most prolific serial offender cases in recent years. Once the press gets ahold of this it's going to make national news." He paused. "You don't want the mayor caught off guard, so I recommend your captain inform your entire chain of command as soon as possible."

Dupree dropped into the captain's chair, just staring into the water. "What the hell!"

"Wait," Bakula interrupted. "Mr. Dupree, how long ago did the tourist, Olivia, see this man?"

Dupree slowly glanced over at Bakula. "Day before yesterday."

Bakula faced Dunham and Oglesby. "He has room for two more heads in this first bag. I think he's coming back."

"I believe you're right," Dunham agreed.

Bakula gazed at Oglesby. "How about we stuff these bags with rocks or something, put them back in the cage, and stake this place out."

"Trap the bastard." Oglesby grinned. "I love it, and how about we use bear traps just to make sure."

Dunham nodded. "Excellent idea—minus the bear traps—but excellent. From a forensic standpoint, we need to test these burlap bags for any possible latent evidence, so we'll not want to use these." He glanced around. "In this environment, we'll likely have little to no success in discovering latent evidence, which is the probable reason he selected it to store his trophies in the first place."

Dupree turned and stared at Dunham. "Trophies?"

"Many serial offenders collect something from the crime scene, whether it's an article of the victim's clothing, a personal possession, or a body part. It allows them to experience the event over and over again in their mind. In some cases, they'll use it to perform some ritual."

Dunham put his hand up. "On second thought, there might be incriminating evidence in the cage, so I recommend we not take the chance of destroying any by placing new bags in it."

Oglesby nodded. "You got it."

"Mr. Dupree," Dunham said, pointing at the burlap bags, "you wouldn't happen to have any large bag that we could use to transport these would you?"

Dupree heaved himself out of his seat, walked over to his storage bin, and opened it. "I just might."

Bakula looked over at a dry piece of land. "We need a twenty-four-hour stakeout starting today . . . maybe over there."

"No one comes here at night," Dupree explained, "not even this killer. It's too dangerous."

"Sunrise to sunset's good for me," Bakula replied.

Oglesby glanced over at Dunham. "I can see why you're mentoring this Rob Faulks. If it wasn't for him, we'd still be in the dark."

Dunham grinned. "He definitely has a gift."

"Like you?" Oglesby commented as he jumped back onto the boat.

Dunham pondered Oglesby's comment.

chapter 26

Palace of Fontainebleau,
Versailles, France,
June 1765

King Louis XV rode his horse around his new courtyard, the Cour des Princes. He pulled back on the reins, halting his horse, and glanced around at his majestic castle, surveying the surrounding courtyards and gardens. He favored this particular palace château, the Palace of Fontainebleau, over all his others—even the center of government, the Palace of Versailles.

The stallion dropped his head and began to graze.

The king leaned forward on the saddle and patted the horse's neck. "Good boy, good boy."

The horse shivered in response and continued to graze.

Although he appreciated the Palace of Versailles, the assassination attempt on his life eight years ago in the Marble Courtyard still lay heavy on his mind. He took a deep breath. Being outside near the fountains and the gardens at the Palace of Fontainebleau was so peaceful, the perfect medicine for these stressful times.

A man hurriedly approached the king, bowed, then grabbed the horse's bridle. "Shall I take your stallion back to the horse farm, Your Excellency?"

The king glanced up at the entrance to the castle and spotted Saint-Florentin and L'Averdy and their entourage rushing down the stone horseshoe staircase straight for him. "No, I believe I'll ride a little longer, Charles. Come back after I've dismounted."

Charles gave a deep bow then hurried away.

It had been five months since the king had announced to all of France that his hand-selected wolf-hunter, the Norman Martin Denneval, would quickly dispatch the Beast. Not only was the wretched monster still ravaging the countryside and feasting upon the peasantry, but the Norman's rude behavior had also created a public embarrassment for the king.

The ministers drew near and bowed. "Your Excellency," Saint-Florentin greeted.

"Well, has the royal court decided upon a replacement for the incompetent Denneval and his son?" The king glared at Saint-Florentin. "This imbecile's indolence and negligence make me look like a fool!"

"We have, Your Excellency," Saint-Florentin answered. "Upon your advice, we interviewed your musket officer and Lieutenant of the Hunt Francois Antoine de Beauterne." He glanced over at L'Averdy. "Antoine explained to us why the hunting strategies of Captain Duhamel and Sir Denneval have failed, and he went into detail about what he will do differently."

"Oh?" the king muttered. "Can you summarize?"

L'Averdy nodded. "Your Excellency, Antoine told us that both Duhamel in the fall and Denneval in the winter based their operations on a failed idea, sending hunting parties to the locations of the most recent attacks. He's convinced that this adversary is too powerful, too fast for any kind of reactive response of this nature. He plans on using a proactive approach by mapping out the Beast's most recent murderous rampages, then identifying any patterns of behavior, possibly revealing its lair. If successful, this will allow him to set a trap." He shot a quick glance at Saint-Florentin then eyed the king. "He did warn it may take a few months to discover a pattern."

"Excellent," the king replied. "Inform all of the ministers of my endorsement."

The ministers nodded and rushed off.

* * *

Two Months Later,
Malzieu, Gévaudan Province, France

Lafont turned his head toward the door as he heard a knock. "Enter."

One of Francois Antoine's fourteen hunting officers, Péilissier et Lacour, entered. "Monsieur Lafont! Captain Antoine has just received word that two young women were pursued by the Beast in a river outside of Paulhac. They fought it and even injured the Beast before it ran off!"

Lafont leaped out of his seat. "How did they manage that?"

"A bayonet attached to a pike. He asks you to meet him at the river. It is a twenty-minute ride. I will escort you."

"Where is Monsieur Antoine?" Lafont asked as he collected his gear.

"The Castle of Le Besset," Péilissier answered. "It's just a little farther, so we might beat him there."

Lafont followed Péilissier out along a mule trail toward Paulhac.

After about twenty minutes, Lafont noticed a dozen horse riders paralleling them.

Péilissier pointed at the riders. "Captain Antoine is waving to you, monsieur."

Lafont spotted the energetic Antoine waving, so he waved back. He was amazed that this youthful man was near seventy years of age.

Antoine caught up with Lafont and Péilissier. "Monsieur Lafont, I'm glad you could make it."

Lafont touched his hat. "Thank you for involving me, Monsieur Antoine."

"It's just around the bend," Péilissier indicated.

As they rounded the bend, Lafont spotted a large crowd near the small river. He noticed three horsemen who clearly had taken charge. As they approached, one of the horsemen turned toward Antoine.

The horseman nodded and pointed to two young ladies sitting on a large log being comforted by four men. "Captain, they're over there waiting for you. Marie-Jeanne Vallet and her younger sister, Paula."

"Have they been injured?" Antoine asked.

The horseman shook his head. "No, although they're still distraught from the incident."

Antoine and Lafont rode over to the young ladies and dismounted. "Monsieur Lafont, will you interpret for me?" Antoine asked.

Lafont nodded. Not only could he speak formal French, but he was also fluent in the local patois.

Antoine bent down and smiled at the girls. "Marie-Jeanne and Paula, may I ask you a few questions?"

Lafont relayed his question.

Marie-Jeanne and Paula both nodded.

Antoine gave them a kind look of concern. "What happened?"

Marie-Jeanne spoke for a few minutes, pointing into the woods and even demonstrating a thrusting action.

Lafont nodded, turned to Antoine, and translated: "She said the Beast came at them from the patch of trees behind us as they were filling up their water jugs. Her bayonet-tipped staff was lying at the water's edge, just a few feet away."

Antoine spotted a staff on the ground. "That staff?"

Marie-Jeanne nodded.

"She rushed from sister's side to retrieve it," Lafont continued, "and as the Beast closed in on her sister, she picked the staff up and stabbed the Beast in the neck."

Marie-Jeanne spoke again in explanation.

Lafont nodded when she stopped. "The thrust caused it to yelp and leap onto the riverbank on the other side. She could tell the bayonet didn't penetrate its thick coat, and after a few moments, the Beast rushed them again, but this time it came after her." Lafont asked Marie-Jeanne to continue with the rest of the story.

When she'd finished, Lafont nodded to her. "As it leaped for her, she braced the back end of the staff under her foot and aimed the bayonet at it, and this time it sank into the Beast's chest. It howled and rolled into the river, as if it were cleaning its wound." Lafont spoke patois to Marie-Jeanne.

She replied to Lafont's question.

"It darted back into the woods from where it came," he summarized for Antoine.

Antoine grabbed the girl's staff and touched the blood on the bayonet. The blood markings seemed to suggest it penetrated about three inches. He stared at her and paused. "That took courage, young lady; a story likened to Joan of Arc, and I shall personally pass it onto His Majesty. I will be recommending a reward for your act of bravery."

Lafont grinned and relayed Antoine's comments to her.

Marie-Jeanne beamed and hugged her sister.

The men turned and murmured to each other, clearly happy with Antoine's comments.

Antoine gazed into the woods where the Beast had run off, then he glanced over at the closest hunting officer. "Péilissier!"

"Yes, Captain."

"Take La Chenay with you and coordinate a series of hunts with the local huntsmen and their hounds. You'll need them in the thick forest. Concentrate your efforts around Montchauvet."

Péilissier bowed to Antoine, and he and La Chenay mounted their horses and left.

Lafont approached Antoine. "Do you believe this is the Beast?"

"Hard to say, Monsieur Lafont . . . it is true at the least that they were attacked by a large wolf, making it a man-eater." He stared into the woods. "I'm a bit confused, though, as to how one young woman fended it off with moderate effort, when in some attacks the Beast easily dispatched three armed, full-sized men, lopping their heads clean off."

* * *

Forest of Montchauvet,
Gévaudan Province, France,
One Week Later

Péilissier sat on his horse upon a ridge next to his fellow hunting officer, La Chenay, and watched his hunting party below in the wooded valley 'beating the bushes,' just as they'd been doing for days.

The hounds could be heard for miles.

"The hounds are excited," La Chenay observed.

Péilissier grabbed the reins tighter, now staring at the woods for any movement. "Yes, indeed."

At that moment, a massive wolf shot out of the woods and streaked across the valley at the edge of a patch of high brush.

"There!" Péilissier shouted.

In an instant, it darted out of the valley toward the opposite ridge, heading north.

"It's headed for the Montchauvet Forest and swamps!" La Chenay bellowed.

The two hunting officers kicked their horses into a gallop and chased after the wolf, maintaining the high ground. After about two minutes, they finally made it over the ridge.

Péilissier scanned the great expanse of the Montchauvet Forest before them, but there was no sign of the wolf.

"It's too fast!" La Chenay yelled.

Péilissier pointed forward. "I expected this possible escape route, so I have three local hunters, Chastèl the innkeeper and his two adult sons, waiting in front of the swamps.

La Chenay glanced over at Péilissier, both still in a full gallop. "They should have encountered it by now. Why haven't we heard musket fire?"

Péilissier spotted all three hunters coming into view, rounding the tree line from the east, their heads barely visible with the thick, high underbrush. "Damn! They left their posts!"

As the two horsemen neared the three local hunters, the three caught their attention and stopped.

"Did you see a wolf run toward you, innkeeper?" La Chenay asked.

The innkeeper shook his head. "No, nothing came."

Péilissier spotted an obvious animal path into the forest and pointed at it. "Why did you leave this area? I specifically told you to stay here!"

The innkeeper glared at Péilissier then pointed to the east. "We thought we saw something over there, so we investigated."

Péilissier faced his horse to La Chenay. "It went in here. I'm sure of it." He glanced back at the path to the tree line, which had a section of tall grasses and shrubs covering much of it. He then approached it and eyed Chastèl. "Innkeeper, will we encounter any difficulties if we enter here?"

The innkeeper held back a smirk, quickly glanced over at his two sons, then shook his head. "No, nothing."

La Chenay rushed toward the entrance through the underbrush, followed closely behind by Péilissier. As they passed the first set of shrubs, the horses immediately sank to their knees in the marshy earth, and both riders flew out of their saddles and landed face first in the soggy mud.

"Ba, ha, ha, ha!" bellowed all three locals.

The innkeeper dropped to his knees in uncontrollable laughter.

Péilissier rose slowly out of the muck then walked up to the innkeeper. As the innkeeper stood, he got nose-to-nose with him, glaring. "You knew damn well the swamp was there! I should have you arrested for such disrespectful behavior!"

"Back off!" one of his sons replied angrily, grasping his musket in a threatening manner.

Péilissier turned and walked over to the innkeeper's son, grabbed him by the collar, and jerked him close. "How dare you!"

Both the innkeeper and the second son picked up their muskets and aimed them at Péilissier.

"Unhand him, you swine!" the innkeeper threatened.

Péilissier saw La Chenay take aim at the innkeeper, then he heard galloping horses coming over the ridge. He turned his head and spotted six of his armed hunting officers nearing them.

The innkeeper noticed them as well and opted to lower his musket.

As the horsemen arrived, La Chenay took the muskets away from the innkeeper's sons.

Péilissier neared the innkeeper, ripped his musket out of his hands, then struck him in the abdomen with the butt of his own musket.

The innkeeper keeled over and grimaced.

His sons took a step forward but stopped when they noticed all of the officers aiming their muskets at them.

Péilissier faced the closest mounted horse officer. "Two of you, arrest these three insolent bastards and take them back to camp. Keep their hands tied behind their backs at all times." He glanced at the woods. "The rest of you, collect your hunting parties. We'll follow the wolf's scent from here. Prepare to get wet."

chapter 27

Vidocq Class, Loyola University,
New Orleans, Louisiana

Dr. Taylor walked around the room, interacting with the students working on their cases. Finally, he approached Rob, Sarah, and Jared. "Guys, Dr. Dunham just contacted me and asked me to pass on some sensitive information."

The three students blinked up at Dr. Taylor.

"He prefers it to be private, at least for the time being," Taylor whispered.

"They must've found something out at the swamp tour," Jared surmised.

"A promising lead?" Sarah asked.

"More than that," Taylor answered, glanced around, then leaned over. "They discovered the decapitated heads of sixteen victims in various stages of decomposition." Taylor pointed at Rob. "You did it, Rob; you uncovered a serial offender on the loose in New Orleans, but the even bigger news is that he's been collecting victims for a while—at least two years."

"Sixteen victims!" Sarah quietly exclaimed. "I mean, we get that he's staying under the police radar by only preying upon the down and out, but sixteen victims? I can't believe no one figured it out until now."

"Ever since Hurricane Katrina," Jared explained, "the Town's had a huge number of homeless. It's hard to keep tabs on transient people, so it's hard to know when they've gone missing." He pointed out the window. "There are entire areas still abandoned, so the killer picked the perfect city to hide his tracks."

Rob glanced up at Taylor. "Did he say what their next step is? Are they starting a task force?"

"Well, the reason why this information hasn't been provided to the public yet is because they're convinced the offender will soon return to his trophies. They want to apprehend him without incident, so they're sending a SWAT team into the swamps." Taylor glanced around the room, ensuring their discussion hadn't caught the attention of others. "If it was made public, chances are he'd abandon his hiding spot, and we'd lose this excellent opportunity to get him off the streets." Taylor paused. "And yes, a task force has been organized."

Rob shook his head. "Well, if this guy brings his animal, I hope the SWAT team arms themselves with long, long dog catcher poles."

* * *

Honey Island Bayou, The Stakeout

A tall, thin man with short, sandy-colored hair pulled into an abandoned parking lot that butted up against the Honey Island Swamp, just outside of Slidell. He parked his van in the far corner behind a batch of trees, blocked from view. He exited the van, opened the back, and pulled out a burlap sack. He peeked into it and stared at its contents obsessively; a freshly decapitated woman's head. He closed it and approached a small aluminum motorboat hidden in the weeds at the base of the moss-draped cypress mangroves growing in the swamp.

A helicopter flew right over the man, headed past the swamp and toward the Pearl River.

The man glanced up and stared at the helicopter, and as it turned, he noticed the word 'Sheriff' written on the side. *Strange*, he thought to himself. *Are they after me?* The man continued to watch the helicopter, and once he was convinced they weren't searching for him, he boarded his boat, started the engine, and pushed off into the swamp. As he motored forward, he reached underneath the seat and pulled out a large machete. After about twenty minutes of traversing through the mangroves, he moored the boat onto a large section of forested dry land. He got out and walked for another ten minutes along the edge near the water line, keeping an eye out for gators.

As the man neared a nine-foot alligator, the creature fled the land and crashed into the water, disappearing underneath the water lilies.

The man spotted his shack, hidden among the thick underbrush. He carefully approached the shack and glanced down at the many huge canine footprints in the sand. He grabbed the handle of the door, ensuring it was still latched. He then peeked in a crack between the door and door frame and grinned. Satisfied, he left his shack and quickly walked toward the water line.

Ten minutes later, he neared his destination but stopped when he spotted the helicopter again.

The helicopter flew straight then turned right, maintaining its low altitude.

They definitely didn't see him, but . . . could his collection of heads have been discovered?

The helicopter pilot glanced at the fuel gauge then frowned slightly. He keyed the microphone on his headset. "Oscar Sierra, fuel level near bingo. Will need to return to base and refuel. Estimated time of return, one hour."

The SWAT team leader, hiding behind a few trees on a large hummock in the swamp, glanced up at the helicopter, adjusted his earplug, then keyed his own microphone. "Roger, one hour." He glanced over at his three team members hiding in strategic locations then stared at his watch. He keyed his microphone again and whispered, "Two more hours until sunset."

His team members made eye contact with him and nodded, all knowing full well that if the offender was coming today, it'd be soon.

The man watched the helicopter leave the area. He waited a few more minutes and noticed nothing unusual, so he started off to add to his collection.

The SWAT team leader scanned the swamp, convinced that their target was either going to arrive by boat or from the forested land area. He had purposely positioned his team for these two possible scenarios. He rubbed his eyes.

Splash, splash, splash.

The leader heard the noise and scanned the water but saw nothing. He eyed the far team member, who had a better vantage point, and noticed he was staring back at him. The team member pointed out toward the water to a cluster of mangroves. He nodded, then stared at the trees. He heard what sounded like a person trudging his way through the water.

All of the team members aimed their rifles at the patch of mangroves.

The man trudged through knee-deep, lily-covered water around the patch of mangroves toward his collection. He was waving his machete and holding onto his burlap bag, completely unaware he had company.

The SWAT team leader stared at the man through his rifle scope. He keyed his microphone. "Target in sight—game on."

The team members repositioned themselves as the man approached the metal cage, continuously hiding from view.

The man neared the large cypress tree, now thirty feet away.

"On my signal," the team leader ordered, waiting for the perfect time when their target had no chance of escape.

The backup team, listening in on the radio, waited in a high-speed swamp boat.

The man trudged through the water and passed another mangrove. He suddenly stopped, raised his nose high in the air, sniffed, then jerked his head ninety degrees to the left, spotting the far team member aiming a rifle at him. His face turned red, his blood boiling. In an instant, he turned and bolted through the cover of mangroves.

"Shit!" the team leader spouted. He keyed his microphone. "Converge on the target! Challenge!"

The team members jumped up and converged but stayed on dry land, paralleling his escape.

The front team member ran along the water line, aiming his rifle into the mangroves to his left. He lost sight of the target but had a good idea where he was because of the splashing noise. He decided to pick up speed to get ahead of the target, knowing his trailing team members covered the back. He then spotted some splashing in the mangroves slightly ahead of him. "Shit, this guy pulled ahead—he's making good time," he announced on the radio. He now ran as fast as he could. "Target's at my ten!"

"In sight," another team member reported. "No, just lost him."

The front team member spotted the man jumping onto dry land just ahead of him. "He's out of the water!"

The man bolted down an animal trail, which veered right.

"Losing sight of him in the thick brush! He's twenty feet ahead!"

"Keep pressure on him," the lead member blurted out on the radio. "I'm going off trail to head him off." He changed direction to the right and ran through the trees, only guessing that the trail turned in his direction.

"Team Bravo en route to assist."

The team leader keyed his microphone as he ducked through the branches. "Take the west channel!"

The second and third team members caught up with the front member, and as they did, they noticed the trail split. All three stopped.

The second team member pointed down at fresh boot tracks. "Go left!"

The front man ran as fast as he could, followed closely behind by the other two members. After about a hundred yards, the trail opened up. They stopped.

The front man spotted a wooden shack tucked into some heavy brush. The door was wide open. "There," he announced as he pointed at the shack.

"The tracks head straight to it," the second team member stated.

The three rushed up to the shack. As they approached the door, a massive, dark-haired, wolflike animal came into view from inside, filling the entire door frame.

The animal glared at the SWAT team members, baring and snapping its massive teeth.

"Shit!" the front team member yelled and tried to aim his rifle at the creature.

In an instant, the animal charged, attacking the front member with a crushing bite to the throat.

The other two members lost their balance during the lightning-fast attack.

As the second member rolled onto his knees, he witnessed the creature pounce on top of the third member, ripping his throat out. The second member raised his rifle for a shot, but the creature streaked into the brush. He shot multiple times at where he thought the animal might be. He then glanced at his two partners, both unconscious and bleeding profusely. He keyed his microphone. "Two men down! Two men down! Attacked by some huge animal—a wolf or dog or something!" He turned and aimed his rifle in the direction of the shack, which was now smoking, but saw nothing.

The animal streaked out of the brush from behind the man and pounced on him, gripping the back of his neck and snapping it.

The team leader rushed through the brush, knowing only to go west. He hadn't heard from his team members for ten minutes and feared the worst. He finally came upon the clearing and spotted his three team members lying on the ground. Behind them was a small wooden building engulfed in flames. He rushed up to his team and quickly realized all three were dead. He dropped to his knees in shock.

chapter 28

Angie's Surprise,
New Orleans

Angie Frazier reached across her dining room table and placed a Cajun dish in front of Dr. Dunham.

"Thank you, Angie."

She then scooped a serving from the large pot onto another dinner plate and placed it in front of Maggie. "Bon appétit, guys!" She scooped herself some of the creamy meat dish and sat back into her own seat. "And there's seconds when you're ready."

"This is marvelous, roomie," Maggie responded, staring at her dinner. "And you prepared it yourself? In another life, I think you were a Cajun chef."

Dunham tasted the dish. "Delicious, Angie. The meat is so tasty."

Angie held back a devilish grin and glanced over at Maggie, who was less skilled at holding back hers. Dr. Dunham, engrossed in his entrée, was oblivious to their mischief. She handed Maggie her wine glass. "I believe I'll have a refill of the wine, Maggie darling."

Maggie topped off everyone's wine glasses.

Dunham glanced around Angie's dining room. "Also, thank you for having the meal so early." He grinned. "Should we call this a late lunch or early dinner?"

"Oh, definitely an early dinner with such a spread Angie made for us," Maggie answered as she raised her wine glass. "To great friends."

Angie and Dunham raised their glasses, and both replied, "To great friends."

"You two should stay in New Orleans for the whole week," Angie suggested. "You get out of that hotel after the weekend and come here."

Dunham nodded. "My job may require that very thing." He took another bite. "So, you two were college roommates in the eighties, eh? How things have changed since then."

"Two divorces later, I'm happy as a peach!" Angie jested.

Maggie placed her wine glass down. "It's too bad we won't be able to meet your boyfriend." Maggie reached over and placed her hand on Angie's. "So, you're dating the chair of the geology department. An anthropology professor meets a physical science guy—at the campus cafeteria no less? Whatever did you strike up a conversation about?"

Angie pointed over at a glass case filled with crystals and fossils. "I'm something of a fossil hound, and the Louisiana Geological Association held their latest meeting on campus. I signed up for one of their summer field trips last year, and George ran it." She beamed. "The rest is romantic history. He'll be back from his Norway sabbatical in three weeks."

Dunham received a text and glanced up at the two women. "I've just been informed the mayor is about to hold an important news conference on all local channels—it's on the case I assisted with yesterday. Angie, do you mind if we watch it?"

"Of course." Angie grabbed the remote and aimed it at the flat-screen TV positioned in the upper corner of the room. "Cable TV is my dinner date whenever George isn't around." She switched it to a local channel.

"Thanks. I'll explain what's going on, but it should become apparent."

The news reporter spoke for a moment until a number of officials took center stage behind the podium.

A clean-shaven Black man wearing a dark suit and burgundy tie stepped up behind the news microphones.

The reporter turned and faced the camera. "And here is Mayor Blumenthal."

The mayor made eye contact with the reporters. "Good afternoon. To my right is Orleans Parish Sheriff Marvin LeRoy, St. Tammany Sheriff John Depew, and New Orleans Superintendent of Police Michael Evans." He faced the other direction and continued, "And to my left is Louisiana State Police Officer in

Charge Lieutenant Brad Wendall and NOPD Captain Cyndy DeBlanc, who is the commander of our Criminal Investigative Division."

"Wow, must be an important case," Angie commented.

The mayor drew his shoulders back. "Before I explain the reason I called this news conference, you should know that I just got off the phone with the governor and debriefed him on recent events. He is in full support of our efforts and has offered all assistance necessary." He took a deep breath. "In the last few days, detectives from the New Orleans Police Department, along with the assistance of the FBI, have uncovered the partial human remains of nearly twenty individuals." Maggie faced Dunham and pointed at him. The mayor paused and scanned the room of reporters, taking on a serious demeanor. "Compelling evidence suggests they are homicide victims, all having been murdered within the last two years," he paused again, slowly eyeing the reporters, "by the same hand."

The room went silent.

The mayor cleared his throat. "There is a serial killer active in the New Orleans area."

The crowd of reporters leaped out of their seats and shouted questions at the mayor, creating a chaotic atmosphere.

The mayor closed his eyes and raised his right hand.

The room slowly quieted.

"Sit down, please; there will not be a question-and-answer period until further notice." He paused as the reporters regained their seats.

"Oh my God!" Angie blurted out. "Is this what you've been doing, Edward?"

Dunham nodded as he stared at the TV screen.

"We're in the process of identifying the victims, but this may take some time. In the meantime, if anyone has knowledge of someone gone missing in the last two years, please contact your respective law enforcement office."

"Are you close to apprehending this serial killer?" a reporter belted out above the again-noisy room.

The mayor raised his hand again. "Sadly, three of New Orleans's finest lost their lives in an attempt to apprehend this monstrosity, but their sacrifice has not been for nothing. We are that much closer to discovering the identity of this killer, but we have much to do." He pointed to the others to his right and left. "State, parish, and city law enforcement officials are banding together and establishing a task force to deal with this serial killer. He pointed to his left. "The task force will be headed by Captain Deblanc, but she needs the public's help."

"Here it comes," Dunham warned.

"Apparently, the offender has been using some kind of large dog or wolf-dog hybrid to kill his victims. If anyone has any information they believe may assist the investigation, please contact us immediately. But *do not* attempt to approach a possible animal threat on your own. Just call in any tips you may have. That is all for now."

The crowd of reporters shouted questions after him, but they fell upon deaf ears as everyone on the stage followed the mayor out of view. The local news reporter faced the camera and reiterated what had just transpired.

Angie lowered the volume on the TV. "Unbelievable! This will definitely make national news."

"Were you there when the three police officers lost their lives, hon?" Maggie asked.

Dunham shook his head. "No. Through a lead, we discovered the offender's collection of decapitated heads in the Honey Island Swamp."

Angie cringed. "Oh, how disgusting!"

Dunham nodded. "So, they quickly set up a stakeout in hopes he would return. A SWAT team was dispatched to the scene first, while the detectives and I went back to HQ and formulated a long-term plan. We didn't expect him to show up so soon, but he surfaced in the late afternoon, which was yesterday."

Maggie put her hands to her mouth. "Oh my!"

Dunham glanced at Maggie and shook his head. "The offender was challenged but successfully escaped, as if he were prepared for such a scenario." He raised his hands. "He fought back ruthlessly, which ended the lives of three SWAT team members."

"Have you offered to help out on the case?" Maggie asked. "I hope so."

Dunham glanced at his watch. "Not officially, but I'm meeting up with the newly organized task force within the hour. Detectives Bakula and Oglesby should be picking me up anytime now. I'm sure they're going to ask me to formally join."

"Don't worry about your wifey, Edward," Angie interrupted as she grasped Maggie's hand. "She can be my roommate again."

The doorbell rang.

"That must be the detectives." Dunham gained his feet.

"No, finish your dinner," Angie ordered and left her seat. "I'll bring them in." She walked to the front door.

"I thought you were working on a big case with the Navy?" Maggie asked.

Dunham cleaned his plate then wiped his face. "Yes, but I believe I can handle both, especially since they're both out of Louisiana. Besides, there's not much more I can do with the Navy's cold case. We've hit a dead end."

Angie brought Bakula and Oglesby into the dining room.

Bakula nodded to Maggie then eyed Dunham. "Hi, Dr. Dunham, are you ready to go? The captain's waiting."

Dunham stood. "Yes." He glanced over at Angie and Maggie. "Ladies, meet Detectives Bakula and Oglesby."

Everyone greeted each other.

Dunham smiled at his hostess. "That was the best chicken I've had in years, Angie."

Bakula stared at the food in the pot on the dinner table. "Dr. Dunham, that's not chicken. Looks like you've been introduced to a Cajun delicacy—possum! I can recognize it anywhere."

Dunham cringed and glanced over at Maggie and Angie, both giggling.

"It was Maggie's idea!" Angie insisted.

"You never want to taste anything new, hon," Maggie said, beaming at him. "So, I wanted Angie to surprise you. It was great, wasn't it?"

Dunham grinned. "Actually, it was delicious—and save some for me." He turned to the detectives. "Ready to go?"

After Dunham said his goodbyes, he followed the detectives out the door.

As they entered the car, Bakula said to Dunham, "The results of the DNA samples collected off of Ol' Danny's brush are in."

"Great," Dunham replied as he put on his seatbelt, "now we just have to wait for the results of the victims."

They made their way to the conference room at the Criminal Investigation Division, which was teeming with law enforcement officers from a number of jurisdictions.

Captain Deblanc glanced up. "Ah, Dr. Dunham, I'm glad you could make it. Let me introduce you to everyone."

At the mention of Dunham's name, everyone abruptly stopped their individual conversations and stared at the new arrival.

Dunham noticed this, but he knew his now-famous reputation was actually an opportunity for this fledgling task force to develop confidence right from the outset.

Deblanc introduced Dunham to everyone, and after a few minutes, individual side conversations built up again.

"Dr. Dunham," the captain said, "I am aware you're a very busy man, but are you able to continue to assist us?"

Again, the room went silent, everyone waiting for his response.

Dunham was impressed that everyone had heard Deblanc's quiet request. "Yes, if you don't mind sharing my time with a few other cases."

Deblanc beamed, as everyone did. "We'll take what we can get, and hopefully we can nail this bastard quickly." She gazed around the room. "OK! I need everyone to take a seat."

Chairs along the long conference tables filled quickly.

Deblanc took the podium in the front of the room. "Thank you, everyone. I believe the key to our success is to maintain a constant flow of communication between our respective departments. When I get something, I'm passing it on." She glanced at Bakula and Oglesby. "Presently, we have an extensive crime scene investigation taking place in the Honey Island Swamp and another in downtown New Orleans at the location of an attack on a homeless person. We've also resumed an investigation in Foliage Park where the mutilation of Frankie Hambone occurred." She glanced over at Bakula with an inquisitive expression. "Any other place?"

Bakula stood up and faced the crowd. "Yes, we are now investigating a probable attack of a sex worker at Jackson Square."

Deblanc nodded. "That's right. Also, we're confident that once the victims are identified, this'll produce some leads."

"Speaking of leads," Bakula interrupted, "hopefully today's news conference will generate some as well."

Deblanc glanced over at Dunham. "Anything to add, Dr. Dunham?"

Dunham stood up. "Thank you, Captain. I spent some time with the investigators at Honey Island and am very impressed by their progress. If there's latent evidence, they'll find it. Even though our offender torched the shed, a significant amount was saved. The fact that he took the time to light up his hideout tells us he believed its contents might incriminate him, so we want to handle it accordingly."

A police officer came into the conference room and handed Deblanc a sheet of paper.

Dunham scanned the room. "Who will be returning to the Foliage Park crime scene?"

An Orleans Parish deputy sheriff raised his hand. "We will, sir."

"We discovered the car of the child molester, Frankie Hambone, in the parking lot for a group of businesses along Spanish Fort Boulevard, which butts up against the woods," Dunham said. "If it's true that our offender followed Hambone from work, chances are he parked his vehicle in the same parking lot. Check to see if that particular business has outdoor security cameras. We may get lucky."

The deputy sheriff nodded as he wrote the information in his notepad.

Dunham turned and faced Deblanc. "And one more thing—do you have a forensic artist who can reconstruct the faces of the most decomposed victims?"

"Sure do. We'll get right on it."

Dunham sat down. "All set, Captain."

"Excellent, Dr. Dunham, and thank you." She glanced around the room. "Anyone else?"

A deputy sheriff from St. Tammany Parish raised his hand and stood. "Yes, ma'am. Currently, we've begun to interview residents in and around Honey Island Swamp, but it's a monumental task. If anyone would like to assist, it certainly would be appreciated."

Deblanc nodded. "Of course. Come see me after, and I'll make sure you have as many officers as you believe you need. This truly is our main focus. Someone must have seen him in the last two years."

"Thank you."

Deblanc scanned the paper she had just been given and grinned. "Thanks to the press conference, leads are coming in. One looks promising. Apparently, three teenage boys were walking through the abandoned amusement park and heard the screams of a woman from inside an abandoned building, followed by screeching noises from what sounded like a large animal."

Dunham whispered to Bakula and Oglesby, "Rob mentioned screeching noises."

Bakula raised his hand. "Oges and I will take that one, Captain."

"Excellent." She addressed the group: "Keep the communication lines open. Last thing—the three law enforcement officers who lost their lives were highly trained SWAT team members, experts in close-quarter combat." She paused. "Don't underestimate this offender, and be on your guard. Dismissed."

chapter 29

Jared's Apartment

Knock, knock, knock.

Jared turned and stared at his apartment door, then tilted his head, confused. He glanced over at Rob and Sarah.

Both were sitting on the couch watching TV. Two open half-filled pizza boxes and empty glasses littered the coffee table before them.

"Were either of you expecting anyone?"

Rob and Sarah glanced at each other, shaking their heads.

Jared shrugged, got up, and opened the door.

Sebastian stood in the hallway, smiling. "Hi, Jared!"

"Yo, Sebastian! Come on in."

Sebastian entered the apartment and spotted Rob and Sarah. "Hi, guys! Did you watch the news conference? You were right, Rob," he said, eyeing the pizza. "Oh, don't mind if I do." Sebastian grabbed a slice and stuffed half of it into his mouth as he sat down.

Jared closed the door. "Sure did."

"We did see it," Sarah answered. "Amazing, huh?"

"Why didn't they give you credit, Rob?" Sebastian asked. "The bastards."

"Dr. Dunham insisted they keep my name out of it, as well as his own." Rob paused. "If the offender was watching, he may come after me—which actually happened last year in Boston."

"So, did they put you guys on the task force?" Sebastian asked.

"They did the opposite," Sarah said. "They were forced to stop our involvement because of the public attention it would receive. That was the first thing the superintendent of police made sure of."

"No worries," Rob added. "Dr. Dunham is helping out, and we have a direct line of communication with him. He prefers it that way."

"So, we're going to continue to investigate?" Sebastian asked, taking a smaller bite of pizza.

Jared glanced over at Rob and Sarah and grinned. "We certainly are, partner."

"We just don't know what we can do to help," Rob admitted.

Sebastian poured some Coke into Rob's glass, drank from it, then glanced over at Rob. "I'm in for some brainstorming. You figured this guy out once, Rob. You can do it again."

"Dr. Dunham is not going to let us get too involved," Sarah explained. "Last time Rob and I helped with a case, the killer almost did us in!"

"Besides," Jared said, "we're no longer in the know. We're now at a disadvantage."

Rob tapped his chin. "I did text Dr. Dunham, asking him to give us anything to investigate, but he hasn't replied yet. We may just have to wait."

Sebastian raised his finger in the air. "Ah, but we can go where authorities dare not tread!" He took another bite of pizza.

Jared, Rob, and Sarah gazed at each other, confused, then stared at Sebastian.

"We're listening," Jared offered.

Sebastian swallowed. "We investigate the possibility of this being the Rougarou."

Jared shook his head. "Sorry, Brother Sebastian, no can do. This is a mundane serial killer with a weird method of murdering his victims, i.e., with a trained killer mastiff or something."

"One second, Jared," Rob interrupted.

Sarah turned to Rob and smiled. "Uh-oh, this happened in Boston. Rob's onto something."

Rob shot a quick glance at Sarah, then back to Jared. "Sebastian might be onto something." He waved his hands. "I'm not talking about the cryptozoology stuff, but offender motive."

"As in, he *thinks* he's the Rougarou?" Jared asked.

"Maybe, or maybe he believes his killer dog is."

Sebastian shrugged his shoulders. "Well, I was hoping for a cryptozoology investigation, but I'll take this."

Sarah stood and paced. "Our offender is definitely not attempting to make the news for attention, and these ruthless murders mean he's satisfying a deep emotional need." She stopped and popped her head up. "If it *is* the Rougarou he's imitating, we need to know more about the folklore."

"There are actually a number of legends of the Rougarou," Sebastian stated matter-of-factly.

"Which one seems to fit best?" Jared asked.

Sebastian paused. "Well, it certainly doesn't conform to a creature punishing Catholics for violating Lent, and for that matter, *any* of the legends used to inspire fear and obedience we can ignore."

"Fear and obedience other than Catholics?" Sarah asked.

"A couple of the stories were clearly designed to persuade children to behave, but this guy is not trying to instill fear."

"That makes sense. Any others?" Rob asked.

Sebastian placed his thumb on his front teeth, staring down at the floor in thought. "A number of legends have the werewolflike creature swayed by the rise of the full moon, but that doesn't fit either. The Foliage Park attack and the Jackson Square attack were not during a full moon."

"How do you know that?" Jared asked.

Sebastian shrugged. "Well, I had to check, didn't I?" He raised his finger. "Now, there are a group of Rougarou legends stating the creature was a man who was cursed with lycanthropy—the usual werewolf story. The curse may have been transferred through the bite of another Rougarou, but that doesn't seem to fit either. This guy keeps on killing. Another has the curse for only a hundred and one days, but this guy's been active longer."

Now Rob began to pace. "As I recall, lycanthropy of legend has the curse being an actual animal transformation—shape-shifting—but lycanthropy of psychology is when someone merely takes on the characteristics of a wolf. The latter fits like a glove!"

"So, our killer believes he's a Rougarou," Jared said. "How interesting; the origin of this particular Cajun folklore may have begun as the later psychology theory, and through successive generations, ended up becoming the more colorful shape-shifting theory."

"I prefer a little flavor," Sebastian admitted. "Curses are so much a part of the human story; they must be true!"

"So, here we have a serial killer in Cajun country," Jared added, "actualizing Cajun folklore." He nodded. "This guy believes he's cursed for sure. Great job, y'all."

They gave each other high fives all around.

"How did the curse start?" Sarah asked. "The one he believes he was infected with?" She glanced at Sebastian. "Are there any legends that answer this?"

"Witchcraft," Sebastian answered then raised his hands. "Apparently, someone pissed off a witch."

"Witchcraft in New Orleans?" Sarah asked. "I thought it was Voodoo here, not Wicca."

"New Orleans has everything, Sarah," Jared answered, grinning, "but a Voodoo priestess can curse, too, and since Voodoo is more prevalent here than Wicca, I'll go with Voodoo."

"I'm on board with that," Sebastian agreed.

Jared nodded to Sebastian then faced Sarah. "Even though Voodoo's background hails from Africa, New Orleans has an excellent reputation of mixing culture and folklore."

"So, how can we translate this into discovering the identity of our serial killer?" Rob asked.

"Not a clue," Sebastian admitted.

Rob faced Jared. "Hey, remember when you and Dr. Taylor gave us a French Quarter tour and we passed the Voodoo store? How about we see what they have to say?"

"Oh, does that mean we have to force ourselves to go back to the French Quarter?" Sarah jested. "I'm in."

"Let's do it," Jared agreed.

chapter 30

Francois studied his well-worn map of the province under the lamplight, while sitting at a wooden table in his chambers. He looked up and stared at the evening sky though the open window, deep in thought. He studied his map again, which was dotted with the locations of the Beast's attacks.

An owl hooted, its sound emanating from the window.

"Is this your lair?" he asked himself, pointing at a particular valley on the map. He knew the locals were annoyed at him for spending so much time studying maps and not hunting the Beast, but he had a strong feeling success was just around the corner.

"You called for me, monsieur?" a man interrupted as he entered Antoine's room.

Antoine glanced over at his huntsman, Péilissier, and grinned. "Yes, come, I want to show you something."

Péilissier approached and stared at the map over Antoine's shoulder.

"I believe I may have found the Beast's lair." Antoine pointed at a location on the map. "Notice the recent pattern of attacks surrounding this valley."

Péilissier nodded. "Very convincing," he replied, studying it further. "Since your hounds have arrived and the weather is cooperating, we should act soon."

Antoine nodded. "Agreed, especially since the second set of tracks is likely a mate he has acquired, giving our hounds the scent of two targets."

Péilissier studied the second attack pattern farther south. "What do you make of these, monsieur? Strange."

Antoine had a strong suspicion there were two man-killers in the province, especially since the southern tracks did not have accompanying tracks of a she-wolf partner. The problem was, no one—from the king and his court down to the locals—wanted to hear this kind of disturbing news. All he needed to do was bring one trophy back to the king. He shook his head. "Our prey merely being ubiquitous, Péilissier, which is why we must surround him at his lair."

A huntsman burst into his room, stopped for a moment, and bent over, gasping for air.

Both Antoine and Péilissier turned and faced the huntsman.

"I apologize for the intrusion, monsieur," he gasped, then he took a deep breath, "but we've spotted the Beast and his mate on the grounds of the Royal Abbey of Les Chazes!"

Antoine whipped back to the map, nearly knocking over the lamp. He placed his finger on the abbey. "I am correct! It is his lair." He turned and said to the two huntsmen, "It's time to bring out fresh hounds. We leave tomorrow morning. Prepare tonight." He rushed out of the room, closely followed by his huntsmen.

Two days later, Antoine, Lafont, d'Archer, Count Morangiès, and a number of other local nobles huddled around a table outside on a hill to the north of the Royal Abbey of Les Chazes. They were underneath a large red canvas tent, staring at a local map. Upwards of fifty volunteers, huntsmen, and their hounds surrounded them, ready for the day's hunt.

Antoine glanced up at everyone. "I have just received word the Beast and his wolf pack are in the Pommier Woods just north of here. We will surround the woods with our sharpshooters in the back, one hundred paces from the tree line. Our houndsmen will move into the woods with their hounds and beat the bushes. When the Beast and his pack try to escape," he glanced around, "sharpshooters open fire." He pointed to the left. "I plan on positioning myself at the Bèal Ravine."

"Monsieur!" a man grasping a musket called out. "How do you recommend we load our muskets for such a monster?"

Antoine nodded. "Excellent question; this is a large animal, so I recommend loading five charges of powder, a ball, and if you have it, many pieces of shrapnel."

Morangiès grinned and leaned over to d'Archer. "Wolf shot."

Antoine turned. "That is correct, Count Morangiès." He scanned the crowd. "Let's be off! Houndsmen in front!"

Hours later, Antoine and his hunting entourage dispersed around Pommier Woods and the Bèal Ravine, surrounded by granite outcrops, which dominated the higher areas. In and around the woods grew thick underbrush.

A huntsman approached him.

"Are we ready, Rinchard?" Antoine asked.

Rinchard nodded. "We are, Captain."

"Excellent," Antoine replied, "Sound the alarm for the houndsmen to advance."

Rinchard nodded again then aimed his musket high and pulled the trigger.

Antoine could hear replying musket shots to his left and his right, then he heard the barking of the hounds. He turned and faced the nobles. "Be at your ready, gentlemen."

Lafont, d'Archer, and Count Morangiès stood a safe distance back, but they all carried their own muskets. "I have a good feeling about today's hunt."

D'Archer grinned. "Hopefully the outcome is positive."

Antoine and the nobles maintained their positions as the hunt continued. They heard hounds from all directions.

After ten minutes, Antoine noticed the barking and howling of the hounds changed pitch and intensity. He glanced to his left and right at the other huntsmen. "If something comes out of the woods toward us, I will take the first shot—but if I miss, open fire."

The huntsmen positioned themselves for a steady shot.

Morangiès faced d'Archer. "The hounds seem to be drawing closer, as if they're chasing something toward us."

Seconds later, a massive wolf burst from the woods and bolted straight at Antoine. Its eyes were fixed on him and its jaws wide open, revealing huge teeth.

Antoine calmly aimed his musket at the large advancing creature and fired.

Boom!

The kick was so great that it knocked him back, and he nearly fell to the ground. Even so, he never took his eyes off the wolf.

The shot penetrated the creature's right eye, and it collapsed.

"Perfect shot, monsieur!" Rinchard shouted.

Surprisingly, the massive wolf got back to its feet and made a dash toward some massive rocks. Rinchard took aim and shot. The wolf dropped again, now completely motionless.

"Amazing," Lafont commented.

Everyone rushed up to the sprawled animal. As they reached it, they just stared at the massive wolf.

"My God, what a beast!" d'Archer blurted out.

"Look at its enormous chest," Rinchard observed, "and its length. This animal is twice as large as a normal-sized wolf from this area!"

"I've been hunting wolves for nearly fifty years," Antoine informed them, shaking his head, "and I've never seen its equal." He bent over the massive wolf and pointed to a relatively fresh scar on its chest. "The brave young woman, Marie-Jeanne Valet, told us her pike penetrated the Beast in this very spot."

Count Morangiès joined him and touched the partially healed wound. "It is a fresh scar, maybe a month old." He stood up, eyed everyone, then faced Antoine. "Monsieur Antoine, it seems you have killed the Beast!"

The crowd of hunters cheered and applauded.

"I want to be sure it's the Beast before I have it stuffed and sent to His Majesty. We will need to have young Valet, her sister, and other witnesses inspect the carcass for confirmation. We'll also need to open it up and identify the contents, which may contain human remains."

"We shall name the Beast 'the Wolf of Chazes' in honor of this abbey!" d'Archer proclaimed.

Three huntsmen rode up to Antoine then dismounted.

"Monsieur," the lead huntsman began, "we chased the she-wolf and saw two massive whelps following her. They are even larger than the she-wolf." He pointed behind him. "They escaped, but we may have hit one of the whelps."

Antoine frowned and shook his head. "We must find them."

"When do you plan on bringing the Beast to His Majesty?" Lafont asked Antoine.

"He and the court will demand to see it immediately," Antoine said, "so I will have my son accompany the stuffed carcass. My job is not done here. Its mate and the whelps must be destroyed, or we will see more attacks in the future."

* * *

Palace of Versailles, Versailles, France,
Three weeks later

Robert François Antoine de Beauterne, son of Antoine, stood before His Majesty and the entire royal court of ministers and parliament. Positioned next to him was the embalmed carcass of the Beast, with a large piece of canvas draped over it. Behind him stood a packed room of nobles and other onlookers, clearly excited to see his prize.

King Louis XV raised his hand to the crowd, and they went silent. He eyed Robert Francois. "We have been briefed on your father's exploits and his successes in Gévaudan."

Robert Francois gave a deep bow. "Thank you, Your Excellency, and priority was for your immediate viewing, thus, he directed me to escort your prize here, as he stayed and finished his royal assignment."

The king beamed.

Robert Francois turned and faced the stuffed creature, gripped the canvas, then faced the king. "Your Excellency, I give you the Wolf of Chazes!" He ripped off the drape and revealed the massive wolf posed in an aggressive stance with its huge teeth exposed.

The crowd broke their silence, awestruck by the absolutely vicious-looking, monstrous creature.

The king stared at the monster for another moment then eyed the crowd and grinned. He glanced over at a beaming Saint-Florentin.

As the king approached Robert Antoine and the Beast, Saint-Florentin turned to L'Averdy and whispered, "All of France will know of this. Their concerned king has come through on their behalf."

L'Averdy glanced back with a look of concern. "Let's hope that this is indeed the Beast, and the killings stop."

"It is the Beast," Saint-Florentin exclaimed. "Look at the size and ferocity of this monster." He paused. "Besides, if the killings do continue, we control the newspapers. We shall ensure the Beast is dead in the eyes of all of France."

* * *

Gévaudan Province, France,
Near la Besseyre Saint Mary,
December 1765

Pierre swatted one of his lambs back onto the snow-covered dirt road with the end of his pike as he and Jean-Claude walked the small herd through the forested area.

Both sides of the valley had steep slopes, and a few rocky outcrops could be seen within the pines. It was late morning, and snow fell lightly on the path.

Jean-Claude glanced back at Pierre. "I hear they finally let the innkeeper and his sons out of jail."

Pierre swatted the same lamb trying to leave the trail, then said, "The man did aim his musket at a royal officer of the hunt. Knowing the innkeeper and his temper, I would've shot him too."

"Ahhh," Jean-Claude blurted out. "Jean Chastèl is as good a hunter as any of those nobles. They were afraid he was going to kill the Beast and take the glory away from them. That is . . . if the creature they stuffed and presented to the king is to be believed."

"It's been two months since they killed the Wolf of Chazes," Pierre contested, "and no more attacks." He swatted the front sheep to pick up speed.

"Then why are we still carrying these weapons, Pierre?"

"Don't," Pierre challenged. "The Beast wasn't the only wolf ever to have killed in these mountains—man or beast." He paused. "Besides, they paid for them, why not use them?"

"You know they're going to order us to disarm soon."

They continued through the forest path for another twenty minutes, conversing all the way.

Jean-Claude peered forward and spotted a thin wisp of smoke rising above the trees ahead. "We're close to the village."

At that moment, the sheep's neck bells rang louder and more frequently.

Pierre noticed all the sheep in the herd behaving erratically, clearly agitated. "Possible predator! Be on your guard!"

Jean-Claude scanned the hillside, grasping his staff tighter. He turned back. "Watch behind you, Pierre!"

Pierre turned and saw nothing behind them. As he turned back, he spotted a large wolflike creature streaking toward Jean-Claude from the right. It leaped at him with its massive jaws open. "It's on you!" he screamed.

Jean-Claude quickly turned, just in time to see a massive set of teeth a foot away, aiming for the back of his neck. He jerked his head away, which caused the creature to miss its target, but it still managed to knock him over with its momentum. Jean-Claude rolled on the ground in the snow, still clutching his pike.

The nimble creature landed on all fours and quickly positioned itself over Jean-Claude with its full attention on his vulnerable neck.

Jean-Claude's eyes were glazed over, stunned by the force of the attack.

Just as it was about to clamp down on its quarry, the bayonet on Pierre's well-thrown staff penetrated the side of the creature. It howled in pain and leaped off its prey, Pierre's staff clattering to the ground behind it. The animal stopped at the edge of the path and turned back around.

Pierre rushed to Jean-Claude's side, retrieved his staff, and squared off with the creature.

It glared at Pierre, gnashing its teeth but maintaining its distance as it slowly circled them.

Jean-Claude finally gained his feet, grabbed his staff, and aimed it at the creature.

The sheep had bolted in all directions, some seeking shelter in the relative safety of the trees.

The creature rushed at the herders, but they both jabbed their staffs at it, and it backed away.

The animal growled and continued to circle the two, seemingly searching for a crack in their defense.

Pierre could see blood flowing down the creature's side where his bayonet made contact.

They jabbed at the creature and screamed, but it still challenged them.

As they fought it off, Pierre couldn't help but notice that the creature looked slightly different than a normal wolf. Its head and chest were wide with small ears, and its reddish fur was quite long, its tail overly long. Strangely, its eyes seemed to sparkle—even glow—red, as if it were a hellhound.

Four men from the village heard the commotion and rushed toward them. As they ran over the hill, they spotted the battle at the edge of the road.

"Look! The Beast!" one of them yelled.

They rushed to assist Pierre and Jean-Claude, screaming and shouting as they ran.

The creature spotted the four men approaching, hesitated, then streaked up the steep slope and out of sight.

* * *

Three Months Later

D'Archer was finishing his meal when Lafont walked into the dining room. "Marquis, there will be no more assistance from Versailles."

D'Archer dropped his fork back on his plate and stared at Lafont. "What do you mean no more assistance? The Beast continues to terrorize the countryside!"

Lafont shook his head. "If you recall, last fall, the king publicly declared the Beast dead—shot and killed by his royal huntsman. It would be an embarrassment to the crown if he admitted he was wrong, and that's exactly what additional assistance says."

"Then we'll go to the governor."

Lafont frowned and again shook his head. "And by this action go against Versailles? The governor would never side against the king."

D'Archer sat back in his seat and stared at the ceiling. "Then we have no other alternative but to coordinate and fund our own hunts." He glared at Lafont. "We will systematically eliminate all wolves from the province."

"I couldn't agree more, Marquis."

chapter 31

La Bête

Detectives Bakula and Oglesby walked through the abandoned theme park with the teenage eyewitness. The detectives couldn't help but stare at the massive rollercoasters and other rides, all abandoned because of the devastation brought on by Hurricane Katrina in 2005.

"I wonder why this place is still abandoned," Bakula said.

"Tax reasons, I hear," Oglesby answered. "Lots of people want their cut before they can sell."

"All while New Orleans citizens suffer not having a cool amusement park like Six Flags," Bakula replied then pointed at some of the graffiti. He glared at the teenage boy. "You weren't defacing private property in here, were you, Jeffrey?"

Jeffrey's eyes darted back and forth. "No, no, sir . . . we were just checking the place out."

Bakula rolled his eyes, fully recognizing Jeffrey's classic deceptive body language.

"Well, don't come back here, young man," Oglesby ordered. "Read the 'No Trespassing' signs."

"Yes, sir." Jeffrey pointed at a small building next to a large roller coaster. "It was in there. We were walking by, and we heard a lady screaming," Jeffrey continued as they approached the building, "and then we heard some kind of animal growling and screeching inside. It sounded huge, if that makes sense."

Bakula nodded. "Stay out here, Jeffrey, and don't touch anything." He put on a pair of latex gloves then tried the handle on the door.

To his surprise, it opened.

Oglesby pointed to a latch on the door. "These wear marks are fresh. Someone had a padlock on this door."

Bakula and Oglesby entered the room, stopping immediately. The smell was overwhelming. Blood covered the floor and bed, and blood spatter marks decorated the walls.

Bakula glanced over at Oglesby. "A scene of torture and mutilation, Oges. Call in the crime scene investigators."

Oglesby touched a latch on the inside of the door. "Looks like our perp locked his victims from the inside."

Bakula pointed at the bloodstained floor. "I see a few footprints—high heels, I think—and a set of large dog tracks. Clearly our man." He stared. "I don't see any large human footprints though."

Oglesby pointed to the shelf opposite the bed. "Something's written on it. It's scratched into the wood and looks fresh."

They headed for the mirror, carefully walking around bloodstains on the floor.

Bakula stared at the writing and pronounced, "La Beet?"

"No, it looks French. *La Bête?*"

"What's it mean?" Bakula asked.

Oglesby pulled out his iPhone. "I'll Google it."

Bakula glanced into the back room. "French sounds right since our perp might very well be a French-speaking Cajun swamp man. Maybe he did write this . . . or the victim wrote it as a warning." He paused. "I just don't think the victim would have had the time to write it once our perp sent the animal in to kill her."

"La Bête means 'The Beast.'" He glanced around at the bloodied room. "Assuming our perp wrote it," he aimed his iPhone at the writing and took a photo, "I bet this is our man."

"So, he calls his man-killing mutt La Bête—or the victim did." Bakula pointed to the door. "Let's get outta here before we step on a key piece of evidence. I want to check the surroundings anyway." As they exited the building and closed the door behind them, Oglesby called it into HQ and Bakula grabbed Jeffrey by the elbow and escorted him to the park's exit. "Thank you, Jeffrey, that's all we need for now. You did a great job." He pointed to a blue house in the distance on the other side of the eight-foot gated wire fence. "That's your house, right?"

Jeffrey nodded.

"Was I right?" Jeffrey asked. "Was it the serial killer?"

"We believe so, but don't come in here again," he pointed his finger in Jeffrey's face, "and definitely don't bring your friends. This place will soon be crawling police, and we don't want any contamination of the crime scene."

"Yes, sir," Jeffrey replied then jogged away.

Bakula glanced to the right and spotted a path in the weeds leading directly to the large perimeter fence.

"They're on their way," Oglesby stated as he pocketed his phone. "Do you think this is the path he used? Makes sense since it's a direct shot on and off the property."

"That's what I was thinking, Oges."

The two walked parallel to the path toward the fence, inspecting every inch of the path.

Oglesby pointed ahead. "Check it out. See the opening cut into the fence?"

On the other side of the fence, blocking the opening from view, was a large wooden crate leaning over the opening.

Bakula grabbed the cut wire and opened the crack wide enough for Oglesby to walk through. He followed him out.

Before them was the side of a garage.

"Looks like our serial killer parked his vehicle between the fence and the garage." Bakula glanced around the area. "The garage would certainly hide a parked vehicle."

Oglesby pointed down at the ground. "Tire tracks." He pulled out his phone and took a photo of the tracks.

Bakula stared down the road into the residential area. "Good catch." He paused. "What do you think the chance is that one of these neighbors spotted our man?"

Oglesby shrugged. "Young Jeffrey said the screams were during the day."

Bakula pulled out his phone. "Time to call Dr. Dunham."

chapter 32

Retaliation,
Early to Rise Donut Shop, New Orleans

NOPD Officer Andy Collette sipped on his coffee in the booth at the donut shop. He eyed the two other police officers sitting in another booth, also taking their break. "How did that bastard get approval to attend the conference and I didn't?" Andy muttered, shooting another glare at the officer.

Collette's partner, Officer Cliff Belfort, sitting across from him, continued to work on his crossword puzzle. "Get over it, Andy, it's not like you deserve to go to the conference," he glanced up and eyed Collette, "cuz you don't." He went back to his crossword puzzle. "You're just pissed he did a better job sucking up to the boss."

Collette bit into his donut, frowning. "Well, why would you suck up to that asshole anyway?"

Belfort snickered, still staring at his crossword puzzle. "To get permission to go on choice conferences like this one?"

Collette peripherally noticed the door open, but no one entered, so he looked back at his partner.

"Well, if he thinks I'm gonna help his ass out on anything, he's got another thing coming."

"He's got another *think* coming; not another *thing* coming," Belfort corrected then glanced at his watch. "In ten minutes, we need to call in, partner."

Collette raised his eyebrows and tilted his head, now curious as to why the door was cracked open. He then noticed a large, hairy snout peeking through the opening; something large was wedging itself into the crack of the door.

A massive dog-like animal nosed its way through the door and stopped just inside the shop.

Collette sat up. "What?"

Belfort glanced over at the door, curious to see why Collette was acting so strangely. He stared in shock at the same massive, dark-haired animal.

The animal glared at both Belfort and Collette and began to stalk them, growling and gnashing its teeth as it moved.

"Shit!" He and Collette simultaneously lunged out of the booth, reaching frantically for their guns.

Collette pulled out his firearm and lifted it with his finger on the trigger.

The animal leaped on Collette before he could get a shot off. It sank its teeth into his neck, snapped it, then immediately released him.

Collette's body collapsed to the floor.

The animal's eyes were now fixed upon Belfort.

The two other police officers frantically left their seats, reaching for their handguns.

Patrons and workers screamed as they rushed away from the horrid scene.

Belfort aimed his handgun at the animal and fired.

The creature attacked Belfort as though his shot had missed. It bit into the officer's neck and immediately snapped it. In an instant, it released Belfort's lifeless body as it had done with Collette's, then rushed the two other officers.

The officers opened fire on the animal.

The animal attacked the closest officer first, knocking him into the second as it latched onto the man's throat.

The second officer fell to the ground from the impact but held onto his sidearm. As he aimed his handgun at the animal, he saw it snap his partner's neck. He took aim and shot.

The animal rushed the officer and bit into his shooting hand.

"Ahhhhhh!" he screamed.

The massive animal released his arm, opting for his throat.

Four police officers lay dead on the floor.

Patrons and workers, still screaming, hid behind two large tables, blocked from leaving the coffee shop by a man-killing creature in front of the only available exit.

The creature glared at the crowd, blood trickling from its chest from well-placed shots.

Everyone huddled together even closer.

The massive animal slowly approached the frightened crowd, its head lowered, gnashing its teeth, as if it were about to attack. It paused for a moment, then it turned and sped out of the coffee shop.

Thirty minutes later, Captain Deblanc pulled up to the donut shop with Dr. Dunham in the passenger seat. Over a dozen police cars now surrounded the shop, their lights flashing. Four emergency vehicles were also parked out front.

"Oh my God!" Deblanc commented. "Looks like a warzone."

Dunham pointed into the shop. "I see Detectives Bakula and Oglesby."

Inside, Dunham counted four bodies lying on the floor with sheets covering them from head to toe; blood blanketed the floor. Tables and chairs were strewn about. "It is a war zone, Captain."

Bakula and Oglesby hurried toward them.

"Captain, Dr. Dunham," Bakula pointed to a group of distraught patrons, "the eyewitnesses reported a large dog-like animal—maybe three hundred pounds—coming into the shop and," he pointed at the two bodies closest to the door, "attacking these two police officers, Andy Collette and Cliff Belfort."

Deblanc frowned and shook her head.

Bakula pointed to two other bodies, "And then attacking the second two officers, George Paddock and Sam Delouise."

Oglesby stared at the bodies. "All good cops. Paddock was a buddy of mine."

Bakula faced Deblanc. "Their chain of command has been notified. Their sergeant is on her way and wants to handle contacting their next of kin."

"As it should be," Deblanc responded.

Oglesby pointed to a man who was giving a statement to a police officer. "That eyewitness said the animal seemed to target the police officers and even ignored the patrons."

"Sounds like they got lucky," Deblanc commented.

"The worker behind the counter recalls someone jamming the door open just before the attacks but not coming inside," Bakula explained. "She's convinced the hands she saw were from a Caucasian male. Seconds later, the animal barged in."

"This bastard is getting us back for discovering him and confiscating his collection," Oglesby interrupted.

The captain turned to Dunham. "Would someone like this be that brazen?"

"I believe so," Dunham answered, "and I also believe he's giving us the message that we're going to have our hands full apprehending him." He scanned the carnage in the room. "He's killed seven armed professionals—these four in a populated section of the city. He's ready for a fight."

"And a fight he'll get," Oglesby growled.

Dunham shook his head. "The control he has over this creature is remarkable . . . to attack police officers and ignore the others."

"This guy is controlling an animal with amazing agility and ferocity." Deblanc took a deep breath. "We are in for a fight."

"He has inadvertently revealed his intentions, though, which may be to our advantage," Dunham commented.

"What's that?" Bakula asked.

"He's not leaving town."

Deblanc glanced over at Bakula and Oglesby. "Just got word; our man did, indeed, park his van next to Frankie Hambone's car at the edge of Foliage Park. The sheriff's department found a security camera pointed at the parking lot."

"Finally, some good news," Oglesby replied.

"All we can tell so far from the grainy black-and-white video image is that it's a light-colored Chevy van, and our killer is Caucasian."

"At least we can match it up to the type of tires we discovered at the amusement park," Bakula added.

"Excellent," Dunham responded.

chapter 33

Marie Bouttes's Voodoo Shop,
French Quarter, New Orleans, Louisiana

Rob, Sarah, Jared, and Sebastian strolled down Bourbon Street, slipping through the crowd of tourists.

"I think we're close, aren't we, Jared?" Rob asked.

Jared nodded and pointed. "There it is: Marie Bouttes's Voodoo Shop."

They stopped in front of the shop, taking in all of the tourist souvenirs and signs. One sign stated, 'Spiritual Readings,' and another advertised 'Talismans and Charms for Protection and Strength, Love and Passion, Money and Success, and Good Luck and Fortune.' Sarah pointed to the second sign. "Hey, Rob, look! Love and passion." She squeezed his hand, and Rob blushed.

"Aww, how lovey-dovey," Sebastian commented.

"Time to go in," Rob replied, smiling at Sarah but quickly changing the subject. He opened the door and held it for the others.

The small room was filled with an assortment of T-shirts, hoodies, shorts, ball caps, and beanies, all having some reference to Voodoo emblazoned on them. To the right were tribal masks and statues.

Sarah made her way to the other wall. "Oh, this is what I was looking for—Voodoo dolls."

"Now, remember," Jared commented, "poking needles in Voodoo dolls to cause pain and injury is a Hollywood myth."

"You are well informed, sir," a Black lady six feet away interrupted.

Everyone turned around and faced her. She appeared to be somewhere in her thirties, her hair was tied back, and she was wearing a traditional Creole dress.

"Voodoo dolls are created to bring health and happiness," the lady added.

"Hello," Rob began, "are you Marie Bouttes?"

"Marie is my mother," she said and bowed her head slightly. "My name is Annette Bouttes." Just then, a young girl peeked at them from the back of the store. Annette followed their eyes and responded, "That's my daughter, Nina." Annette glanced back at everyone. "Do you have any questions? Are you looking for something in particular?"

"Besides a souvenir Voodoo doll for my girlfriend, we actually came here for answers to some questions."

Annette tilted her head toward Rob. "Of course I'll answer your questions, but before I do, do you mind if I hold your hand?"

Rob glanced around nervously. "Sure," he answered apprehensively, "I guess."

She slowly approached Rob, took his hand gently, and closed her eyes. She opened them and gazed at Sarah and Rob. "Young man, I see exceptional good in you." She smiled. "You have a special gift."

"He certainly is gifted in criminal investigation," Jared interrupted.

Annette glanced over at Jared. "Because he has a gift from the spirits to sense evil." She turned back to Rob as she released his hand. "How may I help you?"

Rob glanced over at Sebastian. "Well, my question is kind of strange, but," he paused, "we are working on an investigation and," he paused again, cleared his throat, then took his eyes from Annette's. "Have you ever heard of the curse of the Rougarou?"

"Or who caused the curse in the first place?" Sebastian added.

Annette shot a glance at Sebastian, losing her smile. She faced Rob again. "Why are you here?" She grabbed Rob's hand again and stared into his eyes. "You are searching for the serial killer, aren't you?" She pushed his hand away.

Rob shook his head. "How did you . . .?" He eyed the others.

"Wait here," Annette ordered. She turned away and walked behind the counter, then into a back room.

They heard her speaking with another woman; their discussion quickly turned into a hushed argument.

"What is going on?" Sarah asked. "How did she know we were investigating the serial killer?"

"How about we ask her when she gets back," Sebastian said.

Rob nodded. "I'll do it."

Annette returned, as did her kind demeanor. "I am allowed to answer one of your questions, but only one." She lost her smile again. "You are endangering all of us."

"How are we endangering you?" Rob asked.

"Wrong question," Annette replied then handed Rob a sheet of paper with an address. "At this address you will find the killer, or at least he worked there last week."

Rob's jaw dropped, stunned by her response. He glanced at everyone again. "You know who the serial killer is?"

She closed her eyes as she raised her hands and shook her head, then she glanced over her shoulder at the back room. "We do not know, but no more questions." She held her arms out and shooed everyone toward the door and didn't pause until she had the four of them on the sidewalk. She faced Rob and whispered, "My mother sensed the evil in this man when she was there."

Jared glanced over at Sarah and rolled his eyes.

"She does not know his name," Annette said to Rob, then she pointed at his chest, "but you will be able to sense him." She pointed her finger in his face. "I warn you—he will sense you in return, because of your gift. If he realizes you recognize him, he will kill you and anyone with you."

Rob was generally skeptical about such a supernatural answer, but Annette had impressed him. "How will I make him believe I don't recognize him?"

Annette turned to the large window of her shop then turned back to Rob and stared into his eyes. "I must go. Do not make eye contact with the evil; just ignore him." She turned and rushed back inside.

"What the hell was that about?" Jared blurted out. "You don't believe this BS, do you?"

"Absolutely," Sebastian blurted out. "There is no other plausible explanation for how Annette knew we were investigating the serial killer case just by Rougarou questions and by holding Rob's hand."

"Yeah, that was weird . . . but believing the lady's mom sensed the killer?" Jared shook his head. "That's going too far."

"Rob having a gift certainly would explain why he's been instrumental in capturing the most elusive serial killers of our time," Sarah commented. "Who knows, maybe it's not really a supernatural thing but a gift of heightened awareness Rob and these Voodoo ladies have."

"Rumor has it, the Watchmaker has this gift," Sebastian commented.

"OK, for now, I'll accept the hypersensitivity theory. Now what?" Rob asked, staring at the address on the sheet of paper. "I say we check it out."

Sarah peeked at the address on the paper and typed in her iPhone. "Here it is. It's JR's Quality Auto, a mechanic."

Rob glanced up at Jared. "So, we'll bring your car in, tell them it's making a weird sound or something, and set up a time for them to fix it." Rob said. "The rest of us will walk around and take some pictures, like tourists, but we'll try to sneak pics of all the workers."

"OK, OK," Jared replied. "But if you 'sense' this guy, I'm gonna crap my pants!"

"I'm bringing silver this time," Sebastian replied, "and a diaper for Jared."

chapter 34

Captain Deblanc stood before the podium in the conference room. She placed paperwork in front of her, then stared at the large crowd of task force members. "OK, let's begin. As you are aware, our offender ruthlessly attacked and murdered four police officers while on their break at a coffee shop."

"Now it's personal!" yelled a member from the middle of the room.

Many in the crowd nodded their heads.

Deblanc paused. "This attack is clearly retaliation for our challenge of him in the swamp. He seems to be sending the message—game on."

Oglesby glanced over at Bakula and Dunham and shook his head in disgust.

A sheriff raised his hand. "Captain, will you inform us of the funeral arrangements?"

"Of course." She scanned the crowd. "Now, forensic results have come in, and I'd like to discuss their significance then plan our next steps." She nodded to a forensic specialist sitting in the front row.

The specialist stood, approached the podium, and faced the crowd. "We'll start with the DNA results tested on the victims' skulls. As we suspected, we haven't found matches on too many of them since they'd likely been homeless for quite some time. We did get a DNA match of a female. Her elderly parents told us they lost touch with their daughter around ten years ago. They said she was a lifelong drug addict and preferred a life as a sex worker." He glanced over at Bakula and Oglesby. "We also found a match with a male, nicknamed Ol' Danny, although his true identity still eludes us."

"Any possible DNA samples of our offender?" a task force member asked.

The specialist shook his head. "No, nothing; we even searched for DNA samples on all of the artifacts collected from the shed, but nothing."

"On the table in front of you," Deblanc began, "is a list and photographs of everything we collected in the shed. Most things are scarred or torched, but it's still something. So far, nothing has given us a lead. Be my guest at finding anything."

Oglesby stared at all of the thick chains, clamps, and braces. "Looks like this guy really wanted this animal chained up."

"Detective Oglesby," Deblanc began, "do you have any update on the abandoned amusement park crime scene?"

Oglesby stood up. "Yes, ma'am. As everyone knows, our offender trapped a victim in an abandoned building, and the woman was mutilated. What we'd like to keep out of the papers is the discovery of a fresh set of scratch marks on a wooden dresser, which spelled out 'La Bête'. This is French for 'The Beast,' a clear reference to our offender's prized canine killer." A couple of task force members mumbled to each other.

"We've also identified the tire tracks as those coming from a common set of Michelin tires." He nodded at Deblanc and sat down. "That is all."

Deblanc thanked him, then she grabbed the video projector remote and pushed a button. She pointed at the screen behind her. "Now, I'd like everyone to see the security video showing the entrance to the woods at Foliage Park." She gestured at two deputy sheriffs. "Great find, gentlemen. Tell us what you have."

One of the deputy sheriffs stood and crossed the room as the video started up. Onscreen, a car pulled into the lot and parked near the woods. "We edited the video to first show the Foliage Park victim exit his vehicle and enter the woods."

A full-size van came into view and backed up intro another parking spot butting up to the woods.

"Within two minutes, our offender backed his Chevy van up to the tree line. In a second, you'll see him exit, walk to the back of his van, and open it up."

Just as the deputy sheriff stated, the man in the video left the van and opened the back.

"He's difficult to make out, but he's a relatively thin male, Caucasian, probably wearing a T-shirt and jeans."

"Do we see the animal?" a task force member asked.

The deputy sheriff shook his head. "No, the van seems to be in the way, but we're convinced this is the moment he let it out into the woods."

"It's too bad the video's so grainy," another task force member commented. "That license plate is straight on to the camera."

Deblanc glanced over at Dunham. "We've actually sent the original to the FBI lab to see if they can clean it up enough to make out the face and the license plate number."

Bakula pointed at the screen. "At least we can target light-colored, or possibly white, Chevy vans with Michelin tires."

Deblanc nodded. "Let's allocate our resources and investigate all light-colored Chevy vans. Stop them, and if they have Michelin tires, you have probable cause to search. We might get lucky."

The man came back into view from the woods, rushing around the van.

"We cut to when we see our offender coming back to his van, which is about a half hour later." The sheriff pointed at the screen. "Here, he closes the back of the van, jumps into the driver's seat, and departs."

"Anything to add, Dr. Dunham?" Deblanc asked.

"Not at the moment, thanks."

She scanned the room. "Anyone else?" After a short pause, she nodded. "OK, let's get back to work."

Everyone began to leave the room, and Bakula and Oglesby approached Dunham.

Bakula shook his head. "It feels like he's two steps ahead of us."

Dunham nodded. "This is definitely the feeling in every task force I've been involved with. We just need to be patient. Our video enhancement programs were designed by NASA. I'm confident we'll get a license number—or at least a partial number."

"And there can't be that many light-colored Chevy vans with Michelin tires running around New Orleans, can there?" Oglesby surmised.

chapter 35

Rob's Sixth Sense

Jared pulled his car into the side parking lot of JR's Quality Auto and parked it. He turned and faced everyone. "OK, I'll tell them I'm looking to change auto mechanics and was recommended to come here."

"Don't forget to tell them it seems to be making a funny sound," Rob reminded.

"Yeah, yeah, I got it."

Sebastian patted his pocket. "And I've got my silver ready to go."

"You can hold onto my arm again, Sebastian, if you need to," Sarah jested.

"Let's do it," Rob said, "and don't forget to take photos."

They all left the car and followed Jared through the front door then approached the man at the counter.

He was typing something into the computer and had yet to acknowledge them.

Jared noticed that his name tag: Jeb.

Jeb glanced up and smiled. "Hi, may I help you?"

"Yes," Jared began, "umm . . ." he glanced over at Rob, who nodded to him. "Yes, my car seems to be making a funny sound, and, umm . . . I'm not satisfied with the auto mechanic I've been using so I wanted to see about y'all."

Rob, Sarah, and Sebastian started walking around, as if browsing. Sarah stopped adjacent from the counter and turned to take a selfie, capturing Jeb's face in the background. Sebastian took his cue from her and started making goofy faces into his phone screen, angling all the while to include the employees passing by behind him.

Rob noticed that the large double doors leading into the auto garage were wide open, so he casually approached. He peeked into the garage and spotted at least ten people working on four or five cars. He pulled out his iPhone and surreptitiously snapped a few photos.

Suddenly, a man walked up from the right side, almost bumping into him. "Oh, hi, how y'all doin'," the man said in a loud, pleasant tone.

"Er, hi." Rob said, flustered. He noticed his nametag. "My roommate is over there being helped already. I'm just waiting for him. You must be the owner?"

"That's right!" JR replied, grinning. "We'll take care of your roommate." He pointed to the man behind the counter. "You're in good hands with Jeb."

Rob pointed into the garage. "I was just snooping to get a peek at your operation. Very impressive."

"Thank you!" JR answered. "Snoop all you want." He pointed to a yellow line about ten feet ahead. "Just don't go beyond that line. My insurance company would have my ass."

Rob chuckled. "Thank you." He halted behind the yellow line as JR rushed away. Rob stared intently at each employee, but he felt nothing.

A mechanic walked by and waved to him.

He waved back then frowned. "What am I thinking?" Rob whispered, slightly embarrassed. Had he taken the Voodoo lady's comments too seriously? He walked back to the front room and joined Jared.

"All set?" Jared asked.

Rob rolled his eyes. "Yeah, let's go."

Jared slapped the counter. "Well, thanks for the information, Jeb. I'll come back tomorrow if I choose this place." He grinned. "Take care." He, Sarah, and Sebastian followed Rob out the front door.

Jeb, caught off guard, stared at the four leaving so quickly. "Wha? I didn't even look under the hood yet."

Rob glanced back as they walked to their car. "I didn't get any specific feeling, and I stared at everyone, but I did take a bunch of photos."

They arrived at Jared's car but stayed outside, still talking.

"You didn't really expect to feel something, did you, Rob?" Jared asked.

Rob shrugged, and they all made to get into the car just as a white Chevy van entered the driveway and parked two spots away from them. A tall, thin man exited and began to inspect the inside of the wheel well of his van, as if something were wrong. He sat on the ground and stuck his head deeper into the wheel well.

At that moment, Rob felt a rush of emotions go through him, and the hair stood up on his neck.

Sarah glanced over at Sebastian. "I think we all took a lot of photos, so we could . . ."

Rob turned slowly, as if following a compass, and he felt the emotions were most intense in the direction of the man working on his van. *It's him*, he thought to himself. He grabbed his iPhone and tried to sneak a photo of him, but his hands were shaking too much.

Sarah picked up on Rob's unusual behavior.

Before she could ask what was wrong, Rob put his index finger up to his lips.

She closed her mouth and nodded to Rob.

"Hey, babe, step over here and let me get your picture next to the auto mechanic sign. Your friend JR from back home will love it. Say cheese!" Sarah said on the fly as she subtly aimed her phone's camera just past Rob.

Rob stepped to his left toward the sign and sneaked a glance at the man; his head was still jammed inside the wheel well. He looked to Jared and Sebastian and mouthed, "It's him; let's go, now!"

Jared and Sebastian both peeked at the man then nodded.

The man jerked his body out of the wheel well and turned and stared right at the young man's back. Anger filled his veins, and his stare turned into a glare.

Rob could feel the man focusing his attention on him, but he did exactly what the Voodoo lady had instructed and ignored him. "Well, let's go, we have a plane to catch!" he said loudly.

They hopped into Jared's car, purposely avoiding any eye contact with the man.

Jared started the car, backed up, and drove off. His eyes were locked on the rearview mirror as the man walked into the middle of the parking lot, glaring at them. "What the hell was that?"

Sebastian eyed Rob, who was shaking and sweating. "Jared, I believe it's time to hand you that diaper."

"Just go," Rob directed, then he turned to Sarah. "Did you get the photo?"

"A couple, but they're mostly of his back. I didn't dare take a photo of him when he was staring right at us."

"Very prudent, Sarah," Sebastian approved. "I'll take life over death any day."

"It's time to call Dr. Dunham," Sarah said.

Rob nodded. "I will, just let me relax a bit."

The man entered JR's Quality Auto, walked into the auto garage, and headed straight for JR's side office.

JR glanced up. "Hastings, glad you're back. We need to get that Monte Carlo on the road by the early p.m."

"I'm leaving for lunch. I'll be back in one hour."

"What do ya mean?" JR asked. "You just got back, and I need your help here."

Hastings glared at JR, narrowing his eyes even further. "I'll be back in one hour."

"OK, OK, man," JR replied, intimidated. "I'll have Hank work on it until you get back."

Hastings quickly left the building.

"What a whack-job," JR whispered to himself, shaking his head as he counted a stack of money.

* * *

NOPD Task Force Headquarters

Captain Deblanc stared at Dr. Dunham as he spoke to someone on his cell phone. She knew it must be important, just by his excited demeanor.

"You're sure he was next to a white van?" Dunham asked, paused, then nodded. "All right, Rob, have Sarah text the photo to me immediately. And don't go back there! I'll contact you later." He hung up and said to Deblanc, "Do you remember, Rob, the college student?"

"Of course."

"Well, he and his partners have been continuing their own investigation for the Vidocq class, and they're convinced they spotted our serial offender at his jobsite!"

"What? Excellent! How'd they figure it out?"

Dunham shook his head. "He didn't give me the details yet, but Rob's pulled through too many times to ignore his instincts." Dunham's iPhone buzzed, and he presented the screen to Deblanc. "Here's the photo of who they believe is our offender."

Deblanc studied the image.

Dunham beamed. "Notice the white Chevy van with Michelin tires? I never told Rob about our offender owning a white van."

Deblanc's eyes widened. "This is too coincidental. It's our man, but it's too bad his head is turned. Do they have a better photo of him?"

Dunham shook his head then pocketed his iPhone. "No, they didn't want to be too conspicuous, apparently. He works at JR's Quality Auto."

Deblanc nodded at Dunham, then she moved for the conference room door. "Time to act! JR's Quality Auto—it's just a few blocks away. Let's get everyone we've got and seal that place off." She stopped and eyed Dunham again. "His life-threatening volatility and aggressiveness are justification for a warrant. We need to control the situation immediately, even without the owner's permission."

Dunham nodded. "Agreed, and he won't be in possession of his animal—at least I don't think he'd take that creature to work."

"Just in case he does have it in his van," Deblanc surmised, "we'll block his access."

Within minutes, a dozen police units pulled into JR's Quality Auto and surrounded the place. Officers exited their vehicles and rushed into and around the building.

Deblanc and Dunham climbed from their vehicle and followed the first wave.

"Not good . . . I don't see a white van in the parking lot," Deblanc commented. "Hopefully, it's in the garage."

She and Dunham entered the building.

Hastings stopped his white Chevy van behind a car at the red light, just a few hundred yards away from the auto shop. He immediately spotted the ensuing chaos of police cars. Anger boiled in him, and he slammed the steering wheel and screamed, knowing full well they were after him.

The light turned green, and the first car drove through the intersection.

He scanned the area, and once he was convinced no one spotted him, he drove through the intersection away from the shop.

Dunham walked into the auto garage, stood next to Deblanc, and watched a dozen or so police officers handcuff every employee, their bodies lying flat, face-down. He glanced to the right and spotted a man giving the officers an earful.

"What's the meaning of this?" the man screamed. "This is my shop!"

"I don't see a white van," Deblanc noted. She approached the man and kneeled down. "Are you JR?"

"What the hell did I do?"

Deblanc glanced at the police officer and pointed to a chair. "Let him up and seat him here."

JR slowly stood, with the officer's assistance, then sat in the seat.

Deblanc showed him the arrest warrant. "JR, I'm Captain Deblanc, NOPD. I apologize for the forceful introductions, but it had to be done for the safety of you and your employees." She handed JR a photo. "We're looking for this man."

JR stared at the photo, glanced up at Deblanc, then eyed the photo again. "That's Charlie Hastings. He's out on his lunch break, but I expect him back any moment."

Deblanc frowned. "All right; I want every driver to get their police units out of here! The rest of you stay!"

Officers scrambled out of the building.

"Hurry!" Deblanc glancing over at Dunham. "I hope he hasn't seen us yet." She turned to JR again. "I need every bit of employee information you have on this Charlie Hastings."

JR shook his head. "I don't have much. He's a recluse; he never talks to anyone." He smiled apologetically. "He, uh, only accepts cash, so I'm not sure he has a bank account."

"Hi, JR, I am FBI Special Agent Dunham. Do you have his address or his phone number?"

"Well, he gave me an address and a phone number when I hired him a couple a' years ago, but I know for certain they're fake."

"How do you know?" Deblanc asked.

"I tried calling a couple a' times, but nothing, and he told me to never send him anything to that address because he won't get it."

Deblanc shook her head. "Why would you hire someone if you know their information is fake?"

"Well, I didn't know at first, and he's the best worker I have. Don't want to lose him. You should see how strong this guy is."

Deblanc shook her head. "So, you pay him off the books."

JR shrugged his shoulders. "Hey, I have a lot of overhead."

Deblanc grabbed her handheld radio and keyed it. "This is the captain. Let me know if a white van comes around."

"Roger," a voice over the radio replied.

Dunham glanced into the garage, considering possible DNA sources. "JR, which tools are his? Where is his workspace?"

He nodded toward a Monte Carlo. "Over there. He's our tire and metal worker."

Deblanc pointed to the Monte Carlo. "Make sure no one touches that car!"

"If you're lookin' for fingerprints or somethin', you probably won't find any." JR commented.

"Why is that?" Dunham asked.

"Bending frames and working tires'll rip your hands apart. Hastings always uses thick work gloves."

Dunham approached, searching for work gloves, but he didn't see any. "Let me guess, he takes his work gloves with him."

JR shook his head. "I don't think so, but I saw him workin' on his own van, so maybe he did this time."

A police officer approached Deblanc. "Captain, there's no Charlie Hastings at this address. As a matter of fact, there is no such address."

"Of course not, with our luck," Deblanc replied. "Any luck on a Charlie Hastings anywhere else?"

"There's a Charles Hastings residing in the affluent area of New Orleans," the police officer responded, "and we have a unit on their way there, now."

Deblanc shook her head. "It won't be a match." She glanced around. "We're going to search every inch of this place for DNA samples, fingerprints, and any kind of latent evidence." She turned to the police officer next to JR. "Release him and all the employees, but don't let them go anywhere."

Dunham glanced up at Deblanc. "It's apparent that our offender has made a diligent effort to hide his true identity from his employer, and I don't believe it's a coincidence that he started working here about the same time the murder spree began."

"What are you suggesting?" Deblanc asked.

"I'm suggesting that our offender is not from New Orleans and moved here to kill." He paused. "And if that's the case, we may need to see if we have a similar pattern elsewhere." He turned to JR. "What kind of accent does Mr. Hastings have?"

"Definitely a Louisiana accent." JR shrugged his shoulders. "To me, he looked and acted Cajun."

"That will help narrow down the investigation." Dunham bent over and stared at the license plate on the Monte Carlo.

"What are you thinking?"

"For our offender to own and drive the van, legally anyway, it must be registered by the State of Louisiana, and if it is, the registration could only have been sent to him." He glanced up at Deblanc. "If we can get the van's license plate number, we'll know his name and where he lives locally."

"Let's hope the FBI lab can clean up the video," Deblanc answered.

"We might also get lucky by reviewing security cameras at gas stations nearest to JR's," Dunham said. "Chances are, he's gotten gas around here—or they might have caught him coming and going to work."

"I'll get a couple of officers on it." Deblanc peeked out the window. "I don't think this guy's coming back, so I'll get the criminal investigators here. Looks like we're in for the long haul." She glanced at Dunham. "I'd like to know how your young Rob figured our offender worked here."

Dunham grinned. "My thoughts exactly, Captain. I'll get the details from him."

Hours later, Hastings scanned the inside of his garage, then stared at his white Chevy van. He held a large spray gun and wore safety goggles and a mask.

His white van had painter's tape over the bumpers, wheel rims, side mirrors, and window frames. Newspaper was taped onto the windows and windshield.

He connected the dark-blue spray paint into the gun, positioned it a foot away from the van, then slowly sprayed the van, maintaining an even motion back and forth.

In just a few minutes, his entire van shimmered with the first coat of blue paint.

He took off his mask, stared at his "new" van, and grinned.

chapter 36

Gro Mambo

Dr. Taylor entered the classroom to the sounds of all the students conversing, laughing, and enjoying each other's company. As he neared the podium, he snickered, remembering how different the class was on the first day, so quiet and impersonal.

"Good morning, Dr. Taylor," a student greeted.

Taylor smiled and nodded to the student, then he scanned the room. "Good morning, fellow investigators!" He waited until all side conversations ceased. "On day one, I informed you that the last week of our class was devoted to class presentations. You've all been working hard on your investigations, and I, for one, am eager to see the results." He scanned the room again. "I purposely failed to mention another treat for this week." He grinned. "You are going to meet some of the greats in criminal investigation, and today we're starting with one of the greatest."

Rob and Sarah beamed at each other.

Rob glanced around the class, and it was obvious from the smiles and side whispers that everyone else knew who was coming as well.

Taylor waved at the doorway, and Dr. Dunham entered.

The mumbling from the students got louder.

Taylor opened his left arm to Dunham. "I'd like to present to you Dr. Edward Dunham, chief scientist for the FBI Lab in Quantico, Virginia."

The students burst out in applause and whistles.

Taylor grinned at the class. "You're a hit already, Dr. Dunham."

Dunham dropped his head, donned a humble grin, and nodded in thanks. He then grabbed the podium with both hands, lifted his shoulders, and swept his eyes across his captivated captive audience.

The applause quieted.

"Well, if I knew I was going to receive that kind welcome, I would've come last week and stayed."

The students laughed.

"At first," Dunham continued once the room quieted again, "I couldn't promise availability because of a high-priority case I'm assisting the Navy with, but the stars have aligned, and I'm here." He pointed to Rob, Sarah, and Jared. "As all of you are aware, your classmates discovered an extremely violent serial offender on the loose in New Orleans."

Everyone in the class glanced over at Rob's table.

"Dr. Taylor asked that I discuss career paths and how I became an FBI chief scientist. I certainly will," he paused, "but after that, would it be OK if I walked around and reviewed your cases with you?" He grinned at Taylor. "Maybe I can help you pull an A out of Dr. Taylor."

Applause erupted again.

Taylor grinned. "Dr. Dunham, I believe that's a yes."

Dunham glanced over at Rob's group. "Sorry, guys; you're last."

Jared swatted Rob on the arm. "Great, knowing you two is now a detriment!"

Dunham spent the next twenty minutes discussing his career and entertaining a question-and-answer period. He then began his walk-around with Dr. Taylor, listening intently and giving advice.

After working with most of the tables, Dunham and Taylor stood off to the side of the room and watched the class work.

"You're a hit, Dr. Dunham. Maybe you should consider a career in education in your later life."

Dunham snickered. "My wife's an educator, so I'm sure she would approve." He glanced again around the room. "I have to tell you, Dr. Taylor, if it wasn't for this course, Rob would not have gotten involved, and our offender would still be an unknown."

Taylor beamed. "I'm very happy with how this course has transpired. Hopefully, it's the first of many."

Dunham approached Cedric, Lacy, and Sebastian.

Cedric spoke up and gave Dunham the details of the case and how it was solved last week, effectively ending their ability to help.

"So, did your investigation conform to their conclusions?" Dunham asked.

"Actually, yes," Cedric replied, "thanks to Lacy's amazing attention to detail."

"Great work." He nodded in Lacy's direction, and she dropped her head and blushed.

"The break in the case actually allowed us to help out other teams," Sebastian began, then pointed to Rob, Sarah, and Jared, all three of whom were listening to the conversation at the neighboring table. "These guys asked for my —ahem—'unique qualities,' he jested.

Dunham grinned. "Well, follow me then," he said as he walked over to the last table, Dr. Taylor and Sebastian in tow. "Hello again, Rob, Sarah, and Jared."

"It's true, Dr. Dunham," Jared began, "Sebastian's been a godsend."

"Great," Dunham complimented. "Dr. Taylor informed me he's passed along my updates to the three of you about what happened at JR's Auto Shop." He shot a glance at Sebastian. "Sorry, the four of you."

"Yes," Rob answered. "So, you're convinced he's our man?"

Dunham nodded. "I'm quite confident." He paused. "What I do need to know, though, is the details of what led you to JR's Quality Auto."

Rob, Sarah, and Jared eyed each other but remained silent for a moment.

Finally, Rob answered: "Well, we looked at possible motives for a serial killer using a dog, or wolf-dog hybrid animal, and since local Cajun folklore tells of a similar kind of creature, called a Rougarou, we decided to investigate this angle."

"One of the many variations of Rougarou legends has a witch cursing a poor soul as a werewolf, so we went to a Voodoo souvenir shop on Bourbon Street to ask questions," Sarah offered.

"I don't think Voodoo has anything to do with witchcraft," Dunham commented.

"Yeah, but it's common for locals to call Voodoo queens and priestesses witches," Jared explained, "because they cast spells, charms, and curses, too—and since New Orleans is Voodoo central, we started there." He shrugged, as if still surprised. "It worked! The owner of this place claimed she saw the killer at JR's Quality Auto!"

Dunham shifted his attention to Rob. "OK, but what did she say to convince you enough to check out the auto shop—besides her assumption of having seen this man?"

Rob paused then glanced at Sarah and Jared.

"Because the woman, Annette, claimed her mother made a spiritual connection with the killer when she saw him there," Sebastian blurted out matter-of-factly. "She also said that Rob had some kind of supernatural sight, just like her, and when we got there, he felt him too."

Rob dropped his head and frowned. Dunham, the empirical scientist, would definitely question his credibility now.

Dunham paused for a moment, giving absolutely no hint of skepticism. "I believe it's time for the four of you to take me to this Voodoo shop."

Rob, taken aback by Dunham's accepting response, flashed a partial smile. "Great." He faced Jared. "Can you drive?"

Jared nodded excitedly. Dr. Dunham patted his jacket and pants pockets, suddenly missing Heather's constant assistance. Finally, he pulled out his own keys and said, "I'll follow along behind!"

Forty minutes later, they walked up to Marie Boutte's Voodoo Shop.

"This is it," Jared said.

Dunham led the way into the shop. A door chime jingled as he opened the door.

There were a few other tourists browsing, but Rob spotted Annette waiting on a tourist interested in the Voodoo dolls. "There's Annette," he whispered to Dunham. "She's the one we spoke with. Her mother stayed in the back and refused to speak with us. We never saw her."

"Once the mother realized why we were here," Sarah interrupted, "things became very unwelcoming. Annette practically pushed us out the door."

"Her mother ordered her to kick us out," Jared added.

At that moment, an elderly Black lady wearing a traditional Creole dress appeared from the back room, stood behind the counter, and stared at Dunham.

Annette glanced up, saw her mother's face, then spotted the group. She rushed up to Rob but kept her eyes on Dunham. "Why are you here?"

"This is Dr. Dunham," Rob reassured her, "chief forensic scientist and special agent for the FBI. He insisted we come."

"I'm here to speak with your mother," Dunham stated firmly.

Annette turned and faced her mother.

Marie nodded, then she turned and entered the back room.

"Come," Annette said as she led everyone behind the counter. To a teenage girl stocking a shelf, she said, "Take over, please." The side room Annette led them into was filled with old jars, cans, and small baskets containing a variety of dried plants, herbs, and flower petals. Other items associated with Voodoo, such as small cotton dolls, covered the walls.

The elderly lady, seated in a rocking chair, stared at Dunham.

Annette presented her mother. "This is Marie Boutte, Gro Mambo."

"Gro Mambo is the high Voodoo priestess," Jared whispered to the others.

Dunham nodded as if he already knew this information. "Thank you for allowing us an audience, Gro Mambo. My name is Dr. Dunham. I believe you know why we're here."

Marie got out of her chair and slowly approached Dunham. She presented her hands. "May I?"

Dunham reached his right hand out and placed it into her open palms. She grasped it with both of her hands and closed her eyes. Moments later, she slowly opened them, making eye contact with Dunham. "It is true. You do have a special gift. Powerful," she paused, "and you are beginning to believe it."

Dunham was not surprised by her statement. Two years earlier, a Rosicrucian grandmaster claimed he'd acquired this gift by reading from a special ancient book of all knowledge, sparking his own inner knowledge. Last year, a surprisingly omniscient priest claimed the ability was a charism, a gift from the Holy Spirit. Being agnostic, Dunham doubted these claims, even with countless unusual, unexplainable events substantiating them. Now, a third spiritual leader had corroborated this.

Marie glanced over at Annette then eyed Rob. She grasped his hand and stared into his eyes—this time not closing them. "I see what you mean, daughter. You do have a special gift, young man—yet to be fully tapped."

Rob glanced over at Dunham then at Sarah.

Marie let his hand go and settled back into her rocking chair.

"Is this how you knew the man at the auto shop is the serial killer?" Dunham asked her.

She glared at Dunham. "It is how I knew he was the Rougarou! I did not need to touch his hand."

Sebastian perked up.

"A Rougarou is killing these innocent people," Marie stated confidently.

Dunham raised his eyebrows. "So, Gro Mambo, you're not saying this man is using an animal to kill innocent people, you're saying he *is* the animal." Although the empiricist in him outright rejected this supernatural answer, it made sense in its own weird way.

"Yes."

"I was right!" Sebastian interrupted.

Dunham quickly glanced at Sebastian then back to Marie. "Mrs. Boutte, how is there a connection between you, a Creole, and the Rougarou, a Cajun story?"

"It is time you know what the Gro Mambo have been keeping secret for almost two hundred years," Marie announced. "One of our greatest leaders was approached by a Frenchman with the family curse . . . the curse of La Bête."

Dunham raised his eyebrows again and asked, "La Bête?" remembering that this was the name scratched on the dresser at the theme park.

"Yes, 'The Beast,'" Marie said. "The Rougarou. The Frenchman asked Gro Mambo if she could break this curse because he wanted to marry his cousin. You see, the family knew any children from two cousins, both having the curse, were doomed to transform into the Rougarou at will."

Dunham immediately picked up on a genetic connection to the family curse—a recessive gene. *The shapeshifting, though, is a bit of a stretch*, he thought to himself.

"Wow!" Jared blurted out, stunned by this information.

Marie continued. "The Gro Mambo told the Frenchman the curse could not be broken because it came from his ancestral lands, but her magic was powerful, and she could block the curse with a binding spell. It would work on the entire family line."

"So, a spell was used to bind the curse?" Sarah repeated.

Marie glanced at Sarah and nodded. "The Gro Mambo successfully bound the curse," she raised her finger, "but she insisted that future Gro Mambo hear the story just in case her spell was broken, and the curse was released." She paused. "This is what I saw in the auto shop." Fear blanketed her face. "And the Rougarou sensed my discovery!"

Dunham's eyes widened. This revelation fit the story Malaya Santos told him about what happened in her village years ago, although she called the creature Aswang. The story about Castle being connected to mutilations seemed to begin there. *Might something have happened to Castle in the Filipino village that day that released the curse?*

Dunham thought for a moment, trying to see how this story could help him discover the identity of the serial offender, but nothing presented itself. He pulled out his phone and scrolled to the photo Sarah took. "Is this the man you believe to be the Rougarou?

She stared at the photo for a moment then nodded.

"Is there anything you can think of to help us?"

Marie nodded again. "Trust your feelings." She stood and selected five tiny cotton dolls and handed one to each of them. "A gift; they will help protect you."

Everyone accepted the dolls, and they thanked her.

Dunham smiled. "Well, thank you so much for your time. You've been very helpful."

She nodded a final time and went back to her chair, staring off as if no one else were in the room with her at all.

Dunham led the way out of the shop.

Annette followed them out to the sidewalk. "Please keep those gifts on your person at all times." She turned around and went back into the store.

"What do you make of that, Dr. Dunham?" Jared asked. "Shapeshifting from a human to a Rougarou?"

"Genetics," Dunham answered.

Rob glanced over at Dunham. "What?"

"If true, family members having the," he paused, "shape-shifting gene passed on from only one side of the family will not transform into the Rougarou—although they'd still carry it. If they received the gene from both sides, they would have the ability to shape shift into the Rougarou."

"So, you believe her," Sarah said.

Dunham shrugged his shoulders. "Well, shape-shifting aside, recent research has identified a genetic component to one becoming a serial killer, meaning one may be born a serial killer if both mother and father passed on the gene."

"Expressed as a Rougarou?" Sebastian asked.

"Nature versus nurture," Dunham explained. "If one has the genetic disposition to be a serial killer, or nature, and the family has a tradition of acting like werewolves, or nurture . . ."

"That's called lycanthropy," Sebastian interrupted.

Sarah eyed Dunham. "So, genetics gives them a 'serial killer' family curse, and family tradition gives it a lycanthropy flavor."

"Exactly, which means our serial offender may still be a man using an animal to kill."

"The Beast of Gévaudan," Sebastian blurted out.

Dunham glanced over at Sebastian. "Beast of Gévaudan?"

Sebastian nodded. "She said a curse from the Frenchman's ancestral lands, i.e., France, and in the mid-seventeen hundreds, a wolf-dog hybrid animal killed over a hundred people in the mountainous region of Gévaudan."

Rob faced Dunham. "This gave us the idea that our serial offender was using a wolf-dog hybrid to kill his victims; a precedent case."

"The strange thing is that the nickname of this animal was also La Bête, just like she mentioned," Sebastian said, thumb pointing over his shoulder at the shop behind them.

Dunham stood stunned for a moment. "The coincidences keep piling up. I haven't told you this, but the name 'La Bête' was scratched on a dresser at one of the crime scenes."

"This guy thinks he's recreated the Beast of Gévaudan." Sarah shook her head. "Just great."

"The prevailing theory is that the person who used La Bête to kill," Sebastian explained, "probably for the king's ransom, was a man named Chastèl, an innkeeper. Rumor has it that one of his sons used to breed mastiffs with the European gray wolf."

"I'll need to sleep on this," Dunham said, unlocking his car with his remote, "but at the moment, I have another case that requires me to go to the New Orleans Public Library."

Jared manually unlocked his car.

"Is this the Navy case?" Rob asked.

Dunham nodded. "I'm attempting to locate a former Navy man—a Joseph Castle."

"More coincidences," Jared muttered.

Dunham stopped. "What do you mean?"

"In French, the last name 'Castle' is 'Chastèl'—the same as the innkeeper's name from Sebastian's story."

Dunham's shook his head, his face expressionless. Joseph Castle with the Philippine animal attack, a Frenchman with the New Orleans Rougarou, and Chastèl with the Beast of Gévaudan in France was just too coincidental.

"Are you OK, Dr. Dunham?" Sarah asked, noticing the blood had drained from his face.

"Of course!" Dunham said. "Why didn't I make the connection earlier? It was right there!" He jumped into his car. "I have to go—keep me updated, guys." He pulled out into the street and drove off.

"Nice job, Jared," Sarah commented. "You just gave the Watchmaker another lead!"

Jared slid into the driver's seat as everyone crammed into his car. "Not sure what it was."

Dunham stopped at a light behind four cars, pulled out his iPhone, and touched an app labeled, 'Secured,' then dialed a phone number and placed the phone on speaker.

"One Alpha Charlie," a voice answered at the other end.

"Winfall, One, Eight, Eight, Eight, Eight," Dunham replied.

"Our crypto-translators are in sync and this connection is now secured," the voice said. "Good afternoon, Dr. Dunham. I see you're driving in downtown New Orleans. How may I help you?"

"Hello, Big Brother, I need your help. Do you see anyone with the name Joseph Castle residing in the New Orleans area? He'd be middle-aged."

After a few moments, Big Brother replied, "Negative, but I could expand the search area if you'd like."

"How about a temporal search?"

"I love how you use big science words with me, Dr. Dunham."

"Oh, sorry."

"Just teasing. I'm already checking." He paused. "I have a Joseph Castle living in Lafayette, Louisiana, in the late 1990s, then moving to Baton Rouge in 2000."

"That's him, but I was hoping for something more recent. I have a suspicion he now lives in New Orleans, and he's the serial offender we've been looking for."

There was silence on the phone.

"Nothing more recent," Big Brother answered. "The only other Joseph Castle popping up is one from the early to mid-1990s living in Monroe, Louisiana."

"That's definitely our subject, and Monroe was where he resided prior to Lafayette." Dunham thought for a moment as he turned down another road. "Big Brother, I seem to recall an unsolved series of mutilations, or murders, around Monroe when Castle and his family lived there."

"Wait just a moment." He paused. "Here, I found a series of articles discussing this, but they were mutilations—sheep, mostly—and all found decapitated. They blamed it on wolves entering the area from the Appalachians." He paused again. "Hmm, there was one unsolved murder at the time . . . a man found decapitated, although I see nothing about the local authorities connecting the two."

Dunham grimaced as he drove. "I believe Mr. Castle was just getting started."

"Here's an interesting article from that time. A local West Monroe man by the name of Randy Clay claimed a man mutilated those animals, and he also claimed to know why."

"Claimed to know why, hmm." Dunham thought for a moment. "Interesting! Does this Randy Clay still live in the area?"

"He does, indeed. Looks like he's a local celebrity. He hosts a local morning culinary show out of Monroe, and he's the president of the board of a local culinary school. Shall I book you a flight to Monroe?"

"You're reading my mind, again, Big Brother."

"Would you like a flight out today?"

Dunham got onto the highway. "No, make it for tomorrow morning; first flight. I have to visit with my wife one more night before I leave."

"No further explanation required, Dr. Dunham. I'll text you Clay's address and phone number and your flight itinerary."

"Thank you, again, Big Brother. Out." Dunham hung up then voice-dialed Special Agent Turner's number."

"Hi, Dr. Dunham, nice to finally hear from you," Turner quipped. "I see in the news you've been busy in New Orleans."

"That's why I'm calling you. It looks like we've gotten the break we're looking for. I hope you're holding onto your coffee."

"Why? What's up?"

"It looks like the serial offender we're presently looking for in New Orleans is none other than Petty Officer Joseph Castle."

There was silence on the other end of the phone.

"I'm not sure if I can wrap my head around this," Turner finally responded. "This is unbelievable."

"I'm off to Monroe, Louisiana. My flight is tomorrow morning. Maybe this'll help us find him."

"Good luck, and I'll see what I can dig up on Castle. Keep me in the loop."

"Will do."

chapter 37

Day Trip, First Leg,
West Monroe, Louisiana

"You are nearing your destination," Dr. Dunham's GPS announced.

He stopped his rental car at the end of a long country driveway just outside West Monroe.

"You have arrived at your destination."

He gazed at the white two-story Victorian home at the end of the drive. It had a huge front porch connected to a circular gazebo—and Dunham noticed a man sitting inside, partially reclined in a cushioned chair.

The man had spotted Dunham as well.

As Dunham drove up the driveway, he passed a white wooden fence that surrounded the man's yard and ended at the woods behind his house.

The man stayed in his seat and went back to reading a magazine.

Dunham parked his car, exited, and approached the man. "Hello, Mr. Clay? My name is Dr. Dunham . . . I spoke to you on the phone?"

The man didn't glance away from his *BayouLife* magazine. "Can you believe it," the man said, "they wrote an entire article on me, and they got my age wrong!" He glanced up at Dunham. "If people think I'm sixty-three years old, they'll think I'm over the hill!" He shook his head and stood. "Ah, once they see my gorgeous profile, they'll say, 'Yeah, Randy Clay may be fifty-three, but he's got the body of a fifty-two-year-old!'" he jested, grinning from ear to ear.

Dunham laughed.

Clay approached Dunham and shook his hand. "Don't mind me, Dr. Dunham. My bark is worse than my bite—except on the days I've eaten too many burritos. Ha!"

"It's a pleasure to meet you, Mr. Clay," Dunham said, already genuinely glad to have met this man who so clearly enjoyed life.

Clay turned back toward the front porch. "Follow me; let's get out of the sun. I have a cooler filled with Louisiana's finest lager, Abita Amber. Nectar of the gods, my friend."

"Don't mind if I do, thank you, Mr. Clay. I actually make it a habit to try local craft beers wherever my travels take me."

Dunham sat in a second cushioned seat and scanned the area. "I love your place, especially your front porch."

Clay took a long drink. "Thank you, I'd love to show you around, especially my poker room." He eyed Dunham. "Now, what's so important that the FBI has flown all this way just to see my smiling face? My accountant promised me I haven't evaded any taxes, or maybe it's my success at the casinos? Did they put you up to this?"

"No, not at all, I'm actually here because you might be able to help us on a serial offender case."

Clay lost his smile and stared at Dunham. "Is this about the New Orleans serial killer case that's dominating the news?"

Dunham nodded. "I'm afraid so, Mr. Clay. You see—you've met the prime suspect before, back in the early-to-mid-nineties."

Clay paused, then said, "Joe Castle, am I right?"

Dunham gave an affirming grin but said, "I'm not at liberty to say at the moment, Mr. Clay." He paused. "I read an old article you were interviewed in about the animal mutilations at the time . . . where their heads were missing."

Clay sat back. "Well, I'll be." He took another drink. "He killed that Monroe man, didn't he?"

Dunham shrugged his shoulders. "I'm not sure; I haven't investigated that particular case, but from what we know now, it makes sense." He leaned toward Clay. "You seem to be the only person who claimed a human being mutilated these animals, and now you come up with the correct name, Joseph Castle. How did you make the connection?"

Clay snickered. "My best friend in the early nineties was his cousin, Freddie Castle."

Dunham leaned back. "Oh, I met Freddie and his two boys in Lafayette."

Clay nodded. "Sounds right; after the man was found dead, around 1998, the whole family took off to Lafayette." He took a drink. "Freddie was a good man, but his cousin, Joe, was a piece of gator crap. When those animals were getting mutilated, I suggested to Freddie that we do some nighttime hunting and kill the predator and become famous." He took another drink. "That's when he told me it was his cousin doing the killing." He glanced at Dunham. "It all made sense."

"You didn't report it right then?"

Clay shook his head. "Nope, I swore to Freddie I wouldn't divulge anything until after they left for Lafayette. Even when I did report it, I didn't give Joe Castle's name." He raised his beer to his lips.

"Did Joe Castle own a big dog?"

Clay's head jerked forward, and he pulled the bottle from his mouth, accidentally spilling some beer. "I didn't think anyone knew about that mutt."

"What do you mean?"

"When Castle came back from the Navy, his ol' man got him some mastiff or something." Clay took a small swig and stared out at the horizon. "Nasty thing, too—killed their sheep."

"Did you ever see it?" Dunham asked.

Clay shook his head. "Nope, Freddie said once they got that thing, no one would visit them."

Dunham took a drink. "Do you think Joe Castle used that animal to kill?"

"You'd think, but Freddie said they shot it once it killed their livestock. I think he's right since it was a few years before the man was found dead."

Dunham took another drink and thought for a moment. "Maybe that's what gave him the idea." He put his beer down. "Anyway, it looks like Monroe is where and when Joseph Castle got the taste for human victims."

Clay shook his head. "Nope, far from it."

"What do you mean?"

"A few years before the mutilations, Joe Castle had moved to Vicksburg, Mississippi, around 1995." He pointed east. "It's about an hour's drive east on Highway 20."

Dunham was stunned. He knew full well Vicksburg had experienced a series of unsolved murders around 1995. He grabbed his iPhone and noted the distance between Monroe and Jackson, Mississippi.

"Some folks were murdered in Vicksburg at the same time Castle was there, then he moved back here in 1998, and that's when the Monroe murder occurred."

"Why didn't you report this?" Dunham asked.

Clay shook his head. "I didn't make the connection until a couple of years ago when I was watching *Unsolved Mysteries* and they had the Vicksburg murders on, and then I did. My buddy's the Monroe chief of police, so I told him." He took another drink. "The bastard told me to stick to cooking."

Dunham stood and shook Clay's hand. "Thank you, Mr. Clay. I must be going. You've been more than helpful."

"No problem, Dr. Dunham. I was going to ask you to stay for dinner. The wife's a phenomenal cook."

Dunham tilted his head, confused. "Mr. Clay, I thought you were a prominent chef around here?"

"I made the *BayouLife* didn't I?" Clay belted out a low, guttural laugh. "Can you keep a secret? My wife has all the culinary talent, and she creates the recipes for me. I just do good TV."

Dunham smiled. "Your secret's safe with me, Mr. Clay. I have a two-hour drive to Jackson, Mississippi, and I want to get there by early afternoon."

He shook Clay's hand, got into his car, and headed for Jackson. On the way, he voice-dialed Hobbs and listened to the ringing through the speaker.

"Detective Hobbs."

"Yes, hello, Detective Hobbs, this is Dr. Dunham."

"It's great to hear your voice, Dr. Dunham. I didn't expect a phone call from you. How are you doing?"

Dunham glanced around. "Fine, fine, but it looks like you'll be cursed with my presence again, and hopefully in two hours. I apologize for the short notice."

"You mean blessed. This afternoon is as good a time as any. So, why are you making a trip to Jackson? Engles is safely behind bars, being one with the jailhouse, awaiting trial."

"Well, Mr. Engles is the reason for my return trip. He has potentially valuable information in the New Orleans serial offender case."

"I knew you'd be involved with that high-profile case," Hobbs commented.

"Remember that Engles lived in Vicksburg, Mississippi, in the mid-1990s and claimed his neighbor was the Vicksburg Serial Killer. I'm now convinced Engles was right, *and* this very person is now murdering in New Orleans. I'd like to find out which apartment he and his neighbor lived in. This information just might help us catch him."

"Hmm," Hobbs commented, "if I recall, Engles believes you're the reason he'll be behind bars for the rest of his short life. I'm not so sure he'll want to speak with you. May I suggest I speak with him?"

"I appreciate it, Detective—is there any possibility you can make this happen when I arrive?"

"Sounds good, Dr. Dunham. I'll handle the details. Meet me at the city jail."

Two hours later, Dunham pulled into the lot and entered the jailhouse. "Special Agent Dunham, here to meet with Detective Hobbs," he said to the officer at the front desk, presenting his badge.

The officer stood and shook Dunham's hand. "It's nice to meet you, Dr. Dunham. Follow me. Detective Hobbs is waiting for you in the interview room."

They proceeded down the hall, and as the officer opened the door, Dunham saw Detectives Hobbs and Nebelecky standing, drinking coffee in front of a two-way mirror. He shook their hands. "Hello, it's great to see you two."

"You, too, Dr. Dunham," Hobbs replied.

"Hi, Dr. Dunham," Nebelecky began. "I had to join in, if you don't mind."

"Not at all." Dunham spotted Engles on the other side of the two-way mirror, shackled and sitting in the interview room by himself. "So, the key piece of evidence I need from Mr. Engles is either the name of his Vicksburg neighbor in 1995, or the address."

Hobbs pulled up a map on his iPhone. "After our phone conversation, I took the liberty of locating Engles's apartment building on Google Maps." He presented the tablet to Dunham. "Here it is. This should help us pinpoint which apartment this neighbor lived in."

Dunham grinned. "Great."

"We received approval from Engles's lawyer to interview him, as long as nothing he says can further incriminate him," Nebelecky said.

"Well, let's see what I can find out," Hobbs said as he left the room and entered the interview room where Engles was sitting.

"Here's to a fruitful interrogation," Dunham commented as he stared through the two-way mirror.

Nebelecky watched his partner. "Hobbs is our best interviewer, so you're in good hands."

"Well, aren't you a sight for sore eyes, Detective," Engles commented sarcastically.

"Good afternoon, Mr. Engles, sorry to pull you from your usual routine, but I received approval from your lawyer to speak with you. Do you recall when the FBI special agent interviewed you a while back about trying to pin those Vicksburg murders on you?"

Engles frowned. "How could I forget? That bastard. Why? Is he still trying to pin those murders on me?"

Hobbs purposely ignored answering his question in hopes he'd believe it to be true. "Your lawyer and I are only looking for the truth, Mr. Engles." He paused. "Do you recall the name of this neighbor you believed to be the man that did kill those victims?"

Engles paused and stared at Hobbs. "The guy with the huge, scary-looking dog." He shook his head. "No, never did know his name."

Hobbs presented his tablet to Engles. "Could you identify which apartment he lived in?"

Engles bent forward and stared at the map on the screen for a moment then pointed his finger at one apartment. "First floor, corner unit. Can't forget that."

Hobbs stood up. "Thank you, Mr. Engles, you've been very helpful."

Engles grinned. "Tell my FBI friend 'Hi' for me."

Hobbs returned to Dunham and Nebelecky and placed the tablet on the table. "The great thing about Google Maps, they even give the address to the specific apartment."

Dunham quickly wrote the address in his notepad then pulled out his iPhone, typed the address into a text message, and pressed send. "Thank you, so much, Detectives. I need to rush to the airport and make the quickest flight out of here."

"Hey, it was great seeing you, regardless of if it was such a short time." Hobbs said as he and Nebelecky each shook Dunham's hand.

"Good luck, Dr. Dunham," Nebelecky said.

Dunham rushed back to his car and connected with Big Brother.

"I see you texted me an address," Big Brother commented.

Dunham pulled out of the parking lot. "Yes, this was the probable address of our New Orleans serial offender when he lived in Vicksburg in 1995."

"Let's see what we have here," Big Brother commented. "I have a Jerry Lafont living at that apartment for just a couple of years."

Dunham turned a corner. "Jerry Lafont? Could you check to see if there's a Jerry Lafont living in New Orleans today?"

"Let's see . . . No, I don't see a Jerry Lafont, but I've found something interesting."

"What's that?"

"The very first Vicksburg victim in the 1990s was a Jerry Lafont."

Dunham breathed in sharply. "He stole the identity of his first victim in Vicksburg."

"Once you have a victim's social security number," Big Brother began, "you could register a vehicle and even get a driver's license."

"I hope they've had success in identifying the New Orleans victims . . ." Dunham paused. "Much appreciated, as always, Big Brother. One last request—"

"Your flight leaves from Jackson to New Orleans in forty minutes. I just texted you the flight number, and you can drop off the rental at the airport."

Dunham grinned. "I don't know how you do it, Big Brother. You're the best. Out."

chapter 38

Mayor Blumenthal's Daughter,
New Orleans, Louisiana

Mayor Blumenthal took a sip of coffee as he sat at his kitchen table reading the paper. "Thank you, my dear. You're the best," he said to his wife, who was scrambling eggs on the stove.

"That's right, and don't you forget it," she teased.

Their eleven-year-old boy ran by, chased by his nine-year-old brother, both armed with Nerf guns. The nine-year-old accidentally bumped into his dad but completely ignored the collision.

"Hey, watch where you're running, superhero!" Blumenthal yelled animatedly.

The nine-year-old scowled. "I'm the villain, Daddy. I'm Deathstroke!" He then shot after his older brother.

The mayor grinned as he watched them run out of the kitchen. "Heh, isn't that always the case—the youngest brother gets suckered into being the bad guy." He thought for a moment. "Someday, I should apologize to my little brother."

Carla Blumenthal set the eggs and toast in front of her husband. "Your brother is now forty-three, honey. He probably doesn't even remember."

"Oh, Tom has a memory like an elephant," he commented as he scooped a cloud of egg onto a piece of toast. He raised the toast to his mouth. "Speaking of remembering things: Don't expect me until late tonight, dear. There's that fundraiser tonight," he said, taking a bite.

"Uh-huh, I remembered." She faced her husband, grinning. "That means another night out with my sisters!"

"That means spending lots of money," the mayor growled. "I don't think I like that as much as I like these eggs."

She kissed him on the forehead and sat down to her own breakfast.

Their daughter, Tanya, the oldest of the Blumenthal children, walked in, grabbed some cereal, a bowl, and the carton of milk, and sat at the table. Without a word, she began to eat.

"How's basketball camp, honey?" the mayor asked.

Tanya shrugged her shoulders. "Fine, they run us too much though. Too many drills too." She glanced over at her mother. "You don't have to drive me again, Momma. Yvette's picking me up in a few minutes."

"She's been driving all week. Saves me a trip." Carla shrugged and took another bite.

Minutes later, a car horn beeped out front.

Tanya slurped a big spoonful then stood. "That's Yvette. Gotta go." She got up, put her bowl in the sink, and kissed her parents quickly. "Love, y'all."

"Love you, too, honey," the mayor replied.

"Grab a pastry, honey. Cereal's only part of a balanced breakfast!" her mother ordered.

Tanya rolled her eyes and sighed, grabbed a pastry and her basketball bag, then left the house.

She spotted Yvette's car in the U-shaped driveway and hurried toward it.

Yvette lowered her window and smiled at Tanya. "Hurry up, girl, we'll be late."

Tanya smiled, finished her pastry, and casually walked around to the passenger seat. She opened the back door and tossed her bag into the back seat then closed the door.

As she opened the front passenger door, a man came up from behind her, grabbed her by the hair, and slammed her head into the car.

Tanya collapsed, unconscious.

Yvette jerked her head to the right as she heard the thump and felt the car jolt, just in time to see a man enter the passenger side of her car, headfirst. She opened her mouth to scream.

The man struck Yvette in the face, instantly knocking her out. He pulled back out of the passenger seat and reached down for Tanya.

Yvette's head collapsed onto the steering wheel, blasting the horn.

Unfazed, the man lifted Tanya's body, threw her into the passenger seat, then closed the door.

The mayor heard the horn blaring, frowned, and slammed the paper onto the table. "Tanya and that Yvette might be good girls, but their teenage shenanigans are going to annoy the whole neighborhood." He stood and looked out of the kitchen window at his driveway.

The assailant calmly walked around the front of the car to the driver's door, opened it, pulled Yvette out, and tossed her limp body onto the concrete.

The mayor's jaw dropped as he watched the attack unfold. "Oh my God!" He rushed to the door, calling, "Tanya! Tanya!"

The man put the car in gear, turned his head, and watched the mayor run out of the house toward the car. He grinned ominously as he drove off.

The mayor ran after the car, frantically, right past Yvette. "Get back here! Tanya!" He ran down the road, following the car till the driver picked up speed and disappeared at the end of the street.

The mayor stopped, turned around, and ran toward the house.

Carla walked out of the house and spotted her husband sprinting toward her from forty yards away. She then noticed Yvette collapsed on the pavement. "Wha—? What's going on?"

"Get my keys! Get my keys! Call 9-1-1!"

As Dr. Dunham walked through the gate door into the airport's arrivals terminal, he spotted Detectives Bakula and Oglesby waving to him.

"Dr. Dunham!"

He approached them. "Hello, I see I have an escort. This is unexpected."

"Haven't you heard?" Oglesby asked. "The mayor's daughter was kidnapped this morning, and we think it was our serial killer. We tried to text you."

"I turned my phone back on as we taxied up to the gate just a few minutes ago and saw you'd texted but hadn't had a chance to read your messages. Are we headed to HQ?"

Bakula nodded as the three hurried through the concourse. "The captain's waiting. Headquarters is in chaos. We're convinced our perp will kill her soon, if he hasn't already."

"Looks like he's sending another message," Oglesby added.

"Agreed," Dunham replied. "We need to act fast."

"Was your trip fruitful? Find anything that might help find this Joseph Castle?" Bakula asked.

"I think so. Do you remember those unsolved murders in Vicksburg, Mississippi, in the mid-nineties?"

Bakula shook his head and smirked. "I think I was just graduating from middle school in Grand Island, New York."

"I remember," Oglesby answered.

"It looks like Castle began his serial murder career there."

"Any way this'll help us find the mayor's daughter?" Oglesby asked.

"Maybe," Dunham answered.

They turned into the next concourse.

"Castle took on the name of his first Vicksburg victim," Dunham continued, "stealing his identity and using that alias during the time he was committing his murder spree."

"Ah, so, he may be doing the same here," Oglesby said.

"Yes, and if we can identify the victims from the oldest burlap bag, we might get lucky."

Bakula shook his head. "I believe the captain said we've made no progress in identifying the victims."

Twenty minutes later, they entered New Orleans Police Department Headquarters.

As they walked out of the elevator on the fourth floor, Dunham immediately noticed a flurry of activity.

Dozens of law enforcement officers were rushing around in overdrive. The floor was filled with loud conversations interspersed with actual shouting.

They entered the busy task force conference room.

Captain Deblanc was in the middle of the chaos.

"Over here, Dr. Dunham," Deblanc called and waved him over. Then she glanced at a police officer. "And I want it yesterday!"

The police officer rushed off.

Dunham broke off from Bakula and Oglesby and said, "Hello, Captain."

"I'm sure Bakula and Oglesby updated you on the details of the mayor's daughter being kidnapped. We're sure it was Castle."

"I agree."

"The whole police department's on the lookout for a white van. They found her cell phone smashed to pieces outside of the mayor's home."

Dunham frowned. "There goes any chance of tracing them through that."

"Bakula texted me about Castle taking on the identity of his first victim. Great job, Dr. Dunham."

Dunham nodded. "Have you had any success in identifying the victims, especially from the oldest bag?"

She shook her head. "No, still no luck identifying them. The first bag had one male and three females. We have their DNA results but nothing to match them with. I gave it high priority."

Dunham thought for a moment. "Did your forensic artist finish the facial reconstructions?"

"Yes," she answered, searched through some paperwork, and pulled out four computer-generated facial images and handed them to Dunham.

"Thanks, I'll take just the male victim." He noticed the artist had portrayed long, uncombed hair, and even created a second image of the same person but with a scruffy beard. "Excellent work." He glanced at Deblanc. "I'm going to visit the owner of the homeless shelter. Maybe she can recognize this man."

"Good luck." She glanced over at a group of officers. "Bakula and Oglesby!"

"What's up, Captain?" Bakula called back.

"I need you two to take Dr. Dunham to the homeless shelter you visited." She glanced at Dunham. "He'll give you the details on your way."

Dunham raised the sheet of paper with the facial image reconstruction. "Let's make a couple of copies first."

Twenty minutes later, Bakula parked the police vehicle in front of the Plight of the Homeless Shelter. "Luck has to follow us sometime, Dr. Dunham, so let's hope someone recognizes this guy."

"What's the owner's name?" Dunham asked.

"Marion Thibodeaux," Oglesby answered. "She's been in business for five years or so, so maybe she'll recognize this victim."

Inside, they found a half dozen people either eating at the long tables or sleeping on one of the cots set up in rows on the left.

Bakula pointed into the kitchen. "There's Marion."

Marion turned around as she was prepping another batch of soup and spotted them. She stepped away and met them as they walked toward the kitchen. "Detectives, who ya lookin' for now?"

"Hi, Marie; this is Dr. Dunham from the FBI, and he's helping us find the serial killer."

"Nice to meet you, Marion," Dunham greeted.

Marion merely nodded back, maintaining her grumpy expression.

He presented the victim's image. "Do you recognize this person? He would have gone missing about two years ago."

Marion stared at the computer drawing for a few seconds, then she glanced over at an elderly lady eating soup. "I think Annie'll know him." She walked out of the kitchen and approached the woman. "Annie."

Annie glanced up and eyed Marion.

Marion placed the image in front of her. "Do ya know this guy?"

Annie stared at the image for nearly fifteen seconds. "That'd be Al Buzzard." She glanced up at Marie. "Ain't seen him fer two years though."

Dunham, Bakula, and Oglesby shot each other a glance, clearly excited at the prospect of finally catching a lead.

"Are ya sure?" Marion asked.

Annie nodded. "Sure as I'll ever be."

Marion handed the image back to Dunham. "Al Buzzard." She turned and walked back into the kitchen.

Dunham pulled out his iPhone and texted the name to Big Brother, requesting an address.

"Come on; let's call it in and see what we find," Bakula suggested.

As they rushed from the shelter and crowded into the car, Oglesby called in the name and Dunham received a text.

"There's an Alec Buzzard who lives near the Greenwood Cemetery on Homedale Street," Dunham began. "He moved there twenty months ago, and there's a blue van parked in the driveway as we speak. I just texted both of you the address."

Bakula and Oglesby both turned around and faced Dunham, looking confused.

"That's him, I can feel it."

"How'd you get all that information so fast?" Bakula asked.

Dunham grinned. "Don't ask. Now, let's make the mayor's day and find his daughter."

"I'm in," Bakula replied as he turned the car around and headed toward Homedale Street.

Oglesby read Dunham's text and grabbed the radio. "I'll call in the cavalry. I believe SWAT would like another go with this bastard."

Tanya Blumenthal was lying down on the bed, her arms tied behind her back and her legs bound. She had duct tape over her mouth and stared hopelessly at the ground.

"Mmmm," Castle taunted as he entered the room.

She closed her eyes and moaned.

Castle grinned as he wondered how best to torture the mayor for the next few days. His plan was to haunt the mayor's mind, then crush his heart by having his only daughter discovered in bloody pieces, minus her head—that was his.

Tanya turned and moaned again.

Castle left for the kitchen and opened a can of stew with a manual can opener. He abruptly paused, stuck his nose up high, and sniffed. He frowned and stared out the kitchen window into the twilit front yard, aware something was awry, though what, he couldn't yet tell.

Smash! Crash! Four SWAT team members burst simultaneously into the house through the front door and two windows. All four now had their rifles aimed at Castle.

Castle turned and faced the closest SWAT team member. Anger filled his eyes, and he reached down but his right shoulder jerked back as he was shot by the closest SWAT officer. Castle's body spun as the rifle fire found purchase, then he bolted to the right.

All four SWAT team members opened fire on the moving target.

Castle raced from the room with lightning speed and busted down the back door. Police, positioned in the backyard, began to shoot, but Castle rushed the closest officer, and, with surprising strength, ripped him off his feet, knocking his handgun to the ground.

"Hold your fire!" screamed an officer, fearing a stray bullet may hit the cop being assaulted.

As Castle reached the end of the yard, he heaved the officer into the trunk of a tree and slipped into the high brush.

The officer moaned then collapsed, unconscious.

The other police officers sprinted to their downed colleague as Castle escaped into the darkness.

Inside the house, the four SWAT team members quickly worked their way through the rooms and finally into the spare bedroom, finding the mayor's daughter bound but still alive.

Two hours later, the small street was filled with police vehicles and news vans, yellow police tape separating the two. Crowds of pedestrians pressed against the tape as the news reporters spoke into cameras.

Dunham, wearing latex gloves, squatted in the blue van, shining his flashlight over everything.

"We've got everyone combing the neighborhood looking for this guy," Oglesby informed, also shining his flashlight around. He aimed his light into the glove compartment. "It's like he disappeared."

"My guess is he's at his other location," Bakula added, shining his light under the seats.

Oglesby glanced over at Bakula. "Why do you say he's got another location?"

"Because there's no sign of the big dog."

Dunham nodded. "Mmm." He then glanced over at Oglesby. "Anything in the glove compartment?"

"Here's a notepad," Oglesby said, "and the first page is a list for groceries."

"May I see it?" Oglesby handed him the new piece of evidence, and Dunham studied it. "The watermark on the notepad says AltCom." He glanced at the two detectives. "Does that ring a bell?"

Both detectives shook their heads. Dunham pulled out his iPhone, texted 'AltCom' to Big Brother, then pocketed it, continuing his search.

"Apparently, the mayor wants to get on national news and give you serious props, Dr. Dunham," Bakula commented as he searched.

Dunham shook his head. "I need to keep a low profile. Publicity will adversely affect my ability to assist local law enforcement with serial offender cases."

"I don't think he gives a shit," Oglesby replied bluntly. "He feels you deserve it."

Dunham received a text and glanced at it. "Still, I must stay on the fringe." He read the text again. "It looks like AltCom is a commercial real estate company out of Boston owned by the Marotta Firm. They've only had three business transactions in New Orleans, and one of them is a small auto shop purchased a year and a half ago. A second is a grocery store building, and a third is a warehouse for a casino."

"Castle worked at JR's Quality Auto," Bakula replied. "That's a little more than a coincidence."

"Let's check the auto shop tonight," Oglesby added and stared out at the crowd. "It gets us outta here."

"I actually like that idea," Dunham agreed. "I have the address." He texted Big Brother back about their interest in the auto shop and that they were going to check it out. "One issue though."

"What's that?" Bakula asked.

"We'll need a warrant, and this lead is a long shot. We may not get approval."

Oglesby swiped on his phone. "I'll have the captain get on that. I've never seen anyone convince a judge like her."

"So, while the captain's working on the warrant, how about we grab a bite to eat? I'm starving. Oges is buying."

Oglesby pulled out a five-dollar bill. "My ol' lady felt generous and gave me a Lincoln this time. It's on me!"

"Actually, the tab's on the FBI," Dunham offered. "It's my turn."

"Never look a gift horse in the mouth, I say," Bakula replied.

The three of them sneaked around the news reporters, slipped into their police vehicle, and hurried away from the crime scene.

chapter 39

The AltCom Lead,
New Orleans, Louisiana

Oglesby parked the unmarked police vehicle in front of a downtown industrial expanse located along the Mississippi River.

"Looks like this is the place," Oglesby said.

The fenced-in expanse was at least a half-mile long and a quarter mile in depth, butting up to the river. There were a half dozen huge storage buildings widely dispersed, and in between them were numerous smaller brick buildings, all having dim external security lighting. The darkness between the buildings was dominated by an obscuring mist caused by the muggy evening.

Dunham pointed at the gate door next to the tall metal vehicle entrance gate. "It's cracked open. Did that just happen, or do they keep it open?"

Bakula scanned the area. "You certainly can tell this is after working hours. I don't see a soul."

"So, which one's the auto shop?" Oglesby asked.

Dunham pointed to the buildings to the right. "Well, let's start over there." He glanced at Bakula and Oglesby. "Listen, if on the far chance this is indeed Castle's place, he may very well have his animal with him. The same one that effortlessly dispatched armed SWAT officers, so be on your guard."

Oglesby pulled out his handgun. "How about we call for backup?" Oglesby asked, a serious expression overtaking his face.

"We're already here," Bakula replied, "so how about we quick check it out, and the first sign of Castle and/or his mutt, we call for backup."

Oglesby opened the door. "And to think I'm going to retire soon."

The three law enforcement officials exited the vehicle, handguns drawn.

They entered the industrial area and approached the first building. The interior appeared dark and quiet.

Bakula signaled to the others that he would go left.

They separated, walking the perimeter in both directions.

Dunham abruptly shined his flashlight into a window. Seeing nothing, he turned his light off and walked to the next window, repeating the process.

Oglesby was one step behind Dunham and kept watch away from the building.

Having found no signs of Castle in any of the windows, Dunham said, "This doesn't seem to be the place."

Bakula approached them from the front. "Nothing." He pointed to two buildings. "Let's check out the closest one."

They walked straight to a side door of the next building.

Bakula tried the door, but it was locked, so he indicated to the other two that he would go right this time.

As Dunham and Oglesby neared the front of the building, they heard a clanging to the far left, in the distance. Both stopped and stared in the direction of the noise and just listened.

"That sound was pretty far away," Oglesby whispered. "Probably of no concern."

Dunham nodded as they continued to walk the perimeter.

When they met up with Bakula, he pointed over at the next building.

"Now, this one looks like an auto shop—look at the old vehicles parked in the back.

They started for the building, and when they were about a hundred feet away, they spotted a hulking shadow just outside of the light of the building's overhead security lamp.

The dark figure moved toward them on all fours. It was a massive dog-like animal, which then stopped underneath the light and glared at the three of them.

"Holy shit!" Oglesby yelled.

Dunham aimed his handgun at the creature. "Wait until it's twenty feet away, then fire and don't stop until it's dead," he ordered his fellow law enforcement officers in a confident, commanding tone. Dunham was sure this animal was going to attack.

The creature slowly moved toward them, growling and gnashing its teeth—and suddenly, it bolted straight for them. In a fraction of a second, it was just feet away.

The three fired in rapid succession at the creature.

The animal yelped and fled to the right into the darkness where it continued to growl and screech.

Bakula pointed to the side. "This way! We'll put our backs to the dumpster! Call in for backup!"

Oglesby screamed into his radio for backup as he and Dunham kept close ranks with Bakula.

They reached the well-lit dumpster, turned around behind two fifty-gallon trash cans, reloaded their clips, and aimed their handguns forward, but they saw nothing.

"Castle's out there, too," Oglesby said.

The animal screeched in the darkness, some fifty feet away.

The massive, hairy creature came into view and again slowly approached them, growling and gnashing.

"Didn't we at least wound that stupid thing?" Oglesby muttered.

It leaped forward and Dunham screamed, "Now!" All three men emptied their clips at the animal.

It turned and bolted to the left, back into the darkness, its screech echoing between the buildings.

"What the hell is that thing?" Oglesby yelled. "It's sure as hell no dog like I've ever seen."

"I don't know, but I'm low on ammo," Bakula admitted.

"I think we all are," Dunham added.

Oglesby pointed to the left. "There!"

The animal walked slowly into the light in front of the auto shop building then moved toward them for a third time, running full speed as if it had never been shot.

"Use what you have!" Bakula yelled.

The animal stopped, glaring at the men, then dropped its head as if it were going to charge.

Blam! Blam!

Loud, thundering shots blasted from behind them.

The animal collapsed then screeched. It got back up, still facing the three men pressed against the dumpster.

Two more shuddering shots rang out and hit their target.

The animal dropped again. This time it got up, turned, and rushed away.

A shot rang out, missing the animal and landing just ahead of it.

The animal turned and bolted toward the auto shop.

As it streaked in front of the building to the right, another shot rang out, again hitting ahead of the animal.

The animal turned and ran straight into the building.

Dunham, Oglesby, and Bakula whipped around.

A man holding a high-powered rifle approached them from the darkness. He was wearing dark, military-style clothes, and even in the dim light, they could see that he had short hair and a strong jaw line.

Dunham recognized the man immediately—Drake Brackston, former SEAL Team Six member.

Brackston glanced at the trio as he walked by, just as calmly as if he were waiting for a bus. He drew near the auto shop building, suddenly stopped, then turned around and started walking unhurriedly toward them. He pulled out a remote control device, gave a slight grin, then pushed a button.

KA-BOOM!

The building exploded, causing a shockwave that hit all of them almost immediately. Debris flew everywhere. Everyone, excluding Brackston, dropped to the ground, covering their faces.

Seconds later, Dunham popped his head up and saw that the building was half gutted and in flames. Debris was still falling from the sky landing around them.

He and the detectives got to their feet as Brackston walked away from the demolished building like an action hero in a movie.

Brackston joined the three and said conversationally, "Hello again, Dr. Dunham."

Dunham looked both ways, scanning the area. "Castle!"

Brackston raised his free hand. "Breathe, Dr. Dunham; maintain a calm spirit in the face of danger." He paused. "He's no longer a threat to New Orleans. I watched Castle run into the building just before the animal came out. I noticed he left the door open for the beast."

Dunham took a deep breath. "Mr. Brackston," he glanced over at the detectives, "these are Detectives Bakula and Oglesby. Gentlemen, this is Mr. Brackston."

Brackston nodded to them then eyed Dunham. "I came to finish a job that I should have done back in the Philippines."

"Were you assigned this job?" Dunham asked.

Brackston shook his head. "No, I'm supposed to be overseas." He smiled. "This one's on me."

"Just one—no, two questions," Dunham said. "How did you know to be here tonight, and how did you know to set charges in that particular building?"

Brackston turned and watched the burning building. "Dr. Dunham, who do you think works in the same department as . . . BB?" He grinned again, then turned and disappeared into the darkness. "Good night, gentlemen."

Oglesby stared at Brackston as he departed, then he faced Dunham. "That answered your two questions?" He shook his head. "Who is that guy? And what government department is BB?"

"Long story," Dunham responded as he watched the flames. "My guess is the creature couldn't dodge that one. I bet we find the remains of it and Castle in there."

chapter 40

Vidocq Course, Last Day,
Loyola University, Louisiana

Dr. Taylor stood before the podium and surveyed his students, aware that they were all excited about the last day of the Vidocq course.

Dr. Perry, chair of the Criminal Justice Department at Loyola, stood next to Taylor, scanning the room and grinning from ear to ear.

Dr. Dunham, Detectives Bakula and Oglesby, and Special Agent Turner waited in the back of the room.

Taylor raised his hand, and the class quieted. "Well, everyone, it had to end. Our three-week course exceeded my expectations in every respect, not because of the curriculum, but because of you."

Dr. Perry clapped, prompting Dunham, Bakula, Oglesby, and Turner to do the same.

"Yes," Taylor continued, "all of you have learned valuable lessons by working on real investigations." He presented a thick folder. "These personal thank-you letters you have received from the participating law enforcement departments are incredible." He beamed. "The caliber of the criminal investigators in this classroom boggles my mind."

The professionals applauded the students again.

The students followed with cheers and high-fives to each other.

Rob grabbed Sarah's hand, smiled at her, then gave Jared a thumbs-up. "Team Watchmaker!"

Jared returned the thumbs-up.

"As you can see, we have a few visitors on this last day." Taylor nodded to those waiting in the back of the room, grinning. "I'm sure they would have been here anyway, but in this case, they were ordered to be here," he shot a glance at the door, "by an unexpected visitor."

The students eyed each other with curious stares.

Taylor leaned toward the hallway. "Is he here?" he asked someone out of view, nodded, then faced the students. "May I present to you the mayor of New Orleans, Mayor Blumenthal."

The mayor walked into the room, followed by four other men and one woman.

Everyone in the room stood and applauded.

The mayor took the podium and stared at the students, beaming. "Thank you, thank you."

The students slowly took their seats.

The mayor scanned the room. "Good morning. Before I start, I'd like to update everyone with information hot off the press," he glanced over at his entourage, "although the press has yet to be informed." He gestured toward Special Agent Turner and nodded. "Dental records generously supplied by the Navy have confirmed that the deceased male found inside the burned-out building is, in fact, Joseph Castle, our prime suspect for the serial killings."

The students jumped out of their seats again and cheered.

The mayor beamed then patiently waited for everyone to take their seats once more. "It is truly an honor to see America's best and brightest sitting in this classroom. I was informed that today is the last day of your class, so I wanted to come here this morning and give my personal thanks." He glanced at the others in the front of the room. "As you probably know, my daughter was kidnapped," he shook his head, frowning, "at the steps of my own front door by this maniac, hell-bent on giving my baby a horrible death!"

The room went silent as the mayor composed himself.

"I want to personally thank you, Dr. Dunham," he continued, "for discovering the lead that found my daughter alive and well." He glanced at the woman to his left, then to the detectives in the back of the room. "I want to personally thank you as well, Captain Deblanc, Detective Bakula, and Detective Oglesby, for assisting in discovering the identity of this ruthless killer and getting him off the streets." He faced Team Watchmaker's table. "I want to personally thank Rob, Sarah, Jared—" he shot a glanced around the room. "Wasn't there a fourth?"

Sebastian stood and raised both hands.

The class laughed.

"And Sebastian, for discovering that a serial killer was in our midst." He gazed around the room. "And lastly, I want to personally thank all of you and your instructor, Dr. Taylor, for having this class here in New Orleans. If this class was not in session, none of the aforementioned accomplishments would have been achieved." He moved away from the podium and applauded.

Everyone joined in.

Jared leaned over to Rob and Sarah. "Wow, you can see why he was elected mayor. What an orator!"

Sarah beamed. "You can see he loves his family."

The mayor stood behind the podium again and waited for everyone to quiet down. "When all of you have finally graduated, and if you decide to live in New Orleans," he winked at the students, "ask me for a job, and my response will be, 'When can you start?'"

The students cheered.

"Thank you, thank you, thank you." The mayor walked away from the podium and shook the hands of everyone up front, then he walked through the classroom, shaking the hands of every student individually.

Side conversations broke out as the mayor made his way around.

Bakula leaned over to Dunham and Turner. "Well, they may have found the man's remains, but there's absolutely no trace of the creature in the ruins; nothing. It's like the animal disappeared."

"The fire chief said the explosion was so intense that he wouldn't be surprised if the carcass was completely incinerated," Oglesby added.

"Well, we'll know soon enough if it's alive and roaming free," Dunham replied. "That animal has a taste for human blood."

Turner presented a folder to Dunham. "I thought you'd like to see Castle's dental records from the Navy. There's a photo of the dental remains of the body found in the building too."

"They're crazy—almost freaky," Oglesby commented.

Dunham opened the folder. "What do you mean? Aren't they Castle's?"

"Oh, yes, the dental expert has no doubt," Bakula began and pointed at the X-rays, "but check out Castle's canines. They're huge, like he was a vampire or something."

Dunham stared at the teeth. He studied the X-rays. "That is interesting. He's always had enlarged canines."

"I noticed that years ago," Turner added.

"The forensic dentist claims they're not implants but the real thing," Oglesby added. "Like I said, freaky."

"At least we know they're Castle's charred remains," Bakula responded. He shook Dunham's hand. "Oges and I have to go. It's been an honor working with you, Dr. Dunham."

Oglesby also shook Dunham's hand. "Absolutely, I can retire now. My career ended on a high note, working hand in hand with the Watchmaker."

"The honor is all mine, gentlemen. Teamwork solved this case."

Turner faced Bakula and Oglesby. "Thank you both for allowing me to work with you in closing the Navy's cold case. I'll meet you at headquarters."

Bakula and Oglesby said their goodbyes and left the noisy room.

"And thank you, Dr. Dunham, for solving our cold case," Turner said. "The vice president wanted me to pass his personal thanks to you as well."

"My absolute pleasure."

"Things still don't add up though. I get it that Castle killed those people in the village, but where did he get such an animal in the jungle on such short notice? He was only in the village for a few days."

Dunham shook his head. "Strange, isn't it? I don't have an answer."

"I'm off to police headquarters. It was great working with you."

"Take care, Special Agent Turner."

They shook hands, and Turner left the room.

Dunham couldn't get the image of Castle's enlarged canines out of his mind, as if the Voodoo high priestess was right and the man had been truly cursed with lycanthropy. Maybe Castle didn't control a wolf-dog hybrid after all—maybe he *was* it, shapeshifting into the Rougarou. That certainly would explain why the creature's body was nowhere to be found.

Dr. Taylor waved Dunham over. "Dr. Dunham, come join the party."

Dunham grinned back at Taylor, still pondering Castle being cursed with lycanthropy. "Impossible," he denied quietly to himself as he approached the mayor.

chapter 91

Near the Forests of Mount Mouchet, France,
June 1767

Marquis d'Archer faced the dozens of huntsmen and houndsmen and pointed into the forest of Mount Mouchet. "Gentlemen," he said, "not only are we going to eliminate every wolf in these forests, but there's also a rumor the Beast is near." He glanced around. "Charles, where are Jean Chastèl and his sons?"

"They've already positioned themselves in the east valley, Marquis."

D'Archer paused then nodded. "Very well." He scanned the crowd. "Let's carry out the plan, gentlemen! Gather your volunteers and rid these woods of wolves. Whoever shoots the Beast shall receive a handsome reward!"

Lafont, de La Molette, Count Morangiès, and the other nobles sat on their horses, waiting for the marquis to join up with them.

D'Archer mounted his horse and rode up to them. "Are we ready?"

"I have a good feeling about today, Marquis," Lafont commented.

"As do I, Etienne, as do I." D'Archer rode his horse to the north, and the nobles followed.

The crowd of hunters and hounds dispersed into and around the forests. The day was unusually pleasant, which finally gave the advantage to the hunting parties. Teams of hunters and hounds coordinated their advances, kicking up predator and prey. As wolves bolted from their hiding spots, they were channeled through the valleys and shot, leaving none alive.

After a full day of hunting, d'Archer dismounted and sat on a large granite rock next to the other nobles. "I believe we've had a good day."

"I will celebrate only if one of these wolves is the Beast," de La Molette commented.

A huntsman rode up to the nobles at a full gallop. "Marquis!" He jumped off his horse in front of d'Archer. "Jean Chastèl has killed a massive creature—what must be the Beast!"

D'Archer and the others leaped up and mounted their horses. "Take us there, Antoine!"

The nobles followed Antoine on horseback toward a large crowd in the forest, where they spotted Chastèl kneeling at the carcass of a massive reddish-haired wolf, its stomach sliced open.

The crowd was cheering and celebrating.

They dismounted and joined Chastèl. D'Archer touched the enormous animal. "This is a strange wolf. Tell me how you shot this creature."

Chastèl pointed at a fallen tree. "I was seated there, resting, reading out of my Bible, when I looked up and noticed the Beast advancing toward me. I closed my Bible, took aim, and shot. The Beast fell where he's lying now. We opened it and found human remains in its stomach."

D'Archer slapped Chastèl on the back, beaming. "Congratulations, Jean! If this creature turns out to be the Beast—and I'm confident it is—you shall be a wealthy and celebrated hero!"

Lafont turned to de La Molette. "Even if this is the Beast, I'm not sure it will be well received by His Highness."

"Oh, you are absolutely correct, Etienne, but I no longer care about our king's approval. The health of our province is my only concern, and Jean Chastèl may have just accomplished this when all the king's huntsmen fell short."

The next morning, innkeeper Jean Chastèl approached his barn behind the inn, carrying a large leather bag. He was accompanied by his son, Antoine.

He opened the wooden door, they entered, and then he locked the door behind him.

Chastèl's younger son, Frederick, was lying naked in a pile of hay, blanketed with a tarp. Blood still covered his face. He turned and glared at his father.

"Antoine told me you fed my favorite dog human body parts, only to shoot and gut him near the forest. You killed him!"

Chastèl glared back at his son. "I did it to protect you! I gave the nobles their Beast!" He shook his head. "Your murderous rampages have gone too far, Frederick. You have no control when you change.

Frederick dropped his head.

Chastèl's eyes began to glow yellow. His eyebrows thickened, and hair started to cover his face. Claws sprouted from his fingers, and his canine teeth enlarged. He snarled.

The son looked up and realized both his father and his older brother were shapeshifting. He scowled and began to change as well.

Chastèl glared at his son. "You will either leave forever or we tear you apart right now! Make your choice!"

"Never!" Frederick howled.

Chastèl and Antoine attacked.

Frederick responded, but Chastèl and Antoine were too much for him.

The fight lasted only minutes.

Frederick collapsed, bloodied and exhausted.

Chastèl and Antoine hovered over him, both breathing deeply from the fight.

Frederick shapeshifted back to his human form, still panting. "OK, OK, but where am I to go?"

"You must leave all of Europe. Sail across the Atlantic. Once there, do what you will, but you will no longer terrorize the French countryside."

Chastèl and Antoine shapeshifted back to their human forms and Antoine threw a bag to Frederick.

Chastèl unlocked the door. "Clothes and money are in there. Take it and be gone."

Frederick hesitated for a moment, debating between his family and his bloodlust. His mind made up, he slung the bag over his shoulder and ran out of the barn.